The City Beneath The Earth

The City Beneath The Earth

by
Mark R. Sneller

Published by Fresh Air Press

Visit Mark's website at
marksneller.com

This edition was prepared for publication by
Ghost River Images
5350 East Fourth Street
Tucson, Arizona 85711
www.ghostriverimages.com

ISBN 978-1-7330238-2-5

Library of Congress Control Number: 2020916855

Printed in the United States of America
November, 2020

Other books Mark R. Sneller:

A Breath of Fresh Air

Greener Cleaner Indoor Air–a Guide

to Healthier Living – 2nd Edition

Toxic Exposure

Dying to Read

The Mars Virus

In Progress: *The Fight at the Poker Game*

and Other Stories

In Progress: *The Magical Powers of Lazlo*

Pearce

Dedication:

This book is dedicated to my daughter.

Within a minute, Jess found the trail to the west, accompanied by two wolf descendants, one on each side. They belonged to ages long past, licking flesh from their teeth, looking for more meat to tear, protecting. Jess, in her turn, found herself having devolved with them. For long moments, she wallowed in the feeling of being an early human from 50,000 years in the past, shambling through the muck beneath a dense canopy of trees in the bleakness of a cold dreary death-filled morning—a cavewoman from a past long dead, as a child conceived out of the mists of dawn, lacking only a club. She saw herself thusly, as a convert to surface life—one who had killed another human whose blood had stained her clothing, accompanied by two feral meat eaters as intimate companions.

PREFACE

The fracture lines beneath the earth in Southern Arizona were minimal compared with those of many other states such as Alaska, California, Mississippi and New Jersey. The Arizona-Nevada border, where the Colorado Plateau ends, is the location of the most significant concentration of Arizona fault lines. When earthquakes did occur, they clustered primarily in that northwestern quadrant. Numerous quakes occurred in other quadrants of the state, as well. However, very few occurred in the Phoenix and Tucson areas. That was before The Mars Virus destabilized the planet's major and minor tectonic plates to affect the countless fracture lines associated with them, most of which had not been identified.

Not even Gottlieb and his army of engineers and scientists could have anticipated the extent of the world-wide calamity brought about by the virus. This included the virtual disappearance of the northern and southern hemispheric jet streams, along with the melting of the polar ice caps and the Greenland Ice Sheet. These events were accompanied by planet-wide eruptions of land-based and undersea volcanoes, plus rampaging storms across the globe, all of which led to the disappearance of whole island chains and countries in northern Europe and Southeast Asia. Thousands of fractures lines were activated, more than 100 of them beneath the largest cities in China, home to over 40 million people.

The country of Mexico was situated at the boundary of three tectonic plates. Mexico City, with a population of nine million, was situated over an old lake bed that quivered whenever even a distant quake occurred and where major rivers and their tributaries overflowed annually.

In the United States, major earthquakes, hurricanes, tornadoes, river overflows, sleet, and driving rain did their share of damage. The eruption of the Wyoming supervolcano finished the infrastructure of the nation and was a major contributor to the cold dark years around the world. Every aspect of life on the planet struggled to survive in the unpredictability of atmospheric, ground-based, and oceanic turbulences. The underground city was no exception.

PART 1

ONE

Early March

Except for the time she spent the Yard or the Pen, Jessica Sophia Galloway had never been outside the walls of her underground city. She'd never seen a body of water or touched the sand of the desert surrounding her home. She had never been outside when it rained, seen a fish, or the leaves turn. Whenever it did rain, the summer storms were short-lived. Living underground, she could feel the increase in humidity as the great fan brought in moist outside air during those brief periods.

The discovery of the detailed diaries written by scientists in Lincoln, Nebraska, explained that the global disaster occurred as a result of an entity they dubbed The Mars Virus. A few grains of dust from a meteorite contained the virus. As it spread throughout the planet, it mutated any life form, as it bound with all DNA. The details held in the diaries were public knowledge, that is, what was left of the public. They told about the State of Nebraska many miles to the east where it had all started in what was once called The United States of America, before international boundaries disappeared and before the world fell apart.

Ostracized for her brilliance and dedication to morning jogs, eighteen year-old Jessica inhabited a pod with her parents in a high-class neighborhood well below the surface. Her family had the sickness, as did the other 240 inhabitants of their city.

She hadn't slept at all the night before her departure to the surface world outside her city. Now, examining herself in the polished steel mirror, her once thick and abundant red hair, which was typically held up in a fashionable bun, now lay straggled accentuating her sunken, red-rimmed, green eyes. "Irish to the core," her mother would declare on occasion, whenever Jessica set her mind to do something. Jess was the product of an English father and a mother who boasted Norwegian, Spanish, Italian, and whatever-got-under-the-fence blood. Adventurers and explorers all. The latter may have been a Celtic legacy from western or northern Europe, most likely Ireland, where red hair was not uncommon. Her forehead was gentle, her eyes almond shape with a look of sadness about them, her lips full and inviting, her nose modest—more angular than round. Over all, men found her tall full-figured body attractive. Although her teeth were regular and strong, she possessed the slightest suggestion of a lisp when she spoke, which served as an absolute turn-on to men.

Wherever she touched her skin, it became indented, which took a period of time to reset itself, similar to effects she had read about when people became afflicted with radiation poisoning. Pulling her lips back with her fingers, she examined the prominent teeth—bleeding gums were beginning to recede. "Cute, real cute. For your next trick . . ." she declared, facetiously.

She spoke to her father's reflection. "Daddy, have you ever been in a situation where you were so overwhelmed that you were afraid to do something, so you put it off, but it turned out to be easy when you finally did it?" She watched the image smile and nod in agreement. "The problem is, I don't think this is going to be so easy." She turned to face him directly. Preempting his response, she went on, "I'm overwhelmed with fear, because the devil's chamber awaits."

As mayor of the city and a positive personality by nature, Robert Galloway had over two hundred souls in his charge. Smiling, he offered compassion through the gaze from his own dark, sunken eyes. "Jess, give yourself credit. Your beauty will return, your courage will bolster your effort. Don't get too intellectual about it. Over-analyzing is a waste of time when you don't have enough information. Therefore, either forget about the problem, or get more information. Too much thinking about failure will inevitably draw it toward yourself. Never have any expectations." His thoughts were different than his words. *You're two years past marrying age and you're starting to lose a good man—well, one who is attracted to you, while adventure is all you can think of. Come on, Jess, get over this silliness and give us a grandchild.*

His spoken words struck a nerve. A small laugh escaped her, as though she were a container filled with worry that had been punctured slightly to let out some of the pressure—like tears leaking out pent-up stress.

In contrast to his daughter, Robert had brown eyes and dark brown hair, supposedly dominant genetic traits. He stood of average height at 5'10". His tan tunic and pants were made of well-tailored hemp fresh from the loom and were always stain-free. As the consummate politician and mayor of the city, Robert presented affability on the surface, yet exhibited occasional ruthlessness in meetings while trading favors for necessary votes.

Attempting to bolster her courage, Susan, her mother, got up from her chair and put her arm around her daughter, who was similar in appearance. "Honey, your father has his doubts. I believe what you are about to do is the most grandiose, no, most wondrous adventure anybody in this city has ever attempted."

For an instant, Jess was taken aback. She felt just the opposite of grandiose—even miniscule, perhaps foolish. She refused to consider dealing with the inevitable public derision she would face upon her return. Her outspoken nature had gotten her into this predicament. Other than her youthful exuberance, she took after her mother in the sense that Susan had an exciting element about her. Her years in the underground city had stifled that element. Her mother had been transformed from a businesswoman into an excellent teacher who possessed the analytical mind of a scientist.

Once the public had discovered Jess's intentions to go Topside, she received the Godspeed sign of a letter "U" formed with the thumb and index finger of the right hand, then "L" with the same two fingers of the left hand—abbreviations for their city's name, UL-One, typically called Ulone. Some joked that it stood for "You Live Alone," ignoring its true designation as Underground Living Colony One. More frequently, others made the sign and then jammed the two hands together like linking rings, in order to form a protective force against evil—more recently in specific reference to her. This latter was particularly prominent among the womenfolk who passed her in the tunnels, or saw her in the sweaty, cramped gymnasium. More communiqués were received via her household computer. Whatever she got, she gave it back sign for sign, strength for strength. *If that's what you want, I've got more where that came from,* she thought.

Finished with her self-examinations, Jess gathered her backpack and left the pod with her father. Fearing her own tearful reaction to her daughter's departure, Susan left the pod to return to her work in the Ring, planting a new cultivar of tomato with her best friend, Annie Rostov, head of Hydroponics. She had no desire to follow Jess to the west gate to see her daughter leave the city for what could be a one-way journey.

Father and daughter took the long walk to the end of Spoke 7 to the west, where they climbed the stairs and exited into the Yard. Several people were either walking, running, or playing soccer inside the perimeter of the wall in those early morning hours. Others, including James Okimura, her self-appointed betrothed, were working the pottery wheels, painting ceramics or using the kiln.

As James made a move to stand, his father's hand stayed him. "She knows you're watching," Philip said, stroking his goatee. "Let them have their moment."

Most of the dozen or so occupants of the Yard ceased their activities to watch the pair. Robert walked her to the six-foot-tall steel gate set into the thick red adobe wall and unlocked it. By the afternoon, both lock and gate would be much too hot to touch. The builders of the city did not anticipate the great change—one that would result in scorching heat for an unknown period of time. The gate was always locked from the inside. Although Robert held one of the duplicate keys, the hour of Jess's return was a big unknown, so the gate would remain locked. She would have to climb the hill to enter through Spoke 1, which faced Phoenix to the north.

Watching his daughter walk out into the desert alone and locking the gate behind her, Robert wondered what he had gotten himself into. He should have said "absolutely no" to her endless requests and ended the matter. His own sickness from whatever was going around had left him too weak to fight and now he might have seen his daughter for the last time.

To Jess, the world outside the gate appeared completely different from the one she had left. The desert seemingly went on forever. The brilliant true sunlight of the glaring desert blasted her head downward. Squinting from the increase in brightness, she squeezed her eyes shut, maintaining a head-down posture for several moments until she slowly opened them to slits. Struggling a step at a time, she slowly made her way toward the highway two miles directly ahead, having become a part of the world's grandeur for the first time in her life.

TWO

"It's about the temperature we figured. Not too bad," she muttered, gaining some distance from the wall of the city behind her. In doing so, she saw the sun's tip just rising over the top of the mountain. *If the surface is this bright in the morning, it should be a lot of fun in the afternoon,* she mused. *Where will I be then?* Only three or four people out of two-forty had expressed any honest concern for her welfare. One was her mother; the other Michelle, her best friend. A third was Annie Rostov. To the remainder, if she never came back it might be for the best. Not even James, her self-proclaimed suitor, had faith in her mission.

The temperature of her home proper and the air about her now would be fairly equal. She knew the relatively constant temperature at home almost always ranged in the high seventies, which was no match for the temperature in this surface world that could be scorching in the direct sun, once it got into the summer months. Indeed, the damper in the duct that drew in fresh air from the outside would be nearly closed during those months to keep excessive heat from entering the city.

A gentle breeze blew against her from left to right, similar to the constant breeze down below, where the fan pushed the air throughout the entire structure. She felt the gentle warmth radiating from the surface of the sandy earth. No smell of sweat or perfumes or garlic or other aspects of life could be detected in this place; instead, there were different odors in this Arizona desert. She thought she smelled the slightest tinge of smoke, or did heat waves smell like that?

Jess pulled out the wide-brimmed hat she had fashioned. The long-sleeves she had added to her tan tunic would protect her arms. Now secure in her cocoon of clothing, she walked head down through what functioned as a road path to and from the west gate. It soon became so covered with sand she found herself going astray. Occasionally she ran into a tumble of rocks, unaccustomed to having to step clear of anything, unless it was an item absently left on the floor of one of the corridors during some con-struction project, or perhaps something accidentally dropped.

She felt the unusual give of the hardened and crusted desert floor breaking free when she stepped on it. Grains of sand found their way between her toes, passing through the tightly-woven hemp san-dals James had modified for her to wear. Jess's senses were both dulled and heightened at the same time. Although hammered by the dry air and the brightness of the sunlight, she became excited at the occasional green lizard and brown horned toad as they scampered to safety. She'd studied them in computer movies in preparation for this trek to the big city of Phoenix. Reality presented a completely different picture. Her fascination with life around her did not, however, prevent her from walking head-on into a number of species of cactus. From her studies, she had already recognized these cacti as prickly pears, jumping cholla, and tall saguaros. The latter displayed tiny spiny green arms, each of which took almost a century to sprout and mature. She watched, fascinated, as a brown bird flew into a hole in the central stalk of one saguaro, where it had made a nest.

The jumping cholla broke when she brushed against it, pinning her tunic to her skin. The piece measured some four inches in length by an inch in diameter, with inch-long spines that surrounded its tubular frame. She found a twig from a mesquite tree to pry the pod loose from its attachment to her body. Occasionally, she looked behind herself to gain an understanding of her location and took in the bright, giant dome of sky that called her to return home quickly, lest she become dehydrated, go mad, and then become lost. Playing hide-and-seek as a child might have had been challenging; finding oneself actually lost and disoriented on a hostile planet could be an adventure with dire consequences. There was never the possibility of becoming lost in 8-spoke-wheeled city of UL-One.

At last, Jess came to the broken highway that led slightly northwest toward the sprawling city of her destination. Her emotions became hormone-driven, perhaps triggered by the new challenge to her survival. She had a brief feeling of disappointment with herself for even contemplating the trip in the first place. Then she reconsidered. *No, I'm sick. My people are sick. Communication with the surface is nonexistent. We need supplies. Nobody wants to do the job except me. Simple math.*

Behind her stood the Superstition Mountains, seat of the legendary Lost Dutchman Gold Mine and a former Apache Indian stronghold. To the southwest, Picacho Peak jutted 500 feet above the valley floor where the final battle of the Civil War had been fought. The ancient mountains enclosed a valley that once had grown to be the third largest in the country in terms of both population and square miles. The formation held endless washes, hiking trails, ridges, geological wonders—areas where migratory birds visited, somewhat fewer in numbers than was once the case. Tens of billions had perished when the volcanoes erupted and the weather turned planet Earth into a landscape more in keeping with that of a distant world.

THREE

Jess walked along the side of the broken road heading north. Occasional and unpredictable sandstorms ensured that the road resembled the desert around it, with no vehicular traffic of any consequence to disturb it. For a moment, she saw herself as an Indian guide like Sacajawea, the Lemhi Shoshone woman, who, at the age of 16, guided the Lewis and Clark expedition into unknown territory. In her case, there would be no expedition, no companions. Minor detail. For some strange reason, the escape into fantasy made her feel a little better. She dutifully trudged forward for well over an hour, trying to avoid tripping on chunks of asphalt that presented themselves randomly, until the sound of crunching occurred nearby. A large vehicle with enormous wheels pulled beside her and a female passenger leaned out the window. She appeared to be near Jess's age. "Hey, you want a ride, freako? Where ya goin'?"

Loud music boomed from speakers in the car. Jess quickly realized she must look strange in all tan clothing, with a scarf wrapped so low on her forehead, she might as well be blindfolded. The girl slid over for Jess to climb in next to her. The hair of the woman and that of the male driver had been dyed in streaks of various colors, not unlike people in her city. Both were smoking, holding their breath while doing so, passing a cigarette back and forth.

"This place," Jess showed the woman the address on the module she had pulled out of her pack. The woman glanced at the slate. "Ain't goin' that far, honey, but closer than here. Want something to drink?" Before Jess could reply, the woman pulled out a bottle from somewhere. Unscrewing the cap, she took a drink, passed it to the driver, who did the same. He passed it back over to Jess who took a long swallow and gagged. Trying not to look more foolish than she already felt, she didn't ask what it was that burned her throat, desperately trying to concentrate on the landscape as the vehicle entered the outskirts of the big city. The smoke in the vehicle irritated her eyes and lungs. The insanely raucous music grated on her nerves; music absent flutes and gentle drum beats or soft melodious voices. Instead, she heard screeching.

Jess felt true terror for the first time in her young life as her vehicle traveled at, what was to her, an exceedingly high rate of speed. Scenery rushed past. Her need to vomit became pronounced. Closing her eyes, she took the slow deep breaths one needed in stressful circumstances, as her gym instructor, Mara Page, had advised. Opening her eyes two minutes later, dead vegetation and leveled buildings filled her vision in this desolate city that might have contained many millions at one time. Little greenery remained, other than the mesquite and paloverde trees; both desert natives.

The vehicle soon reached a street where several stores stood in a row. "This is it, freako. We're outta here." When the vehicle came to an abrupt stop, the girl reached across to open Jess's door. The moment her feet hit the pavement, the couple drove off. Feeling dizzy, Jess guessed the hour to be approaching 9:00 a.m. Few people walked the streets. The occasional women she saw wore short, colorful dresses, ostensibly for the warmer clime. She looked down at her own bland outfit, feeling oddly out of place. Many on the street must have found her to be a curious creature, undoubtedly high on drugs.

Feeling disoriented, her head hurt. The taste of the liquid lingered and made her thirstier than she had ever been. She reasoned her headache might be attributed in part, to signs of dehydration, having read about it in preparation for her journey.

When she tried to relate her purpose to people, the dryness in her mouth made it a challenge for her to form words. Pulling a container of water from her backpack, she took a small drink to wet her lips. People turned away as she approached; children ran from her. She wasn't accustomed to insects alighting on her skin, desperately seeking moisture that would evaporate as soon as it formed. *What a strange world. How can people live here? Almost every store is closed.*

She walked along the row of small buildings until a larger one came before her with a handful of patrons pushing carts on wheels. Jess realized she must appear to be some creature that had broken free from a horror movie to ravage a city's populace with her red hair, green eyes, hat, odd clothing, and sandals.

She warily entered the store, perhaps the size of the triple-pod hospital or gym back home. If she had any choice, she would have stripped naked and danced in the relative coolness of the store. As she would find out later, this store was among the few buildings that employed air conditioning. Jess ran her fingers along a number of cans on the shelves, amazed at their assorted contents and wondered how to open them—there was not a single earthen jar to be seen. She read the labels. Every single one had an expiration date of 20 years before. Whatever that meant, it didn't sound good. Glass jars with food were in relative abundance with a notice on each to return the jar to the store because no more were being manufactured. She could find no expiration date on these.

Most surprisingly, three children tagged along behind a single mother, who stood looking at the produce. *It must be nice to have as many babies as you want*, she reflected. She pulled the module from her backpack and displayed the address on the screen to several persons who turned away from her.

Finally, she approached a middle-aged man who stood by a shelf of jarred goods reading the labels. He gave her an appraising look, grinned, and pointed in the direction she needed to go to find Salvage Enterprises. She had some suspicions about the directions he provided when another man came to the first and they laughingly spoke. When she considered the lack of communication she had received, she would have no other choice. She would have to go in the direction the man had directed.

Similar to a visitor to a botanical garden, or a native of a third-world country visitor who finds himself in an indoor supermarket, the produce section attracted her. Captivated by the odd selection, she took two large peaches and added something called a banana, which she also placed into her pack. A section with bottles made of actual glass, labeled as pure spring water, caught her eye. Never having seen a screw-cap before, she played with the top for some time until she got it loose, cautiously putting it up to her lips while recalling the experience she'd recently had in the car with another clear liquid. Finding the contents of this bottle as advertised, she drank it all. She replaced the cap and had set the empty back on the shelf, as requested, when the power went off. None of the shoppers made a comment, as though it were a common event. Neither did Jess, accustomed to such outages. They were tied to the same grid.

Jess left the store, followed by the stares of incredulous customers, passing several counters which displayed signs that read *Self-Checkout by*

Microchip. Another sign read, *Smile for the Camera*, whatever that meant. She walked out into the increasing warmth of the day, already much warmer than she had ever experienced. She felt guilty about not leaving a note regarding what she had taken to trade for credits, but had found no paper or writing instrument with which she could write on.

She headed in the direction given to her by the patron and strolled until she found a used book store, where she feasted on holding books she had only heard or read about. After some time, the proprietor asked if she was going to buy something or stand there all day. Jess left reluctantly and after twenty minutes of walking down the endless corridors of pavement, deeper into a section of homes with no stores to be seen, it became clear she had been deceived. All the homes were abandoned with windows broken, doors wide open, or displayed old, dismantled vehicles in the yard. Jess found no person to speak with, no bench upon which to sit and rest. No traffic could be seen in the neighborhood. Her legs and head hurt. Afraid to look at her feet where the straps of the sandals had cut into her skin, she had no choice. It was time to turn around and go back to the area of the stores.

A half-hour later she returned to the bookstore. Summoning her courage, she asked the proprietor for the directions to Salvage Enterprises. She showed the man the address on her module. He pointed her in the direction opposite to that given by the grinning man in the market.

Tired and forlorn, Jess walked as she had been bade, zombie-like, without inspiration almost forgetting her purpose, passing a women's clothing store that displayed an electric sign in front that read Temperature 91. Curious, she paused a moment to look at the clothing styles. Men of all ages passed her and would make suggestive remarks. Of this, at least she was familiar, and managed to rebuff their advances with practiced skill. The buildings around her were one and two story—each huge by her standards—with stacks of tumbleweed backed up against them. Taller buildings stood in the distance. Her imagination saw them as gargantuan soldiers of an invading army preparing to march over the smaller buildings to crush all beneath them.

Jess shook herself. She had been in this world since shortly after sunrise. Her brain had ceased to function properly. Her weary bones and swollen feet were too tired and blistered to take her much further. At home, she would be starting her two hour hydroponics rotation shift. Hoping to be home by nightfall, she was relieved to see it wasn't even 10:00 a.m. *You have plenty of time to get the job done*, she thought, although, thus far, she had gotten nowhere. The man in the store told her Salvage Enterprises was at least a two or three mile walk. This would take her a good hour or more at her present rate of speed.

She had walked perhaps a half-mile when she stopped. Leaning against a building, she removed her sandals and shook them out. Walking barefoot, she continued for another quarter mile until good fortune guided her to a park across the street. She surmised it might be for public usage because the ground was covered with asphalt similar to the public roadways. A single small building stood in the immediate area. A sandy area about the size of her home pod had some gym-type equipment that appeared to be for use by children. A row of paloverde trees bordered the front of the park along the street. Trees were in full bloom, with yellow flowers lending contrast to their green branches and trunks—photosynthetic throughout—all able to convert sunlight to energy. A few mesquite trees were also scattered within the park, including a large one located just to the west of a bench outside the building.

Inspecting the building, Jess found it to be a restroom. The sinks were not working, but the commodes contained water. She noticed that the small amount of urine she voided had turned dark yellow. *This is something new,* she thought. *I must be getting sicker.* Casting aside her inner reflections, Jess forced herself to remember her mission. Standing on painful feet, she felt lightheaded; suddenly a cramp gripped her right calf muscle. As she leaned against a sink to stretch it out, she stared into one of the mirrors and took a close-up look at reality, transfixed. She mused: *Nothing has changed, Jess, just the same beautiful diseased face you were looking at this morning and last month. Is there a trace of madness in those eyes? If so, I sincerely hope there is madness enough to cope with whatever is coming next.* A sense of sarcasm overtook her. "*Why, no,*

Jess, it's just real life. Simple solution. Quit looking in the mirror.

Her mind wandered to her home. As mayor of the city and head of the city council, her father had obtained an upscale pod near the middle of Spoke 6. The location did not provide for maximum air flow from the ducts, but at least it was distant from the foot traffic on Spoke 7 that led to the Yard. Her daddy's personal contacts in the city had created the carpet with woven pictures of yellow and red snapdragons; and, along with the wall hangings, provided the house with a colorful and cheerful environment.

On the door to the tunnel hung a decorative beaded curtain made from hemp and compressed leaves, preventing passers-by from looking in. Every home had a curtain. Theirs had a design of the red tomatoes grown in the gardens.

Jess always possessed a bent toward science and experimentation. She understood that when something grabs onto you and won't let go, then you have to take care of that thing, otherwise it can gnaw at you at all hours. She thought about it for so long that there was nothing to stop the gnawing, except to do the thing before it ate her alive. She defined the thing as a trip to the surface—a forbidden fruit.

FOUR

Jess laughed out loud at her own entangled thoughts and she spent several minutes trying to comb her hair; fruitlessly hand-pressing the sweaty rumples from her tunic. She did pull the sleeves from it to cool her arms somewhat, folded the sleeves into squares and placed them in her pack. Bitter reality struck, as a youth might feel reality when he goes to sea for the first time, with ruffians for shipmates, and sees his land-based home slip away over the horizon, realizing his childhood is gone forever.

Once outside and barefoot, she carefully surveyed the land around to ensure she had a good sense of her bearings before sitting on the bench. With great delight, she noticed actual birds bathing in a water fountain. Some were blue, others red or varied in shades of mottled brown. A larger bird stood in one of the troughs at the top, dipping its head beneath the water, fluttering its wings. She recognized it as a quail with the curled feather at its head.

Something was wrong. She concentrated on their faces and saw all with eyes and ears misaligned, their wings were set higher than those she had seen in the computer movies—Sider bird mutants infected by The Mars Virus. Back home none had alighted long enough for her to notice their features. A chill coursed through her. *So they're real, not make believe fairy tales invented to scare children.*

She swung one leg over the rim of the fountain and pulled herself into a seated position. She soaked her bruised and swollen feet, while scooping water to splash it onto her face and her neck, after removing her hat.

Remembering the fruit in her pack, she took a small bite from one of the peaches. Its sweet juice forced her to eat as slowly as she could, lest she devour it in seconds. Its unbelievable richness of flavor overshadowed the tasteless quality of the fruits grown at home. She saved the second peach, although her hunger drove her to make an attempt to eat the banana. The outer portion of the fruit could not be bitten through. She did find that if she squeezed the banana hard enough, the innards would ooze out of the dents that had been made with her teeth, weak as they were and painful as it was to bite the hard skin. Once she pulled the skin apart she could access the fruit more fully.

She recalled reading that one of the mistakes the builders had made in planning the construction of UL-One was the creation of a Tilapia fish farm in an area within the ring designated for aquaculture. This mistake in judgment turned out to be one of many as they rushed to complete her city, already occupied. The Yellowstone explosion halted their final touches. To her people, the fish farm turned out to be an impractical venture in terms of maintenance. Within months, a disease destroyed the entire farm, forcing the area to be re-purposed.

Jess pulled out a small ceramic container of salve, which she had personally prepared. To her feet, she applied the anti-inflammatory mixture of powdered leaves and roots from calendula, thyme, cloves, and rosemary infused with CBD oil. This was the best her mother and Annie could concoct. She soon found that, instead of lessening the pain significantly, the salve had a minor effect. *Even these plants have lost their potency,* she reflected.

She washed her sandals in the fountain and laid them on the edge to dry. Wrapping wrapped her feet in gauze, she gingerly limped over to the bench to stretch out in the shade of the tree. She drank a small amount from her stash, removed the hard objects from her pack, and rested her head against it to stretch out for a short rest, promising herself she would resume her search for the business once she arose. Wasn't she Jessica Galloway, daughter of the mayor, and daughter of Susan Galloway, the most popular science teacher in all of UL-One? Wasn't she, Jessica, a teacher of science, a physically fit woman, a dreamer longing for adventure? She could do this.

Jess awoke hours later drenched in sweat. The

sun had not reached the midpoint in the sky when she first lay down; now she saw that it had advanced considerably to the west. In her estimation, the hour neared 4:00 p.m. In another two hours at home she would be eating dinner on the second of three shifts.

What might Maggie, the kitchen chef, have prepared for dinner tonight? Because Wednesday was special treat day, she could expect curry-flavored cricket powder sprinkled into a salad of lettuce, okra, spinach, water chestnuts, and radishes. Slices from baked potatoes seasoned with oil of cloves would provide the proper mixture of greens, starches and protein necessary for a healthy diet. If Maggie was in a good mood, she would serve sugar beet slices for desert. If she wasn't, the masses would have to contend with radishes sprinkled with sugar crystals.

Jess knew she was delirious and understood the signs of vitamin deficiency; especially the onset of scurvy from a lack of Vitamin C. Everyone else in the city had the same problem. She had researched the subject and when presenting her findings to the doctors, found they already had knowledge of the issue, although neither of them had experienced the problem before. The three were in agreement. Their food was played out. It had little of nutritional value anymore. Everything had to be replaced with fresh strains—or it needed to be revitalized in some manner.

"So much for getting stronger from eating spinach," she mumbled, recalling the cartoons she had seen about some sailor who had been created by spinach growers to sell their product.

Compelled to get some food into her stomach, Jess pulled out a couple of nutrition bars from her pack and ate both of them slowly, along with the second peach, washing them down with a good drink of water from her corked jugs. Afterwards she felt much better, yet frustrated at herself for sleeping so long. She decided against continuing her search for Salvage Enterprises this day because the place would likely be closed by the time she got there. The night promised to be a long one, so she resolved to remain at the park until morning, when she could resume her quest.

Jess pulled out her reading slate from the back-pack, then placed the pack behind her head as a pillow. After some time, stores began to turn off their interior lights, which were few to begin with, yet no street lights came on—despite the presence of the poles.

She had trouble divesting herself of the memory of the way people looked at her. She knew her clothing and hair separated her from the others, but why the stares when she was taking the fruit or drinking the water in the store? *You're in another culture*, she told herself. *Pretend you're in a story of old where people on one side of the world visit another; where different peoples congregate according to ethnicity.*

As Jess relaxed, her mind wandered. She had said to her father, "Daddy, you know how it is when you're a kid; that everything is supposed to be the way it is? If your parents are handicapped or fight all the time and others are getting divorces—it all seems normal. You see people who live differently right around you, so just because we know that people live on the surface, that shouldn't affect our own lives. Yet, somehow it does, because we've always relied on them, despite the fact that we don't know a thing about what's up here, and we will always rely on them, and that's what hurts me the most."

To which he replied, "You're right. We've taken our easy lives for granted. To me, life demands a struggle. There must be adversity to overcome, which is not defined as juggling shift times to work in hydro or the kitchen."

Jess also remembered the eye roll her mother had given him when he said that—which was followed by her bark, "Robert, you are so full of it. You wouldn't know what to do for excitement or a struggle if you didn't juggle shift times or play cards at night. Why don't you create something or learn to play chess to stimulate your mind?"

"Are you complaining about your lifestyle?" he replied, angrily.

"No, I'm complaining about you," she retorted.

"Here we go again," Robert flapped his arms, looking at Jess as he did so.

Making the move to the underground city had not been easy for anyone, although some had adapted more quickly than others. Some couldn't make it work at all. Robert had stepped into a good job as mayor, which seemed to satisfy his lackadaisical manner; wife's interest in horticulture and her practical approach to problems gave her an instant friendship with Annie. They had remained close for the past twenty years.

Everybody called her Annie because of her diminutive and matronly manner, although bull-nosed when running her business. Her real name was Anna Rostov from Kiev, Ukraine. In search of a better life, her family had moved to Phoenix three years before the Yellowstone explosion, dubbed the Great Catastrophe. Her husband had applied for a number of jobs and found one in Phoenix in his line of work—operating a machine shop and mechanical repair business for a bus district. Similar to Jess's mother, Anna operated a horticulture business. The family moved to the States bringing with them their nine-year-old son, Gregor. All three spoke broken English. Large for his age, Gregor was not unaccustomed to fighting, finding it necessary to practice his skills in school once they reached the States. One week, some three years after their arrival, an unusually large storm struck Phoenix at the time when the world was racked with radical climate changes. Anna's husband died in a one-car accident coming home from work during that storm.

Then, at twelve years of age, Gregor happened upon a poster announcing the opening of UL-One. At the top of the poster was the statement that the builders were looking for people to move into the new underground city. Gregor mentioned this to his mother. After making an inquiry, she accepted an offer to head the hydroponics division of the new city.

If her mother considered her father to be a slacker, Jess could say the same of James, who relentlessly pursued her hand in marriage. How many times had she told him she wasn't interested, and she didn't care if her father supported his efforts? The guy wouldn't go away. Maybe she should find another man to marry to be rid of him. Her problem lay in the fact that she had no interest in marriage—to the consternation of available men.

At last, Jess gave up her musings. She fell into a restless sleep in full acceptance of her present state of adversity. The only clue she slept was the memory of tortured dreams——dreams that featured vehicles rumbling through the streets of UL-One with people running over one another to avoid being struck, many of them unsuccessful at the attempt.

Whenever she awoke, she saw stars outside the cover of the tree she slept under. Many of them were familiar, as she had seen them late at night from the Yard, when she had occasionally gone there to look at them after Lights Out. Sometimes she would go in the opposite direction to the end of Spoke 3, to climb the stairs to the Pen, an outdoor covered area large enough to hold everyone in the city, an area that had been enclosed in steel-mesh fencing. Those rare occasions were not like this. She forced herself to painfully hobble outside the tree canopy to look up.

Night had drawn down gently and the stars began to shine more brightly, striking a chord in her soul.

Some undefined emotion served to bind her with the surface, then pull her back to her memories like a ball that moodily bounced back and forth, never staying in one spot for long. On this moonless night, the Milky Way shone edge-on in all its glory. She found an area on the ground to lay upon and soon found Venus and Jupiter, then identified a number of constellations. At last she fell asleep once again, this time beneath the stars.

A wind gust awakened her in the early dawn followed by a brief rain shower. Doused by the short cloudburst, she saw lightning for the first time. Jess clumsily scrambled to her feet as a crashing sound occurred, as though every piece of cookware in the central kitchen had fallen to the floor at the same instant. She became totally terrified for the second time in her life—not just scared, but as fearful as the sky was big. Frightened for her life, Jess stared at the passing storm clouds. As a further welcome, a branched lightning bolt shot through the huge black cloud from top to bottom followed by another more distant boom.

FIVE

Jess tried to cover her eyes from the rising sun. She reflected, *This nightmare world is filled with obtuse events, of tasteful fruits and large skies; a bizarre world that contains magnificence beyond imagining along with events that threaten to kill you.*

Despite these observations, a primitive sense of fulfillment suffused her, another emotion she had never experienced before. Had she gone back into the darkness of an earlier age? Had she time-traveled into a future built upon random events and total chaos? Either could be true. Those wondrous few seconds would serve to fill her soul for the rest of her life, more so than the entire adventure. *Who is to say how much a few seconds changes one's life for the better or worse?*

Jess tried to stretch out her tight muscles using the bench as a prop, working her legs, hips, and shoulders. Minutes later, with no sense of immediate purpose, she walked over to the fountain, where she plunged her head into it and scrubbed her face. Her dinner of the night before had lessened her headache.

Gently applying more salve on her feet, she changed their bandages and drank the last of her water. Carefully she replaced her sandals. Her legs, feet and shoulders hurt more than she had ever believed possible. Her mind made up, Jess reached into her tote and pulled out a small container. Opening it, she dipped her finger into the CBD oil used as a pain-killer and placed several drops under her tongue. It contained a trace of THC from the *Cannabis indica* strain grown amongst the foliage of its sister hemp plant. Intended for medicinal purposes, the mixture served to decrease the activity of neurons, yet stimulated their sense of creativity. Her mother had obtained a few grams of it from Annie. However, this treatment, too, failed to work as expected.

Steeling herself, Jess began to limp in the direction of the location given her by the man in the book store. She stopped for a moment to look at the playground set in the sand. Clearly, it called to her. After some experimentation on the swing, she managed to get herself propelled into the air, swinging to-and-fro, listening to the regular squeak of the chains, until her sense of duty caused her to halt her laughter and cease the small pleasure.

With hat on head, she crossed the street, wary of any speeding vehicle. She saw none. Once safely on the other side, she passed boarded stores until she found a bakery. Like a living thing with clutching tentacles, the splendid odors pulled her inside, where a handful of patrons sat; many of whom stared at her and withdrew, as though she were a ragged apparition who had spent a night on a park bench.

She noted a middle-aged man and woman seated at a window. They had to be Sider mutants, whose parents had not escaped the plague and had not taken Randolph's Vaccine as had hers. One eye and ear was lower than the other, mouths, canted slightly, backs slightly hunched. The woman appeared to be of Asian descent. Jess averted her eyes immediately, almost afraid she might catch what they had. Word had it just speaking to a Sider or looking at one too closely would bring bad luck.

Jess turned her attention to the showcase. Drool borne of undisguised hunger must have been evident on her countenance as she tried to make a comparison with desserts back home. There could be no comparison. These screamed sweetness. A man who appeared to be in his forties, smiled at her from behind the showcase and offered her one of the larger varieties covered with something dark and oozing something red. He also handed her a small glass container of what appeared to be juice.

"For you," he offered, gently. She returned his smile and tried a small bite of the object she held in her hand. Again, she wanted to devour it in one mouthful. Restraint came to the fore and she ate it slowly standing in place.

Jess thanked the man profusely. Was there no end to surprises? In UL-One, sugar was made in a very limited quantity. A little taste of it is the most one can expect in a bakery that specializes in sweets. Not so in this world. The dark brown and red jelly-like ingredients were also new to her. More curious items filled the showcase.

"I wish you a good life here," the man said softly, gently; his few words uttered with a perfect UL-One accent, as he wrapped another sweet and gave it to her, whispering, "For your journey." The man must have thought she, too, had been ejected.

Jess looked at the man, agape, speechless, totally confused. The books told of a world that might become incomprehensible, of continents flooded by tidal waves, ocean floors splitting, terrible storms and terrible deserts—wasn't she in one now? Yet, here stood little innocent Jessica Sophia Galloway, along with everybody else she'd seen so far, eating a sweet treat or living their lives as though nothing had ever gone wrong in a city where *everything* had gone wrong.

Jess felt compelled to take the treat and return to the park across the street like a dog given a bone to hide in a secret location. The fatigue of the previous day and the troubled sleep had left her spent. The pain in her feet subtracted from her energy. Thanking the man again, she placed the other treats in her pack.

Limping toward her destination, she ate the second sweet and sipped the orange juice, watching, absorbing, comparing, her thoughts swirling, remembering. For the first time, she looked at her life and her own city objectively. The vantage point of a woman who finds herself pulled into a powerful movie to become part of its adventure, unable to escape.

SIX

Jess crossed the street an hour later to enter the building that had no sign, but it did have a number in the front that matched the address Annie had given her. A strong wind gust had blown the hat from her head soon after leaving the sweet store. Her tan tunic showed a darker brown where sweat had stained the jute. Hair stuck to her forehead and neck.

The office she entered equaled three pods in size. In addition to a desk, a large sofa stood in front of a picture window. A tall upright fan swung back-and-forth in the non-air conditioned room. A door at the far end of may have led to a restroom with a large back door that led to the rear of the building. She noted a peculiar unpleasant odor she couldn't define.

Jess approached a physically-toned, handsome woman who sat at an actual wooden desk with drawers, not the pull-down metal types that always needed the hinges repaired. The woman appeared to be fiftyish, similar in age to her parents. Her dark hair had been cut short. She possessed light brown eyes above pink-rouged cheeks and lips. Two small red hearts were tattooed on the back of her left hand. She wore a pink short-sleeve blouse with blue pants and white shoes. Staring at her, Jess thought for a moment she might be looking at another version of her mother, in fact, an older version of herself. The woman gave a half-smile, not knowing what to make of this apparition, and said, "Yes, and how can I help you today?"

"My name is Jessica. You can call me Jess. I'm from UL-One and this is Salvage Enterprises, is it not?"

The woman's eyes opened wide and she held up a hand to pause the conversation, vacating her station and walking into a back area through the double doors. After several moments the woman emerged, followed by a very tall man who could be the same age as the woman. He had a full head of black hair parted down the middle. He also wore bluish pants and a short-sleeved tan shirt. He wore a gun at his side. *This man fits the size of this larger world,* Jess reflected, feeling embarrassed, knowing her appearance must be interesting.

"Hello, I'm Ken Richmond, one of the owners of Salvage Enterprises." He put out his a hand and the two shook, as Jessica introduced herself. She gave a firm handshake, somewhat to Ken's surprise. "I believe you already met my wife, Beth," he said, nodding at her. The athletic woman's eyes sparkled with intelligence.

"Before you two get too much farther along, let's ask the young lady if she would like a glass of cold water," Beth said.

"Right you are," Ken agreed. He found a large ceramic cup and filled it with water from a cooler. Jess gratefully accepted the gift and thirstily drank the entire offering, then handed back the cup and said, "I am from UL-One. The reason I came is because your company brings us supplies twice a year. Yes?"

"Please sit." Beth offered her chair. Jess eased the pack off her back and placed it on the floor, taking the proffered seat.

"Correct," Ken replied.

"Then you are our contact. Our people are dying," Jess informed him, flatly, without emotion. She had to look up sharply to see the tall man's eyes. Ken and Beth looked at each other in amazement and Ken asked, "How so. What's happening?" As if on cue, he pulled out another chair and sat on it backwards, facing her.

Jess explained to him about the onset of disease, the crops they raised and the lack of nutrition. Beth inquired, "Surely you have a good source of protein."

Speaking with a note of pride in her voice, Jess responded, "Oh, yes. We raise crickets and use the same coir for the base that we use for our food products. We have a stable population maintained at about 100,000 of them. Annie, our chief horticulturalist, tells us that it takes some 4500 to make a pound.

That will serve a lot of people when mixed with other foods. We first heat them in the oven to kill any parasites, then grind them into a flour to use for seasoning or baking. Our variety contains 13 percent protein, some 5-to-6 percent each of carbohydrates and unsaturated fats, plus calcium, phosphorus, iron, thiamine, riboflavin and niacin. It also contains nine amino acids. Locusts are a good nutritional source, too. Although they have a greater body mass, they also take up more space."

Beth laughed. "You certainly memorized your facts."

Jess responded, "Not memorized. Learned. By the time everybody graduates elementary school, they have to learn the names of all the amino acids and the nutritional value of the foods we grow. Annie sees to that. If you don't learn, you don't graduate. It's the same thing for most of our subjects. She's the one who has always insists on being the person to communicate with Salvage Enterprises and is the person who gave me your address. It's her link to the past."

Ken mused, "We don't even have crickets at Luke Air Force Base. It would be nice to learn from you. We've always had chickens along with a few cattle and pigs." Then he changed the subject. "Why didn't you contact us about your problems?"

Already red-faced from her short time of sun exposure, Jess's blush was evident, as she replied, "We didn't discover the computer link to you was down until Annie tried to use it. The only way to contact you was in person."

Beth asked gently, "How did you know how to find us?"

Jess told the story of hiking to the road, walking toward the city, getting a ride from the couple of crazy people, her misdirection, getting the proper direction from the man in the bookstore, the night in the park with the birds and rain, the sweets store, and, finally, the trek there in the heat.

Ken was contrite in his apology, "I don't know of any resources to help your problems. Almost all the food in our city is supplied by the greenhouses on base and they don't have much to spare. There aren't any serious production facilities or power sources left anywhere we know of, either."

"What's the matter with solar panels for resources? I've read all about them. We could have them in my city," Jess contributed. She couldn't figure out why she had changed the subject from food to energy. She had thought about food, but by the time it traveled the distance to her mouth, it came out something else. James called it a word blurtation.

Ken shrugged. "We've got the panels. The problem is that you need batteries when you run solar and all the batteries around are at least 20 years old. Most are deader than dead. We've tried recycling a few with some success. Trust me when I say we scavenge a lot to find an occasional battery that is usable or reparable."

"That explains why your cars still work," she offered, enlightened.

"Correct," stated Ken. "Plus the fact that electricity generated from solar panels is sent back to the grid, which is then redistributed to users of that electricity. If the grid goes down, everybody is without power, solar or no solar. Everything anybody uses now is recycled.

"As the saying goes, you dodged a bullet getting here with that ride you took. Anybody who drives a vehicle has the means and the smarts to get fuel and reconstitute it. We know about that couple. They're bad people. They probably didn't think you had anything of value or you might have been beaten or worse. There's another one, an old farmer named Willy Hancock. He and his wife live down in Gila Bend between us and Tucson. He comes up here to scavenge like we do. He's a tough old coot. We know him. He's okay. There are another one or two good people from the base to come to trade and a couple I'd like to shoot on sight."

Beth gave Ken a quick glance. He quickly added, "Just kidding," without too much sincerity in his voice.

"What's the trade?" Jess asked.

"Sharp girl." Ken chuckled. "Food is the answer."

Jess folded the fingers of her hands on top of her head, painfully leaned back in the chair and looked at the ceiling, contemplating Ken's words. The man had dumped a lot of information on her. He knew a lot more about UL-One than he was revealing at the moment. The Underground Living Corporation had been formed to construct the city by Wilbur

Gottlieb, who partnered with Jason Randolph. By Randolph's own admission, he personally brought about the calamity. A large part of the underground city was to be constructed of sheeting made from the shells of the virus. Where she lived, slide-out walls would be utilized to make larger rooms, and what once began as doodles on paper had become a reality. Gottlieb named several cities to be built. The first was designated as Underground Living Number One or UL-One. It took years to find the proper land, build the city and try to overcome start-up problems, even while its population increased. Gottlieb wanted commitment. He wasn't concerned with profit. If the human race failed to survive on the surface, perhaps it might do better beneath it. Jess and everybody else in her city knew Salvage Enterprises made its home in Apache Junction in eastern Phoenix, off I-60, just to the west of the Superstition Mountains. One of Ken's jobs was to ensure no harm would come to the inhabitants of her city.

UL-One's population had always been isolated from the surface world as much as possible. Medical emergencies were an exception to this, although minor surgeries could be performed in their own medical facility. With rare exception, the relatively young population had not yet suffered a medical emergency such as acute and inexplicable pain, heart attack or sudden tumor development. If any of those occurred, Ken's office would be notified and the patient would be picked up outside the west gate, off the Yard, the same gate Jess had used to leave.

A single child per family would be permitted, after which the men would be rendered sterile. Prospective occupants were heavily screened, as much as conditions would permit, to ensure lack of criminal background. Once accepted, they could expect a lifetime of free housing, medical care, and food.

Ken and Beth stared at this forlorn girl. At the moment, he felt deep remorse and questioned whether the creation of UL-One had been the right thing to do. When he looked around him at the abandoned water-less oven they called a city in which he and his wife lived, he wondered if they were any better off than those underground.

"Wait a minute." Beth held up a finger. "Tell me what you think. I've got two ten-pound bags of fertilizer for our own greenhouse at home. I'll give you one. Although it's meant to be used for citrus, I'll bet if you dump it into enough water for it to soak, then filter and dilute it a thousand or ten-thousand fold, you'd get enough nutrients in the liquid to jump-start almost all your plants. It should work for the misters, too. You can mix the remaining solids with the coir. You did mention it, I believe."

Jess nodded. Virtually the entire one-mile-long rim of the city housed food-related growth, along with the processing of the food, including the production of their byproducts. Potatoes, tomatoes and citrus, cabbage, lettuce, beets, and virtually any food grown on the surface could be grown in one of two methods: hydroponically in media, and aeroponically by spray-misting the roots.

Jess could remember Annie's lecture, almost verbatim: "Several things are required to grow photosynthetic plants: water, nutrients, oxygen, light and carbon dioxide. What they don't absolutely require is soil. Its purpose is to hold nutrients, which become available when water is present. Instead of soil, the gardens used coir, the leftover fibers from the outermost shell of coconuts. It stores unused mineral anions such as phosphates and nitrates, and cations such as calcium, magnesium, and potassium, along with copper, zinc, and boron."

Once used for floor mats and a variety of other products, tons of these fibers had been provided in five-pound bricks at the construction of the city. These bricks were currently in storage along the west wall of the north corridor, otherwise known as Spoke 1. Recyclable, the fibers were in no danger of becoming depleted anytime soon. A threat to their supply meant a threat to their food production.

With aeroponics, suspended plants receive 100% of available oxygen and carbon dioxide to the root zone, stems, and leaves. They don't require replaceable containers, such as with traditional hydroponic techniques. The pulp could be dried and pressed into pellets for snacks, or mixed into salads, or powdered as an addition to drinks. Proportionately, more products and oils could be made from the skin of the larger fruit. These products included cleaners, soaps, degreasers, teas, fragrance, art colors and décor, plus whatever the imaginative mind could create from the rind. The health benefits from all aspects of the larger fruit would be enormous.

What the experts didn't count on was years of genetic inbreeding weakening the plants' defense mechanisms, causing a reduction in their vitamin content.

"Well . . . thank you for your time," Jess muttered. "I guess I will take that fertilizer." She stood up slowly. Grabbing her pack, she prepared to leave.

SEVEN

"Jess, we'd like you to stay and rest before you go," Beth offered. "If you're in the mood, you can join us for lunch. Afterward, we'll pick up the fertilizer and give you a ride to your doorstep. Will that be all right?"

In no mood to walk the distance home, Jess answered, "Of course. That will be fine." Accustomed to living under crowded conditions, she asked, "By the way, I don't see many people here."

"You won't because there aren't any," Ken replied. "This city used to have millions, now maybe a couple of hundred live here. Unfortunately, they're not all good people—all clustered in this little area."

"People left because of the heat?" Jess queried.

"No, they left because drinking water, fuel, food, air conditioning and services were hard to come by. About 60 miles from here is the Painted Rock Dam, also in the hot zone. There's no inflow into the dam anymore, so the water flows out enough to generate power at the Solana Power Station. This gives us all a little electricity. The water in the dam is warm and full of algal growth like a bad swimming pool. Once that one goes, we could be finished."

He went on, "I know your parents must have told you about all the changes in the world that were occurring for several years before they got accepted and moved into UL-One. Between the Yellowstone explosion and the fracture in the aquifer shortly after your city's construction, that pretty much capped it off for living on the surface. The ash cloud knocked out power in twenty states and the whole world went cold for several years. Here in Apache Junction power got partially restored because we're in a relatively safe pocket——safe from earthquakes, hurricanes, tornadoes, and serious weather, aside from blistering heat. I've seen it get well over 120 degrees, maybe close to 130. Just wait a couple of months. When people left they thought it would be better somewhere else. Few made it back alive. Anyway, why don't I show you our warehouse?" Ken motioned for Jess to follow him through the swinging doors to the rear of the building.

Jess was about to stand when Beth commanded, "Stay right there." From her desk drawer she pulled out a hair brush and a comb. Walking behind Jess she began to gently work on her hair, noting the manner in which the strands easily came loose. She walked around to the front of her guest and said to Ken, "What do you think?"

"A definite improvement," Ken grinned. "That's

one good looking lady. Hot, I would say." He gave Beth a wink.

Jess did not feel that good looking. Unable to hide the pain in her feet and her calf when she stood, Jess cringed at the effort, as she followed Ken through the double doors. A loading dock stood at the far end of the huge expanse. Machines, tools, electrical equipment, generators, wiring, and electronics were on shelves four tiers high. Larger machines were situated along the walls, while high windows brought in light. At the rear, a man driving a forklift placed pallets of equipment from the warehouse onto a flatbed truck parked in the alley behind the building.

Jess held her nose. "What's that smell? I noticed it when I first entered your building."

Ken ushered his limping guest into a golf cart, steering the soundless cart slowly down the aisles. "You're probably smelling grease and oil from machines. The hot air makes it more volatile. We work directly with Luke Air Force Base located a good 60 miles from here. We loot any unoccupied building. Believe me, there are a lot of those. Our job is to obtain survival equipment for anybody who needs it there or in town. We get it either legally or illegally. I'm not sure there's a difference anymore."

Jess scratched her head. "I don't get it. Why is there even an air force?"

Ken replied, dourly, "First of all, it's in name only. Nobody flies anymore for a lot of reasons: no personnel to maintain the planes, no place to fly to, and the fact that there are few people left who know

how to fly. I'm one of the few. It's an air force combined with an army. It's all that's left of anything
cohesive and organized. There are no countries,
anymore. People have to survive. Years ago, outlaw
bands tried to infiltrate the base. Let's say Carter and
I reduced their number significantly."

"Carter?"

"You'll meet him in a minute," Ken answered.

Jess struggled to comprehend imaginings beyond
her grasp; armed bands, subterfuge, a warehouse full
of metal. She swallowed the flood of questions that
came to mind, captivated by what she saw, heard and
remembered. One of the positive aspects of underground living was the intensity of education. Seeing
all the machinery and equipment made Jess think
about James. She considered him to be the mathematician, she the scientist. Both were plodding and
meticulous in their work. While he saw the universe
in quantitative terms, she saw it as something that
could be tinkered with to reveal its secrets through
discovery. To James, the engineer, the mathematician, there was an absolute answer to be found as
long as one looked hard enough. To Jess, the explor-
atory scientist, discoveries never revealed the truth,
because there was none. Their common ground was
their inquisitive nature and their endless efforts to
achieve a reasonable amount of subjective success.
His problem lay with himself. She saw it as a personal problem; one that might never be resolved. He
didn't like to look people in the eye for a prolonged
period. As her friend, Michelle, had once remarked,

"If you want to look him in the eye, you have to lay on the ground or stand to one side to do so."

Ken said, "In a minute, you'll meet Jay Whitmore. He's the head of our meager repairs division. They don't have universities anymore, but in my eyes he might as well be an engineering professor," stated Ken, as he slowly drove up one aisle and down another. Moments later, he turned a corner and almost ran into a man pulling an instrument from a shelf. He was accompanied by another stockier, middle-aged man with strong shoulders and thighs. The first man appeared to be the same height as Ken and broad shouldered, well-muscled with a square jaw and military-style crew cut. He, too, wore a gun in a holster. Jess dearly wanted to ask about the weapons; now was not the time.

"So, how was Sedona?" asked Ken.

"Making good progress, despite our ineptitude," quipped the shorter man, genially.

"Carter, Jay, I'd like you both to meet Jessica, our guest from UL-One," Ken offered.

Jess focused her attention on Carter, trying to divert her gaze from the same Sider she had seen in the sweet store seated with a woman. Carter walked over and leaned down next to Jess. "Please to meet ya," he offered, looking deeply into her eyes and shaking her hand. She gave him a firm hand shake as she had been taught, although a flush came over her when she pictured her tortured appearance from Carter's point of view. First impressions are lasting. There was something about the man that grabbed her—a spark jumping from one pole to another.

She refused to present herself as a whipped slave and managed to ask a straight question. "Are you one of the people who get all this equipment?"

"Yep, me and my friend here," Carter said, patting his holster. "We let Ken come along once in a while. This is our chief engineer, Jay. He helped construct your city."

Taking her eyes off Carter, Jess forced herself to look squarely into the eyes of a Sider. Jay Whitmore. Where had she come across that name? Jay merely nodded, avoiding the handshake to Jess's great relief. That's all she needed——shake hands with a Sider and bring life to an abrupt end. At the same time, another part of her argued with herself about the ridiculousness of the superstition. She'd have to wait and see. She wouldn't have to say anything about it when she got home.

Ken said, "I'm going to finish the tour with Jessica and get her some lunch. I'll be back soon." Several minutes later they had returned to the office.

Beth looked up from her work and smiled, cheerily. "I have an idea. Why don't you stay with us tonight, honey, at our house? We'd love to have you. We can take you home in the morning. You can shower and I'll wash your clothes."

Shaking her head vigorously—her eyes dark and sunken. "I'm sorry, no. I have people at home waiting for me to return, although I will admit, some don't want me back." She explained about those in her community who wished her bad luck because of her journey to the surface.

"Ah, small towns are the same everywhere, are they not? " Beth admitted.

The three boarded Ken's SUV he had parked in an alley at the rear of the warehouse. He drove a short distance to a diner they visited on occasion. A single upright fan moved the hot air around. Two other patrons were present, a man and a woman. The man gave her a quick up and down look and said something to the woman, who gave her a quick glance in turn and made a comment under her breath.

Beth chose a window seat, helping Jess select from the three items on the menu: hamburger, BLT, and grilled cheese. After a minute of careful deliberation, Jess said, "Help me here. Cheese comes from milk which means cows or some other animal; so does hamburger, and bacon comes from pigs. This is from Luke, right?"

Ken explained, "Yes. When the meat is prepared, it is immediately sent out to the city or used on base. There are no manufacturing plants to make anything anymore such as canned goods or glass containers. Our company supplies them with plastic wrapping materials. There is almost an infinite supply of plastic remaining in homes and stores."

Satisfied with Ken's explanation, Jess ordered the hamburger with cheese; the others ordered the BLTs. To Jess, it seemed as though the pendulum that dictated events made wide sweeps here, not the easy tick-tock life of her city.

Once in the warm car, Ken pulled down the sunscreens from the windshield and drove off with no vehicles in sight. Jess stared out the window, deep in her own thoughts.

Within minutes, Ken turned into a side street in front of a home with an eight-foot- high wall topped with razor wire with a solid-iron gate in the front. Jess immediately thought of its similarity to the wall surrounding the Yard, less the razor wire. A quick pang of homesickness swept over her. Ken remained in the car with the A/C running, while Beth went through the gate and soon returned carrying the bag of fertilizer. Ken made a U-turn and drove down the interstate until he reached an unmarked turnoff to UL-One.

"The gate is locked. You'll have to go to the west entrance," she directed.

"I know where it is," Ken nodded. He wended the car through the desert vegetation as far as he dared. Numerous rocks had fallen from the mountain to litter the desert floor. Once the car stopped Ken opened the glove box and took out something. He reached across the back seat and handed it to Jess. "Here, take this. It's a radio." He showed her how to send and receive calls. "It will not work through concrete walls. It will work if you call me outside from the Pen or the Yard. Call anytime about anything, all right? Keep it private. Others might not understand that you can communicate directly with us. If I call you about updates and delivery schedules it will be on, say, Thursday nights at 9:00 p.m. That way you don't have to carry the radio with you. Remember, you'll have to be outdoors to receive any call. Will that work for you?"

Without waiting for Jess to reply, Beth handed the girl her sunglasses. "And take these."

Ken accompanied her up the rock-strewn sand several hundred feet to the north entrance to her home in the brightness of the afternoon, carrying the bag of fertilizer, then bid her farewell. Fearing someone had locked the latch from the inside behind her, she reached into her pack and removed one of the sleeves of her tunic she had torn off the day before. Using it to grab onto the latch handle, she twisted to pop it loose. She slid the hatch open and breathed a sigh. She took one last look around at the world that, in a single day, had provided enough adventure for a lifetime of memories.

A dark SUV remained a couple of hundred feet down the hillside where it had left her off, pointing in her direction. She gave it a quick wave and descended down several steps, closing the hatch behind her. Her great pain had been replaced by a great numbness. A terrible fatigue washed over her, once again accompanied by a great sense of inadequacy. How weak she had become in a few hours exposure. How weak they had all become compared with the Topsiders who lived all day every day in this terrible world.

Hobbling, she walked the length of the down-sloping corridor over a distance of 200 yards into a cooling breeze. A duct blew the cooler exhaust air up the shaft to an exit grate located next to the hatch through which she had entered. The dim light of the central kitchen hub ahead of her beckoned, somehow presenting a surrealistic picture after her absence of a single day.

Once she reached the more populated area of the hub, many persons gave her the bad luck sign. Too tired to argue, she ignored them, ambling around the circular central kitchen to her home, 6F, on the right side of Spoke 6. Her father would be at the computer preparing notes for the next council meeting, as was his habit in the early afternoon. Her mother would be teaching.

It's good to be home, she thought, parting the beads. "Jess, my dear, you've come back," Robert said excitedly, and gave her the UL sign with his hands, hurrying over to her slumping frame.

"I could use some water, please," Jess said weakly, releasing the pack from her back, letting it fall to the floor.

Robert promptly filled a small urn with cool water and brought it to her. Jess told him only the final result of her efforts, pulling the bag of fertilizer from her backpack. She understood that any details she told would be retold in full. The story would be spread throughout the community, with embellishments, until every detail had been exaggerated to the teller's wont.

Robert turned on the red light outside their pod to call a trolley for pickup. When Jess arrived at the hospital minutes later, Danny Gomez immediately ordered a large cup of soup warm from the kitchen to begin the lengthy hydration process. Then he made preparations to treat her injuries.

Robert remained for several minutes, told the doctor about what his daughter had brought with her, then left to find Susan. Once he was gone, Danny examined her back where the pack had taken the skin off her shoulders. He cleaned the area around the injuries and directed Jess to take a shower, trying to avoid getting water on the torn skin and told her to change into hospital garb. Afterward, he more closely probed her battle-scarred feet and applied the necessary dressings.

Jess struggled to find words of explanation. "Danny, I hurt. My head hurts worse than my feet and my shoulders. I heard screaming music and saw lightning. I felt so insignificant the whole time that I'm not sure about my sanity right now. It's absolute total craziness up there." Something had changed deep within her that was unrelated to the adventure. It would take time for her to sort it out.

Danny listened with the compassion of a friend. "I believe you. Right now, your brain is a mess. Give it time to decompress and rest."

For his part, Danny Gomez was astounded at the accomplishments of the stalwart girl. In a single day, she had gone forth into the maw of the unknown and had returned with a single reward that could change the health of the people. Her injuries were treatable, and if one of them should go forth again, they would be better prepared, thanks to her experience. However, in UL-One, there is usually a downside.

Doctor-dentist that he was, reality dictated he would soon be dealing with backlash from naysayers who would seek Jess's expulsion from the community. His counseling services might be required. Perhaps he'd better relegate that to Alex, his good-looking son, who had a way with words.

The adventuress spent some minutes sitting on the bed, slowly sipping the dark vegetable soup laced with cricket powder. When wake-up time did roll around the next morning, she was in a semi-sleep, trying to feel secure once again, as long as she didn't try to move. Images flashed. Her semi-consciousness presented her with a terrible nightmare. *Had it really happened?* A mental level above that proclaimed, *Is it all bad?* One thing she felt confident about: She was never going back to the surface.

Her mother came to the clinic, saw Jess sleeping, went to breakfast, and returned to find her awake. Pulling up a chair she demanded to know every detail. Jess's tale went smoothly leaving out the part about seeing the Siders. When she got to the part about arriving at the warehouse, she explained about how she must have looked to the couple who greeted her. "They were very nice. He said his name was Ken—quite tall. I'm trying to remember her name—Beth, I think."

Susan stared at her daughter for a number of seconds and softly prompted, as if speaking too loudly might dissipate the tale like a dream one tried to remember. "Did she have any distinguishing marks, like, say any tattoos?"

"Yes, she had two small red hearts right here." Jess took her mother's left hand and touched her hand where the hearts were located.

"Oh my, oh, my," Susan repeated.

"What, Mom?" Jess asked, now concerned for her mother.

"Was their name Richmond, or do you know?"

"Yes, that's it. How did you guess?"

"Oh my, " Susan repeated. "It's my lost sister and brother-in-law. I haven't seen them in over 20 years. All this time I thought they were dead, and they're right here in Phoenix," Susan began to sob, putting her hands to her face.

EIGHT

"If you want to talk to them, you can. Ken gave me a radio. It's in my backpack down there some-place," Jess offered.

Susan looked down to find the pack stuffed be-tween the night stand and the bed. She handed it to Jess, who retrieved the radio and showed her mother what Ken had told her about its operation. "He said to call him anytime. If he could answer he would," Jess inserted. "You have to go outside to use it. Oh, and don't let anybody know you have it——you know, making contact with surface people."

Jess didn't have to finish the sentence. Susan stood and said, "I have tell your father," and left the room. Jess lay back down, perplexed.

Later that day James came by for a visit and an-nounced, "Hi, Jess, I checked in on you last night and guess what? You were out cold. So tell me all about it."

Jess repeated her story, this time dispassionately,

without delving into impressions or deep philosophical implications—something she had yet to sort out for herself—permitting this particular listener to draw his own conclusions. She had known James Okimura literally her entire life. He doted on living vicariously, he shunned exercise, he had a great talent for mathematics, and he clung to Jess like a leach because she was the mayor's daughter. For him, marriage means a pod in a better location. And, lest Jess forget, James was all about himself. She saw him as a shallow man with no emotional growth potential. She needed to tell him off with finality. If she told him now, he would ascribe her statement to her condition and appeal to her parents. Other realizations had come to her, subconscious though they might be. James served as a superficial layer for her appealing in its appearance, but could be blown off like froth on a drink. A deeper stirring had begun in her—a seed planted, the suggestion of a sprout—a wild weed among established grasses.

The following morning, Susan appeared once more in the clinic with a look that bespoke both pain, expressed in a frown, and excitement, in the sparkle of her eyes. Gingerly raising herself to a sitting position, Jess demanded. "Tell me, Mom."

Susan composed herself and poured herself a cup of water from a flask atop the nightstand, turned and closed the inner and outer doors to the room and launched into a tale of her own. "We talked for a long time, until the battery on the radio ran down. She said they'd replace it when we meet outside the west gate tomorrow morning."

"You're meeting Beth tomorrow morning?' Jess asked, surprised at the speed of events.

"Yes, with Beth and Ken. Maybe something like 25 years ago, the four of us lived in Tucson in our own homes. Ken ran an automotive repair shop. Your father sold real estate and I had a small horti-culture store selling plants for landscaping and home decor, sort of like what Annie did once. Beth was always terrific in math and electronics and worked for a company called Heath. She designed computer packages that the company would sell to enterpris-ing people who wanted to build their own home de-vices. The weather turned bad real fast and it rained like crazy. All at once, the two of them decided to join the Air Force and, next thing you know, they went somewhere for basic training and got sent to Houston, Texas, where Ken began to work on planes and generators and military vehicles and Beth got involved in satellite imaging. She could access just about any American satellite we had in order to check their real-time images. The military was busy checking weather patterns around the world and told her they were concerned about an attack against the country, what with national weather emergencies occurring daily everywhere around the world. Beth told me Houston got pounded by two hurricanes back-to-back. That's when everybody got trans-ferred out. The two of them got sent here to Luke Air Force Base doing the same thing they were doing there. They got to Luke before Yellowstone exploded and stayed through the dark years when Phoenix lost virtually all its electricity."

"If there was no power, how did any of them survive," Jess asked, pulled into the story, reliving it with her mother.

"I asked Beth the same question. She said they had a good hundred thousand gallons of gasoline, kerosene, and aviation fuel and plenty of generators to do what they needed, which was basically to give them light, heat, and food, plus there was some power from what was left of the grid. While she worked at her job, she saw power grids and communication systems around the world fall one after another. Ours was one of the most antiquated and the first to go after New York, Chicago, Houston and Los Angeles. Tokyo went down, followed by Beijing, Cape Town, London, Paris, Sydney, Moscow—nobody was spared. People were dying by the billions. The really sad part about the Yellowstone explosion here was that nobody had any warning. Virtually all communication systems were down everywhere. There was no way to tell people to take shelter. They just saw ash raining down like heavy snow. When they first left for Houston, we all promised to keep in touch. Unfortunaely, it never happened. Landlines didn't work, cell phone towers were down, and shortwave transmission was nearly impossible with the atmospheric conditions almost randomized. Somewhere in there your father and I decided that with Tucson getting flooded out by a chain of tropical storms coming up the Gulf of California and with schools closed . . . well, nobody was selling or buying property, wishcome and ifcome weren't income, so we thought it would be a good time to try out Phoenix, to see if we could make things work. We heard about UL-One and it sounded perfect. Now I find out they've have been here all along taking over a business that was run by an employee of W.G. Corp., the same people who built UL-One. Frankly, I seriously doubt that W.G. exists anymore."

"How did they meet Carter?" Jess was longing to obtain more information about the man.

"Who's Carter?" Susan inquired.

"Oh, just somebody I met at their warehouse." Her sudden mention of Carter's name stirred something in Jess like a glimmer of light in a deepening well of despair, and she was disappointed about not being able to learn more about him, while chastising herself for her fantasies about the man.

Susan thought for a moment. " Beth did mention somebody close to them who had served in the Army Rangers."

That had to be him. Moments after mother departed, Jess pulled out her slate and looked up what she could about the Rangers. They were described as a specialized branch of the U.S. Army that trained intensely for four months in small arms fire, archery, hand-to-hand combat, stealth, mountaineering, and water skills, before being sent to a war zone. Their mental training was just as rigorous as the physical training. Suitably impressed, she felt a pang of disappointment, knowing she would never see the man again to ask him about his life.

When both her parents visited the following morning, Robert leaned close to his daughter and almost whispered, "Honey, you mother and I are thinking about moving in with them."

Jess pulled her head back from her seated position as though her father had chewed several raw garlic cloves. "When?" she inquired, stunned. Her parents were bedrock Ulonians, respected and needed by the community. To voluntarily leave the city and start a new life Topside was crazy talk—absolutely unheard of. "What will you do? What will happen here? I mean . . ."

Her mother placed a hand over hers and said, "Right now, we're just talking and weighing the possibilities. We may not do it at all, although, we both have to admit, it sounds pretty good." Susan gave a loving look to her husband. Jess understood it would mean the world for her mother to reunite with her sister. What would they do after the initial joy wore off? The options were few: to never see Beth and Ken again or to visit for a few stolen minutes on occasion in the desert sand. What kind of frustrating life would that be? Nobody would agree to either of those. It would be all or nothing. What would she do if her parents left and she told James to leave her alone? She saw loneliness and bad luck signs in her foreseeable future.

The following morning Susan said her good-byes and left to join her sister. By city charter, if she quit the city voluntarily, she would not be permitted to return. Robert remained behind to gather his thoughts and wrestle with his dilemma. He pondered about what to do. Should he follow his wife—Beth and Susan really weren't all that close to him——it seemed like the proper thing to do—or should tell her he decided to remain here to manage the city and maybe join her sometime in the future? At least she had left him the radio.

Tremors rattled the city while Jess slept. The work crews, accustomed to such earth movements, went about repairing cracks in the concrete walls of the corridors. After three more days, Jess returned home where she spent the better part of a week taking it easy, staying off her feet, having her meals delivered. She hobbled from a torn muscle in her right calf, a legacy from the initial cramp she had incurred in the park and then walking with it. Doctor Danny Gomez explained her right hip hurt because of her limping. He could tell she also hurt in ways more related to emotional anguish than to physical distress.

NINE

Jess and James sat drinking lemon tea in a small café known as The Hub Junior, located at the end of Spoke 3, with the hospital immediately across from where they sat. The operators of the café were the Contee family, originally an immigrant family from Nigeria. The home of James and his parents was situated a hundred yards away in the central portion of Spoke 4. His family operated a successful ceramic business and supplied the kitchen with most of their replacement cups and plates along with making household decorative tiles. His desire was to create parts for the ceramic still, but the Russo family, originally from the Bronx, a densely populated borough of New York City, had that locked up.

Like other open-air cafés, The Hub Junior never had to be concerned about weather changes and could operate from Lights-On till Lights-Out every day of the week, when the proprietors weren't working in the Ring. The business served as a perfect people-watching location, as the populace found its way to and from the central kitchen and the main nearby business district at the beginning of each wheel spoke.

Their main competition was Drink More, which specialized in the hand-whipping of drinks to provide them with a slight froth, plus the addition of various seasonings and tiny pieces of citrus rind as a topping. This was located next to The Magic Store, both of which were located on the ends of Spokes of 5 and 6. The Magic Store specialized in slight of hand, card tricks, mental magic, number magic, phrenology and palm reading. This successful business found that most of its customers were among the most superstitious and who enjoyed skirting the edges of reality.

Artwork adorned the walls of virtually all pods in the city, residential or business. In The Hub Junior, a large four-by-six mural had been painted by the Contees onto finely-loomed jute to portray aspects of the kitchen's exterior. The surrounding streets were presented in the color of concrete. Persons strolled nearby, wearing their traditional short-sleeve tunics with occasional variations that included shaved and painted heads, and tattooed arms.

Jess disregarded her father's occasional declarations of her beauty, or looking hot, as Ken had stated during her visit. In her view of herself, her features were not striking, yet she was graced with a small nose and penetrating eyes. She was not quiet and introspective. Rather, she was a goal-oriented person always in search of an accomplishment. In contrast, James possessed the dark eyes and high cheekbones common to Asian peoples. A not unattractive man, his coal black hair hung loosely down to his shoulders. Jess took the occasion to break the news to him. "My father is trying to decide whether to stay or move Topside."

"It's a joke, right?" James began laughing, the vision of looming disaster evident in his eyes.

"No joke." She told him what she hadn't told him before—that Beth was her mother's sister and how the discovery had come about. She did not tell him about the radio. Instead, they launched into a discussion of what the city would do without Robert and whether the couple would find happiness away from UL-One.

"I want to go to the surface like you did," he informed her, expecting her to recoil in shock at his pronouncement.

"Go for it. See if they let you leave. I'm fine right here," Jess stated, flatly. If nothing else, James was true to form, wanting to do what other people did, absorbing their experience and acting as though it were his own.

James did not reply to her dismissive response and waited for the lemonade to be served by a tall, long-haired beauty named Abike Contee, whose first name meant *Born to be Treasured* in Nigerian. Her father had immigrated to America two years before the founding of UL-One. With flawless, dark-ebony skin, she had been admired by men all her life. She and her father, Onoyu, operated The Hub Junior and were extremely popular because of their outgoing personalities and the African dance and rhythm they brought to the city, along with their dynamic personalities. Her mother had died during childbirth, some two years after moving to the city, a terrible tragedy at a time when two hundred others were struggling to adjust to living underground. The pair exhibited boundless energy and always provided a spark to city life. While always having been attracted to James, she had been friends with Jess all her life. She had the grace to accept that Jess would be his soulmate and held no grudges. Given the chance, however, she would stand with James at a moment's notice, at least, according to him. She sensed the time was near to make a decision, based on rapidly developing events. On more than one occasion, her father had told her she was playing nursemaid to a bird with a broken wing. She needed to send her hot blood in a different direction.

"There are rumors about you going around," James said, indelicately picking a bothersome piece of lemon rind from between his teeth with a fingernail.

"Such as?" Jess asked.

"You're bad luck," he answered, candidly, although he feld torn. As a staunch believer in luck—not the good kind—he felt compelled to support Jess, against his better wishes.

"Oh, that. Who . . ."she began.

"Brenda Russo."

"I should have known Miss High Society Drama Queen would start something. She's always looking for a chance to jump on trouble's bandwagon, aside from starting trouble herself." Jess gave a wave of her hand, clearly dismissing the entire notion.

James had to smile. Jess did have a way with words. "Come on, that's not like you, even though what you say about her is true. You saved our city from a slow death and fortune knows, it wasn't your fault everybody started wasting away."

As luck would have it, Brenda entered the café at that moment with her latest boyfriend. She might be described as the perfect stereotypical New York Italian, complete with the mannerisms, abundant hair, speech pattern, family orientation, and a demeanor that screamed, "Don't mess with me." Her problem lay in that she had watched too many gangster movies about New York Italian Mafioso and tried to identify with them. She saw the couple and mumbled something to her partner, who turned with her and left the café.

Overhearing the conversation, Abike shook her head sadly, maintaining silence. She was on Jess's side and would feel badly, if her friend got ejected. A single journey to the surface for a day should not be cause to cast a spell upon that person. To their detriment, such was the thinking of those like of Brenda—sometimes obtrusive, rarely subtle, quick to find fault, slow to find good.

Abike, her father, and whoever they asked to work their business, considered it politically expedient and best for business to stay neutral and maintain a separation from their customers' conversations and basic gossip. This did not mean they didn't remember conversations and discuss them after-hours between themselves—all in strict confidence.

"See what I mean?" said James.

"What can I do about it?" Jess asked, in all earnestness.

"Nothing you can do. Their memory won't fade. It's something you're going to have to live with. Hopefully, at some time, people will see that you brought back good to the city, at least enough to make them have second thoughts."

Jess grimaced at his words of wisdom, knowing they were said to placate her. "I thought I just did that. True, people want something more concrete, you know, not as hard to prove as better health—perhaps something tied in with good luck or positive opinion."

"Good luck with that," he replied, sourly.

James was all about James, especially when it came to letting her bear the brunt of trouble, rather than sharing it together as a married couple would. Obviously and thankfully, it appeared he had given up on her without her having to say it.

No. It was more than that. James's problem was his shallow personality. The fact that he couldn't discuss anything on a philosophical level was one thing, the fact that he had no interest in anything except numbers or social interactions was another. She saw a piece missing from his thinking pattern, like a broken cog in wheel that wouldn't let the wheel rotate all the way around. He would flip-flop from being shallow to over-analyzing everything. Jess could make up a crazy idea about how to achieve something that may never have been done before and James could mull it over and come up a procedure to get from A to Z with the tools at hand. If asked to make it happen, he couldn't do it. He was his own worst enemy. A knock on the head might not be enough.

Leaning toward him, she said excitedly, "Oh, with all that was going on I forgot to tell you. When I was Topside, I saw a Sider." Her plan was to shock him into leaving. For some reason she couldn't tell him flat out. She was befuddled in understanding how she can have such great courage to adventure forth into an unexplored world and remain a coward in terms of facing a personal issue. The latter was definitely more difficult.

James pulled back in surprise, then leaned in again, "You actually *saw* a real Sider?"

"They looked just like in the pictures." She neglected to tell him about Jay Whitmore. She had looked up his name on her slate while lying in the hospital. Jason Whitmore: He eschewed the name of Jason and had taken the name of Jay. One of the first Siders to be born. Worked for Jason Randolph before being kidnapped by Wilbur Gottlieb and sent to England; became a biochemist and later worked for Gottlieb to retrain as an engineer. Helped with the construction of UL-One, an underground city in the

Desert Southwest of the United States.

She also left out the mention of Carter, who had occupied her thoughts continually since their meeting. Her discomfiture came from the fact that she already had more fantasies about him than she had ever entertained about any man. She would never see him again. One and done.

"You didn't tell anyone else about seeing a Sider, did you?" he inquired, with great concern.

"Not even my folks. Like I said, I just remembered."

"If that gets out, people will put more on your plate. They'll probably be on me, too," he snorted. "Rumor has it WG Corp. was all for the Siders at the start of it all, only to screen them out when they applied to live in UL-One. WG thought it could lead to internal strife, the last thing the new city needed with all the social and worldwide upheaval back then."

Jess saw James glance at Abike occasionally without him realizing she was watching him. In fact, she didn't care.

"If your father leaves, how is he supposed to know when the house is ready?" James tried to compute, but was clearly puzzled.

"Uh...I guess they have some kind of system worked out. There's more," she added, changing the subject. "My science classes are being boycotted, thanks to parents who don't want their children near me."

James was a good theoretical engineer like his father, although he lacked the drive to learn the applications of this knowledge. He preferred to apply his skills toward pottery and sandal making. Although he had a tender side, James also had rough edges that annoyed the heck out of her. She liked decisive people, which wasn't James. For as long as she had known him, he had let other boys intimidate him. Others took boxing and marital arts classes. He preferred to read about construction.

The following day, Jess was readmitted into the hospital.

TEN

Signing up to join UL-One sounded like a great idea until the screening process came into play, which eliminated many of the most talented people who wanted to live in the new city. Even after being accepted, many became disillusioned and left, with no place to which they could return. Depression and claustrophobia were two reasons cited most for leaving. Similar to any new neighborhood, this one gained stability over time. The enlistment of a good doctor presented itself as one of the most challenging tasks the founding fathers had to overcome. Typically, the rare physician who decided to spend an entire lifetime underground in a closeted community found that a wife or husband would have something to say about it. No doctor of decent (or even indecent) training wanted to be cross-trained in dentistry or care for totally routine injuries every day. These might include cuts from the kitchen staff, chapped hands from pottery making, exercise-related injuries, or an assortment of complaints from a pedestrian who had walked in front of a hand-operated trolley or had sprained an ankle while jogging. Furthermore, living in a tiny single-room home without a view of the outdoors for the rest of their lives suggested a prison setting.

The son of a Baltimore-trained physician, Danny Enrique Gomez followed in his father's footsteps. He had traveled with his parents around the world, as Doctors without Borders, who treated the sick and wounded. His father passed shortly after attending Danny's graduation ceremony from medical school. Danny became intrigued with treating minorities and the opportunity to spend his entire lifetime serving a small number of people over their entire lifetime attracted him. He was enthusiastically welcomed into the community. Unmarried at the time, Danny soon found a suitable mate in the city, who gave birth to a son, Alex, who became trained over time. Seriously diluted though Alex's skills might be, his intuition and gifted skills at communication were adequate enough for the community at large, enough so that he began to be called Doctor by the city's denizens. What nobody had anticipated was the desire of citizens to care for themselves. There were always those who sought attention, medical or otherwise; however, to the great consternation of the doctors, many leaned toward self-medication and self-healing, even sprains and bone breaks.

Medical and dental instruments were gifted by W.G. Corp. initially, while Salvage Enterprises provided dressings along with badly needed additional instruments upon request; at least when they were available, which became a rarity as the civilized world died. Initially workable at the hands of the physicians were plant-derived topical and ingested painkillers, antiseptics, and antibiotics, until even these had slowly lost their potency, as Jess had surmised. The most conservative citizens agreed with the builders of the city: Total isolation could lead to death of the city, whereas too much dependence would do the same. There existed too many things the citizens could not provide for themselves. If the Topside world died, so would they, given the radical climatic changes in progress. This strongly suggested they strive toward as much independence as possible—a cause that Jess had almost single-handedly taken upon herself to pursue.

The central medical office consisted of a triple pod situated the end of the southern corridor designated as Spoke 5, with doors separating the units earmarked for reception, overnight stay, and surgical and dental procedures.

Danny Gomez, a convivial man with great compassion, felt his patient's forehead. "You've definitely got a fever, my dear," as Jess coughed slightly feeling embarrassed at having to return to the doctor for medical care a few days after she had gotten back on her feet.

"Other symptoms?" asked Alex, whose black pony tail had been tied with a piece of red-dyed hemp rope.

"Bad headache, light sensitivity, coughing, runny nose…" answered the patient.

"Good old cold," said Alex. "Maybe a touch of flu. Maybe it's the same bug doing both. "Incubation period is about right," he added.

"Right for what?" she asked.

Danny began. "There is an incubation period from maybe two-to-several days and a seven-to-ten-day course of infection."

"Starting from when I went to the surface?" Jess asked, suspiciously, as she pushed a strand of hair back from her sweaty forehead.

"Yes. Between us, we are concerned," responded Alex.

Colds were not uncommon in the underground city and made their rounds periodically. Occasionally, latent strains residing in the human would emerge, seemingly without a trigger to set them into an infective mode.

Danny continued with his explanation, frustrated that this knowledgeable and inquisitive woman hadn't chosen the path of medicine rather than teaching. "Coming in contact with viruses that are resident in people on the surface is a new experience for us, even those who have gone there for surgery. Nothing like this has happened to us after they returned. It might be going around Topside now. We know it's an infection, we just don't know the extent of its virility."

A shiver ran through Jess as she heard the doctors' words. She thought about the fish once grown for food in the early years of the city. *The fish became contaminated by something from the outside and the entire stock died.*

Danny saw her sudden flush, thinking it part of her symptoms, and said, "See, it takes three things to react to a foreign agent: state of health of the host—that's you and me—level of exposure; that is, how long a person is exposed to how many agents, along with virility of the infecting agent itself. In other words, is it alive or dead? How powerful or weak are the destructive agents? Right now, down here, the last two are a given. The real problem is the third factor: state of health of the host. We're immunologically weak from lack of exposure to foreign germs. Plus, our immune systems are also weakened from improper nutrition."

"For the present time, wash your hands frequently and thoroughly, keep your hands away from your face, and don't touch anything you don't have to touch. Also, stay away from group gatherings, including those in the central kitchen. Stay isolated until your symptoms clear and wear a mask when near others."

Alex interjected, "I will add that you should to try to keep down the fever. Wipe your forehead, neck and forearms with water frequently. The constant breeze in the city will help cool you."

Once Jess left for home, Danny said softly, in case the walls had ears, "This isn't standard stuff. We could have some real problems."

"Look at the bright side, Dad. I've never seen

tuberculosis or any number of diseases we've read about. She might have just as easily brought back one of them that could kill the lot of us. Let's hope it's a simple respiratory infection and it stays that way."

Two days later Jess began vomiting. As the disease spread, the four hospital beds became filled overnight. Danny lived across the street from the hospital and was forced to have a trolley stationed outside his home so he could make house calls. Somehow, Alex escaped the illness; not so his own wife and young son. The trolley drivers were kept busy making food deliveries to homes until they, too, became ill.

Danny ordered all lights in the city on dim during waking hours in order to lessen the severity of the eye's reaction to light and the subsequent headaches that could be ascribed to this disease. He even suspended the nightly meeting of the men's and women's card, cribbage, checkers and chess groups held in the kitchen. Over the next several days, fifteen persons reported none-to-minimal symptoms of the disease and were placed in charge of food preparation which would consist of a single meal a day.

The library experienced a run on its books unparalleled in recent history. Scores of leather-bound volumes were checked out containing the works O'Henry, Lewis, Cervantes, L'Amour, Grey, Howard, Hugo, Tolstoy, Dostoyevsky, Socrates, Plato, Gibran, Clancy, Heinlein, Asimov, and various artists, scientists, inventors, and writers of flesh novels and children's stories. By the end of the epidemic, two deaths had occurred, both infants. It would take longer for the symptoms of the initial sicknesses from vitamin deficiency to abate. As such, recovery from the problem of poor diet went unnoticed in the light of the present crisis. Jess made the call to Ken to make arrangements to pick up the bodies for burial at the Apache Junction cemetery.

A cause and effect relationship could not be denied. Jess had gone to the surface and brought back with her an illness to sicken an entire city, thus confirming the old adage: Bad luck is communicable.

As a native of UL-One, steeped and bred in its logic, Jess had to admit there was a point to that line of thinking. She could carry on a persuasive argument to prove that bad luck could be transmitted. She knew a number of people who were surrounded by negative occurrences, whether it be to chance or poor choices on their part. Those occurrences also tended to affect those who associated with them too closely. It may have some relationship to playing a game with a poor player who brings one down to their level. Her extension of this logic called for the communicability of good luck for the same reasons. Unfortunately, the latter was in short supply at the moment.

Over the course of the next couple of weeks after Jess's return, the outer ring became more active than ever as the gardens immediately responded to the nutrients supplied by the fertilizer. Soon, the crops produced healthy seeds. Corn, radishes, okra, squash, spinach, all manner of legumes, citrus, hemp—all grew faster and with more color. The tomatoes were larger than anybody could remember. Even the crickets became larger because they were fed healthier leaves from fruits and vegetables. Annie morphed into a different person, becoming compulsively bossy, taking care of her charges, trusting their problems had come to an end.

ELEVEN

An acrimonious backdrop existed with Jess as the target. Superficially, life continued. Although many forgave Jess, few forgot. Their pity went out to James, who might marry the witch and had probably caught a terminal case of bad luck. Rumor had it, the couple was having their problems. Popular sentiment also had it that it might be a good idea to give James a wide berth. In case Abike didn't know it already, maybe somebody might want to slip in a quiet word, encouraging her to accidentally run into him a little more often. Somebody thought they heard somebody say that the red witch was never going to get married, not to James, not to anyone.

Prejudices and popular sentiment aside, many believed the addition of a few new-age medications would be helpful. How to obtain them in a world gone dead was another story, if Jess's tale could be believed. These medications were denied them by the religious principles held by the founder of the city, Wilbur Gottlieb. These principles were absolute and written into the city charter: No synthetic agents for health-related issues would be acceptable—including painkillers, anti-microbials, anti-inflammatories and anti-depressants. In his diary, the engineer described his own immunological issue and he shunned anything artificial. Only naturopathic remedies were acceptable.

As good fortune would have it, Rogers, a conservative on the city council, resigned, ostensibly to take up with Brenda. Another man named Jim Page, husband of UL-One's head gym instructor, Mara, also resigned. Rumor had it she nagged him to leave for the sole purpose of petitioning herself to become a member. Once Jess's father left, the position of mayor would become available—a post coveted by Brenda.

Robert petitioned for Jess to be voted for acceptance as a council member, as did Mara for herself. He believed that it might be harder to eject Jess, if she were on the council.

Council meetings were held on alternate Mondays in the dining room after the last of the three dinner shifts, the single evening when the game players were not permitted to be present. A dozen paintings hung on the walls, which displayed this month's theme of flowers. Clanging and scraping sounds filled the corridors as the kitchen crew prepped for the morning meal.

Once Robert called the meeting to order, the council reviewed old business. This included some pilfering of sweets by occasional employees of Jean's Hair and Nail Salon and obscene pictures painted on shaved heads by the operator of Head and Body Painting Ltd., what to do about illicit transactions of cannabinoids, and special awards for outstanding students. Both Mara Page and Jess were voted in as new members. Well-known to float in any direction the wind blew, Mara had her own agenda, which included close ties with Brenda and removal of bad luck from their beloved city.

At the conclusion of that particular council meeting, Robert announced he would depart the city the following morning. After packing his meager belongings, he returned the radio to Jess and the following morning left the city. By the next meeting, Brenda had gathered her forces and was voted in as the new mayor. She quietly suggested that Jess bring up the issue of the city's need to be upgraded. Twenty years is a long time to ignore infrastructure. With Jess as a contact with the surface, the opportunity to do so might be ripe at the present time. After all, weren't they all on the same side? Jess knew Brenda was using the subject as a ruse to get her into further trouble. If Jess played it right, she might get the measure to pass.

The grape fields in Santa Rosa County, California, were washed out. Left with nothing but their wits, the Russo family applied to WG Corp. for entrance to UL-One. The new city didn't need wine experts; however, it did need chemists. Because this was as good as circumstances permitted, Barry, Alicia and their ten-year-old daughter, Brenda, joined the growing population.

The intent was for them to work the soil chemistry side of hydroponics. That never happened. Instead, shortly after moving to their new residence, the entire Internet disappeared, as did virtually all surface communications, save a single line to a WG sponsored warehouse in Apache Junction called Salvage Enterprises. Given lack of direction, the Russos did what they did best—turning sugars into alcohol. Whether it came from grapes, beets, or fruits, all sugars fell victim to their talents—to the delight of the populace and the consternation of the ruling class, including the mayor, Robert Galloway.

In another life, Brenda might have become a chemical engineer, or, at the least, owner of a successful winery. In this life, she fell victim to her own products, finding the need to over-taste the alcoholic products her family produced. Having been warned on a number of occasions about her excesses, at the age of 30, she found herself in Unit 7 for two days. With a lot of time to think on her hands, Brenda swore she would remake herself—to an extent. Once released, she stopped drinking entirely and found illegal cannabis usage more to her liking. She cut and styled her hair and found solace in rumor mongering. Her figure had always been attractive to men; now she began an exercise program in the gym and hatched a long-term plan. Brenda went back to work, making the most potent alcohol possible under the confining circumstances. There were no glass reflux condensers, copper coils, or wooden casks available.

Since moving their operation to the underground city, headaches and other side-effects became a common complaint among users of any alcohol produced by the Russos. In defense, the family maintained that nothing could be done about it. The side effects were due to the presence of chemicals known as aldehydes and ketones, most prevalent in red wines. The majority of the problem lay with cooling and condensation, rather than the source product.

Historically, while the Okimuras made cups and plates for dining, Brenda asked them to create flasks and tubing from Brenda's designs for the purpose of improving cooling. She requested them to produce double-sets of porcelain coils. Experimentation soon found that spray misting the coils, along with blowing air over them with a small fan, dropped their temperature significantly and produced a purer product at a faster rate. No complaints ensued when she used a large supply of coir to make filters which removed some of the alcohol and a high percentage of the side products. Most of the headaches disappeared. The new Brenda could do no wrong.

A sense of regret overcame Brenda. Jess's aptitude tests were exceptionally high—one of those people you love to hate, someone who was genetically endowed with physicality, looks, smarts, and drive. She would have made an excellent student of Brenda's with her penchant for science and her inquisitive nature. When combined with Brenda's knowledge of chemistry and almost Germanic sense of exactitude, they would have made a great team. Alas, destiny dictated otherwise. At the moment, Brenda needed Jess as a contact with the surface to institute a makeover of the entire city. She knew in her heart what the city required. Brenda planned to get the credit, viewing the ejection of Jess to be a foregone conclusion.

"Will you stop your pacing?" Philip requested.

"I'm thinking," James answered.

His mother inquired, with hope in her voice, "About what? Maybe moving out?"

"That's a laugh," Philip replied to her question. "Move to where. Nobody wants to live with this guy." Turning to his son, he said, "Why don't you go to the gym or exercise, lose some weight, and quit being such a dullard."

"You haven't even worked at pottery for several days. What's with that?" his mother pestered.

"I'm tired of digging out the clay pit," James retorted.

"Oh, poor baby," his father gibed. "Before she passed, my mother used to say James was born with a wooden spoon in his mouth."

James ignored his parents, not an unusual circumstance. "Talk all you want. I've got a plan. You'll soon change your mind about me. I'm going to go to a council meeting?"

"And?" his parents asked in unison.

"And you'll see," James shot back.

At James's pestering, Jess requested permission for him to visit the proceedings. It was not an unusual event for one or more guests to be present during a council meeting, although they would not be able to vote. Many wondered why she permitted him to badger her. Friendship did have its limits. She wondered the same thing.

Brenda and Jess spoke to each other about their concerns for the city during the next meeting and under New Busines, Jess received permission to speak. She told a small falsehood. Although she had spoken to Ken on the radio the evening before in a corner of the Pen, she said he had told her when she was in Phoenix that he had acquired a large amount of tubing and sprayers from a storage facility at the abandoned campus of Arizona State University. He wanted to donate them to replace the old calcified units currently in use in hydroponics. When she relayed the information, 55 year old Maggie Nolana, head of Central Kitchen, complained, "Excuse me, don't we have bigger concerns? In case you hadn't noticed, everyone got sick and a two people died." She did not take pride in this girl's flighty schemes and had been vocal about them on numerous occasions with Susan, Jess's mother.

Of Chinese decent, Maggie had been named Nolana at birth by some unidentified person because of a cloud in her birthing information. Her father was unknown and her mother died at her birth in Baton

Rouge, Louisiana. Hence, No Last Name or Nolana was officially ascribed to her as a surname. Her mother's parents took custody of her and thought the last name of Nolana had a cute lilt to it and left it alone. Maggie grew up waiting tables and cooking at her grandmother's restaurant until she struck out on her own at the age of thirty, where she was hired on as a full-time cook at a diner in Phoenix. After five years, she saw an opportunity and joined the underground city at its inception, responding to the enticement of heading its food services.

Jess expected Maggie's words. Both she and Maggie were staunch traditionalist and a bitter defenders of UL-One. The difference was that she saw herself as a realist and a progressive. This time she looked at Annie Rostov, who had complained for some time about the lackluster appearance of plant leaves for as long as Jess could remember. Annie was definitely interested in the acquisition of the new lines.

Alex Gomez, assistant head physician of the city, raised his hand. "Maggie, our nutrition-related illness is diminishing almost daily with the fertilizer Jess brought back. Is that not true?"

"What's more important, illness or misfortune?" Maggie's retorted, raising her chin in defiance, her salt and pepper hair falling back onto her neck. She rarely agreed with anyone about anything.

Reluctant to join the fray as a true member of the old school, Robert had raised his daughter in that manner and had strongly opposed her trip to the surface. After lengthy and painful deliberations, her logical arguments swayed him. This was not always the case. As an experienced politician, Galloway could stand rooted in his spot regardless of who might be presenting their case—if it went contrary to his intuition. When his daughter had argued in support for her voyage into the unknown, she beat down every objection he put forth and demonstrated a strength of resolve he had never witnessed in her before. Her strength persuaded him more than did her arguments. Sadly, he also understood he could lose her, if she left the city by herself. He thought, *if she's old enough to marry, she's old enough to take the consequences for her actions.*

"If you want to talk about luck, Jess, if it wasn't for your father and only because of him, we let you come back at all," sneered Maggie.

Brenda remained quiet, watching, letting the pot boil.

"Then you're not going to like this," James proclaimed, interrupting. "We're talking about going back to the surface again, the two of us."

Aghast at James for making that statement, Jess tried to maintain her composure, wondering what body part he had pulled the statement from. *He* wanted to go Topside, not her. He was the one who vicariously relived her tales, trying to badger her into another trip, this time with him, playing his game to the max, teasing, knowing she would never do it. Uncharacteristically, he had stepped it up a notch. She felt betrayed and publicly humiliated.

A slow death through nutritional starvation would have been preferable.

TWELVE

James was tired of Jess's hemming and hawing about getting married. Now it was too late. Robert had departed. Although Brenda had the authority to marry them, what would be the point? Perhaps some good might come of it for the people of UL-One; that is, if she did consent to go to the surface with him. It would provide him with a lifetime of interesting memories and could provide him with a needed boost of respect in the eyes of the public. Rumor had it he chided her for her physical weakness over a simple one day journey.

Jess glared at James—a look that said it all. "Why did you have to stick your nose into it?" The room remained in total silence. Maggie directed her gaze at Jess to snidely declare, "Go and stay. Don't plan to come back. The history of this city is about maintaining ourselves without influence from the surface. I'll give you that we do receive occasional supplies. That aside, anybody who leaves can stay out. You're no different. We made that mistake once by letting you back in and it almost killed us. We won't make that mistake again."

Before Danny could say anything, his son asked, "Exactly what do you expect to accomplish by going out again?" This was the last question Jess wanted to hear.

James had boxed her into a corner and she had to think fast. Was there anything down deep she could pull up without publicly rebuking James, although the damage had already been done? He had undercut her to make her the laughing stock of the city. She went deep into her well of feelings, as she present- ed her case. They would be words which, hopefully, would die of old age before she took any action to implement any of them, despite her previous con- versations with Brenda about the matter. "All right, here is what I think." She looked from one to anoth- er with her eyes boring into theirs, like a fighter or a drill sergeant looking down into a person's soul through their eyes. "We were all dying. Our food tasted like paper. That problem is gone. Yet, we're weaker by the year. Our computer system is hang- ing on by a thread and our knowledge of the outside world is totally lacking." *Because there is no outside world,* she wanted to add. "We use their water and their energy. There's an entire planet we know noth- ing about. Why? Because our forefathers wanted to keep us ignorant of life out there and created rules to keep us separate."

"That's the whole point of UL-One, in case you

hadn't noticed, my dear. And life goes on, doesn't it?" retorted Maggie, sarcastically.

"I'm not going to let us die," proclaimed Jess. As she said that, she wondered what lay beneath those words. Her recent return from a nightmarish experience had made her vow to never go back. She swore to herself she would do her best to return her people to better health. What she had brought back didn't come close to what they needed. She had argued against her own doctrine of independence; a doctrine that wore the badge of failure. Hard as it as to admit, her new mantra had become: You have to be dependent before you can be independent.

"She's right," said Alex, who had a magnetic personality and a great bedside manner. The well-worn word around town was that before he was married, he wasn't good at just bedsides.

Maggie turned to Alex, "Which part?"

"All of it," Alex replied with confidence. "From the standpoint of my father and me, we could all use better medications and better instruments to aid in our diagnoses and treatments. How about better lighting so we can see what we're doing when we're drilling your teeth, Maggie."

James added, "Jess made some friends up there. We'll appeal to them for help. Look, UL-One is our home. We're not moving away, if that's what some of you may want. To my mind, we must be revitalized, isn't that right, Annie?"

Jess stared at James. Obviously, the man was trying to convince himself, without appearing to be a fool. Too late for that.

For an unexplainable reason, Jess felt invigorated after her diatribe. Heads turned to the woman who understood, perhaps better than anyone, the need for upgrades. If the rest could be done to those standards, she was all for it. Reluctantly, she nodded in agreement. Visiting a Topside city was forbidden, unless surgery at the base hospital required skills beyond their skill level. Jess had gone once, and, all right, an exception had been made. Now two of them wanted to go.

"I say let them go. We'll discuss their ejection when they return." This from Mara.

"Why don't we discuss it now?" asked Maggie.

Danny nodded. "Brenda, you've been pretty quiet over there. What are you thinking?"

"You know me. I'm a believer in the old ways, as we all are. It hurts me to say she's right. Gottlieb may have had this city built, but his experts were wrong in many ways. They thought we could farm fish, until the fish died. Where would we get the food to feed the fish? How much space would it take to filet the fish and recycle the parts, or how would we obtain replacement pumps for filtration and oxygenation? They made mistakes. I understand it was because they were in a hurry because the world was ending. Maybe someday we can be totally independent. For now, if we don't make serious changes soon, we'll die down here. I believe that."

"Okay, say the two of them go," said Maggie, not ready to give in. "What's the goal? Is there a plan, or is it hit and miss? Is it trial and error? You know, like they used to say, 'Make an error, we take you to trial'."

Although she was used to it, Maggie's sarcasm bit at Jess. She did her best not to let it show. "We don't know for sure, yet." said Jess. And she didn't. Damn James for opening his mouth and getting her into this. If she wanted to go back to the surface, which she didn't, it would be on her terms. Now he had taken that choice away from her.

"Really," replied the head of the central kitchen. "Do you know whether or not you'll be bringing back another virus to kill a few more of us?"

Brenda had heard enough of her vitriol. Trying to maintain order to the meeting, she interjected, "That's enough, Maggie. You're out of order. There's no place for those accusations here." To her credit, Maggie ran a very tightly regulated program and had done so over those many years. No sickness had ever been ascribed to her kitchen as long as she had been in charge. On the opposite side of the balance sheet, she knew very little about anything else, save gossip. She dedicated her free time to conversing with people on the streets, asking how they might be feeling this fine day (even though all the days were the same) and trying to glean suggestions for better tasting food, her store of cookbook information for the masses having been depleted long ago. While doing so, she might inquire about who said what to whom and what whom had thought about what who had said.

"What turned your head, Brenda?" Maggie snidely remarked.

"Do you want a barb, Maggie? How about that little personal stash of beet sugar you have hidden in the kitchen. That's an offense against the community," Brenda tossed back.

Maggie actually blushed. That in itself was worth the price of admission. "So what. Everybody stashes something," she managed to spit out. True though the statement might be, Maggie was quite sure of herself, almost narcissistic. Nobody called her out like that without the favor being returned.

Returning to enter the devil who patiently waited had little attraction to Jess. She could accept her own personality flaws, but self-punishment had no place among them. She offered, "In answer to your last question, Maggie, we don't really have a plan, other than to save ourselves from ourselves. Our founders were caught short and didn't have time to get prepare us for the long haul. Another two years preparation time wouldn't have hurt. It's up to us to do that. We're not talking about going right now, anyway; we're thinking maybe sometime in the future." Yes, that was it. If she could stall long enough, perhaps the entire issue would melt away.

Her mind flashed back to how she might have acquired the disease. How many Topside citizens had she come in contact with, perhaps in the market or in the sweet store, perhaps even Ken and Beth, or people on the street whom she had asked for directions? She had to verbalize her feelings. "What we do know is that our children and their children will become less than human beings, losing the sense of taste, smell, sight and hearing. How many generations will it take for this city to die? How about a smart reply to that question, Maggie? When was the last time you were in the Yard getting sunlight or exercising? Come on, give us an answer. As a matter of fact, why don't you come with us to a bizarre nightmare world that, strangely enough, has what we need?"

Jess surprised herself at her candor. She knew she was both right and wrong hoping that Maggie, in all her ignorance, wouldn't realize the truth and the lie in Jess's statement. In truth, their senses had dulled and would continue to do so. At least their wide mixture of population groups would provide for a very deep gene pool—one that wouldn't become the victim of in-breeding as would one in which the population consisted of all white, black, Asian or Hispanic people who inbred within their own small community for generations. She had brought this up with Alex in the past and he had agreed with her. Now he remained silent, although he gave a slight encouraging nod of the head. The lie was that it might not take several generations for the city to die. It could happen in a moment's time, if a large earthquake replaced the occasional tremors.

Maggie blushed for a second time, pursed her lips and remained silent for a moment. Things were not going well for her today. She retorted, without answering the question, "Can you promise you won't bring back more sickness? I almost died."

Mara Page declared, "I'm with Maggie. It's made up nonsense. If it ain't broke, don't find an excuse to fix it. Everything's fine and suddenly nothing is good anymore. Well, I say no."

Danny, whose sense of adventure had faded years before, could see the point. The city did need work. If laws can separate church and state, what separates fact from fiction, practicality from superstition, necessity from religion doctrine?

Before anyone could reply, Brenda said, "I move we vote on obtaining assistance to upgrade the city as described by Jess."

"I'll second the motion," said Alex. The vote was taken with Brenda, Jess, Annie, Alex and Danny in favor; Maggie and Mara against. The motion was approved.

After the meeting, Maggie remained behind to check on the kitchen staff's preparations. Jess watched her linger in order to catch any after-meeting gossip, ensuring that her friends heard the latest whispers.

Jess and James loitered on their own to exchange a few words with the others, then Jess nodded to James to follow her outside. Once in the walkway surrounding the kitchen, Jess took several steps to the right to stop next to the kitchen wall. Passers-by saw the couple emerging from a council meeting. Jess smiled broadly, a trick of her mother's—before she quietly ripped her father to shreds.

"Who told you to speak for me?" she demanded,

teeth showing in the happiest of all smiles, as though they had finally agreed upon a wedding date.

"I wasn't speaking for you, Jess, (he had stopped calling her various endearing names after Robert's departure) I was speaking for the city," he began, defensively.

Appearing in a good mood, she countered, smiling, grinning broadly. "No, you spoke for me and for yourself. You were an invited guest. You were there to observe the proceedings, not to present what your fantasy allowed."

James looked around him at the prying eyes of the passers-by who were visiting the various boutiques. He grinned in turn. "All right, I got caught up in the conversation. I said what I felt. Come on, Jess, you do want to go back, don't you?"

"Hug me," Jess commanded, sweetly. The couple hugged, lovingly. Jess whispered in his ear, without answering his last question, "Don't you ever do that to me again. And by the way, we're finished. After we get back from the surface, if we go, you can run to Abike, or you can do it now. I don't care. I never did. And if we go, we'll do it when I say so, because you haven't got the guts to do it on your own. I'd love to watch you try."

To James, it wasn't so much the reproach that stung him—he could take criticism—he'd turned a blind eye to it all his life. It was the tone in which she said it, almost as though she had been waiting for a moment to beat him over the head. At one time he might have been disturbed to learn there was no future for them together beyond friendship. Now he felt relief. The single problem he had with Abike was her father, who believed him to be of weak character. He preferred to roll with the punches. At the same time, he chastised himself for blurting out a fantasy he entertained about going to the surface—in a council meeting of all places. He already had serious misgivings about his blurtation. It also disturbed him to think that both he and Jess would be ejected.

It was over for Jess, as well. She did not understand why her thought of marriage to him, or to anyone, had a rough edge to it. The cloak of marriage had always felt uncomfortable. Something beckoned that lay beyond marriage and settling down. She couldn't understand her reticence. Her own parents had argued endlessly for her to move on with her life, while she gave feeble arguments in riposte. Her father always told her that if you don't know what decision to make, then make no decision at all. She knew James would try to go to Abike and try to withstand the onslaught from her father. If she did go to the surface, did she need James to go with her? Did she even need go at all? All she had to do was to say no to the entire idea and everything would return to normal. Reluctantly, she decided to hold her cards for the time being. Not so deeply buried was the thought: *Dear game player: Identify each of the numerous back luck components in this picture.* With James gone from her personal life, was her destiny to become a spinster like Maggie?

THIRTEEN

Mid-June

The elevation of the sprawling megacity that once carried the name of The Greater Phoenix Metropolitan Area stood at 1086 feet above sea level, although the nearest seas were the Pacific Ocean some 367 miles to the west and the Salton Sea some 277 miles closer, also to the west. The sea had merged with the Gulf of California during the great earthquake that split the San Andreas just prior to rushed completion of UL-One, over two decades before. The great heat had settled over the valley during the long summer months that began in what used to be spring and stretched well in what used to be fall.

James had offered her no respite since his untimely declaration during the council meeting and her subsequent berating, so she angrily relented. *All right, mister. Let's see what you're made of. Let's do this and get it over with.*

Heavily weighted with food and water, both had

ensured the straps on their backpacks were suffi-ciently padded. Jess had the flash of thought to call Ken for a ridE—an idea she immediately rejected. What was the point of James having an experience if there was nothing to experience? If they did get into trouble, unbeknownst to James, she maintained the radio in her pack.

Jess had her concerns for James, who struggled through the sand of the desert. He had always been overweight and physical exercise was not one of his strengths. The sun hung a half-a-hand above the mountain behind them, the temperature already in the low nineties, the maximum she had reached during her earlier visit. James frequently looked up-wards and around himself, clearly in disbelief at the grandeur of the world, one that proclaimed him to be just another ant no different than the others smaller than he—ants that also ran into little holes in the earth.

At one point Jess admonished him. "James, stop gawking and watch where you're going." Continu-ing to look up and around he stepped on a flat rock, slipped and fell on his rear landing on a piece of jumping cholla that stuck his pants to his butt cheek. His left outer forearm struck the edge of the rock and pulled off a flap of skin, which he failed to notice at first. The cactus stuck into him drew his attention first. Not seeing what it was, he reached behind to pull it off and stuck his fingers into the spines. Waiv-ing away Jess's attempt at assistance, he regained his footing to stand, which caused the spines to dig in more deeply. "Don't move," Jess directed, almost laughing at James's antics. She pried the pod loose and showed it to him as it fell to the ground. Not at all amused, James continued walking, occasionally massaging his rear end, until Jess saw the blood dripping from his arm.

"James, stop. Look at your arm." Jess halted him. A one-inch piece of skin had torn off and hung loose. She gently pulled up the skin over the wound and pulled a piece of gauze from her pack to wrap it with. "We need to go back and have the doctors look at that. "

"No," I'm not going back," he declared, almost shouting. "We just started. All the bad luck got out of the way just now so we're good to go."

"James, it could get infected."

"No, I said."

To Jess, circumstances can be more difficult when pain or shock is expected. Neither is something any sane person looks forward to, whatever its guise. She wondered from which direction it might come this time. She had no doubt it that come it would. As if to confirm her thought, a strong warm wind out of the south blew sand onto them. Their long-sleeved clothing protected them well, albeit adding another unneeded element of warmth.

James possessed no eye protection; Jess wore the sunglasses Beth had given her. Both wore wide-brimmed hats fashioned by James. Reaching the broken pavement of the highway, the couple began to walk along it. No vehicle approached from either direction. Nearing the outskirts of the city ninety minutes later, and with the wind increasing at their backs, Jess stopped to set down her pack, pulling out a container of water and taking a long, slow drink. James did the same and chanced to look behind him. He placed a hand on his Jess's arm, and asked, "What's that?" pointing to the lower sky. The lower quadrant of the southern sky appeared black. Sweat ran in rivulets down both of their faces. Jess took off her hat and waved it over her head and face to add a small element of coolness.

"If I had to guess, I'd say it's a dust cloud," she conjectured, remembering an old movie she had watched depicting just such a scene. It must have been shot from near their location. Reportedly vehicular pileups had been common. She teased, "Do you want to go back?"

James declared, "I came here to see the surface and that's what I'm going to do." His determination was admirable, although at times he tended to be full of himself—probably because he made such good quality drinking containers and plates. In any case, his false bravado was obvious.

The couple sped up their pace, marching along the edge of the cracked roadway. A single vehicle came their way from the south. By stopping and waving to it, they were able to attract a great deal of attention to themselves and a pickup truck pulled alongside them. The pair looked in the window and saw the driver was an elderly long-bearded man wearing coveralls with a handgun on the seat next to him. After inquiring where the freakos were headed, the driver told them to get in the back of his pickup.

To the man's surprise, Jess said, "You're Willy Hancock, aren't you. You have a farm in Gila Bend." The wind gusted making her hair stand straight up for a moment, almost blowing off her hat and giving her a diabolical appearance.

The man picked up the gun. Jess added quickly, hoping she wouldn't get shot for saying the wrong thing to the wrong person, "Ken Richmond of Salvage Enterprises told me about you last time I was here. He said you were one of the good guys. Beth said the same thing."

The farmer nodded, suspicion clouding his face. He said, "I'll take you into town. You're on your own after that."

The pair climbed in the back of the truck and had barely seated themselves when the vehicle lurched forward. "What's the matter with that old guy?" James huffed.

"It's called suspicion, James. We look like freaks to him. We got a ride, didn't we?"

The first set of buildings they passed belonged to a major shopping center destroyed in its entirety by a single supply-line gas explosion. To their eyes, it presented no more than the burned out hulk of blackened-building-skeletons. James expressed his fascination with their size and they discussed the issue in a philosophical manner. One of the qualities she did like about him was his willingness to delve deeply into a subject when it was warranted; although, admittedly, he sometimes delved too deeply when there was no call to do so. She called it the engineer in him.

Their vehicle headed northward, while the wind and storm approached rapidly from the south with gusts moving faster than the vehicle itself. Fully half the sky had darkened and when the vehicle made a turn, the wind and sand hit them hard. They hunkered down below the side walls of the truck until the driver stopped with buildings blocking the direct force of the sandblast. Sliding open the rear window, the driver declared, "That's as far as I go. Say hi to Ken and Beth for me, if you even know them."

The couple departed the bed of the truck some distance from their destination, as it drove around a corner and disappeared. They became absorbed with looking at other blackened buildings. Colorful clothing and multi-colored hair appeared to be the norm among those few people they passed, all of whom were hurrying to escape the oncoming sandstorm. The wind had increased and the main body of the dust cloud approached rapidly. The east-west streets were virtually free of wind, while the north-south streets proved to be wind tunnels, causing them to double up for protection

"We've got a good two-to-three mile hike from here is my guess," Jess stated. "It's straight up this street and then a right turn."

The game plan was to rely on luck, which was no game plan at all. If they returned empty-handed they might both get ejected; then she'd be stuck with him permanently. The one card they held was that Ken and Beth would respond to their entreaties. What specifically they might entreat was something neither of them could define, despite their lengthy discussions on the topic.

She marched them along the street with the wind at their backs. James began to pay more attention to the wrap on his arm. "Does it hurt?" she asked.

"Starting to burn," he replied, morosely.

Their hats were blown off their heads to join the litter getting swept up the street. All the stores had closed their doors to the elements, which left the couple with no choice but to hurry forward. At last Jess led them around a corner and pointed. "It's that building. The one with no sign and the big window." The single story structure occupied half a city block. Two boarded up businesses were attached to Ken's building, one on either side.

She led them across the street. Few standing buildings remained on their right to block the wind. Not a single vehicle had been present during their walk. James pulled the door open and declared with a rasping voice, "That wasn't so bad."

Jess glared at him. His face said otherwise. Something had blown into his right eye and he rubbed at it. Blood dripped from his wound. Her first thought was that she probably looked like he did. Entering the building, Jess feasted on the faces of Beth and her mother who were working at separate desks. Her mother had gained some color and a little weight. She looked strange to Jess, wearing blue jeans and a short-sleeve blouse. Both women looked up at the entry of the couple, hot and sweating with sand falling off their clothing.

Jess hugged her mother and Beth and then introduced Beth to James, who appeared surprised at being part of a puzzle that was rapidly adding more pieces. Jess had not told him of that familial bond, considering it private information. Outside, wind-blown tumbleweeds blew past at a high rate of speed. The dust-laden sky had turned the day into a yellow-brown netherworld.

"What's the matter with your arm, James," Susan asked.

"Fell on a rock," he said.

"We'd better take a look at it. Just a second," she requested. She went through the back door and within a minute, emerged with Ken and Robert. James crinkled his nose as the door opened. He held back to watch Jess and Robert give each other a great bear hug. "James, welcome to our new workplace. A little larger than our last one, don't you think?" Robert stated, grinning, sweeping his hand out and around.

Jess introduced James Okimura to Ken and then played out a drama she had rehearsed. In a tone befitting comedy relief in a tragedy, she announced, "If you will please remember me, my name is Jess. I was here some months past and desired your help and you were so solicitous as to give me assistance. Because of your help we are regaining our strength and our entire community wished me to send thanks to you." This wasn't true at all. It would do under the circumstances, and her playful usage of the language brought laughter to the group.

Susan declared, "My goodness, those backpacks look heavy. Set them down and let's get you both some water and fix that arm.

Ken said, "Just a second." He left the group and returned a moment later with a number of items.

"What's that?" James asked.

"Mercurochrome, iodine, gauze, and alcohol. Why?

"I can't use anything that's not natural," James confessed.

"They are natural," Jess chided. "Mercury and iodine have atomic numbers of 80 and 53 respectively. They're elements, James."

Susan chimed, "James, there's dirt on the bandage and probably underneath it. We should pull that flap of skin back and treat the wound directly."

"Will it hurt?" James became concerned.

"It'll sting like hell, but, hey, pain never hurt anyone," Ken stated. Beth gave him a sharp glance, as was her habit.

"Then, leave it," James insisted.

"Bad decision," Susan warned. She cleaned the wound and applied the germicides. James almost cried in pain when the alcohol hit the wound. She wrapped it in gauze. "Check it later. Okay? We want air to get to it so it'll dry."

Once that task was completed, James thanked her and asked, "Would any of you be willing to help us sell or trade these artworks from our home?" The pair began to unload them, spreading the contents atop Beth's desk. Grains of sand cascaded from their tunics and hair onto the materials, and they dutifully brushed them off onto the floor as they appeared.

Susan and Robert weren't surprised at what they saw: a pile of woven, stitched and decorated goods. Most of the bright colorful scenes detailed the underground world and the shops—comings and goings of people in their various activities— riding trolleys, growing produce, men and women exercising, conversing in the pods, and a priceless and wonderful depiction of parallax as the trolley tracks narrowed in the distance of a tunnel toward the central kitchen in the distance.

James watched Beth trace the tracks with her finger and said, "Euclid's Fifth Postulate basically states that parallel lines will never meet. However, in non-Euclidian geometry . . . "

"Not, now, James," Jess chided.

"Oh, sorry," he said.

Ignoring him, Beth touched a corner of one of the pieces and examined it more closely. It wasn't made of cloth as she knew it, definitely not cotton and definitely not a synthetic such as nylon, rayon, or polyester. It was more akin to a plant-like material—jute perhaps? If so, it suggested the use of looms. She gently fingered each piece, as though she were running her fingers through a chest of gold and jewels. "Did you make these yourselves?" she inquired, looking up at her visitors in wonder.

"No, ma'am . . . Beth." James responded. "Well,

Jess and I did make a couple. Mostly, they represent the artwork of our people. That one there is my favorite, the one that has the different designs on the plates."

Ken might have laughed at the comment about plates, except for the geometrical presentation of the different colored and differently-fashioned drinking vessels, from small to large, presented in the cloth artwork. They were laid out in a pattern very strongly suggestive of the planets of the solar system in orbit about a sun, which, in this case, appeared to be the yellow hub of a wheel. Beth appeared to be delighted beyond measure. She had always been an art lover who could realize unique quality when she saw it.

"You made this?" Beth gasped in awe.

"Well, actually, yes."

Ken asked, "Do you know anything about astronomy, James?"

"Sorry, sir, it's not one of my areas of interest," James answered, who seemed to regard the question as curious.

Listening to his response, Jess asked herself for the hundredth time, *How can a person be a creative and a smart mathematician, yet be a complete social dud at the same time? Of course, there is always me—a cold blooded creature who slides out of the darkness into the light of the sun to get burned. How does that work?*

Ken excused himself and walked into a small side room. A moment later he returned with money in his hand. "Here, take this money. It may help you buy what you need while you're here. We still use it when we don't have any other medium of exchange."

The couple now had money in their pockets and, just as importantly, many pounds of weight off their shoulders. "Well, thank you both," said James, as he looked around the front office area. He had to ask, "Uh, what do you make here?"

"We don't make, we give or trade. Go on back and take a tour," offered Ken.

"Mind if I come too?" Jess asked, grasping at the opportunity to see Carter, whom she had forgotten about for a couple of minutes; just for one more look, a word or two, a positive memory to take home in case all else failed. Beth lovingly refolded the treasures to gently place them into a carton. Her actions were suggestive of a person who was accustomed to the handling of precious goods.

Jess turned to her mother's sister and asked, "Oh, Beth, may I borrow your brush and comb, please? I must look a mess."

FOURTEEN

Once in the warehouse portion of the building, Ken said, "Jessica, you've seen it, so why don't you drive and show James the different sections?" He explained the operation of the battery-operated cart to her and offered to the visitors, "Friends, I invite you to peruse the warehouse at your leisure and plan on spending the night with us at our home. You can stay here until later this afternoon or go out on your own. We'll meet you back here at 5:00 o'clock. As for the dust storm, it might last for an hour or last for a day. Nobody knows. Feel free to wander. If you want to eat, there is a small diner down the street where we ate before. It may or may not be open for lunch today and their menu is skimpy, as you know. In a little while, the four of us have to go to the base for a few hours. Jess, they've asked me to bring your parents to teach them some of your hydroponic techniques." At that, Ken departed to enter the office.

"What's that smell?" James announced, seating

himself on the passenger side of the vehicle.

"It's a combination of grease and machine oil," she said. "The heat makes it more volatile." She began driving slowly up and down the aisles of the hot building, stopping on occasion so James could get out and examine an object. She explained what Ken had told on her earlier visit months before, forgetting nothing, and looking, hoping, to run into Carter. She didn't know how James would react if Jay was with him. She talked, driving at less than walking speed. As she did so, a part of her mind wandered. She had been satisfied with the relative dullness of her life until the idea of helping her people became an overriding force. The weeks following her single day's adventure Topside were filled with memories, feelings, and self-examinations, all of which led to this second visit—all were building blocks for something she knew not what, except to say, in her heart, she knew her youth was over. She found herself on the high seas of life being rocked by the waves, trying to stay afloat. The mind, stamped with impressions of events, came to its own conclusions. The great adventure had begun. As for her traveling companion, his veneer showed obvious signs of cracking.

Jess's frequent evaluation of others usually led to self-evaluation. She recalled a time in the early teen years when she began to associate with a tougher and older group of kids. She told one of them she didn't feel comfortable being with them, to which the other kid had replied that maybe she had found her element, but didn't want to accept it.

A few moments later, rounding a corner to head down another aisle, she saw the two men ahead of them some fifty feet away, standing, logging data in a notebook. Trying to maintain her composure, she commented, trying to keep the thrill of seeing Carter from being obvious. "The tall man is Carter, the smaller man is Jay. Both work for Salvage Enterprises. Come on, I'll introduce you." She found her momentary excitement to be accompanied by a concern regarding the introductions, both mingled with a sense of amusement. Any embarrassment would be on the part of James, nobody else.

The men looked up as Jess drove nearer and stopped next to them. Carter grinned broadly at the couple. He came over to Jess, leaning down beside her. "Well, hello, Jessica. You look a little different than the last time we met."

Jess blushed. She had regained her vigor—although sweat beaded her brow, par for the course. "It's Jess, and you look the same as I remember you," she replied, keeping the meaning behind that to herself.

"And who do we have here?" Carter asked, nodding at James, who was stupidly fixated on Jay.

"That's James," she replied. "He wanted to come with me this time. James, meet Jay and Carter."

Jay stared back at James. "It's all right, James. Haven't you seen a Sider before?"

For the fun of it, Jess desperately wanted to force James to shake hands with the Sider. She had thought long and hard about her earlier prejudices relating to Siders and had shrugged them off as gossip, unlike her companion.

"Uh, no, I haven't. Sorry. It's all good," he said, knowing it wasn't.

Jay gave a genuine laugh at James's statement. "I hear you're a superstitious bunch down there. Get over it."

Jess climbed out of the cart and let James deal with his own problems. Carter stepped back and they stood face to face. "How have you been? How's business?" she asked, stalling, keeping the moment alive.

Carter lightly touched her elbow and said, with a great smile, "Come on, let's take a walk. Let them work things out."

Over the course of the next half-hour, Jess explained the needs of her city. She found Carter to be a serious listener, respectful, and intelligent. Beneath it all she saw a new type of character in her life—a very tough man who would fight, literally and figuratively, a man with a military background who stood in front of her with a gun on his hip carried in a well-worn holster. She told him about her love of reading and that someday she'd like to spend time in a real bookstore. Tired of speaking about herself and her problems, she asked, "What about you, Carter. What have you been up to? Shoot any bad guys lately?"

"As a matter fact . . ." he began, laughingly, then continued, "not lately. Mostly salvaging, scavenging. Ken, Jay, and I go up to Sedona whenever we can—that's up north—to work on a little project. Maybe you can go with us next time," he threw out.

Jess blushed again. "Sorry, we can't just come and go from UL-One. I'll be lucky if I don't get thrown out after this trip."

"That might not be so bad. You're parents seem to be doing fine, although your father keeps talking about people he misses and events in the past. He appears to be a lonely man. Not so your mother."

Now comfortable with the dialogue, Jess said, "I'm happy for them. For me, I've got to try to get the city rebuilt."

"Give Ken the go-ahead, and he could probably do it by himself," Carter snorted.

"You're kidding."

"I'm not," Carter insisted. "I've learned so much from him. The guy's a workaholic. I think that's why he and Beth get along so well. 'Life is for living', is their motto. Both of them like to create."

"What doesn't he like?"

"Who, Ken? Lazy people who want others to do their work for them; seditionists, traitors, any kind of disloyalty. He's not your intellectual, deep think-er kind of guy. He's a simple soldier who will lay down his life for you—that is, if he thinks you're worth dying for. Ken once told me that in his young-er years he would get mad when he shouldn't and didn't get mad when he should. That got him into a lot of trouble. To solve the problem he decided to either be mad all the time or try to be calm all the time. He chose the latter. I learned a lot from him."

What a stark world these people live in. Dying for one another, no less. What an absolutely new concept, Jess thought.

Carter continued, "Beth told me Ken was an all American swimmer in high school at Michigan. When I asked him about it, I said he must have had all the girls after him. He laughed and told me that he got seconds because two of the guys on their team held world records. He felt better about himself after he met and married Beth, who he calls his a trophy wife. She fell in love with him for the same reasons I told you about."

After unsuccessfully trying to wrap her mind around the location of Michigan and swimming pools, where people raced in water, she politely chuckled as though she understood.

"So who's this James?" Carter nodded over toward the next isle. "Your boyfriend or something?"

"Ex-boyfriend, sort of."

"Ah," Carter said in reply, noting the relief she expressed in that short statement. Not willing to lose the moment, he asked, "Tell me about yourself. What are your strong and weak points? What kind of life goals does a person have when they grow up underground?"

The moment of truth. Jess took a deep breath and began to reveal herself to this man whom she would say goodbye to in a few minutes. Carter listened patiently and made no value judgments. She opened up to him about her love for science, the influence of her parents on her life, her desire to be better at something—she knew not what—the scandals in her city, and even her confrontation with James about coming back. He stopped her occasionally to interject some comparison with his own life. Two strangers had broken down a barrier and entered the sacred ground of trust.

At last Carter sighed. "Well, my dear, it's been a pleasure. We'd better get back and see how they're doing." He held out his hand for a shake and she took it. He placed a warm hand over hers for a long moment, then released. The couple casually walked back to see Jay and James standing side-by-side, writing in a notebook and discussing the implications of various physics' equations. Their presence was ignored as the engineers wrote and translated one equation into another, occasionally expressing a point with a gesture, with James trying to dominate the conversation.

Carter found Jess's hand and gave it a quick squeeze. She returned the gesture, her heart pounding. *What the hell am I doing? Hey, I'll never see this man again, so flirting is free.*

"It looks like you worked out your differences," Carter grinned.

"It's more like we discovered our similarities," James answered.

Carter said, "Well, folks, I hate to break up the party. Jay and I have to finish logging data from our most recent truckload of items, so we'll leave you two on your own for now."

The two men watched the couple climb into the cart and drive off, with Jess giving a wave. At that, Carter asked Jay, "So what got you two so chummy?"

Jay shrugged. "Nothing complicated. I asked him what he did in UL-One and he said he was an engineer. I told him I was too and no more than that. It turns out he has a great memory for formulas with little knowledge of their practical application. I asked him if he knew why air or water flowing through a pipe actually created negative pressure. He said he did and explained it to me. He was spot on and off we went. I will say he was a little full of himself. He talked to me like I was lower than dirt."

"Did you tell him your background?" Carter laughed.

Jay chuckled, "Nah, I didn't want to hurt his feelings."

Carter grinned. "I get the sense that Jess may have to set him straight at some point."

Jay gave his own lopsided grin. "How'd that go? You've been talking about her enough since the first time she came. Then she shows up again. I can't wait to hear the sordid details of your conversation."

Carter looked at his friend sheepishly. "Man, I swear she's special. She's the whole package. I think she likes me, too."

Jay canted his head. "And you're going to let her walk away just like that?"

Carter paused, bit his lip, and said, resolutely, "No, damn it, Jay, I'm not."

With noon hour approaching, James insisted on seeing the park where Jess had spent the night. Their packs contained nutrition bars and water, the latter having been replenished prior to leaving the office. The darkness outside had become profound. The wind had settled into a sandy breeze and the temperature was nearing 110°. The pair exited the warm warehouse to enter a blast furnace. Their knees sagged, as the world of reality re-introduced itself. Recovering more quickly, Jess led the way across the street to a small, all-purpose grocery store. She had explained about the curiosity of patrons at the other market when she had walked out with some of their produce. James conjectured that one had to pay for everything in this world, as opposed to bringing one's own goods, or to trade time, for bartering. Armed with this realization, they managed to struggle through the purchasing process where James acquired his own pair of sunglasses and Jess selected two peaches, two bananas and something called cob corn—all products of the numerous greenhouses at the air force base. No chits. Cash only. No bartering. No government assistance.

More than an hour later, the sweaty couple came to the park and the bench that had been Jess's bed on the previous visit. She was worried. She could feel her strength of resolve flagging once again. Self-doubt began anew. She forgot about her frivolous few minutes with Carter. *What have we accomplished? If we come home empty-handed, we would surely be asked to leave, either voluntarily or invol-*

untarily. Regardless of what we might accomplish, it might happen, she worried.

James read her thoughts. "Don't be so concerned, Jess. We're laying the groundwork, that's all."

To Jess, his words did not sound reassuring. Beaten and dehydrated, his confidence had long since dissipated. His internal dialogue had reached crisis proportions in this surreal, nonsensical world. His brain felt like it would explode to release the pressure. For a moment he thought of himself as a clinician who had lost his mind and who had been tasked with the evaluation of the sanity of inmates in an insane asylum. With him was a woman who appeared to be taking everything in stride. *Not to mention whatever she had been doing with this Carter guy, while he got stuck with a Sider, no less.* He had a problem trying to understand this world and had absolutely no desire to adapt or adjust. Now he understood why Jess had not wanted to return. He felt deep regret for insisting they come here, especially knowing they would face ostracism and possible ejection. There had to be another way to accomplish their goals; yet, here he was, now an inmate within the asylum who was charged with the impossible mission of evaluating himself.

Remaining in the shade beneath the large mesquite, they talked, ate, and watched the birds flutter in the pool. At last James asked, "What do we do with time?" She knew what he meant. In the underground world there was no need for timekeeping devices. If they saw one, they wouldn't know how to read it, let alone set it for the correct hour and minute. The lights went off at ten and came on at six. Hourly tones rang throughout the city for schedules to be met. A longer deeper warning tone went off at 9:00 o'clock, an hour before Lights Out. Continuous beeping tones might occur at any time and signified a tragedy or accident, an indication to check computers for updates. Other chime codes denoted special notices. Now they found themselves in a world where the exact time had a true meaning. Other than movement of the sun, there had to be a way to discern time in order to keep their appointment with their hosts. The solution was obvious. "I guess we'll have to ask someone," she replied.

On this trip, no passing storm welcomed their presence and, in an inexplicable way, Jess felt derelict as a hostess. She was not able to supply the requisite thunder, lightning, and rainfall she had previously experienced and, indeed, had received endless questions about. To some extent, the birds made up for this when a group of tiny finches flew both singly and in groups to the fountain, where they repeatedly stuck their heads beneath the water and fluttered their wings; some hopped, others walked. Larger plumed gray quail visited the fountain to dip their beaks into the refreshment. James was astonished and laughed out loud, to Jess's great amusement. "What a strange world this is," he declared.

Suddenly, the tiniest bird with a long beak came from nowhere and fluttered with great rapidity about Jess's head. The bird's white-brown color was overlaid with red iridescence covering its head and throat, with more iridescence on its back. She withdrew out of surprise, then froze, watching, soon realizing there was no danger after all. The bird hovered patiently, inspecting.

Could it be a hummingbird and that it was attracted to the red of my hair? Jess wondered. Why? There had to be a message there, an omen or a warning. Was the bird warning them to go home—or might it be welcoming them to its world. Things like that didn't happen at home. She gave the UL-One sign with her thumbs and forefingers for general protection, just in case.

Upon looking at the bird closely as it hovered, James shrank back. "Its eyes are messed up." He had the sudden urge to give himself a thorough cleansing. The time he had been forced to spend speaking with Jay had given him a dirty feeling that a good shower and scrub might not wash off.

"Of course. Why wouldn't their eyes be askew?" Jess retorted to the man next to her, who seemed to refuse to accept what the virus had done to life on the planet, indeed, to the planet itself. She resisted the urge to launch into a lecture. You can't teach a man to see, if he chooses to be blind.

The couple left the park to cross the empty street. Occasional pedestrians appeared and within moments, a foot-covering store caught their attention. Staring for some time, they marveled at what people chose to wear and moved on to the next store, which was the same one Jess had entered on her first visit, entering the place where she had encountered actual printed books.

"Look, James," Jeff exclaimed. "Here's *Fahrenheit 451* by Ray Bradbury, and *David Copperfield.*"

"And here's an intermediate-level book on calculus," James declared. He picked up the book, scanned the pages, nodded and set it down. He found another one more advanced and slowly turned the pages, mentally photographing the pages, studying the book, as Jess became enamored with a collection of sea stories by Jack London.

They now had money to purchase actual books and magazines. Weight considerations limited their purchases. The couple settled on numerous copies of a magazine known as National Geographic, which they knew would completely satisfy their clients. Even so, their weight would be considerable. James paid for the books and the couple split the load.

A display of books on sale just inside the door caught Jess's attention. She had missed it coming in. She abruptly stopped to stare. James ran into her. "Sorry," she mumbled, mesmerized by what she saw. The title on the edge of a large hard-cover book blared their words like klaxons: *Great Underground Cities of the World* by Wilbur Gottlieb. She pulled out the book from its slot and slowly thumbed through its full-color pages to read awe-inspiring descriptions of each diagram or photograph. . "My God, James, is there anything this man didn't do?" she muttered. "I have *got* to have this book."

FIFTEEN

Armed with foreknowledge, the two entered the sweets shop. James had stored this part of Jess's adventure at the front section of his memories—a must-do after he had forced her to repeatedly recite her experiences to him. As luck would have it, Jess's old acquaintance sat behind the counter, who stood to meet them. "I see you've returned. There are two you now. How interesting," the man stated with questioning eyes. Dark bags lay beneath them.

"Sir, I don't know your name, but this is my friend from UL-One. We are here for . . . business. We will be happy to buy some of these items from you as well as several of those bottles of water you have there," Jess said, ignoring James who stared at the showcase.

James looked up and asked, "You have a UL-One accent. What brought you here?"

"I joined there when I was in my twenties," the man replied, wiping his hands on a stained apron.

"Things were not adventurous for me. I needed more excitement. I left twelve years ago. I've regretted that decision every day since," the man explained, spreading his arms out wide to include the entire world.

James slid into a booth with Jess sliding into the booth opposite, each nearest the window to enable them to stare out at the strange world outside, feeling both part of it and insulated from it by the glass. They resisted pulling out their bookstore purchases, fearing they might look even more peculiar than they already appeared.

James spoke first. "Twelve years ago would have made us both six years old. "Do you remember anybody leaving our city of their own volition?"

She shook her head and shrugged. "No. UL-One is a small town. Come on, if anybody does anything or says anything, everybody knows about it." In a moment, the remembrance came to her. "That's it," she said, talking around the sumptuous bite of chocolate donut filled with strawberry jelly. A trickle of jelly ran down the corner of her mouth. James pointed to it and she wiped it off, licking her fingers thoroughly.

"It is?" he replied.

She leaned forward. He leaned toward her in turn. Under her breath, she offered, "This is the guy who was taking things when people weren't around and not leaving a chit for a fair trade item."

James's eyes lit up. "Right. A thief. It was well publicized." They both knew better than to look at the man. The couple went back to their feast when, moments later, Jess exclaimed, "James, look, a Sider. She's coming toward me. Don't look. Okay, now look carefully so she doesn't see you looking," she teased, knowing his attitude toward the mutants.

James caught little of what she had said, as though his ears, as well as his mouth, were filled with glaze—except for the word Siders, which he caught. Through their sunglasses, they saw a middle-aged woman who held two leashes with a Sider puppy on the end of each. James said, "Somebody pinch me. A real dog. Idiots," he mumbled.

"What?" she queried

"Siders. Idiots," James repeated.

"You're serious."

"Sure. Even the guy, Jay, I was talking to. I had to teach him physics."

Jess had heard enough. The time had come to say what was on her mind. "Excuse me, Doctor Know it All. That man you just called an idiot has a Doctorate in Molecular Biology from Cambridge University. He studied under Jason and Linda Randolph *and* under Wilbur Gottlieb. If it wasn't for him working for Gottlieb as an engineer with a thorough knowledge of useful and practical physics, something you are totally ignorant of and refuse to learn, neither of us would have a city to live in. You disrespected the wrong person. I hope you apologize, if and when you ever meet again. The man must have thought you lower than a bug—no, dumber than a bug. I'm surprised he didn't laugh in your face."

James's jaw dropped. No words came out. Instead, he stared out the window and let Jess's words sink in. He ran a hand across a metal table top as if to smooth it out. "I guess maybe I might have been a little too judgmental."

"Yeah, welcome to the surface world." Jess thrust. She did not chastise herself for her outburst. A different phraseology could have been used. To her mind, James needed a hit over the head. With James, however, though he might be conciliatory for a short period of time, he wouldn't change for the better. She had known him too long to believe otherwise. On the other hand, why was she coming to the defense of Siders, steeped as she was in the tradition of bad luck associated with them? Could it be that by meeting the legendary Jay Whitmore, she had done a complete turn-around? She'd have to think about it. "By the way," Jess added, "this coffee isn't too bad. I could get used to it."

"Too bitter for me." James made a wry twist of his mouth. He continued to sip at it, thinking, then declaring, "I've read about them. They're supposed to be extremely athletic. According to history, the Siders messed up sports big time. One announcer said that he'd have to retire because he couldn't describe the action fast enough, and when Sider horses entered the races you could make good money by betting on them."

She knew he hadn't read Randolph's diary. In fact, other than studying anything related to numbers, he didn't like to read. How many times had she read about the wonderful scientists of the world, men and women who were relentless in their pursuit of answers, driven by forces they couldn't control? Each time she read of Pasteur, Newton, Bohr and Archimedes, she became supercharged, yet she had no real laboratory to pursue…what? They were gone and so were all the laboratories. If any were functional, regardless of their procedures, their cultures, test tubes, and counters would be contaminated with the virus. She could read between the lines to see that Randolph belonged to that group of the very greats. Beyond his feeling of guilt, he had taken the invasion of the virus into his laboratory as a personal attack against him and his house. He had spent the better part of his life in the pursuit of its eviction.

Completely sated after their luxurious meal and feeling somewhat hyper, the couple wandered the streets, walking slowly, going in and out of the few remaining stores, dodging the heat to find a lesser heat. These shops consisted of a hair salon, Jess's market, and a variety store displaying miscellaneous objects humans had manufactured, many of which were unidentifiable to them.

A thermometer in the window of one store read 112°. With hours to kill before their appointment time and with money in their pockets, James suggested that they go to an early afternoon movie at a theater they had passed. The marque called it a 3-D SuperScreen Three-Sided Wraparound special showing of *War of the Worlds* starring some guy named Tom Cruise.

The old building proved to be the size of a single pod. The couple purchased tickets. Entering the theater room, cooled by two upright fans, they encountered two rows of five seats each and found seats in the front. The top of the screen was torn in several locations. After two hours of the feature movie, the screen finally went black. The couple remained motionless. The well-worn movie skipped and stopped at times. These factors did not affect their experience. Stunned with explicit scenes, explosions, monsters coming out of the earth to harvest human blood—all with surround sound, they wished for complete silence and darkness.

Slowly they arose as one, inquired as to the time from the clerk at the front, then emerged into heat now measuring 118°. The couple trudged through the streets back to the warehouse. Lights flashed in their heads, movie scenes froze in place or sped by to the next scene, aliens bellowed, moans of the tortured or the loved—their overloaded systems screamed for peace, yet were caught up in something much larger than their ability to take it in stride. Ducking, crying, laughing, angry—and thunderstruck at the absurdity of the enormous experience, the couple had been wrung dry of emotion.

The walk to the warehouse turned into a lengthy torture chamber. Their shoulders sagged under the weight of the books they carried. Somehow, without words, they made it safely back, as emotionless robots might trundle from one room to the next. Out of their element, two wasted human beings collapsed on the sofa in the office area by the window, neither spoke as they slowly drank water obtained from the cooler. The hour neared 4:30. Jess thought about the theme of the movie: aliens versus humans. *Exactly who are the aliens in the world we are in, us or them?* She felt herself being consumed one large hunk at a time. Ever since she had entered this world, she'd had to deal with her worst fears: that her soul might erode, her decision-making ability hampered. Yet, every so often, there emerged a suggestion of thrill in it all.

James had put himself on autopilot and, books or no books, once again seriously regretted his decision to come Topside. He had been warned. The good seemed so superficial, the bad so overwhelming. There existed no predictability in this world of randomized events; no chimes to serve as reminders; no guideposts; nothing familiar, whether it be sights, sounds, smells, or even the simple measure of time.

At a few minutes after 5:00, the two couples returned to find the adventurers seated on the sofa, solemn, sipping from glasses of water and chewing on nutrition bars. "How did your day go?" Robert asked.

"Interesting," James mumbled. "We ate at the donut shop, actually saw another Sider. After that, we watched a movie."

"Siders, huh. What do you think about them?" Ken asked with a curious smile on his face.

"They give me the creeps. I say they're bad luck," James stated in a morose tone.

Jess gave him a look of disgust. *Well, at least he's back to his default setting. I feel so much more secure now,* she thought, facetiously.

Ken shook his head sadly. Changing the subject, he asked, "What did you see at the movies?" The community had a single theater that rotated six very old movies, all of which had been made before the Great Catastrophe.

After Jess told him and James interjected his opinion of the film, Beth offered, "If you liked the experience, we have a larger selection on our screen at home, although, admittedly, the movies will also be old."

When he saw their sour faces, Robert became somber. "You know, guys, you can't tell anyone about that experience, or even the one that happened this morning.

"Why not?" asked Jess. "What's wrong with that?" Instantly, she knew she had asked a bad question. Once a single person knew, everybody would know and the entire city would be privy to the information and spin countless webs around each point. It would be considered bragging and showing off, in that she and James had experienced something no person in UL-One had ever dreamed of: movies, jelly donuts, birds, dogs, Siders—and real danger. There was nothing like making yourself the center of attention by talking about an utterly captivating movie that presented new dimensions in perception and sensuality. They would be considered pariahs and cries for ejection would gain momentum from the majority of the populace, even those who privately wished they could learn more details, because they secretly identified with the pair of adventurers.

Beth peaked out the window to see an old four-door Mercedes-Benz sedan stop in front of the building. Smiling, she suggested to the others, "Let's go home. It's time to make dinner. We'll all go out the back." With raised eyebrows, she said quietly, "Jess, your ride is here."

Jess didn't understand. James held back wondering the same thing. Beth grabbed his arm, "Let's go," and began to haul him toward the rear door into the warehouse and then to the alley where their vehicles were parked, leaving Jess alone to figure it out.

She walked out the front door heading toward the car. As she did so, she looked from side-to-side, trying to see into its interior. Heat waves presented distant objects with an underwater appearance. When she reached the passenger window, it rolled down and a grinning Carter asked, "Need a ride?"

James looked back in time to see Jess stoop down to peer in the passenger window of the car. She smiled broadly, opened the door and climbed in. An instant later she disappeared as the vehicle drove off, leaving clouds of black smoke shooting out of twin exhaust pipes.

SIXTEEN

Ken pulled his SUV into the outer drive of his home and unlocked the double metal gate. Slinging both gates inward, he drove up to the house. A moment later, Carter drove in with Jess. Robert and Susan immediately headed upstairs to change out of their sweat-stained clothing.

James desperately wanted to ask Jess what the ride business was all about, but that would have to wait. The interior of the home's immensity held their fascination, their heads swiveling from side-to-side. An instant later, a white, curly-haired terrier came running into the room. Cute as it was, Jess thought James was going to have a heart attack as he shrank back from the Sider dog. When he saw Jess put her hand down for the dog to lick, he relaxed and experimentally tried putting his hand down as she had done. Sadie growled at him and shrank back. Jess picked her up. "Wow. A real dog."

"That's enough, Sadie," Ken commanded. "I

don't think she likes you, James. You can put her down, now" he told Jess. "She's hurting. She's very old. We don't expect her to last much longer."

James looked around him, and confessed, "This house is a little spacious for us. You know, we come from small places. If I may ask, is it just you four living here"

Beth said, "Yes. Until recently, it was only me Ken. Our sons are grown and have moved out. We haven't heard from them for a long time." She gazed with sad eyes at Ken, whose hardened gaze revealed his recollection of a hard memory.

Jess saw the sad look and understood the hurt they both felt about their children. James didn't get any of it, as he stumbled on, clumsily, lost in his surroundings, missing the important points, "I mean, how many square feet is this house altogether?"

"About 3500, not counting the garage," Beth replied, recovering from her lapse.

"Our home is maybe about 450 in total and it's a single room," James returned, objectively, coldly.

Ken gave a slight shrug. "No apologies. In fact, I'm jealous in a way. Set down your things and I'll let Carter show you around while I help Beth in the kitchen. He'll show you both floors, exercise room, outdoor patio, upstairs deck and three-car garage. Sorry to say the swimming pool is drained."

The visitors understood perhaps a fraction of the words the man spoke and wondered whether Ken was showing off, teasing, or just being objective. They had seen swimming pools in the old movies and could not grasp the significance of jumping into water. What an incredible waste of water.

"Let's start here," Carter began.

James felt very uncomfortable with his unexpressed observation that everybody smelled like they had gone to Mara's gym and hadn't showered for days afterward. At least their clothes did. As a matter-of-fact, so did his. And this Carter was the same guy who took Jess off for a private conference in the warehouse and now he's giving her rides.

"This is the entry and family room with basic 65-inch television," Carter began. The room contained a large sofa, two single armchairs with books on a table next to each and three reclining chairs that were joined. Each had a cup holder and a flat, pull-out tray.

"Have a seat," he said, doing so himself. "TV on," he declared. The large screen came alive with animals running in and out of the picture in full color. Dynamic music seemingly came from everywhere. Try as they might, they could not discern the sources of the music or disguise their terror.

"TV off." At first bemused, it appeared that Carter became concerned for the mental health of his tired guests and bade them follow him. "Sorry, I wasn't thinking. Back before the last century they used to have different shows all the time. What we have now is stored in the memory. We don't watch it much anymore. That said, there is a good show about what was once was called The San Diego Zoo. We never get tired of observing the life we'll never see anymore."

The walls of the master suite downstairs were adorned with paintings of Western subjects such as horses, cowboys, rodeos and cattle herds. The size of the bed itself reminded Jess of a book she had read by Jonathan Swift, first published in 1726, about a person who suddenly found himself in a land of giants. The closet was nearly sufficient in size to start a half-pod walk-in business for one person.

When the trio had entered the master bath, Jess and James almost asked simultaneously, "What's that big white bowl?"

"That's called a bathtub," Carter replied. Sensing the blank looks of the couple, he continued, "That's where the basin is filled with water. For people to sit in."

"And?" Jess obviously did not understand.

"And then people wash themselves with soap to get clean and relax."

"What do you do after you wash yourself with soap and get clean?" Jess asked.

Carter replied, "Then you dry off."

"None of that makes any sense," she retorted. "You sit in water, wash off dirt that accumulates in some kind of soap, get out of the bath and dry yourself. Why don't you shower it off afterward or just take a shower to start with?"

"It's a cultural thing," replied Carter "We've never used it. For one thing, it uses too much water—water we don't have. We'll take showers with slow-running water. Washing clothes takes a lot more, so we don't do that very often. Does that answer your question about odors, James?"

Jess had to laugh. James's effort to maintain distance between himself and the Topsiders had been obvious. She, too, had felt a sense of revulsion on her initial visit. Now she completely understood. Where she came from, multiple odors were the norm. To her people's way of thinking, odor-free air was unclean, almost lifeless air.

James blushed. Pretending to ignore the jab, he asked, "If that's the case, how do you put out a fire? Aren't there supposed to be fire engines?"

Carter realized he knew just as little about their world as they did about his. He also wanted James to go away. "Most of the time we let it burn itself out. We have no other choice. It's either that or waste thousands of gallons of water. You need to understand, our reservoirs are gone. At one time, we once held twenty reservoirs of water at six million gallons each. All of them are dry now. We lost a lot when water mains ruptured after the Big Catastrophe. Hundreds of millions of gallons of water flooded areas of the city for weeks—months, in some cases. Homes and businesses were lost, in part because skilled workers were dead and in part because materials to make repairs were lost. Nobody knew how to turn off the pumps to certain areas until a couple of survivors turned up to help shut off valves to the city. The repairs never happened. By chance, the damage to the mains and outlying pipes was minimal here in Apache Junction, which is why we're clustered in one location.

"Everybody here lived on the air force base some years ago. We had plenty of generators and fuel to get us through the dark years, enough to heat the greenhouses and provide artificial lighting for them. The virus that infected the plants seemed to be happy, because the plants grew quickly. Once things warmed up, a lot of people moved out and tried to begin a community here. Problem is, there are a lot of bad people among them. With a shooting every couple of weeks, we're going to run out of people pretty soon.

"In this part of the country the climate change has brought about what looks to be a permanent drought. According to more than three decades of satellite downloads by the military, which were copied and organized by Beth with Jay and Wei's assistance—that's Jay's wife, Wei—animal life is struggling. We believe most of it is extinct because their ecosystems were erased. No person or living thing on the planet is immune to the changes. These changes are in the beginning stages. They could last for tens of thousands of years. The Randolph virus caused it."

The young couple from below looked at each other, each with their own conclusions. For Jess, it was: *My God, it's not only us in our little underground world. The entire planet, civilized or uncivilized, populated or unpopulated, is undergoing a change greater than had ever happened in recorded history. The entire deck of cards is getting reshuffled, with us as a single card in the deck. And we're asking them for help? They can't even help themselves.*

For James, it was: *These people kill each other and they're killing time, simply waiting to die with no future in the offing, no programs in place to better life's condition. How good luck smiles upon us. Let's get our stuff, go home, and hope we don't get thrown out.*

"So, why are you here?" James asked, bluntly. "I mean, if things were that bad, why don't you . . . what's the term . . . bail out?"

Carter stared at him. He disliked this man intensely. Without elaborating, he answered simply, "Actually, we are making plans to do just that."

Then James displayed an acidic side of himself that Jess had never seen before, when he asked, "Help me with something here. Wouldn't you call this a snake pit?"

Jess surmised that he had obtained the phrase from somebody and was waiting for a chance to use it, because there were no snakes in their city and she had never heard of it being referred to as a pit. James saw the puzzled look on Carter's face and added, "From what little I've seen, people here live in constant fear. All I see is hot, dry weather; it's frequently windy; there are fires with no water to put them out with people trying to make it day-to-day, hoping to have enough water to drink. In short, the true quality of life is diminishing."

"What's true quality of life, if you would be so kind as to educate me?" Carter replied. A momentary flash of anger passed through him, Jess be darned. "At least we can see the full open sky day or night and feel natural weather, and have ability to travel at all, a physical reality you totally lack." He was tempted to say that in order the see the entire sky, James would have to climb out of his hole. He bit his tongue. The statement could turn Jess against him, the last thing he wanted.

Hammered by Carter's words, James returned, "At least some of are trying to save a city. You couldn't do it if you wanted to."

Carter shrugged. "All right, if you want to get philosophical, maybe we're just folks trying to make it day-to-day in our world, like you are in yours. Hey, you're the one who is here asking us to help you. Oh, as a slight aside, there may be a way *you* can help us. We'll wait on that. For now, let's go upstairs. We have more bedrooms to see."

Heading up the stairs, they passed Robert and Susan coming down wearing a change of clothing. Susan's hair was wet. "See you in a few minutes. We're going to work on dinner," she announced.

The tour completed, with Sadie at Jess's side and Carter past the point of wanting to strangle someone, the three returned to the downstairs area, where Beth asked Jess to help the others in the kitchen. James flopped into an armchair and, to everyone's relief, soon fell asleep.

In the kitchen, Jess had no words to describe the tools at hand and the food selections available for meal preparation in an appliance that kept food both cold and frozen. Beth saw Jess's undisguised awe as the girl examined the refrigerator and the small freezer on top. Beth explained the benefits of freezing foodstuffs, then walked into the garage, where a chest freezer stood just outside the kitchen door. She reached showed it to Jess and explained, "Before you were born, people used to eat meat from cattle and pigs all the time. Those farms don't exist anymore, at least none we know of, so Ken and Carter go hunting whenever we need meat, other than chicken."

"Where can you hunt around here?" Jess inquired, mystified.

Carter explained, "Not around here. We drive up north to cold country. Flagstaff, Prescott, and the Verde Valley are all gone, not the wild game. There are some hot springs up in that locale keeping the local vegetation warm enough for game to exist. Above that, almost all of northern Arizona is frozen over and may be that way for many years to come."

"What are hot springs?"

"Water gets heated when it finds its way down to the mantle of the Earth. Sometimes it's heated near boiling, sometimes it comes up as steam, or in a spouting geyser, or as a warm pool of water. That's what we have. It's warm enough for purposes of warming our buildings when we finish them."

Jess had lot of questions. "I thought there was little power to run these things." She pointed to the freezer.

Robert stopped chopping carrots. He started to

say, "There's fuel to run our generators when the power goes out," then decided he'd better stay out of something he didn't know anything about. People issues were his area of expertise.

"By the way, where's Jay? Doesn't he get invited to family get-togethers?" Jess asked. She saw the others look at one another and grin. "What?" she wanted to know.

Carter told her, "Jay and Wei, his wife, found a couple of puppies they need to care for. They were abandoned—a male and a female. He's saving one for you. Her name is Carla."

Tears formed in Jess's eyes. "I can't . . ." Suddenly, she realized the puppy must be one of the two she had seen with the Sider woman when she and James were at the sweet shop.

"I know. Just in case," Carter put his arm around her and gave her a squeeze.

Jess recovered herself. Pulling her mind away from having her own puppy, she inquired, "Where do you get all of this food, Beth?"

"We traded Susan's hydro intel for meat at the base," Beth divulged. "We've got deer burgers, pan-fried potatoes, plus lettuce and carrots. Take it or leave it."

Carter asked, suddenly, "Are you happy, Jess?"

Jess leaned her head back, thinking. "Honestly? "Yes. Well, one can always wish for more. For example, this two-level home contains four occupants. If my numbers are correct, there are enough square feet to encompass perhaps seven or eight of our homes. How many rooms do you need to survive and be happy?"

Beth looked at her sister's daughter and laughed. "Given that survival and happiness are two different entities? Honey, it's not really ours. When we left the base, we found an endless number of abandoned homes. People were running scared all over the world, grabbing what they needed and taking off for parts unknown. Who could blame them? Many of the homes could be repaired without too much trouble. We decided we wanted this one, Carter found one for himself, Jay and Wei, found another. It's a roof over our head. Nothing complicated. Now let's eat."

Robert confessed, "I doubt if we'll ever get used to it."

Jess held up a hand, relieved at hearing Beth's statement that Carter had found a home for himself, not one for him and a wife or girlfriend. "Wait a minute. If you're running out of water, does that mean we will, too?"

Ken nodded. Jess saw something in the pause he took before he responded to the question. "'Yes' is the answer. You could run out before we do. You're at the upper end of the water table near the mountains. We've got a lot of emergency water stored out in the garage. Do you?"

Beth saw Jess beginning to revive, as solid food took effect. She and James had come for help. They had also come to get educated. What she had to say needed to be heard by Susan and Robert, as well.

"After the cold dark years, the excess of CO_2 in the atmosphere that remained from the volcanic eruptions held in a lot of heat. As the dust began to settle out, oil slicks on the surface of the oceans absorbed the sunlight. Those occurred, in part, when thousands of ruptured marine-based oil rigs leaked or were ruptured. Along with other factors, the warming of the planet occurred faster than anybody could have imagined. Life began to struggle and adapt with the new, world-wide weather patterns. The upper limit to hurricanes used to be a Category 5. Now, what remains of many coastal regions around the world are commonly getting 6s. Rainfall up in the western portions of Oregon and Seattle is 50 inches, sometimes more, when big Pacific storms roll in. Northern Europe is a frozen wasteland, southern Europe is dry as a bone. Even the city of Tucson, 90 miles to the south, got flooded out. According to satellite photos, we can't find people alive anywhere outside our hot zone, which we think, may get even drier and hotter. There is some sort of magnifying glass lensing-effect occurring.

"That's why we're making plans to get out of here as soon as we can."

SEVENTEEN

As she spoke, Beth realized that none of this was known to those from the underground city who had spent their lives without communication with the surface. The Randolph and Gottlieb diaries were written well before the occurrences Ken or she had described. Any true knowledge they had about the climate and living conditions on the surface world ceased the day UL-One opened for business, because nobody had access to Internet. From what she could find out, spotty electronic communication between proximal locations could not be ruled out."

Ken went on to explain that, from what he could tell, UL-One did possess Internet initially, which died with the rest of the communication networks. Land lines were a memory; airport runways were either swamped, fractured or piled with debris; tens of thousands of airplanes were all parked and dead, as were all ships, trains, cars and trucks. All major roadways were either destroyed or presented various types of road hazards. If there were any functional isolated areas, nobody knew about them—other than those who lived within them. One exception was the Desert Southwest of the United States. Even the Randolph/Gottlieb enclaves in Lincoln, Nebraska, had succumbed to the annual repetitious rainfall and the great flood of 2019 that wiped out the croplands of the Midwestern United States. Military bases existed in name only—places where people could get a meal and a place to sleep. The one in existence they knew of was Luke in Phoenix. The oceans roiled; higher magnitude earthquakes and volcanic eruptions commonly occurred. Despite it all, plants grew at a faster rate, thanks to the virus that caused it all, as they replaced the carbon dioxide produced by volcanic eruptions with oxygen. Everything considered, the visitors didn't know how lucky they were locked in beneath the earth.

Jess said, "You mentioned Oregon. That is up north just below Washington State. Right?"

"It is, at least on the map. Compass-wise it's not north. The magnetic poles of the planet appear to be reversing. What used to be the magnetic north is now in the middle of the Atlantic Ocean and heading south someplace. Doubtless, navigation could be messed up, if there was any place to navigate to."

During the discussion, Ken had started a portable evaporative cooler where water trickled over moist pads in a metal box with a fan blowing the cool breeze in their direction.

"So who's the new mayor?" Robert asked, changing the subject.

"Brenda," Jess replied.

"Brenda——well, good for her. How's she doing so far?" Susan asked.

"Considering that she is arrogant, self-serving, conniving, deceitful and treacherous, I would say she is doing surprisingly well," Jess responded.

Robert shook his head. "Not surprising at all. You need to learn to read people better, my dear; and not make decisions based on what you see on the surface."

"By the way," Beth stated happily, "please note my use of paper plates, not real ceramic ones that require water to clean them. We are conservative and environmentally conscious and we never use plastic when we can help it. As concerned citizens, we avoid pollution whenever possible."

At that, Jess looked at her, not understanding, while Beth and the other four broke out into hysterical laughter. After it had finally died down, one of them would start laughing during the meal which would be picked up by the others to introduce another round of hooting.

Robert said, "Don't worry, Jess, it's a long story. You already know the ending,"——a statement that caused the others to break out once again.

"Boy, did I need that," Susan declared, wiping tears from her eyes.

Thirty minutes later, the six arose from the dining room table and eased themselves into the various chairs around the television. Ken started a second and larger evaporative cooler. "Before we show you our movies, which I can guarantee will be more educational than the one you watched today, I'd like to hear from our guests about their city, from their perspective, not from those of our two new borders. Whatever you want to say is fine."

Seeing that James was still sleeping, Jess began her description of the city layout, the daily routine of the citizens, its homes and businesses, the good people and those who would like to see her ejected. "We've got maybe fifteen or twenty half-pods or full pods available for business operations. The number varies, as they fail or succeed. These include arts and craft supplies for those who want to make their own creations at home or right there in the store; we have a rope shop, two electronic repair facilities, several cafés and a massage parlor. There's pottery making; we have pods for the infirm, although most of our people are below the age of sixty. And yes, we understand that is something we'll have to prepare for. We have separate pods for single men and single women; there is a learning center where our teachers have regular hours to meet with inquisitive students. They're always busy. We also have exercise classes, boxing, martial arts and a variety of dancing classes. Also, we grow just about anything necessary for survival. We have hair and nail salons, two palm readers, a magic store, three fortune tellers, two body painting businesses, laundry, gymnasium, library, and jail—we call that one Unit 7 because it's at the very end of the seventh spoke. The band calls it The

Band Room. Unruly students and hostile people get threatened with Unit 7. That usually keeps them in line. Occasionally, somebody goes in for a day or more. It's like being in solitary in the old movies. They get food and have nothing to do except to think about what they did wrong. So far, that tends to set things right. Your gift, Beth, fixed the nutrition part. Thank you for that."

Jess continued, "We have a tough educational system with home computers and slates that act as encyclopedias. They also have movies embedded in them."

Ken then spoke of his years growing up on a farm in Michigan and their military jobs, while Beth revealed her own background, which Susan had already discussed with Jess when she was in the hospital. Humbled, Jess felt pride in associating with such people, experienced as they were in the hard surface world. She couldn't imagine what fortitude one must have to survive up here, even though they lived in such a wasteful manner. You can find good people anywhere. It came as a surprise when Carter said to the other four, "We surface people admire your humble lifestyle, your simplicity in terms of finding happiness and your acceptance of what you have."

Jess was about to explain that a growing number were not happy with what they had, which was the very reason behind their visit here, when the power flickered. In the blackness, Beth explained, "During the cold, dark years, Ken and I were fortunate. As I told your parents, Ken, Carter, and I were stationed here at Luke Air Force Base.Power outages were not uncommon. When Davis-Monthan Air Force Base in Tucson got hit with tropical storms, the base shut down and some of their operations transferred here where it was safer. Most of the storm fronts couldn't push through the high pressure dome protecting this valley."

With no questions forthcoming, Ken said, "It wouldn't stop raining in Mexico, so people came north to find that El Paso, Houston, San Diego, and Tucson were uninhabitable. Initially, outlying militia besieged the air force base when we were there. Four years later the sun began to shine. We found ourselves trying to live in a ruined city with little electricity. Most of the water mains had frozen, then broke, and the city became flooded. Fire from ruptured gas lines took out virtually all the remaining city. The dams were gone around the country—around the world for that matter—except for one here, so that's why we have a little hydroelectric power."

"You said something about slates. Do you have one of them with you?" Beth asked unexpectedly. Susan replied, "We all have one. Why?"

Jess retrieved her pack and accessed a side pouch to retrieve the unit. Beth looked it over, hefted it, found the turn-on button and perused it, as the others watched. Her eyebrows went up on occasion. She handed it to Ken, who mirrored his wife's actions.

"I'm surprised this works," he stated, scrolling

from item to item. "This belongs in a museum. Even back then, they made better slates than these." He handed it to Carter who had seated himself next to Jess.

Susan touched her husband's arm. "Robert, we haven't looked at ours since we've been here."

"I think our priorities have changed," Robert responded, acidly.

Susan bit her lip in response. She wanted to rip into him, but in so doing, understood she might ignite a time bomb that had been ticking inside her husband since he had joined them. He needed help.

Ignoring her father's comment, Jess explained, "Not many of them work anymore. I'm sure it's affecting the education of our people," Jess confessed. "We need help. The problem is, we're not sure exactly what kind." There it was.

"We'll get to that," Ken said, gently. "One thing at a time." Ken handed the black module back to Beth, who toyed with it again for a few moments.

"Be right back," she said. Beth got up from the table and returned in a moment with another slate slightly larger, thinner and more flexible than the one she had been given. She handed it to Jess and ushered her through its operation. "I don't know where Gottlieb's people got the ones you're using. They must have been in a hurry to grab anything."

While Beth coached her guests on the use of the slates, Robert and Susan got up from their seats and hovered over Jess's shoulder. All three were astounded; not simply from the standpoint of speed of operation, but also because of the unbelievable vast nature of its content and its color. Then Jess began to cry softly. The others watched on. Jess managed to hold up a hand as if to say, "It's all right. Let me be."

Beth wasn't about to let her be. "What's wrong, sweetheart?"

Extremely embarrassed, Jess looked at the others and declared, "What's wrong? Bigness. Big houses, big problems, over-abundance, even big under-abundance, that's all."

The others looked at each other with perhaps the same thought. It was as if Jess had finished reading what was in the home library and had been led into the library of a large university. Beth slowly nodded to Ken, who received the unspoken message married people use to communicate. He made the comment, "Look guys, I've got to run to the office for an hour or so. Beth, honey, show them the contents of the slate and let them play. Back soon."

For some reason, he winked at his wife. Jess knew that a wink was a secret message. Ken left the home through the front door, opened the gate, drove out, closed the gate and drove off. At her husband's departure, Beth led the others in to the family room, inquiring, "Do you want to wake him?"

Jess waived away the question. She had no interest in waking James. "Leave him. He needs the sleep and we need the peace."

Robert gave a short laugh at his daughter's dismissive attitude. Her show of resentment added a new parameter to her personality he had not seen before. Something was going on with his daughter. He thought: *It must be communication with the surface that was affecting her judgment. He'd better have a talk with her when he got a chance.*

Jess, apparently having recovered from her crying episode, explained, "There are no pets in our world, nor have any of our people seen real animals in person—except for those who weren't born there. Right, Mom, Dad? There's just not enough food for them, no way to clean up after them, or provide all that would be required for their health and welfare. Our own psychologists tell us that this is one reason why we are so closely bonded as a people. We have to look out for and care for one another in the absence of personal pets."

Jess was about to ask where Ken had gone when she heard his car pull into the driveway. Darkness had fallen.

"You will stay with us for a while, yes?" said Beth.

The issue of how long they would stay had never entered their conversation. Their work was not completed—nor had it even started. The details behind their visit required discussion. "What time is it now?" asked Jess, sensing the lateness of the hour.

"Just after eight o'clock," Ken replied, walking in the door.

With nothing to gain by leaving early, Jess made the decision to spend the night.

EIGHTEEN

How weak we are, Jess thought, *living dull lives beneath the ground with no sunlight and without endless streets to roam. No gas line explosions for excitement. No dogs. The torturing heat.* Puzzled by her conflicting thoughts, Jess decided that the surface world was not something to which she would want to adapt. It grated on her to even have to deal with it at all, but the survival of UL-One depended on their mission. Jess had nagging doubts as to whether she would be able to survive in this world. Her inquisitive mind demanded she learn more about this treasure trove of information she had discovered through Beth and Ken, and yes, Carter.

Jess gave Ken her full attention. "I've been trying to visualize what you've been telling me about changes in the world. It's not working. Can you be more specific?"

Susan moved over in the sofa to be more in the line of fire of the cool air blowing from the cooler. "I'd like to see what you have on your screen. Wouldn't you, Robert?"

"Not particularly," came the dour response. "If the world's gone it's gone."

Susan gave him an annoyed look, almost one of disgust. "Then why don't you go someplace else so the rest of us can get an education," she suggested.

Robert humphed and remained seated.

Suppressing a grin, Ken turned to his wife. "My dear, this is your area."

Beth frowned, as though reluctant to proceed. "All right. This is a rough idea of what has happened over time. These are records Wei and I pulled from the military and meteorological satellites. TV on," she commanded. "Limit screen size to five-by-four. Night satellite image of Earth 30 years ago on the left compared with today. Rotate."

The screen came to life with the lights of the world's cities numbering in the thousands on the left side, with no lights on the right side screen. "No electricity," was her statement. She walked to the screen and commanded, "TV—Infrared of world thirty years ago compared with today."

Beth pointed and explained. "Red is warm, yellow is a little cooler, green is more cool, and blue is cold. Jess, I understand your fascination with events surrounding the Great Catastrophe. Here's what I saw before we left the base. We have to start someplace, so let's start in Greenland. They had stored a vast storehouse number of seeds that had been collected for years from around the world for just such a disaster. By the time the catastrophe occurred, nobody thought the seeds would be needed with it raining so much; either that, or nobody could get to them except for the Greenlanders, who had their own problems. Enough ice had melted on the island to expose countless of tons of nuclear waste stored there. This caused the North Sea to become highly radioactive."

Jess's knowledge of geography was better than her knowledge of history. Woefully out of date, she fully realized she had no access to what had happened to the world since before she was born. In her mind, the world appeared to be unrecognizable and its people may all be gone, with the possible exception of isolated pockets, a tight little area of the Desert Southwest being one of them. *How absolutely alien.* She had to ask, "Radioactive waste from what? From nuclear power plants?"

Beth explained about unintended consequences, "Yes, and from the production of nuclear weapons, along with the purification of uranium, plutonium, strontium, and cesium—that sort of thing. Another example of this is what happened in Hanford, Washington, where the Department of Energy maintained a waste dump for some two million gallons of radioactive materials, plus evil chemicals known as PCBs, in a couple of holding tanks. Hanford is the place where 12 pounds of Plutonium were purified for use in the atomic bomb that was dropped on Nagasaki. When the Seattle Fault split and leveled the city, the fracture zones traveled the length of the state and ruptured the tanks. All the waste entered the Columbia River and flowed out to the Pacific Ocean. Seattle was some 600 miles from Yellowstone, so when the volcano exploded, that finished off the city. Same thing for Portland, Oregon. Pacific storms picked up the radioactive water and dropped it inland.

"See the polar ice caps are blue and the oceans are greenish? It's easy to distinguish the continents simply by their yellow to red color differentials in most cases. See how red it is in Alaska, Siberia, and northern Russia? Those are more than ten million square miles of forest fires caused by an extreme amount of heat baking those regions."

Beth ordered, "TV—IR image of Earth today."

This time a different image appeared, one that was almost entirely green or blue-green. "Notice the absence of the polar ice caps and the Greenland Ice Sheet. Russia is solid blue because of ice; South America is blue from rainfall and over-vegetation; the same with the African continent. See how difficult it is to distinguish the continents as determined from their coastal outlines? Also, note that the continents are smaller than they used to be by some 20 percent. That's because low-lying land has been covered with water, and there is a greater quantity of ocean water, more large lakes, and many more rivers. Warnings were given to move away from coastal areas some years, even decades prior to their flooding."

Susan asked, "Is it my imagination, or are there

warmer colors in the central United States?"

"It's not your imagination," Beth replied. She got up from her seat next to Ken and outlined an area on the wall with her finger. "The Yellowstone eruption occurred here and spread volcanic ash over this area. The thick ash retained some of the heat from the blast that took out perhaps ten states and portions of many more. The sulfurous cloud acidified the oceans to the extent that we have no idea whether there is any life left in them. Also, notice a localized red area, which includes us, and extends to the Mojave Desert in Southern California. There are others deserts in Chile, Australia, China and the Middle East. The world's land mass used to be comprised of 30% desert. It's more like 35% now.

"While we're on Infrared, let's look at something else." She requested the TV to show areas in Russia, China, Africa, Italy and the American Midwest for specified time periods. "Initially, when the weather began to heat up, these areas were red. One to two months later rapid regrowth of plant life occurred. They were hit by plagues of ants, locusts, beetles and other insects that ate everything in their path. In some cases, swarms of spiders came to eat the dead insects."

Jess glanced over at James who had his eyes open. She was about to return her gaze to Beth when he said, "I don't believe any of it."

"Any of what?" Beth asked, shaking her head slightly, not understanding the statement.

"Any of what you're saying. It's like that fantasy

movie we saw today. It didn't happen."

Jess shot, "James, it's history and besides, nobody here cares what you think. Do us all a favor and go back to sleep."

James gave her a dirty look and slouched down further in the sofa to follow her advice.

Jess saw Ken and Carter look at each other, rolling their eyeballs upward. She bit her lip. This was not the James she knew. This new James had sprung a leak. To her, uncouth as he might be, he was absolutely correct in that the episodes shown before them were surrealistic. How did the saying go: It has to be real because you can't make up something like that?

"What are all those little red dots along what looks like coastlines?" asked Jess, perched at the edge of her chair, eyes riveted to the screen.

Beth replied, "Oil tankers run aground. On any given day there were over 10,000 of them in the oceans carrying oil from one part of the world to another. Each one could hold up to 80 million gallons of oil, depending on size. A lot of them are probably at the bottom of the ocean. Thousands got run up onto the coasts. From what I could research, the oil originally came up out of the ground quite warm, maybe 150 degrees, give or take, and retained that warmth inside the cargo vessels. That's why they show up orange-red. Now watch." She grabbed a remote from inside the sofa armrest and scrolled the screen to a particular point, then amplified the image until the picture became obvious. Scores of ships lay beached. Billions of gallons of crude oil had washed onto the shores. "Let's say the oil is shifting its location from beneath the earth to the surface.

"This was once called the Straits of Hormuz, where a high percentage of world's oil shipping occurred. A tidal wave initiated by a magnitude 7.8 quake in the Arabian Sea washed into the Persian Gulf and took out scores of ships at once. Many were thrown onto land, as you can see, while others sank and actually caused the gulf to dam up. A number of us watched it happen through the eyes of satellites. As a comparison, back in 1989, an oil tanker called the Exxon Valdez ran aground and lost nearly 11 million gallons of oil. That represented about 20 percent of the oil it carried. A literal drop in the bucket, so to speak, compared with what happened worldwide."

"In addition, the Trans-Alaskan pipeline carried some 80 million gallons of oil a day until it ruptured. Multiply that by the myriad of pipelines around the world to get an idea of the amount of oil on the surface of the earth."

Robert stood up. "This is all very interesting. I'm going to bed. See you in the morning."

Both Beth and Ken gave a wave of the hand in dismissal. Carter ignored him while Susan actually flipped him off behind his back. Not knowing the meaning of the gesture, Jess turned her attention back to Beth.

NINETEEN

Beth continued with her narrative. "In the Norwegian Sea, before the Big Catastrophe, the jet stream and the main ocean currents either originated from, or were largely influenced by that region. It's also noted for at least one other point of interest. In 1969, a Russian nuclear sub sank in those waters. Last time we checked, the radioactivity from the sub was 100,000 times greater than one would normally expect under those circumstances. The radioactivity carried throughout the oceans of the world and increased in intensity as more of the reactor became exposed to sea water. This added to the countless megatons of radioactive waste buried in drums beneath the ice in Greenland, which is now gone. In effect, the nations that mined scattered pockets radioactive elements, highly concentrated them, and dumped them to our oceans and rivers."

She proceeded to show them a red point in the Norwegian Sea and several larger red zones in

Greenland. Each of the red areas possessed one or more tails of varying lengths and widths depicting different rates of leakages from the different sources. "We can safely assume that widespread death to mega-trillions of phytoplankton, algal cells, fish and sea mammals occurred.

"Questions so far?" Beth looked at her class, who sat stupefied. She portrayed a doctor who was explaining to students her interpretation of a full-body scan of a patient, in order to reveal the worst possible outcome to that patient—in this case, Planet Earth.

With a sigh, Beth continued her presentation, "Before this all began, there were around 14,000 nuclear warheads—let's call them packets. Those packets, along with the radiation in the nuclear reactors worldwide, plus that which was being purified, can all be affected by environmental conditions, whether they be salt water, tidal waves, earthquakes or time itself.

"Beijing, China, went nuclear. That is, both radioactivity and hurricanes lay waste to the city. At the time this happened, 450 nuclear reactors were in operation around the world for the generation of energy with another 60 under construction and another 150 planned. In Beijing, there were eight nuclear reactors up and down its east coast. The three nearest the city went into meltdown when literally a hundred fault lines began to vibrate in and around the city. The effect on the reactors was many times greater than Chernobyl. This is because onshore breezes moving east-to-west blew the radioactivity over the city. The winds shifted and washed back and forth over the Yellow Sea between mainland China and Korea some 1300 miles to the west, finally carrying the radioactivity to the west coast of the United States. That's one reason why the ash cloud from Yellowstone became radioactive. Between Beijing, Shanghai, nearby Korea and other areas, perhaps a quarter-billion people were lost within a few short weeks.

"Let's shift focus. TV—show global wind currents of Middle East dust storm from four months ago." Wind arrows dominated the areas specified. They flowed in patterns running through Iran, Iraq, Syria, Egypt, Lebanon and Israel. Outlying arrows flowed into the central stream. Sets of numbers appeared in various places. "Dust storms have always been present in this part of the world during hot, dry conditions, historically occurring at least two-to-three times yearly. In today's world, it's not uncommon for them to occur more often. See those numbers? The top one is wind speed, the bottom is air temperature." She pointed to one set and said, "This one reads winds at 93 miles per hour at a temperature of 123 degrees Fahrenheit. The heat index makes it feel like it's above 150. No mammalian life on the surface can survive under those conditions.

"TV—show hurricane pattern Eastern US for last June." More wind arrows appeared with tight swirls located on the coast of Texas and Florida, plus a third off the coast of South Carolina and a fourth northeast of the Bahamas. "The swirls flow counter-clockwise, which is normal for the northern hemisphere. We won't split hairs over whether they're called tropical cyclones or hurricanes. The fact is, their number doubled in the last twenty years, and their size and velocity of rotation increased. Hurricanes are actually borne from the rising of hot air in what used to be Ethiopia, by the way. The air crosses the continent to enter the Atlantic region. Even in the old days, were places in that country where the ground temperature could reach 150 degrees. The storms depicted on this screen all dumped tens of inches of water inland. I can show you the same thing for Australia, the South China Sea, or Mozambique."

At that moment James woke up again, rubbed his hand over his face and asked, "Am I missing anything?"

Jess, annoyed at the disturbance, was in no mood to deal with the nay-sayer told him, "Not much. Only the end of the world. Go back to sleep."

James did no such thing. He stared, glassy-eyed, at the screen with not even a porch light on to suggest that someone was home.

Beth displayed portions of what had been a stable planet compared with what might have been an exoplanet. "If it wasn't for the iron core, Earth might be mistaken for a smaller version of a gaseous world. We can look at temperatures, rainfall, snowfall and the changing composition of the atmosphere.

"Let's look at one more thing, then we can talk

about what you have on your minds." Here she looked at both of her guests, James stared ahead, expressionless. "TV—today's spring, summer and fall weather map of Arizona." The image flickered an instant then appeared. "We're at the upper right of that red oval-shaped dome where the lower portions runs into the California desert. Tucson and the higher desert some 100 or so miles to the south is at the edge of the bubble. They get both very heavy and unpredictable rain combined with overwhelming heat, especially in early spring through late fall. I'm not going to say we're the only ones with electricity or water anywhere. I will say I can find no others. Above us is bitter cold and ice except for a small warmer pocket slightly below Flagstaff, in the area of Sedona. We call it a tweener. It's in-between the hot and the cold—totally unpredictable weather from one day to the next, although milder in general than areas surrounding it. Outside our pocket, in what used to be the United States, Canada, and Mexico, according to the latest satellite data we have, the daily weather is hostile to human existence."

Jess asked, "It seems to me there was a reddish cast to some of those pictures. Is that the screen or my imagination?"

Beth explained, "The reddish cast is from the Mars Virus. If you'll remember, in Randolph's diary, he said that when the virus reproduced, it released a reddish by-product. This chemical made the solution in the flask turn red. His team created the serum from that chemical extract to prevent people from becoming Siders. Well, that flask is now our planet. That's why we now appear reddish from outer space."

Jess recognized the symptoms of sensory overload, the study of which had been included in their middle-school psychology class. Once this occurs, the brain is given to random disconnected thoughts one moment and brilliant insights the next. During the sleep period, the brain spends time sorting out and pigeonholing the mess, which provides the subject with some answers, more questions, or both.

Jess stood up and stretched. At this point in her chaotic day she had a difficult time focusing on anything. "To think we missed all that by living underground so long."

Beth shook her head, "You didn't miss anything. You wouldn't have seen it. Anybody who was there to see this is probably dead by now. Aside from you down there and an equal number up here, that could be about it for people anywhere."

Coming to life, James said, "First of all, I don't believe it. Okay, we're inside that small red oval of heat. Looking at that picture, I wouldn't know if there was life inside the oval or not. Maybe there is life inside other desert areas."

Carter responded. "Unfortunately, we can't find evidence of anybody else. If you ever get up north with us we'll show you what we mean. Obviously, images are scanty, given the ability of a variety of satellite cameras to penetrate occasional openings in the weather."

"God knows, we try every day to find some sign of human activity," Beth inserted softly. "I try to dedicate time every evening to finding people on the shortwave radio. Let me show you."

She walked over to a closet. Opening the door, she pulled out a desk on rollers topped by an ancient, bulky, tube-operated Zenith Transoceanic Radio measuring perhaps sixteen inches in length by eight inches in height. Susan remained seated. She'd seen it. A loud crackle interspersed with a whining noise occurred when she turned it on; it was receiving signals sent by a transmitter as they were reflected from the ionosphere. After setting a knob to one of six frequency band widths, she removed a folding chair from the closet, opened it, and sat before the radio. Pulling out a drawer, she removed a well-worn book and turned to a page. Conscientiously, she wrote down the time and date and began to turn the dial to the first of a dozen numbers listed on the inside front cover of the book and also listed on a booklet attached to the radio.

Beth explained, "Good shortwave radio transmission and reception requires good atmospheric conditions, for a lot of technical reasons. Those conditions don't exist anymore. After I try certain frequencies, I do a general scan over all the bands. So far, nothing. Even if I heard something, I'd have to figure out the language."

Turning to her guests, Beth concluded, "The problem is, I've never gotten anything. And that's the quickie tour." She turned off the radio and returned the desk and radio to their dark home. Once she had closed the door, she turned to her guests. "Do you know anything about astronomy? Not too long ago, the world had decent telescopes of various varieties. One thing we learned was that of 1300 stars within 50 light years of Earth, there are none that have a planetary system capable of supporting life as we know it. Farther than that, consider it would be very long round trip for a visitor to make it here and get back home again, given that you couldn't travel faster than the speed of light. Therefore, it would take far longer than 50 years. Maybe thousands of years. Maybe never." Beth quickly added, "Which basically means that we are *it,* and soon to be no more, unless you and I survive. Now, show them, Ken."

"You mean our *collection*?" Ken asked, canting his head and clearly indicating his reluctance to show the couple a small portion of what life used to be.

"Show them," Beth repeated, not harshly, but encouragingly.

Beth's words triggered a memory of the Randolph diary in which he had recorded a statement made by one of his chief biochemists, Dustin Jones, who said something like: "Nobody is going to save us. Of the 400 billion stars in our galaxy or even in the greater universe, nobody gives a damn whether we live or die or what kind of soda pop we're going to drink or whether we go to church or not."

Ken saw Jess and Carter holding hands, as he began showing videos of a countless mackerel fed upon by porpoises, of dark swirling masses comprised of billions of anchovies fed upon by millions of swallows dive-bombing them, of hundreds of thousands of birds in a single black murmur that swept and shifted into Rorschach patterns, of melting icebergs, of birds migrating in mass as black as the darkest cloud, of Monarch butterflies flying thousands of miles, jelly fish, polar bears and penguins, endless miles of forests, of locusts and ants in the billions devouring everything in their paths, of birds feeding their young.

Beth took a deep breath and stared at her audience. "That's the short version of what we used to be. I watched a lot of it happen. I watched the oceans regurgitate from the bottom up, volcanoes erupt, and tidal waves make islands disappear. I saw the lights go out," Beth summarized, wistfully, with no hostility, only regret, as though she might have done something to save it had she been given the chance. "Now you understand there is nobody to save us. We didn't do this. The Mars Virus did it to us. Make no mistake, if it hadn't interceded, we would have done it to ourselves."

Jess rubbed her face with both hands and asked, "Can we go to bed now?"

Of course." Beth nodded. "I'll give you a long nightie to sleep in and you can give me your clothing to wash. How about if we leave James to his own devices. As you saw, we do have rooms where our sons stayed. Your parents are in one of them and there's too much junk in the other. That sofa converts to a sleeper and I'm assuming you two might want to talk. James, there's food in the kitchen. Let me get this sleeper sofa set up."

James lumbered into the kitchen, where he could be heard pulling out a chair to sit at the table, where a bowl and a plate of cold food awaited him.

Jess walked Carter out the door to say goodnight and gave him a peck on the cheek. "Thank you," she whispered. At 12:30 a.m., Jess, declared "Lights Out." The room went dark and two tired visitors crawled beneath the covers, with Sadie sleeping on Jess's side of the bed. The wound on James's arm had swollen to turn an angry red.

TWENTY

The same morning, Saturday, the travelers were roused at 8:30 a.m., well past their normal waking hour. Neither slept well. Sadie had taken to her own bed sometime in the early morning hours. Upon awakening James asked, "Guess I missed a lot." Jess grunted, not knowing where she would even begin.

Slow to arise, the couple individually luxuriated in the downstairs master bathroom with a hot and soapy shower, albeit under slow-running water. James favored his left arm, which throbbed with pain. Beth offered him the opportunity to change into surface clothing, while she washed the clothes he had worn to bed. He opted to continue to wear the same; however, she had washed and air-dried Jess's. Both guests had mixed feelings as they attempted to understand how their luxurious surrounds integrated with a dying world. Did they have it too good in their own world where it, too, was dying?

"Now, let's take a look at that arm," Beth told

James, who laid it out on the kitchen table for all to see, while Beth took off the bandage. He looked away as she did so. "That's nasty," Robert declared. "Don't they have antibiotics like penicillin at the base?"

"These are Mars Virus germs," Beth explained. "They have virus DNA mixed in with their own, like everything else does. That's why they're growing so fast. Besides, antibiotic-resistant strains were taking over, even in the old days. Now, I'd say it's a waste of time trying to find antibiotics. We can use common sense, too."

Susan spoke up. "UL-One has more than a half-dozen plants with antimicrobial activity, including ginger, cloves, garlic, and a number of others. The doctors make up a pain-relief balm from them."

James was sick of it all. He felt awash in the "I have to kick myself for getting myself into this mess" syndrome. Jess didn't look forward to the ostracism she would soon face at home. In a sense, both felt as though they were betraying their own people by not returning sooner. They had accomplished nothing, other than to vent their worries onto others who had their own problems and to bring back a few books and magazines. What would they report to the council, to the populace, who would ask for all the sordid details of surface life? Jess felt like turning her ire toward James for getting her into this. If he hadn't, she would have settled into life at home and let the memory of her single visit fade. Then she thought about Carter, whom she had begun to have strong feeling toward—a man totally different from any she had ever know, born and integrated into an environment beyond her wildest imaginings. The sense of thrill coursed through her again.

Seeing the frowns on the faces of the pair, Ken announced, "I almost forgot. I have a little something for you." He arose from the table and returned a moment later carrying a small handbag. He opened the bag and pulled out a slate, similar to the one Beth had shown them the night before. Holding it up, he announced, "I have 200 of these for you to take home. We recovered them from the library at Arizona State University."

Jess and James stared at each other. This gift helped lessen their feelings of incompetence. The material goods they had accumulated contained knowledge for the improvement of education and would provide better quality living, yet there remained the overriding eternal nightmare of bringing back another round of bad luck. Somebody would surely ask Jess if she had seen her parents. "Oh, sure, they're living it up in a big mansion with lots of food and television and a big car," she would answer. Right.

Breakfast concluded, Beth asked, "Do you want to visit the San Diego Zoo? We have it on the TV. It'll be over in a couple of hours. We'll drive you home. Besides, if you walked, it would take longer than that, anyway."

"We haven't seen it either. Stay with us a little longer," Susan implored, tears beginning to form.

"We don't know when we'll see either of you again."

Robert inserted, "Trust me, in the long run it won't change their opinion of you, whenever you decide to return home. You can't talk about it anyway, so what's the difference?"

As the group adjourned to the family room, Ken held Jess back. "Take this and hide it. It's a special slate marked with a white "X" in the corner. It's for your eyes only; not anybody else, especially not James. Keep it separate. You'll know when to discuss what's on it. Carter and I added some special information you will find in the UL-One section. It is the truth. If this information ever gets out to our world here, you could lose your city overnight. Is that understood?" He was stern in his admonition.

Jess nodded her acceptance, saying nothing. She took the slate and slid it into her freshly laundered tunic. At that, Ken then handed her a flat metal case with ear buds. "Here's something else for you alone. It's from Carter. It's called a CD full of his favorite Classical music. He hopes you'll enjoy it. I also have some bags of materials for you out in the car."

Jess found her pack, brought it back to the kitchen, and slid the two small items into it. Beth turned on the TV. Within moments, the expressions on the faces of the guests reflected their incredulity. The acres of lush vegetation vastly exceeded anything the Ring could ever offer along with the wide variety of bird and animals species serving to add more information to be processed. James sat as though he were a statue whose sole purpose was to stare straight ahead.

The day had become oddly cold. Before the six left the home for a trip to UL-One, light snow began to fall. Within minutes the snow turned to sleet as a hard wind blew down from the north. Beth gave the pair a couple of jackets and scarfs.

Noting the worried look on Jess's countenance, Beth put her arm around her. "Hopefully, you'll return a hero, what with what you're bringing back."

"I doubt it. I wasn't a heroine the first time when I brought back a cold virus, along with the bag of fertilizer you gave us." She quickly added, "Did you ever read Gorky?"

"Maxim Gorky? The Russian author? I did many years ago," she answered.

"He wrote that 'Perhaps the heroism of heroes is merely the extreme expression of man's despair and that, almost certainly heroism is a desperate feat of a man afraid'. So, no, I don't want to be afraid or in despair and I don't want to be a hero. I want to be concerned for my people and change things for the better, whatever it takes. And showing off some bit of knowledge or trying to share a happy experience with a lot of people doesn't work for me."

James stared at Jess, "'Whatever it takes' are strong words."

"Here, James, I want you to have this to remember us by," Beth said, reaching behind her neck, unclasping a chain. A small lion pendant hung from it. Awed, James examined the golden lion closely. This was something personal, representing a strength he always wanted to have. A sheltered life in a small world left little time for the expression of strength and courage. The last thing he wanted was to flaunt the lion above his tunic so everyone would think he was showing off, perhaps thinking he believed himself to be the lion, or bragging that he was part surface-dweller. He shook his head, not as a rejection of the gift, but as an expression of thanks. He gave Beth a hug, while Jess hooked up the chain.

Thanks to Ken and Beth, the couple were bringing back reading modules geared more toward science and technology rather than the old ones which had served mostly as book readers and writing tablets. The slates would help their independence through a vast improvement in their education. They also contained a large section on recipes that might take some of the bite out of Maggie. Even though UL-One couldn't grow in physical size or in population, at least they could be a healthier, smarter people, given the proper leadership.

Also in the bags that Ken provided were a thousand feet of micro-thin copper wire, micro-solder and micro-solder guns for computer repairs, along with magnifying lenses. Both explorers had a pack slung over each shoulder, while Ken and Robert carried other bags. Ken drove them as far as he dared, even with his four-wheel drive, and the men helped them with their loads as far as the west exit and down the ladder to the hauler trolley.

Robert gave his daughter a hug and a kiss on the cheek. "I'm jealous. Remember, my dear, you will have a place to stay with us if it doesn't work out for you."

"I know, Dad. All I can do is my best." She kissed him in return and climbed down the ladder.

Jessica Galloway and James Okimura returned to a new normal, not as secure as they'd like to be in their own little nest. They returned to the city they loved, a city created for loyal citizens, which did not include them in the eyes of many, where superstition trumps reality.

People walked both sides of the corridors, trying to stay off the trolley tracks, hanging new curtains in their doors, shopping at the various stores, exercising in the gym, growing and preparing food, decorating concrete walls with designs and murals where decades of art lingered—art created with natural plant dyes with the use of brushes made from plant fibers—drinking out of cups made from cellulose or clay, arguing, negotiating, teaching, learning.

The conservatives exercised their right to resist the changes and wallowed in denial, as is the human condition. They were surviving fine (even though they weren't) with no reason to change anything (even though there was). Change can only lead to more bad luck, at least in the eyes of Brenda, Maggie, Mara, and a growing number of others. According to Abike and her father, James admitted his mistake in going to the surface. He would always express regret. "It's a bad place. It is hard to find good there," were his words.

Accordingly, people conjectured that foreigners

might soon might be overrunning their city. This fact could neither be confirmed nor denied. Apparently, James is seeing Doctor Gomez Senior about something. Maybe he picked up a disease on the surface.

Onoyu Contee had no use for James. There were others in the city who were much more suitable as a mate. Unfortunately, the good ones were already married. Tall, rangy, and athletic in build, he could have passed for a small point guard in the NBA. The man's powerful and dynamic personality lent an air of uplift to others. Where he and his Abike's mother came from, a man must prove his worth. If his wife were alive, she would staunchly declare that love conquers all. Onoyu would respond by saying there was no true love on either side, to which everyone might have to agree. Not long after Abike's birth, the world fell apart and her mother died.

For Jess, nothing at home returned to what it once had been. Although the new gifts led to an air of excitement for her people, she would soon discover that death for them all might be imminent.

TWENTY ONE

A number of nagging memories of the surface stuck with Jess after her return. One of the most obvious was the heat and the concomitant lack of energy to cool the indoor environment. The lack of water served as another niggling remembrance that foretold the darkest future of all, a memory tempered by the delicious few minutes she had spent with Carter. And what was all this talk about a project up north with a dog that was being saved for her?

In the midst of the hectic activity at home, Jess realized she had completely forgotten about the special slate Ken had given her. She closed the door. Nobody would enter. She found a pair of earbuds inside the case of far better quality than their standard city issue. The inside cover of the case had a note pasted over a card. The note read: *Let me know what you think.* The card beneath the note listed various names of authors and their most notable pieces: Tchaikovsky, Beethoven, Mozart, Brahms, Puccini's *Madam Butterfly* and numerous others. The last entries listed were: *Battle Hymn of the Republic* by the Mormon Tabernacle Choir and *The Hallelujah Chorus* from Handel's Messiah.

She placed the buds in her ears, turned the volume on low, and began to listen, slowly paging through Gottlieb's book. Within seconds, Jess learned that the idea for underground cities was not original. It astounded her to find that one of the most famous ancient cities, named Derinkuyu in Turkey, had been constructed in the 11th Century before the Christian era. At a depth of some 300 feet, it was comprised of up to eighteen levels and could house as many as 20,000 or more people, along with their cattle, food and water supplies. They had established schools, churches, and homes, made their own wine and burned linseed oil for lighting. The city was connected by miles of tunnels to other underground cities. A newly discovered city in the same area was found to be even larger and could hold as many as 60,000 persons. Indeed, over 200 of these settlements had been discovered in Turkey alone. Puzzled, she could find no mention of what the diggers had done with the dirt. Ostensibly, the cities were built to hide from invaders. But wouldn't the same invaders see piles of dirt—even dirt that had been spread out? At least in UL-One, the creators had constructed a walled-in yard from the materials removed from a single relatively small level.

A wave of emotion passed over her. Once again, she felt inconsequential, certainly far from unique. She read more. Some underground cities dated back perhaps 5000 years, not the meager 20 years UL-One had been in existence. She found them to exist in China, France, and Poland. In reading Gottlieb's book, Jess wondered if WG Corp. might have succumbed to the weather or had abandoned UL-One for some reason. It could not be found in print. Rumor had it that the man had tried to build another city in Sedona, Arizona, a place where her new friends frequented.

She discovered the answer to one question in the secret texts Ken had provided in the slate. First, he reported that their common aquifer was the fourth largest in what used to be the USA. It included Southern Arizona, parts of Southern California, Nevada, Utah, and New Mexico. Its center lay in the Lower Sonoran Life zone—basically a desert area for many years. It could be reached by drilling some 350 feet below the surface, that is, another 300 feet below UL-One. Jay held the theory that deep-earth quakes split the granite base of the aquifer. This probably caused the water to leak into the surrounding limestone, thus traveling into a number of magma chambers up north which led to volcanic eruptions seen by Beth's satellite images. When she had seen the violence, it made Jess feel as though she were watching the beginning of creation, itself.

Jess paused in her reading to concentrate on the conclusion of Tchaikovsky's *Marche Slav.* Flushed with a surge of adrenaline, she resisted the urge to pump her fists and shout out something to the world. She replayed the piece and listened to it intently.

Once it had concluded, she returned to her reading.

Ken didn't say how Gottlieb found out, but apparently during the construction of the city, and thanks to a new generation of ground-penetrating radar, WG Corp. had discovered another aquifer some four hundred feet below the primary one. Its existence had been masked by a granite stratification. Revealing this discovery could revitalize the city of Phoenix, such as it was. WG Corp. remained silent because it was buying property for pennies, and when the time was right, the discovery of water would be announced and dollars would be made from the pennies invested. In fact, when the Great Catastrophe hit, Wilbur Gottlieb and WG Corp. had earned their fortune through sales of products they developed from the virus that had caused it all. He held one-quarter share in the venture, with Randolph holding the other three-quarters. The company waited patiently and began to purchase cities from bankrupt states, and even from other countries. Both Phoenix and UL-One would be in their death throes by that time. WG Corp. was intent on purchasing the entire Phoenix metropolitan area, once home to nearly five million people, when the time was right.

There were several problems with the grand scheme. Shortly after the plan hatched, the world died, or at least, communications did. No people remained to which the property could be sold, so far reaching had been the catastrophe. From what she could learn, W.G. Corp. died along with everything else when the Midwest got flooded out multiple times.

She stopped reading and skipped the CD to the last two pieces on the list. At each of the powerful conclusions, she began to cry. It was as though the core of her being had been punctured to lose what once existed to be replaced by something so strong and inescapable that, at first, she refused to accept the truth. This truth was deeply mired in the mu-sic——music that pulled her into another dimension of feeling bursting with flavor and richness, of goals yet unimagined, of an undefined future wrought with danger. She almost yelled, *Damn you, Carter. It's your fault.* He had sent music as the messenger.

In the solace of her pod, her emotional pendulum swung. She fell into the well of darkness, mourning for mankind, for the world. None of her people had been witness to surface events, enclosed in their own cocoon. A stream of questions flooded her mind. *How had it happened? It wasn't our fault. Was the virus an enzymatic catalyst to speed up the changes man had begun? If the human race had been puri-tanical from the start and had maintained the planet in pristine condition, it still wouldn't have changed what the virus did. What can I do?*

The inescapable truth slammed her hard enough to make her feel as though she had been awakened by a gunshot. She caught her breath. Her brain had sorted the various randomized puzzle pieces to cre-ate the picture hidden from her consciousness.

She didn't belong in UL-One anymore. She be-longed on the surface. So be it. The vaporous and mysterious entities referred to as surface people had taken on human form. That was something she was prepared to deal with. When and how to make the move was up to question.

Jess needed to tell Brenda about the aquifer and let her decide what to do. She figured there were too many details and she would be caught, if she tried to lie. It was easier to tell the truth considering the severity of the situation. Therefore, Jess would explain to her that when she was Topside the first time, Ken had felt badly that there was no way UL-One could communicate with him anymore, in case of emergency, so he had given her a radio. The second time she was there he had given her the slate that explained about the aquifer, which she had read.

Brenda was not one to tolerate deceit. The end result would be Jess's ejection, except for one thing: Jess was their link to the surface, which meant it would be foolhardy to ignore the water issue, if the information were true. On top of that, the city did need repairs and upgrades.

Jess planned to tell Brenda in time——not yet. First she needed to talk to the doctors and then call Ken.

The affable Alex had untied his ponytail and his long, black hair, graying at the temples, hung loosely at shoulder length. It boasted a sheen and scent suggesting a trace of vegetable oil steeped in lavender. Affable as he might appear, he was not a person who enjoyed having to answer to a forceful teenager, even a spinster in the making—one who had turned nineteen years of age. Logic dictated that he give careful consideration to the plan she had in mind. She wanted to give the surface one last try. In order to do that, she would claim to have a female problem. This would would require hospitalization at the base hospital.

PART 2

ONE

Carter made a quick stop on the way to pick up Jess. When he arrived at UL-One, Jess saw her mother seated next to him and climbed in the back, where a puppy wagged her tail excitedly. "That's Carla," Carter said. "She's a present from Jay and his wife, Wei. She was found recently with her brother, no mother or father in sight. They appear to be a mixture of German Shepherd and Alaskan Malamute. She'll grow to have the understanding of a six-year-old child and, as an intelligent Sider dog, she will be exceptionally protective, strong, and fast."

Over the years, Jess had seen many types of dogs in the movies she had watched on her slate or on her computer, not knowing what name to ascribe to any of them. This one had long straight fur, with short, triangular-shaped face. The whitish face was demarked by a brown skullcap that ended with a point between their eyes. The back was pure white, the body and legs were black. The green iris color of her off-set eyes, with the dark pupils, gave them the appearance of targets.

Jess giggled as Carla licked her face relentlessly. Carter felt pleased with himself for providing two beings with instant mutual love. "According to Jay, dogs are descended from the wolf, which originated in the lush North American continent in ancient years, along with the horse and the camel. They all migrated outward. The dog and the horse returned. She hates the heat, but she should love where we're going."

"Which is where?" inquired Jess.

"Sedona," answered Susan. "You're going with the men. Beth, your father and I are staying here for the time being." Without further explanation, she provided her daughter with a pair of blue jeans and a short-sleeve blouse, along with socks and sneakers for comfort. As they drove, Jess changed into the foreign clothing and voiced no complaints regarding the restrictive feel to the jeans and shoes. When they parked, Susan gave her a set of work socks, boots, and a long-sleeved corduroy shirt to carry to Carter's truck he had parked at the rear of the warehouse. The hour was 7:00 a.m.

Located at 4350 feet elevation and with a former population approximating 10,000, sans tourists, Sedona, Arizona, once served as a garden spot of the country, if not the world. Thirty miles south of Flagstaff and some 2700 feet lower in altitude, it was rife with those who completely understood the healing power of crystals and the positive effects of meteorites, both of which were readily showcased. Sold there were knives inlaid with turquoise, opal and coral that were created by Native American Indians. Numerous experts of every ilk could sculpt one's mind into any improvement the seeker of truth was willing to pay for. Mostly, it was known for its awe-inspiring red sandstone rock formations that could turn bright orange when the sun struck them at the proper angles.

Jess sat in the back seat of Carter's six-wheeler, four-door diesel pickup with Carla on her lap. He turned off the air conditioner and began to adjust the heater. A low-profile camper shell stood level in height with the cab to minimize the effect of wind turbulence on the vehicle. A trailer hitch in the rear and a winch in the front were affixed to the truck's frame. Four large spotlights adorned the roof. In front of Jess sat Ken with two rifles to his left—one a Marlin 336 C lever action; the other a Winchester .270 Model 70 bolt action. Both were suitable for hunting deer, elk, and other larger mammalian species.

The drive from UL-One to the Sedona worksite was not a simple straight line from point A to point B. The entire journey would involve the following: A 20 minute drive from UL-One to Ken's house; a thirty minute drive to the outskirts of Phoenix on Highway 17; a one-hour drive to the northern outskirts of the megalopolis until starting up the pass over a broken road with low desert on either side where hawks refused to ride the thermals after midday. This was followed by a 90-minute climb of some 2000 feet over what was once a curving high-speed freeway——now a treacherous, broken-pitted highway with a steep mountain wall to the east and a 1000-foot precipice to the west, where mother nature gravitated toward her bitch tendencies.

Carter negotiated the four-lane mountain road, trying to avoid fallen boulders. The sweeping curves were a far cry from the 180-degree, five-mile-per-hour hairpin switchbacks one encountered when traveling from Rapid City to Mount Rushmore, South Dakota, but were just as treacherous, because they invited one to speed off the edge—the guard railing long gone.

The drive time to state highway marker 260 was around three hours. After another 45-60 minues to breach the pass, another two-hour drive brought the vehicle to the Sedona turn-off. This was followed by another 45-minute drive around six traffic circles to their site. Variables included weather of the day, vehicles being towed and relative recklessness of the driver. Total driving time approximated six and a-half hours of concentrated effort. Shift-work among drivers was recommended.

For too many miles, the edge of the roadway had degraded so much that portions of the outer two lanes had collapsed. To pull a trailer through the area required first gear, slow speed. All the holes were water or ice-filled. A larger vehicle would cut it between them by inches. Beyond this area was the Big

Hole. Initially, when the men explored the area, they had stopped at the hole to measure its depth, thinking perhaps they could drive through it. This turned out to be not the case, as the size and depth would devour even a large tire. When they did skirt it on this occasion, Jess knew with a certainty they were going over the edge. She forced herself to suppress a laugh at the irony, as she thought, *I spend all my life on the flat and level beneath the surface of the earth, only to die by falling off a cliff.* Her mind wandered to the words of some unsung poet who had written: I *have emerged from the Stygian darkness of a seemingly eternal night to find myself festooned by the glaring brightness of mediocrity. Well,* she reflected, *this world is a far cry from being mediocre. If anything, her own home would better fit both of those descriptions.*

The weather quickly turned ugly. A Cat 6 hurricane had come in from what was once known as the San Francisco Bay Area. With a diameter of some 500 miles, the gale force winds spread far inland, and the outer rain bands rocked the slow moving car as it traveled northward through the mountains, 450 miles from the Pacific Ocean.

"Can't see a damn thing," Carter announced, turning on his headlights and the four spotlights.

Ken asked, "How long since marker 260?"

Carter looked down at the odometer, which he had reset to zero at the marker. "Eight point two miles," he said. "Another two tenths to go."

"What are you two talking about?" Jess asked,

frightened, quivering with fear, while attempting to console a shaking dog.

Ken said, "There's a hole in the road up here. If we get stuck in it, that'll be the end of us."

"How did the hole get there?" asked Jess.

Ken explained, "If there are cracks in the asphalt, rain water gets into them and the ground underneath it gets soaked. Then it freezes and expands, causing the road to crack. When it warms up, the road is already soft and a heavy vehicle or heavy snowfall or hail can cause it to pit and rot away."

Jess wanted to ask why water expanded when it froze, but let it go. Her mind flitted to some obscure remembrance of a comedy series she had once doted on. *What was it Oliver Hardy used to say to Stan Laurel, "Well, Stanley, here's another fine mess you've gotten me into.*

The rain fell in a torrent for some time, then stopped for a few seconds, then fell again. Sleet began to pelt the vehicle as the northernmost portion of the rotating rain bands moving left-to-right came in contact with frozen air less than a hundred miles up north and brought them around the circuit. Watching the odometer carefully, Carter and Ken stared ahead until Ken declared, "I see it."

"Got it," Carter replied, then inched around to the left to avoid the hole as strong wind gust rocked the heavy six-wheeled dually, doing its best to push the car into it. The potholes resembled impact craters made by beach balls, sometimes coalescing with one another, dark and shiny, all filled with water to an unknown depth, like spiders of different sizes luring prey to enjoy a broken axle. These weren't like the roads in Phoenix, or even those that led up to this point from Phoenix. Those were simply degraded from tortuous heat seasoned with occasional dashes of monsoon rain. These were nerve-wracking, demanding total concentration, requiring slow negotiation.

Once past the hole, Ken checked the collection of CDs in the console, pulled one with a Willie Nelson and Waylon Jennings CD and turned the volume down low. Jess looked out her window trying to see the countryside through the falling ice. A cooler sat on the seat next to her with bottled water and sandwiches. On top of the cooler were three parkas with hoods. Blankets and camping equipment were stashed in the rear of the truck. In the old world, a weatherman might be tempted to say that the jet stream associated with the Norwegian Sea had dipped down to their area with bitter cold to its north and warm air to its south. In the new world, the statement would be incorrect in that the planet no longer possessed a jet stream, a Norwegian Sea, or a weatherman.

Jess felt as though she were an explorer out of a science fiction movie riding in a land rover on another world belonging to a distant star, similar to the feeling she first engendered on her first trip to the surface. There were no other vehicles, wild horses, stray cattle, or hitchhikers—no sign of animal life.

"It's comin' up, Carter," Jess heard Ken announce.

"Yep, next song," Carter replied, cheerfully.

Jess listened and watched the men sing together along with lyrics to the song, "As near as I can tell, the whole world's gone to hell and I'm going to miss it a lot . . ." The men sang loudly, slapping their knees. Carter's deeper voice predominating. Jess didn't know whether it was crazier outside or inside the car, yet, somehow she captured the spirit of the moment and felt less melancholy because of it.

At last, the arduous, energy-draining challenge of the pass was completed and Ken took over the driving chores. Straight ahead lay another stretch of pock-marked highway that, in days gone by, given no cops were around, a person might be tempted to floor it, to see how quickly the speedometer or tachometer could be pegged.

With Ken at the wheel and the rain and wind still assailing them, Carter permitted his mind to wander. He remembered the days as a child when he would visit an uncle down in Galveston. He and some friends would dodge giant jellyfish that had washed up on the beach during a storm. They would run through the tentacles, playing hop-scotch, dodging the body and the tentacles that splayed in all directions like starfish. Step on a line and you're out to nurse your wounded foot; fall down and you may not live long enough to tell the story.

Those were the good old days. Today, if he could get to eastern Australia, he might enjoy the miles of algal bloom off the desert shore that had washed up onto the sand to stink it up. No, closer would be the red tide in what was once Florida. A hurricane would pick up the redness, dumping it hundreds of miles inland. And there was always Beijing and the east coast of China.

To his mind, surface people thought about such things. What did they think about down below with no knowledge of this world? He considered Jess the lone exception, one who risked being cast out to leave of her own volition, seeming to take death in stride. She might have made a good Ranger.

As they turned from 17 north onto 179A northwest, the landscape began to change. What had been solid white became spotty white. "Snow melt. Good for us," Carter declared, noting that the rain and wind were easing up. As they came closer to the dead city, escarpments, buttes, mesas, canyons, gullies and washes flowed past the windows. So did their red striations, which were comprised of iron oxide that had begun its deposition 350 million years in the past. With the last of the traffic circle behind them, Ken took them into downtown Sedona.

Buildings on both sides of the street were down, thanks to the work of a new-age tornado. Ironically, one building still stood almost in its entirety. The rapid growth of plant life caused by The Mars Virus, seemingly unaffected by the cold clime, had caused the forest to move into the city. Randomized pieces of lumber, bricks and other building materials were strewn about. Occasional piles of debris could be found amongst the trees and underbrush that occupied places where houses and businesses once stood.

Ken stopped the vehicle and left the engine running. A wooden sign swung in the wind by a single attachment point. It read, CHAMBER OF COMMERCE—WELCOME TO SEDONA. Carter grabbed his rifle, pulled his cap down tightly, and left the vehicle. Pulling out his sidearm, Ken laid it in his lap, rolled down his window and watched the other man enter the building.

Carter returned moments later and offered, "Nobody home and all intact." He got back into the truck and Ken drove off the broken road, cruised up and down the hilly neighborhoods for several minutes, looking for signs of life. Heading east on 89A, he soon arrived at the Munds National Forest Area. He pulled off the highway, drove across a stout bridge wide enough for a single vehicle to cross over a running stream about 10 feet in width. Shortly after the bridge, a branch of the road led to the left. They stayed straight.

Ken explained, "That's Oak Creek we passed over. It originates from underground springs a little farther north and isn't tied in with the Colorado, so it runs all year. Not far from us, near the bottom of a canyon there used to be a trout lake a few miles east. Once we get organized, we'll start pulling fresh water from the creek and look for trout. We should be able to set up a screen of some type to catch them near our home. It's on our list of things to do."

Engrossed in looking out the side window, Jess did not know what to expect. Any description would fall short of what lay in front of her. Northward, jagged pillars of red rock stood perhaps 50-100 feet in height, as well as in width, forming a semi-circle. These tied into a low, red-striated mountain almost pyramidal in shape, with occasional spires of red rock projecting from the top. In total, the height might be 250 feet. The mountain was split down the middle with a small gap of several feet separating the two halves. Other gaps separated the various rocks. The road they were on led to an opening in the outer edge of the circle. All the rocks were colored orange at the bottom, banded with horizontal striations and capped with red. The area within the circle of rocks encompassed some 15,000 square feet. The temperature on the dashboard read 25 degrees when they had driven over the pass. Now it read 50 degrees.

Basically flat, the area looked like a patchwork quilt where a nearly-completed brick home stood at the rear. As far as Jess could see, the home lacked only windows for its completion. A partially-completed brick building to its left lay beyond three small structures. Next to those stood an oval-shaped metal object supported by two wheels, with the front end propped onto bricks. To the right of the home, she saw a naked, square area of concrete. She noted what looked like rows of trenches covered with tarps, dirt piled to one side of each, plus an empty slab in front of and to the right of the home. At the front end of the trenches nearest them stood a small front-end loader with a backhoe. Tarpaulins anchored to the ground covered other objects.

"What's that thing?" Jess pointed.

Ken said, "It's called a mobile home. This one is a called an Airstream, maybe sixteen feet long. We hauled it up last time and plan to search for more when we get a chance."

"And what's that thing over there? And that thing way up on the other side. The big metal thing?" she pointed from one to the other.

Carter answered, bemused, "A dozen years ago, Ken and I began to hunt up here. We found some hot springs and this protected area. Ken got this idea to build here and we ran it by Beth, Jay and his wife, Wei. Since then we've been coming up here to work for weeks at a time during the warmer weather. It's not as if we're Adam and Eve having to start from scratch. We've got the benefits of civilization all around us—benefits we can help ourselves to. Because of the open space leading to the river and that crack in the big mountain, we can get some nice wind turbulence when it comes down from the north, next to where the windmill is standing."

Carter pointed. "That's the thing you're seeing, fifty feet high, outside the crack in the mountain. It's a three-bladed wind turbine for energy production. We didn't have the materials to get it up any higher. It's on a base and is held down by guy-wires that we'd run into if we set it up here, inside the compound. It's on a vane, so it can rotate to face the wind. The higher we get it the better it works. That's because the wind speed is related to energy generated: double the wind speed and get eight times the energy delivered, up to a point. Because the few things we'll need power for are a food freezer and items like lights, floor heaters, and pumps, we'll have a lot of electricity, as long as the wind blows. Frankly, I don't think I've ever encountered a day or night when it isn't blowing at least five-to-ten miles per hour. We even have some piping going up to the turbine to keep the motor and gear box warm in the winter. As far as the trenches, there are pipes inside them that are tapped into a heat source I'll show you in a couple of minutes while we hunt."

The men opened their doors and exited the truck, taking their rifles with them. Carter opened the rear door behind him and removed the parkas, handing one to each of the others. Carla jumped out, followed by Jess, who changed into the work boots and put on the flannel shirt. Carter handed her a baseball cap similar to the ones they wore, each with a different NFL team logo. The instant she stepped out of the protection of the truck, Jess became aware of familiar odors given off by moist vegetation. This combination of odors was comprised of both living plants and piles of vegetation in the process of microbial degradation. In addition, there was a scent of pine oil and a suggestion of mint. Carla ran off to mark various locations important to her.

Once out of the truck, Jess pulled up a tarp to look beneath it. Several rows of pipes lay side-by-side, forming loops at the base some nine feet in depth.

Ken offered, "See those small shacks next to the house? Those are called outhouses. They're bathrooms." He pointed. Then he said, "Now, let's go get some dinner. You stay with Carter and go that way." He nodded to the left where the rocks were separated by three feet. Slinging his rifle over his shoulder, he walked away,

TWO

Carter slapped at a mosquito on his neck, handing Jess a gun. "This is called a .22 caliber rifle." He showed her how to load a round into the chamber, line up the sights and properly pull the trigger.

Jess took the rifle, as though it were a piece of hot metal. He stood behind her and helped her put the rifle up to her shoulder, using both arms to reach around her. Resisting the magnetic pull of his body and scent. She permitted him to hold her closely, perhaps for a longer period than necessary, while the man instructed her on how to kill. Another set of conflicting emotions rushed through her.

Satisfied that she held the weapon properly, Carter said quietly, "Let me know if you see a bird, rabbit or squirrel. Before you shoot, let me give the okay. I'll deal with anything larger." At that, he tied a small bag to his belt and grabbed his own rifle. "You'll want to wear these to keep the insects off," he said, handing her a pair of surgical gloves and a pair of large one-piece swimming goggles.

The two began to walk out of the sheltered area on the far west side. With the exception of the rocks at their back, heavy vegetation surrounded them on all sides. The landscape had transitioned from the low desert to the high desert, with numerous new plant species surrounding them. The insects had discovered their presence and began their attack in earnest. Infected by The Mars Virus, these were more problematic for their prey than any before them— save perhaps those that lived during the age of the dinosaurs. Slapping at her neck, Jess looked at her hand. "Mosquito," she observed.

"How do you know about mosquitoes?" Carter inquired.

Jess laughed. "Really, Carter, I'm surprised at you. Everybody in my city is an expert on insects. Remember, we have an entire mile of moist vegetation encircling our city. We're always on the lookout for beetles, caterpillars, certain types of spiders, and such. Sometimes ants seem to come out of nowhere. We cultivate ladybugs to eat the aphids off of leaves. Mosquito larvae develop in standing pools of water. We grow crickets to eat."

"My apologies, madam," Carter smiled and made a deep bow, thoroughly chastised. "I must warn you, however, that you'll need to be wary of what we call stingers. I have no idea how widespread they range. They're larger than the ordinary mosquito, with a long proboscis. You can hear them coming from their loud high-pitch. The damn things inject some sort of enzyme into the host to dissolve the skin. They're very nasty. When one stung me, or whatever they do, I had a crazy psychedelic reaction for a couple of hours. I was on the bed for the next day or so after that." He rolled down the glove on his left hand to show a round scar on its back.

"Positive or negative mental reaction?" Jess asked.

"Bad. You do not want them in your face. The good news is they appear only during the early fall months. Don't ask me why——maybe it's rainfall or temperature-related."

"Which means us now," Jess added, unnecessarily.

"Correct."

Jess paused. "My guess is that it's the females that cause the problem, like it is with regular mosquitoes. They're the ones that suck the blood. The stingers may want to turn around and deposit their eggs as soon as they dissolve your skin. Your mental reaction to them doesn't figure into their survival mode. It might be a little fun, side-effect for you."

"Nice."

"What happened, exactly?" she asked.

"First I heard a whine. Then it stopped. I felt a sharp sting and in instant later my hand burned like hell. I saw this thing on it and slapped it to death. I guess that was before it could deposit its eggs. By the time I got back to camp, the skin had turned from red to black. I poured alcohol on the hole in my hand and wrapped it. I was in a cloud that whole time.

Ken had to nursemaid me. That was two years ago. Whenever I press a finger on the spot, the thing still hurts." He showed her.

Jess deliberated. "I don't think getting slapped to death by a human is integrated into its self-defense mechanism, so it's not targeting humans alone. Good thing you didn't get stung by two of them, or that it didn't lay eggs."

"What do you think would happen if it did lay eggs?"

"My guess is that they'd either burrow into your skin to turn into who knows what, or leave your body to survive on another host of some type."

Carter rubbed the back of his hand. "Fantastic. I feel better already. Oh, then there are the greens. Those are two-inch-long caterpillars that drop off onto you from the cottonwoods and other leafy trees when you jiggle the limbs. We brush them off out of habit. Got to watch out for the other guy, you know. That also happens during the fall months. Fortunately, both types are very rare. Still, it's best to keep an eye out. That's one reason I keep my head covered. Just don't get one of the greens on your skin. Last year Ken and I saw a squirrel flopping around on the ground with one of the worms stuck onto its back, trying to burrow in."

Jess took his hand in hers for a closer look. "Both of those creatures may be in reproductive mode rather than attack-defend mode. The second one is probably green in color to match the color of leaves, in order to hide from birds. My guess is that it carries the poison for the same reason. From what I've read, there were no reports about new species created by The Mars Virus, only the development of faster movement, larger size, and higher intelligence with existing species. Experts could be wrong. It wouldn't be the first time. A lot of things got rearranged since I was born."

"You think?" *These are new days and new rules,* Carter thought. *Today there are no experts to confuse us.*

Jess added, "The two may be connected as part of a life cycle."

Carter looked at her in disbelief, surprised at the extent of her intuitive knowledge and her sense of deduction. Jess looked at him, reprovingly. "Insects have a life cycle, too, where I come from, you know. There may be more troublesome mutants out there. Anything else I need to know about?"

"Yeah, but you're not old enough." Carter grinned, hiding his acceptance that he was the student, she the teacher.

Something didn't set right with Jess. "What came first, the greens or the stingers?"

"Hmm, can't say. Ask Ken. Hell, I don't know. Why?"

"No reason," she replied, feeling every reason to be concerned.

Absent the buttes and mesas, as far as the eye could see, the thick landscape consisted of ponderosa, lodgepole and other pines, cottonwood, blue spruce, birch, several species of juniper, agave, and grasses, along with more than a score of other species. Thoroughly disgusted by the flying bugs so numerous they clouded vision, the group donned their hoods as they entered the surrounding forest. With the wind in their faces, they heading north, the compound a quarter-mile behind them. Carter put on his swim goggles and Jess followed suit. Carla fell to swiping at her face.

After three minutes, the three arrived at a hot spring, where a body of water bubbled out of the earth, giving rise to steam in the cool air. The spring measured some 30 x 50 feet. A ledge ran around the side where they stood, with an imposing drop-off just past its ledge. A copse of thin-leaf cypress surrounded the pool, unable to support the presence of greens.

Carter told her, "This place is dotted with these, and they keep the temperature on the ground and in the air warm enough for animal life to continue. That includes right through the middle of winter. We think it covers a fairly large area. One of these days, we'll take the time to find out how large. It might even extend beyond the bridge to the south. There used to be one of these, maybe 90 minutes away in the Verde Valley. Then fissures in the ground suddenly appeared here, which exposed the ground water to the heat of the earth. Now we have a rare little ecosystem and a lot of animal life. There's a really fun part I'll tell you about later."

Carter watched with amusement as Jess walked to the other side of the spring and picked up a handful of pine needles, letting them flow through her fingers like sand. She looked up, He followed her gaze to see pine boughs swaying in the wind and a clearing sky beyond. She plucked off a cluster of needles, counting their number, examining their length and their attachment to the sheath. Looking downward, she examined some shelf fungi growing from the side of a tree and plucked a mushroom from the ground. They were everywhere. "Look, Carter," she cried. "Bring the bag. We'll have mushrooms for dinner. They're *Agaricus*. The gills haven't opened yet, so they'll have a lot of meat in them."

Enjoying her curiosity, Carter come over to her and they placed a double-handful of mushrooms into the bag. "Beats the heck out of peanut butter sandwiches," he announced.

"What's peanut butter?"

"Later. Right now we're looking for some solid food. Expect to see squirrels, mule deer, jackrabbits, and possibly an elk, if we're lucky—larger birds, too. Let's keep moving." Slowly and as quietly as possible, weaving through the pine boughs, Carter lead her deeper into the forest for several minutes until he made a motion to stop, whispering, "There's a rabbit." He pointed. Jess nodded. It had emerged from the brush and stood next to a cottonwood tree some 20 feet away.

Carter got behind her and put his arms around her, helping Jess sight the rifle. She did not resist. "Safety off. Now, squeeze the trigger, don't yank it," he whispered.

"I can't see," Jess complained. "Goggles are in the way."

"No, they're not. Look straight ahead. Concentrate and focus," Carter whispered. Reluctantly, she did so, and the rifle gave a small crack. The rabbit fell. "Good girl. Tell Carla to fetch rabbit," he said.

"Fetch rabbit," Jess ordered. Carla bounded to the fallen animal. The dog found a good purchase on the back of its neck and returned with it, tail wagging happily.

"Good girl," Carter said, taking the rabbit from her and stroking Carla's head. "Nice. A fat jackrabbit. It's tougher eating than a cottontail, but I'm not complaining. Keep going," he urged, taking the dead animal from Carla.

Jess followed along, as in a daze. She felt absolute revulsion. She had never seen a live rabbit before. When she did, she had allowed herself to kill it. She wondered about what controls life on the surface of this planet that it should grab her in its clutches in such a manner? How had she permitted Carter to introduce her to this killing? At the same time, she felt another emotion akin to thrill; something called survival instinct. How to reconcile the two might be a problem.

The pair walked on quietly for several more minutes until Carter stopped them again. Pulling his rifle off his shoulder, he smoothly chambered a round, froze in place and fired, with foliage blocking much of his view as a mule deer ran from left-to-right, out of sight. "Damn Sider animals are too fast," he groused. Moments later they heard the crack of another rifle shot. Carter pulled out his radio and said, "Did you get a hit?"

"Affirmative," came the reply.

"He got a hit. I'll bet it's the same one that ran from us," Carter said. "Let's see if we can find him."

They located Ken ten minutes later, He had dragged the deer close to one of the springs. Looking up, Ken noticed Jess carrying a rifle slung over one shoulder and carrying a rabbit. She did not appear to be pleased.

"Well, young lady, you certainly brought us good luck," Ken said, happily.

Jess felt confused. She was trying to determine how killing something could be associated with luck. This world had completely different rules than the ones she knew. *Just take it at face value*, she told herself. *At least I didn't have to carry the creature I killed. Next, they'll ask me to eat it.* Jess's original thesis revolved around her null hypothesis, taking the side of what she didn't want to believe—that she belonged to this world more than to her own. How could she decide when confusing events constantly assailed every aspect of her life on the surface?

Ken stood up. "Tell you what. Give me that critter and hand me your rifle, Jess. I'll take the rabbit back and get it ready to eat, once I get the pit cleaned out. Carter can show you how to field-dress a deer." He handed her his knife. "I've got another one back at camp."

Under Carter's tutelage, Jess cut open the animal, feeling another wave of revulsion at the sight of the insides gushing out. He noted, "We're going to leave what we don't want for the other wildlife to eat. Trust me, it'll all be gone by morning. They need the food and so do we."

When the deer had been cleaned, skinned, and quartered, Carter dipped the skin and portions of carcass in the hot spring to wash them off, then the couple made two return trips to camp, where he cut off a piece of thigh meat, which he gave to Ken, along with the mushrooms. Carter put the animal portions on the roof of the camper where they would freeze overnight and tied them down with a tarp. Ken washed off the mushrooms and placed them in a pan along with some deer fat after he had stuck the thigh meat on the spit next to the cleaned rabbit. "In the morning we'll put the frozen pieces in the big cooler I have in the back," Ken remarked.

"Won't some other animals want to go after it?" she inquired, thinking that perhaps the same animals might want to come after them.

"In all the years we've been coming up here, I've never seen a bear, if that's what you're referring to, although I can swear I hear and occasional wolf amongst the coyotes when they start yipping. You'll be sleeping indoors, anyway. You'll get the trailer. That's the warmest and the most comfortable."

"Where are you and Ken going to sleep?" she blurted without thinking, now feeling a tinge of embarrassment.

"We'll be in our sleeping bags in the house," was

the reply. Carter resisted the urge to ask her why she was asking.

"Did you ever bring my parents up here?" she asked, quickly changing the subject.

"Not yet," Ken said. "Let's finish eating and get to work. We've still got daylight."

Working quickly, Carter showed Jess how to prepare mortar. Once a supply was available, they fell to laying bricks on a partially completed structure while Ken installed windows into the home. A cold wind spun the windmill outside the gap between the two halves of the mountain, which brought a cold draft into the compound to flutter the fire.

With shoulders and lower back aching, Jess knew she wouldn't feel sore until the next day—and worse for days afterward. Jess shared her meat with Carla, who sat next to her, begging, continuously wagging her tail. Jess tried not to think of what she ate as having been a living creature. A chicken is a bird. A rabbit is a mammal. There's a difference. She did have to admit that gnawing on a piece of rabbit and a large hunk of deer meat was nothing short of divine. Ken had given her some salt and pepper, which she added sparingly to her food. She saw herself returning to her human roots, tearing into the flesh of animal meat with her teeth, something she had never experienced before. In some undefined way, she felt wholesome, as though her teeth were biting into the essence of life itself. It wasn't the meat alone—the cold, snow, and sleet were new to her, as well. She was going to miss this moment once she returned home. She had the fleeting thought that maybe her people weren't meant to live underground indefinitely. If she remembered right, temporary habitation also occurred in Derinkuyu. She wondered how many years, if not generations, would be necessary before her people could taste the life she now tasted. Would any of them care to do it? More importantly, was she willing to invest more of her time to learn how to survive in this new world, or was she on a simple binge she had talked herself into, one that would end as quickly as it had begun?

Jess was starting to fade, although the chimes for Lights Out would not occur for some time. Carter offered, "If you want to wash up, you can use the trailer. It has a sink. No toilet. Hang on a second." He went to the truck and brought out a metal bucket with a handle, along with a flashlight. He walked out of the camp and returned some minutes later with a bucket-full of hot water. He retrieved a towel and a bar of soap from a dopp kit and handed them to Jess.

Night had fallen in this new world. Jess noticed sparkles in the air. "Fireflies," Carter said. "Those are the males trying to attract the females."

"So that's how they do it," she replied, giving him a sly look, and walked off to prepare for bed. He smiled in return and went back to the house, where the two men spoke for some time of plans for the next day until Carter said, "Guess I better check on her."

"Yep," Ken replied.

Carter got up and abruptly sat down again. "Nah,

let her sleep."

Jess thought she would pass out instantly. Instead, she lay awake for a long time, hoping there would be a knock the door. Her thoughts turned colorful, even tending toward the lurid, until both woman and dog fell into a deep sleep.

A knock at the door woke up the pair. Dawn was breaking. Jess took a few minutes to make herself presentable before emerging from the trailer, followed by Carla, her new soul mate. She found the men drinking coffee from a pot on the campfire and reading a road map. She made a bathroom run, took several minutes to stretch and joined the men for a quiet cup of coffee.

"How'd you sleep last night? "Carter inquired.

"It took me a long time to get to sleep. I had a lot on my mind," she admitted.

After several minutes, of light chatter and remembering to take her rifle, she grabbed the bucket and headed off to the nearest hot spring. Once there, she sensed a motion behind her. She turned to see Carter. "I have a confession to make," he said, pulling his parka around him tighter in the cold morning air.

"Oh?"

"I thought about getting into the trailer with you. Would that have been a problem?"

Jess laughed. "Not at all. I have a confession to make, as well. The reason I stayed awake so long was because I was hoping you would come to check on me." She reached behind his head and pulled it down closer to her. They kissed lightly at first, then hungrily. She tried to wrap her arms around his bulky parka to no avail, while he had no trouble wrapping his arms around her. A patch of clear blue sky opened between clouds directly over their heads.

"Now for the surprise I told you about before," Carter taunted. "Take off your clothes."

"What?" Jess stared at him, stupefied. No man had ever spoken to her like that before.

"We're going into the water," Carter stated, removing his boots. Jess looked away as he slowly undressed, carefully placing his clothing on the ground for easy access later. Turning back, she stared at him, as he stood naked directly in front of her. The man had the broadest shoulders and strongest chest muscles of any man she had ever seen. He smiled as he saw her look him up and down before easing himself down onto the ledge in the hot spring, with the water just covering his shoulders. She had entertained fantasies about his body since the first moment she had seen him in the warehouse and the dreams had become reality, as though her thoughts had made them come about. She had to be honest with herself. She had fantasized about a lot more than that. Casting aside caution, Jess followed suit and, an instant later, she felt a flash of panic at the unusual feeling of sitting in hot water, then fell prey to its qualities. These were different qualities from the oppressive heat of the desert, or the cold in the morning, or the wind that might whip at her at a moment's notice. This cloak of warm feeling comforted her and welcomed her with all it could offer.

Jess basked in the first hot bath of her life. Soon, she resigned herself to the soak and found her body adjusting to the temperature. Carter put his arm around her and gently pulled her close to him. She did not resist. Not to be ignored, Carla sat on the warm ground, head hanging near to Jess—the steam serving as protection from flying creatures. Soon Carter began to gently massage her shoulders and back, to her great delight.

Jess closed her eyes, and allowed *things* to escape—bad things. She remembered the ridicule she had encountered upon returning from the surface and didn't care. Something was rapidly changing inside her; not something that might evolve over time, but something evolving at the moment. She belonged here with this man, whoever he might prove to be. Opening her eyes, Jess reached around and stroked his cheek. She didn't resist when he wrapped his arms around her and pulled her onto him.

Not long afterward, the couple hastily dressed. Still flushed, they returned to find Ken at the campfire. Ken spoke first, "I was wondering where you were."

Carter put on a straight-face. "We were enjoying the springs."

"I'll bet," Ken leered.

Feeling embarrassment, Jess hastily asked, "Will one of you please tell me what you're building here?"

Carter answered, "Aside from a 1200-square-foot

home with three bedrooms, kitchen, and living room warmed by geothermal energy and a windmill? The steel pipes you see are carrying water from the hot springs throughout the area to include meeting hall. It will have large room for a number of people to eat together along with a couple of rooms that can be used for a kitchen or sleeping. Those pipes in the trenches will also serve a greenhouse. Hopefully, we'll start actual construction of that next time we come up."

"You mean you have to bring up materials from Phoenix?" Jess tried to fathom the ambition of these men, so far beyond her experience. *What had been the biggest ambition of anybody she ever knew, before coming here?* She wondered.

"Yes and no," Ken answered. "A lot of it we can get in Sedona by demolishing some of the few standing structures. There are also old brickyards in the area. We load the stuff into a 24-foot truck we have parked outside the warehouse back in Phoenix. Do you know what a hydraulic lift gate is?"

"No."

"It's an automatic platform that drops down and let's us load stuff onto it—so we don't have to walk the stuff up a ramp or break our backs lifting it up to the bed of the truck. We didn't bring it on this trip because of your limited schedule. We have bricks stashed on pallets on the other side of those rocks. Before we leave, one of us will get down into those ditches and check the fittings for leaks. That's why we left them open. They're tarped so they don't fill with water. Once we're satisfied there are no leaks, we'll fill the ditches with dirt, pack 'em down and let the pipes warm the earth. Under those other tarps are bags of concrete to pour a slab. There's also a cement mixer and a power generator to run the mixer."

"What's a slab?" Jess inquired.

"A slab is a big flat piece of concrete that serves as a base for a building," Carter answered.

Jess walked over to the nearest tarp to look down in the trench. Why are the pipes down so deep?"

Carter chuckled at her inquisitive mind and glanced over at Ken, who smiled in turn, looking down at the ground and shaking his head. Carter replied, "That's about nine-feet in depth. When you get down that far, the ground temperature stays the same, summer or winter, so the water in the pipes will stay the same temperature summer or winter. In this case, hot, because they'll be connected to the hot springs and they're down deep enough to pick up the warmth of the earth beneath them. A great deal of the heat gets transferred to the surface."

Ken poured her a cup of coffee and provided packets of sugar, which she used with great delight. "So, what's the plan for today? Going up north more?" she asked.

Ken turned down his mouth. "Not for a few days. When we do, we can't go too far. It's a frozen mess and we have to do work while we're here."

"That's great. This should be fun," Jess announced, cheerily.

THREE

Although the sun brightened the sky for three days running, workdays had become long and arduous. Jess found herself wearing work gloves as she mixed morter and trowled off excess mortar., laid bricks and constructed wall. Midday temperatures were in the low fifties, hardly noticeable during her work efforts, unless she stopped to rest, which was rarely. From Jess's perspective, the summer nights outside their sheltered circle of rocks were colder than anything she could have imagined when wind chill became a factor, especially noticeable when she collected buckets of hot water away from the shelter of the rock circle.

On the fourth morning she rode with Carter to the city of Cottonwood, 20 miles to the southwest, to slosh through the debris on the floor of an old Home Depot. The couple picked up sheets of heavy plastic for the greenhouse, several water pumps, and a large quantity of construction materials that weren't water-damaged. Jess's muscles screamed with the pain of overwork, pushing herself to her limits. Nightly massages and other ministrations by Carter helped alleviate this problem. The night itself posed no problem in terms of silence. She had grown up with that. The days were another matter. She had known constant noise from 6:00 a.m. until 10:00 p.m. There existed a world of difference between something present and something absent.

Returning from a hot soak one evening, she saw Carter heating a pot of coffee at the fire. She heard music coming from the truck and understood. Her man had become a songbird calling its mate. Returning to the compound, she heard sounds of pounding coming from inside the house, which told her that Ken was working on the final touches to the kitchen cabinets.

"What is that delightful tune?" she asked.

"It's a little something from the old days called 'Lover's Concerto'. Come over here for a second." He stood and took her hand, leading her to the truck. "I almost forgot." He opened the rear gate to the truck. One of the outermost boxes had Jess's name printed on it in black marker.

"What's this," she asked.

"It's a late addition," Carter told her. "When we first met back at the warehouse, you told me you liked to read, so I got you some books."

"Really? That's fantastic." She gave him a big hug. "I hope you got some mysteries. I love them."

"You did say that," he replied, smiling broadly

enough to rouse her suspicions. He picked up the box in two hands and carried it over to the light of the fire.

Jess pulled open the box and pulled out several books: *The Mechanics of Wind Farming, Electricity for Dummies* and *Basics of Meteorology.*

"Gee, honey, you shouldn't have," she quipped. "I suppose the rest of them are like these." They were. She began to laugh. Reaching the bottom of the pile, she picked up a massive tome, and before reading the title guessed, "Let's see; what's this one? *How to Put on Sandals for Dummies?*" Instead, the title read: *The Complete Works of Agatha Christie.*

Jess's mouth opened. She looked up to see a grinning man. "Before you get too involved, I got you something else, too. I never had any use for these before," he said, handing her a wooden box with a lid and a latch. It measured six inches in length by four inches in width and four inches deep. Jess gave him a puzzled look and unlatched the box to find it filled with jewel: diamonds, emeralds, rubies, bracelets, necklaces and rings.

"These are real jewels, aren't they?" Jess remarked, as she tried on a number of rings. Some fit, some didn't.

"They better be or I'll file a complaint. They're on permanent borrow from a jewelry store. Pick out a couple for yourself to claim the title of the richest woman in the world." Carter beamed. He left her alone to play with a ring she found to fit nicely on her middle finger. She opted to put in on a gold chain to wear around her neck so it wouldn't affect her daily construction work.

Later, Ken remained in the house in front of a heater reading a couple of the books in their new collection. Jess lay in Carter's arms at the campfire, playing with her ring, trying to get used to the night sounds. The crackle of wood burning, the chirping of insects, and the occasional fluttering of wings served as background noises.

Carter Lawson looked at this girl with whom he had fallen in love—this beautiful creature, hungry for knowledge, yearning to grow. How had this happened? As if reading her mind, he spoke softly, "You know, baby, I spent the first 18 years of my life in single-wide trailer outside of Dallas, Texas. I played baseball and football in high school and fixed cars for loose change until I left home to join the military and then the Army Rangers. It was the dream of my life. I lost that dream when I hurt my shoulder during the last week of training. The doctors told me it could take me up to a year to heal. I could go through training again after that, if I wanted to. That was in Fort Benning, Georgia. About that time, the entire region got pounded by a terrible hurricane. I got sent to another base outside of Houston. I was a good mechanic, so I got trained in repairing planes and military vehicles. The next year Houston got hit twice with back-to-back hurricanes, and I got shipped to Tucson, where I met your folks, along with Ken and Beth. Everything was a big circus because of people getting shifted from one place to another and nobody knew what the other guy was doing. Some people never made it to their new destinations. Anyway, Ken and Beth had also been in the military and wound up getting sent to Tucson just before I got there. Then we all went to Phoenix."

Reflecting on his life, with the trace of philosophical insight only painful memories can provide, he saw that he was poor growing up, poor in the military, poor out of the military, and now everybody was poor. Curiously, at the moment, he felt richer than ever with a good woman at his side and a new home almost completed, albeit in a world almost devoid of human life. Having a number of close friends counted for a lot, too. Ironically, compared with almost everybody he knew, he might be called a very wealthy man. What was it his daddy used to say? "Just give me a rockin' chair, a good dog, a good book, a jug a sippin' whiskey, and a shotgun to keep the revenuers away. Don't get no better'n 'at."

"Carter, I realize things have to be big here, but you're building a lot in this compound for a couple of people to live here once in a while."

Carter chuckled. "It didn't start out that way. At first, Ken and I thought it might be nice to build a house here for just him and Beth and me to get away during the hot summer months. We started the house and grabbed the trailer as a freebie. When things got really hot in Phoenix and they ran out of water, we got Jay and Wei involved, and pretty soon we all started to think about moving up here permanently.

Now your folks are part of it. Maybe you'll join us, too."

Jess pulled the necklace from beneath her work shirt and examined the ring in the firelight. She asked, "Carter, were you ever married?"

He remained silent for a full minute. She could feel him twitching, thinking, then replied, wistfully, "Yeah, a couple of times."

Jess was taken aback. She lay in the arms of this man, who was tough, rough-hewn and gentle at the same time, unshaven, protective—but she didn't know him, not really. "You were?" Jess almost sat up, shocked to discover that her dream man had been with other women and surprised at her own naïveté in pretending he hadn't been. "What happened?"

The first one was to a woman who lived in the same trailer park we did. We were kids, who thought marriage was the thing to do. I went into the army and told her I'd see her soon. It never happened. She had my baby and both of them died when a tornado swept through the park. I hate tornadoes."

"I'm so sorry," Jess replied. "What happened the second time?"

"When I hooked up with Ken and Beth in Phoenix, there were a lot more people. I met a woman, one who seemed like the perfect match for me. She was gritty and smart. She didn't have the looks, but I saw beyond the superficial. The marriage lasted three years—until she and my two-year-old son died when a storm swept through the city and a fucking tree fell on our home while I was working at the warehouse. After that, I swore I was done with women and got along just fine for a lot of years—until I met you and changed my mind. Jay was the one who encouraged me to go after you."

Jess couldn't imagine what Carter had gone through, losing two wives and two children. She had never lost anyone close to her through tragedy.

"Did you love them?" Jess thought it a legitimate question, wondering where she fit into the picture.

"The first one, no. When it's the thing to do, there is no love, although it tore a piece out of me when they were killed. It was thinking about her that caused me to lose my focus during Ranger training and messed up my shoulder for a long time. The second one, yes. She was a good woman. She loved me in return. That one hurt bad. That's when I started drinking."

"You did? But you don't do it now, I mean, not really, do you?" Jess asked, trying to figure out how she would fit into the equation, if he were a drinker.

"Not now, no. Back then, though, I had developed this philosophy. I tried to stop. It didn't work for a long time. Whenever the stretch of abstinence got to me, I would tie on a bender. That fixed the problem and I went back to abstinence. Eventually the problem went away."

Jess felt hollow. She felt like another woman in the long line. "Why me? Because I'm young?" It was an accusatory question, meant to hurt, borne out of a jealousy of dead women, that he had made love to them, that they had borne his children——a shallow question meant to sting a man already hurting—and she knew it. She had never experienced the feeling of jealousy before. The moment she said the words she deeply regretted them.

"No, your age has nothing to do with it and neither does your beauty," Carter stated. Those are pluses to your main attributes of intelligence, insight, courage, and willingness to succeed against all odds. Then you give me love in return, appreciating me as a man. Do you want me to go on?"

"Yes, please, and, oh, honey, I'm so sorry for what I said." Tears starting to form, self-loathing coursing through her for an instant, until Carter began to speak, taking it in stride, un-phased, as though nothing could hurt him anymore.

"All right, here's another one. Twins ran in our family. I had a twin brother and we had this game where we would switch off taking rewards or punishments for the other one. About the time I got mixed up with my first wife, I also got in with a bunch of new friends and we went out on the town. It turned into an armed robbery. That wasn't my thing, I just got sucked into it. My brother took the fall because it was his turn. He got sentenced to a year in jail on a first offense. He died in prison, along with millions of people behind bars when the world went south. It should have been me. Still want me to go on?"

A big world with big trouble. Pain and suffering. Two more ingredients added to the stew of real life. "No, Carter, I want you to make love to me," Jess cried.

On the fifth morning, Jess suddenly stopped adding wood to the fire and looked to the west between two boulders. Something had caught her attention from the corner of her eye. "Guys, come over here and look," she pointed. Both men came over to look. She pointed. Ken walked to the truck and pulled out a telescope and a pair of binoculars. Climbing to the top of a series of rocks, he lay on the top and patiently took time to focus on the area. Trees partially blocked his view of a broad boulevard and a parking lot in the distance surrounded by low mounds of building rubble. Climbing down he said, "Grab your rifles. Let's go."

Jess opened the back door for Carla to jump in and she followed. Ken got in next to Carter. "What do flashes of light mean?" she asked.

"Life," he answered simply. "We checked out a number of B and Bs—those are bed and breakfast places where tourists used to stay, along with any other partially standing buildings near where we're headed. At that time, there were no humans or indications that humans had been there. Things might have changed."

"I'm sorry you didn't find anybody." Jess was crestfallen.

Carter started the truck and Ken said, "Don't be sorry. That's good news."

"How can that be good?" Jess asked, befuddled. *These surface people talked in riddles.*

Carter continued with the explanation. "In general, finding people is good because it lets us know we aren't alone. If we find a few survivors, it means there will be many others. For us, personally, it's not good for a couple of reasons. For one, suppose we drive up here one day and find one or more cars in our space with armed people living in our house."

Jess didn't have any idea of how she might proceed. "I don't know. What would you do?"

"Take it back from them and ensure they don't return. Another thing is this: We've explored more than a couple of square miles with a lot of hot springs to keep them warm. My sense is there are a lot more of them in this entire region, with plenty of edible vegetables. Suppose we find shell casings on the ground. We wouldn't know how many people we would have to deal with or if they were watching us to see where we went. We would never be able to sleep well, either here or back in Phoenix. We'd be thinking about what we'd face when we woke up here, or when we drove back up. I still wonder."

"I'd think you'd want them to join us," Jess offered, now seeing a dark side to Carter.

Ken took over—a one-two punch. "Look, Hon, anybody we find will have survived for 20 years, just like us. They didn't fly in here for a happy weekend vacation to look at the colored rocks. You're not going to survive that long without good weapons, a lot of ammunition and a lot of smarts. They'd likely have more ammo than we have with us. Yes, we can get better weapons and a lot more ammo. That's not the point. You don't survive by being friendly and opening your house to strangers in today's world.

If you do, you could lose your house and your life. I didn't make up the rules for survival, nature did. The end of the story is that if we see signs of people, we'd better be scared. I don't even know how to secure this place enough to keep out serious intruders, especially since we're gone most of the time. Do you?"

Jess swung her head slowly back and forth, wondering if she would ever be called upon to shoot somebody. The way things were going, she couldn't rule that out.

Carter said, "That's why we're looking, my love—in the hopes we don't find anybody. There are a number of cars in that lot. We're going to check it out. We'll go in the back way."

Carter slowly approached the area of concern and pulled into a side street two blocks away, slowly working his way through the overgrowth. The three got out of the car into a light breeze blowing from west to east. Carla sensed the need for stealth and kept close to her master. The group walked one block to the south and up to the broad boulevard where they stopped behind a copse of cottonwood trees. Pulling out his telescope, Ken looked to the left and then to the right. On the right he saw the boulders of their compound in the distance. He looked to the left for a longer time, then handed the telescope to Carter, who looked and smiled, then handed Jess the telescope. She saw a pendant hung from the rear view mirror of an abandoned truck with its windows open, the breeze blowing the pendant around and around as it reflected the morning sunlight.

Jess breathed a sigh of relief, knowing she would not have to be engaged in an armed battle, until the words of her science-teaching mother came to mind. "You don't have enough data points to make an assessment. The day is still young."

FOUR

Jess was in no hurry to get home. Of those whom she had known to get medical assistance not available in UL-One, many had gone to the base hospital to stay for up to two weeks, or longer. She felt compelled to remain with the men—to observed and to learn.

On the sixth afternoon, Jess assisted in pulling the tarps off the ditches. Carter climbed down a ladder into one end of the first trench and began to closely inspect the pipes' connections. After he climbed out and went into the second, Ken started the engine of the front-end loader, inviting Jess to stand behind him and hold on. Clinging on for dear life, she watched in fascination as Ken drove the machine to the start of the first trench, to begin shoving the dirt over the pipes. He repeated the process until the job was completed, finally driving the machine over the ditches to tamp them down. Carter added more dirt as necessary, carefully avoiding the projecting pipes that would provide more surface warmth to the future greenhouse. After that, Jess watched Carter check the fluids of the truck and the level of diesel fuel contained in drums Jess had not noticed between two boulders. He explained each step to her as a teacher to a student, insisting she do what he had done. "We filter the fuel to remove both sediment and water. We mix it with a small amount of either aviation fuel, also filtered, or with an organic solvent, such as acetone or xylene, to keep the lines clean."

On the seventh morning, Carter looked at the sky. He walked over to the trailer where he had attached a barometer to the wall just inside the door. "We've got weather coming in. It's time to leave."

The four clambered into the truck with Ken behind the wheel. Ken addressed Jess. "There's a truck stop outside of Flagstaff with 18-wheelers we can steal gas from to top off our tank. Keep your rifle handy." He knew she didn't understand the terms he used, but it wouldn't take her long to put the pieces together.

Carter continued, "In answer to your concerns, we want a house to live in and a greenhouse to grow and dehydrate food to use during the cold months, all supplied by geothermal heating and wind energy. We prefer a cooler location—a place promising life, not death. Living in an oven doesn't excite any of us. Didn't you ever want to get away?"

Jess did not expect a question. "To be honest, I didn't want to get away until this last trip. The first two didn't count because they were directed toward my city. That remains, but this time I included a few selfish desires, eager to learn about your world. Also, admittedly, there is a sense of mystery and danger here." *And possible true love, because I needed to meet you again,* she wanted to add. *Actually, I believe I've found what I was looking for.*

Jess grabbed her parka, bunched it up, put it behind her head and soon fell asleep. She awakened an hour later when the vehicle slowed. She saw what might have been the truck stop Ken had mentioned. To the right side stood two broken, abandoned buildings and a number of large vehicles she took to be the 18-wheelers. With Carter standing guard, Ken poured a can of something called xylene into his gas tank, siphoned gas from one of the trucks into their own and within minutes they were on the road again. Jess went back to daydreaming about the fact that she did, indeed, have female problems, as she had cajoled the doctors into saying, but they were the good kind.

The nights were different when she had nightmares of Central America disappearing under tidal waves from the Pacific Ocean to the south and from the Caribbean Sea to the north. It was as though the Earth were a toy ball filled with water and little white flakes, shaking back and forth, and occasionally stopping to see how the flakes settle out, then shaking the ball once again. If she had been a surface dweller, she might have thought the flakes to be billions of tons of plastics, goblets of oil, and radioactive materials shaken free from the oceans and landfills, or worse—lifeforms.

After seeing those pictures, she had dreams of rainfall tripling the normal amount, of Category 6 hurricanes averaging over 200 miles per hour, with twice the band width they had in the old days, carrying water nearly 500 miles inland; of terrible deserts, of nuclear reactor meltdowns, and of a single habitable hot spot in the Southwestern United States where a handful of people lived—many of them prepared to shoot it out with others.

Minutes later the wind increased and began to rock the eastward-heading vehicle. Now in New Mexico, dark clouds loomed before them. It began to rain heavily. Thunder cracked and rolled. Carla whined and sought solace in Jess's lap. She gently stroked the dog's head and said soothing words to calm the animal, if not so for herself. The rain turned to sleet, which turned into hail. The stones soon became large enough to cause serious damage to the vehicle. Fearful the windshield would not hold up to the assault for long, Carter checked the map and directed, "Better take 191 up ahead."

Ken turned southward and drove as quickly as he dared until the hail lessened to be replaced with heavy rain once again. "I can't wait until the rainy season starts," he muttered, sarcastically.

Jess was stunned, as she contrasted her stable life at home with the constantly changing scenes outdoors. Instead of a card player at home flipping from one card to show another, in this world, the weather flipped. *Ladies and gentlemen, place your bets. What will be the next weather card to appear? How many weather cards had she seen so far?* She counted at least nine or ten, with several suits to each card occasionally melding them together. *How hard or long will it rain or snow? What will be the temperature when it does rain and from which direction will it come? Will sleet be mixed in? What will be the size of the hailstones?*

Two hours later they passed over the mountains into the blistering heat of the New Mexico desert, still part of the high pressure heat dome. Ken turned off the heater and turned on the AC. Jess put on her sunglasses as Ken pulled over into what was once a rest stop, now complete with non-functioning toilets and several empty vending machines long since punctured with bullet holes that had rusted along their edges. The trio exited the truck, the lone vehicle in the lot, and went into their respective bathrooms. Carla stayed by Jess's side—watching, protecting.

The building stood largely intact, having been constructed of slump block. The steel door still stood affixed to its hinges, although much of the roof had either blown off or had collapsed. The terrain around them lay barren with the occasional cacti and creosote bushes breaking up the bleak landscape. Buttes and mesas stood in various sizes before the horizon. During the cretaceous period, 66-150 million years before, the visible land had been underwater as part of the Great North American Seaway that split the continent into two parts, stretching from the Gulf of

Mexico to the Arctic Ocean. Today, only dinosaur fossils and sand remained as a legacy of that geological era.

Inside the bathroom, apparently unused for many years, Jess stared at herself in the mirror, as she had done on her first outing to the surface. She saw a vast difference. Her complexion had color, her hair had been styled short like Beth's, and no bleeding gums or sunken eyes stared back at her. Her face had good color, not from being flushed as it was during her first outing, but activated by melatonin from being in the sunshine, enhanced by biting cold wind. A little soak in the tub combined with love making didn't hurt. For a person whose medical issues required her to be sent to the hospital, she was looking pretty good, which could become a problem later when she returned home. Although she liked the color, to the citizens at home, she would clearly stand out.

Exiting the restroom, she joined the men. The small cooler from the back of the truck stood on one of the concrete table seats. The large cooler with the deer meat remained safely stowed. The three stood and ate sandwiches made with bread that Beth and Susan had prepared with soy flour, along with slices of deer meat. The three paced to stretch their legs with little conversation between them. All three ensured Carla's rapid growth would not be stunted.

Carter took over the transportation duties, driving them across the floor of the desert through Sitgreaves-Apache National Forest, climbing in elevation once again. Search as they might, they found no indication of human life. After Sitgreaves, they descended into the lower desert where Carter stopped the vehicle in Lordsburg at another truck stop. They filled the gas tank once again. Straight highway lay ahead.

"We can take 10 and go east to Las Cruces or west to Tucson," Ken said. "Your call, Jess."

She had never heard the name of Las Cruces. She had heard of Tucson, because Ken had mentioned it. "Tucson," she announced.

"All right," Carter acceded. "If we go to Tucson, I do not recommend we go straight south from there because that will take us into Nogales, Mexico. Every time we try it, we get hit with so much rain it's tough to escape from. If you go too far west, you'll run into the Mojave Desert. Even the lizards don't do push-ups there. It'll get to 140 in the shade—and there's no shade. It probably hasn't rained in that part of California in ten years. You'd think you were in Australia. So we'll take a point in-between and go right through Tucson, then head straight north back to Phoenix. That said, I'm going to take a nap; and, by the way, you're driving."

While Carter dozed, Jess endured Ken's patient explanations and his proclamation that they weren't going to get in trouble for going faster than 20 miles per hour. After that, she quickly evolved into an excellent driver, as long as no turns, stops or starts were involved, a problem that repetitious drills finally resolved. Ken made certain to include driving in reverse in his lessons. This was in keeping with his opinion that women's internal GPS might be fantastic at finding a particular store in a shopping mall, they couldn't drive in reverse to save their lives.

Avoiding occasional obstacles in the road, Jess made the curve on the elevated interstate entering downtown Tucson from the east and headed northward toward Phoenix. On the long drive, the men told her a tale of horror about the local Davis-Monthan Air Force Base, where sacks of grains originally stored there were either rain-rotted or eaten by rats. The place had been vacant for years.

Where there once had been a city of over a million people, she saw a glistening sea with portions of buildings sticking up through it, despite the fury of the sun. Those who had migrated in any direction surely perished. Of those who traveled north, they would be met with gunfire, as survivors desperately tried to hold on to what was left, which, according to the men, had included themselves in their defense of Luke. There was no hydroelectric power of note because all the dams were gone. The Colorado River, once providing water from up north along a viaduct, had frozen over and what little did reach them was contaminated with volcanic ash.

In another mood swing, Jess felt curiously displaced from her people, engrosed as she was with the tragedy of the surface world, which she felt an increasing need to join. But she had to absolutely positive about her feelings before she made such a bold move. Impressed with the plans these men had for building up their compound, Jess wished she could have stayed longer to help them. She looked from side-to-side, aghast at the devastation. *What did normal used to be like?* Other than what she had seen or read, she would never know. *Who were these two men? No, more than that, who was she?* When she looked at the big picture objectively and took her emotions out of it, a repeat realization struck her. These people were more trapped than were her own people. In less than a day, they had explored the boundaries of their surface world and could not ask for outside help. There wasn't anybody there to improve the quality of their lives, to give them more power or water or better quality food. The burden was solely on their shoulders. She glanced in the rear view mirror at Carter, who now sat awake with eyes to his binoculars looking, searching. A rush of hormones sent another thrill through her as she wondered, *Was it simply the wish for one night stands of such magnitude one would remember them forever, or had she fallen in love with a tough, sensitive man, one who was trying to make it from one day to the next like the rest of them?*

FIVE

In 90 minutes, Jess could be underground. She didn't want to go home yet. She had been released on a medical leave of absence and might never have this opportunity again. She took her foot off the gas pedal and put on the brake, stopping the car in the middle of the interstate. "You're supposed to pull over to the right when you want to stop," Ken said, looking around him.

"Why?" Jess replied.

"She's got a point," chuckled Carter.

"Can't we go further west or more to the south?" she queried.

Ken shook his head vigorously. "There is no point in wasting gas going into one of the great deserts of the world."

"True," Carter contributed. "If you're that interested, I can show you pictures of rolling sand dunes as far as the eye can see and the pictures won't beat up the car or put us at risk of a breakdown, with no chance of being saved. The last time I called, the auto club said they were pretty busy and to check back later."

Ken laughed. Jess didn't get the joke. "South, then," she insisted, not willing to give it up without a better understanding of the extent of their world. "I know you told me the weather is bad, but…"

"What do you think, Carter?" Ken asked, looking back at the other man around the headrest.

Carter shrugged, thinking, then said, "We could go southeast to Sierra Vista and hit Fort Huachuca." He looked at Jess and added, "We tried it a couple of times and got rained out both times. We could try it again and see what the Command Center or Bliss Army Hospital has to offer. They might have supplies we can use. Plus, we do have enough food, water and gas for the trip."

"While we're at it, we can find out if there are any armed soldiers with orders to shoot strangers on sight," threw in Ken.

"There is that," Carter agreed.

Jess retraced their route back along US 10 to 90 South and turned toward Sierra Vista. Once they passed the Huachuca Mountains, as though they represented a line of demarcation, the skies darkened. All three remained silent, watching the weather and the road ahead.

Once again, Jess's mind wandered to home. Tonight, her people would hold the biggest party of the year, Founder's Day, the day when the charter was adopted and UL-One became an official city.

Preparations had begun weeks before, with an over-abundance of alcohol not so secretly prepared. The orchestra will play, Onoyu and Abike will sing African songs, and Maggie will write good wishes in Chinese, which will be hung on the dining hall walls next to Philip and James's lettering in Japanese, next to Annie's good wishes in Russian Cyrillic. People will be dancing throughout the night, no Light-Out tonight. Tomorrow will be a day of recovery, and Unit 7 will have its share of customers for a day or so.

She knew this when she opted to claim her illness. *"Why not wait until after the party?"* she had asked herself. Why had she missed the best that civilization had to offer just so she would expose herself to a place where no civilization existed? Was it self-punishment for some unspecified reason, or simply that something else overrode the event in its importance?

In Khalil Gibran's *The Tempest,* a recluse disavows civilization because people of that world sought unrealistic and unattainable goals, ignoring the beauty of simplicity—the world of God. None of that applied to her. In her next life she wanted to be any animal that didn't have to intellectualize a thing.

Ninety minutes later, Jess drove through the west entrance onto the base that once served as the staging area for South American military operations. No soldiers were present to greet them, armed or otherwise. As she slowly negotiated the car around numerous potholes, they passed the airport, where two small planes lay cast about like toys and several military vehicles stood in a line. The multi-story Command Center, once occupying nearly half-a-million square feet, had been leveled onto a jumbled heap of construction materials with nothing immediately visible that might be salvageable. Nearby stood the hospital with surprisingly minimal damage.

"I'm thinking they might have blown the building on purpose," Carter suggested. "The destruction looks too even all the way around."

"For what reason?" Jess asked.

"They knew they weren't coming back. Maybe there were too many classified materials to take with them on short notice. Why not the hospital, too? Can't say. I also don't have any idea about where they went or when they left," he concluded.

At Ken's instruction, Jess parked within feet of the entrance to the hospital, where the doors stood askew on their hinges; many of the windows broken or missing. The three travelers warily exited the vehicle, looking about them on a day that had seen them travel through numerous climatic zones. At the present time, they faced dreary, overcast and cold conditions. Ken pulled the keys from the ignition and locked the pickup.

Finding a map of the hospital on the wall just inside the door, Jess traced it with her finger. "Perfect, just what I want," she muttered, and headed off down one of the corridors, with Carla and the two men following, cautiously, lighting the way with flashlights. She led them to pharmacy, microbiology, hematology and surgery, each area assaulting them with the mustiness of mold. All drugs had been grabbed, ostensibly when the building had been vacated. However, the other areas provided riches. They found it necessary to find sheets and pillow cases in which they could haul out their loot. This included surgical instruments, stainless steel trays, scores of suturing packets, and a small autoclave for sterilization. They kept an assortment of items for their own use later in Sedona. To the delight of the men, numerous cans of ether were found, which they coveted, in order to reconstitute old diesel fuel. In their experience, old gasoline had too much water condensation or rust in it to make it practical for use; plus, the evaporation of short-chain hydrocarbons over time tended to turn it into varnish. Diesel fuel worked better for their purposes and all their vehicles were diesel powered.

They returned to the lobby and Jess sat behind the desk. She began opening drawing while the two men dragged boxes and pillow cases full of supplies into the area when she said, "Gee, this looks like one of yours," and began to pull out a heavy weapon from the bottom drawer. Carter looked and was about to tell her to set it down when it went off, sending a round between him and Ken, striking the wall beween their heads and blowing gypsum into their faces. Jess had dropped the weapon onto the desk and was holding her right wrist when Carter reached her in two bounds. He picked up the gun, dropped the magazine, ejected the next round in the chamber, reinserted it into the magazine, and put the gun in his belt and the magazine in his pocket.

Jess sat dazed and in shock.

"Colt .45," Carter told Ken, who found himself brushing fragments of plaster board from his hair and shoulders.

"I could have killed you! I could have killed you!" Jess began to cry, tears streaming down both cheeks. "Oh, Carter, Ken, I . . ."

"It's all right, Jess. It's my fault. I should have schooled you on handguns when I had the chance." He pulled her up from the chair amidst the uproar with Carla barking madly. "Is your wrist all right?" he asked, while watching her shake it out, trying to hold her at the same time.

"It's fine," she declared, backing off his from attention.

Ken cautiously walked to the entrance, checking outside to see if the shot had attracted attention.

"Relax, it's over," Carter said. He reseated Jess and checked the other drawers of the desk where he found a nearly full bottle of Jack Daniel's. He tossed it to Ken.

"Liquid refreshment." Carter laughed, trying to mask his shakiness.

"Death by friendly fire," Ken muttered, taking a long pull and handed it to Carter who did the same. He gave it to Jess who took a drink and gagged. The men laughed. Comedy relief in a tragedy. To Jess, he said, "I like to laugh in the face of danger. Hopefully, there will be time to cry afterward."

For the men, the episode had ended. Looking at the wall behind Jess, Carter commented, "According to that calendar, they vacated this place in June, 22 years ago."

Jess had entered a new dimension of reality. She had learned that, unlike her own world, on the surface, a bad decision in life can lead to an instant death. Already feeling slightly imbibed from her small drink, while still fixated on guns and death, she asked, "Something I don't get. You always have guns with you and you lock the car. Why? So far we haven't seen a single person. You said you never saw anyone except when you were away from home."

Carter responded, "You haven't asked the question, so I'll answer it. In our world there is a thing called Murphy's Law. If we don't have our weapons, we will be attacked and trapped, defenseless. If we do have them, then we won't be."

"Oh, sort of a bad luck, good luck thing," Jess returned.

"It's more like the worst kind of luck versus nothing happening," Carter answered. "In addition, once in a while you run into a wild animal that needs to be taken down. Maybe it has rabies, or something."

"What's rabies?"

"It's a terrible viral disease. You can't get it unless you get bitten by, say, a bat, or a skunk, or dog or cat. There's no cure. It makes you go crazy. It's very scary. Sometimes, even the slightest movement will cause the animal to attack."

The late hour dictated that they either load the

truck and drive back to Phoenix, or stay where they were. Nobody had a schedule, so they set their treasures near the front entrance, having decided to do more reconnaissance in the morning. Carter removed portions of the deer from the cooler and grabbed some bottles of water. The three sat in the cab of the truck slowly eating and reviewing what they had salvaged thus far and deciding what more they could do tomorrow.

"Anybody want a shot of hooch?" Ken asked, unscrewing the bottle of liquor Carter had found. After taking a swallow, he passed the bottle to Carter, who did the same, then passed it over to Jess, who began to wave away the bottle, thought about it, then took a small drink. She had never been a drinker and found no need for alcohol, until the present time.

"Where's Carla?" Jess asked, looking around, wiping alcohol that had run out of her mouth with the back of her hand, while trying to ignore the laughing men. It took a moment for her to realize they might be laughing away the danger to themselves.

All three began calling the dog's name, searching indoors and outside. Ken checked the truck again. The dog had gone. Jess was about to suggest she take the truck and go looking for her when the pup suddenly appeared from a weedy lot behind the hospital with a rabbit in her teeth.

Wagging her tail she received praises from her masters, who exited the vehicle. They voted to prepare the rabbit and feed most of the spoils to the victor, who will soon grow to weigh 85 pounds and stand 20 inches at the shoulder.

Feeling warmer and more relaxed, all three found comfortable hospital beds where they could get a good night's rest. Not inclined to use the moldering bedding, they removed the sleeping bags from the truck and unrolled them onto the beds with guns at their sides.

SIX

After coffee in the morning, the trio made their way to the dental area, where Jess discovered an x-ray machine that, according to the manual, would provide instant views of any given tooth on the accompanying screen. The machine and manual were taken to the truck, along with the other items they'd recovered from the day before.

"Let's check the basement," Ken suggested. In addition to finding the machinery necessary to operate the building, they also located several gallons of 80% rubbing alcohol, along with numerous bottles of merthiolate and tincture of iodine, which they took to the vehicle.

"We missed the kitchen," Jess proclaimed.

The searchers soon found closed aluminum cabinets filled with packets containing powders of mixes, gravies and sauces, along with numerous jars of freeze-dried coffee. There wasn't enough to feed a city. There was enough to serve two men and their close associates for a long time very nicely, adding to their kitchen larder up in Sedona, which, to this date, housed only salt and pepper.

"Let's find the commissary," Ken offered.

"We're getting tight on space. We'll have to save that for another time," Carter replied.

Jess inquired, "What happened to everybody? Aren't there supposed to be skeletons, at least?"

"General evac," Ken said.

"For what reason?" Jess asked.

Ken replied, thoughtfully, "You don't just close a base on a whim. It takes congressional approval. Davis-Monthan and Houston, I can understand. Maybe this was closed for the same reason—weather." He got behind the wheel with Carter seated next to him. "Let's look around a little more."

Fifteen minutes later, they pulled into what remained of the vehicle maintenance building. The men assigned Jess the task of checking the belts, hoses, and fluid levels of the truck. With a tire-pressure kit he kept in the truck, Carter plugged it into the utility outlet on the dash and ensured the tires were at their required pressure, again guiding Jess through the process, watching her repeat it. After topping off the tank and selecting a few tools to take, the three left the base in a heavy downpour and headed northeast once again to I-10, then drove west through Tucson and north toward Phoenix, with Jess at the wheel. Carla let it be known that she would sit next to her master.

A great sense of relief suffused Jess. She had

promised the doctors back home that if they would give their approval for her medical release, she would do her best to bring back whatever she could to aid their practice. Their truckload of supplies ensured her promise would be kept.

A four-hour drive brought the three to Ken's house. To the excitement of Susan and Robert, the treasures were unloaded from the truck and brought into the kitchen, where the autoclave and dental imaging equipment was checked out. Everyone participated in the meticulous cleaning of every item, boiling the surgical equipment and carefully packaging the pieces. The deer portions went into the freezer, with the exception of what Beth warmed and served for dinner. Jess said nothing about the weight she carried, about nearly killing one of the men she had grown so close to.

In the morning, after the truck was loaded, Jess changed into her UL-One clothing and said goodbye to her parents, both of whom gushed over her. "Sweetheart, go do the right thing," her father offered.

"Jess, follow your conscience and your heart," her mother offered. Neither of those comments was helpful.

Susan understood the growing bond between her daughter and Carter. Staying Robert with her hand, she said, "You two go. We'll be all right."

After they had left, Robert said, "She belongs down there. That's her home."

Susan laughed. "Don't be silly. She'll be back."

Carter began to drive Jess home with Carla in her lap. She held Carter's right hand with her left. Ken sat in the rear to help with the unloading. "Before we take you home, we have something to show you to assist in your education," Carter mentioned, before turning off the main roadway. He drove some miles to a fenced-in area with barbed wire strung at the top of steel barriers. An armed guard came out of shack that held a small window air conditioner. He approached the vehicle as it came to a stop. Carter displayed credentials. The soldier looked through the window, then waved them on. Carter gave salute and slowly crunched over the gravel road past a raised barrier. In front of them were large-diameter gray pipes arising out of the earth. They elbowed outward at ground level to feed into other pipes, which branched off to either side.

Carter explained, "I know you have your doubts, so let us help you dispel them. This is the last water-pumping station in operation in the entire city. It serves a few hundred. This water also supplies the people, the greenhouses, and livestock at the base. We're good for maybe another two or three years; that is, as long as there is enough electricity to operate the water pump. Then there will be no more water—ergo, no more food for us or for you."

Carter exited the area and passed a lone Sider walking into a small dwelling. Testing the waters, Jess remarked, "I apologize for my people, who believe even looking at a Sider brings bad luck."

Ken said, "Yeah, we know, if it wasn't for a Sider

you wouldn't be alive today. None of you would be. Doesn't anybody there read history?"

"You mean about Jason Randolph? More times than I can count. Did you ever read Gottlieb's diary?" she asked.

"Sure," Ken replied, as though to say, "Who hasn't?"

Jess continued, reciting common knowledge, not all that sure he or Carter had read it. "The big sticking point in the completion of UL-One was hydroponics. Wilbur Gottlieb's two experts were killed in a plane crash and Gottlieb needed somebody very smart and talented, so he contacted Jay Whitmore. Even for an intelligent Sider, Whitmore was brilliant. Randolph wanted Jay and his wife to join them in their fortress in Lincoln, Nebraska, as they prepared for the worst environmental conditions to hit the planet. Linda Randolph wouldn't have it. Whitmore had deceived them, and she never forgave him for that. So, Gottlieb built his own fortress in Lincoln and retrained Whitmore, who was a biochemist and had developed a method to quickly degrade the ocean's plastics. Once Gottlieb got him in tow, he turned him into a horticulture expert almost overnight. It was Whitmore's design we are use today, in the rim, to feed our people."

"I knew that," replied Ken.

"I'd respond to that, but there's a lady present," Carter rejoined.

Carter turned off the highway and drove two miles across the desert to stop outside the west gate where the men deposited the boxes. "It would have been nice if Brenda had given you a key," Carter said, sarcastically. "I mean, especially since you're coming back from the hospital."

The pup remained in the car, whining, as her friend and mistress hesitated before leaving the car. "I know, honey, I feel the same way," Jess whined in return.

Jess faced a dilemma. Ostensibly, she had gone to the hospital. Now she brought back a load of supplies. Therefore, she would be forced to lie. The official story would have to be that, during her stay in the hospital, the men had obtained the supplies on their own and returned to the hospital to pick her up. Her facial skin color told differently. The story concocted on the drive to UL-One was that the medications she received for her problem had side effects. The medical issue itself was personal and she didn't feel like discussing it. There was nothing she could do about suspicions regarding her story.

A second and more severe problem presented itself. She would never be permitted to leave again. She had this sudden flash of herself years in the future speaking with a grandchild, who might aspire to loftier goals. Jess might lapse into some silliness about the time she had been close to ejection and was forced to give up this crazy fantasy of spending time Topside building homes and greenhouses in some faraway land called Sedona. She would explain that, in time, she came to realize the futility of that dream in a dying world, as she struggled to become a stable member of the community. *Oh, and yes,* she projected, *there was this man. It took me a while to get over him. Down below, those kinds of fairy tales don't exist. There is no way to express such a dream. That's the part of life we've all been missing. Our stew only consists of broth.*

She would never see her parents again, or any of the others. Carter and Carla would fade into painful memories, unless she quit the city entirely. When would that be—a month, a year? *Make up your mind, Jess.* The remembrance of feeling an imaginary cloak of warmth with Carter by her side stood in stark contrast to a life underground. A familiar impulse grabbed her and shook her like a dog shaking a rag doll. The report from the gunshot still rang in her ears.

She thought about superstition and how it transcends rational thought. It is a basic underlayment of human behavior and may be inextricably bound with instinct. It is a widely held, unjustified belief in supernatural causation leading to certain consequences of an action or event, or a practice based on such a belief. It is also a guiding force superseding intellect, providing a rationale for various behaviors. It satisfies a need to understand events, especially those pertaining to one's own life. It can be argued that it is as old as ancient memory. Its expression can be singular, or in mass, and may appear instantly.

If she knew anything at all, it was that hard work, along with taking chances, can lead to success, and that luck is a matter of perception. She would need to make another leap of faith and follow her intuition.

Jess took her hand off the door handle and said, "I've made up my mind to join you. Nobody in our city has ever left voluntarily. I've done it three times. I'm the perfect definition of a pariah. Within days, I could get ejected. I want to leave on my own terms. This isn't about me, anyway. It's about how to get the most done for my people and getting into big arguments down there won't accomplish that. I'll meet you back here in three hours. I have some unfinished business to take care of first."

The two men looked at each other and smiled. Carter said, "Three hours it is."

"Oh, one more thing," Jess said. She exited the car and walked around to the driver's side window, motioning for Carter to roll it down. He did so. She leaned forward and with her right hand, reached behind his head and pulled it forward to plant a lengthy kiss full on his mouth.

"I think she likes you," Ken grinned, as Jess turned to the left and walked up the hill. The opened the hatch, entered the city, found Brenda, and gave her the information she had been withholding about the water. She would be happy to tell the council, if they held an emergency meeting at the moment. Shocked at the revelations, Brenda called for the meeting.

Maggie and Mara didn't believe a word of it. The women contended that it was a ruse by the surface people to infiltrate their city under the pretense of constructing equipment for a hypothetical problem. What they had to gain by doing so was something they had to think about, but she had no doubt a valid reason could be found. Next thing you know, they'll be coming down here trying to fix who-knows-what.

Maggie observed that, while the recipes found in the new slate Jess gave her were popular, her vote could not be bought. James was given a pass. When called to the council meeting to testify, he confessed to having made an error in judgment in his earlier proclamation of wanting to go to the surface. Yes, they had brought back educational and other valuable materials. No, he had no desire to go back and never would do so again. He told the council that it was Jess who wanted him to go with her and sure enough, as luck would have it, he hurt his arm and if it wasn't for the UL-One doctors, he might have lost it. The discussion devolved into a 'he said, she said' confrontation after Jess erupted in anger at his accusation. She told him that his cheap confession ignored the help the surface people gave him and his words were merely a ploy to win Abike, who had finally left him, and by the way, for everybody's information, so had she.

Adversities are frequently brought about by poor decisions. James's temporary efforts toward bravado led him to feel foolish in his own eyes and in the eyes of others. The trip Topside had torn a large piece out of him. Unfortunately, neither he nor the doctor could define which piece was missing or how to fix the problem. At the meeting, Jess told James that she thought he was shell-shocked—something to which she feared her own father had succumbed.

During the meeting, Jess told the doctors about what the surface people had obtained for their new medical supplies that awaited them outside the west gate. She followed that information with the announcement. "Brenda, I'm going to save you the trouble of trying to eject me." She handed her the radio, declaring, "As soon as I say goodbye to a couple of close friends, I'm leaving UL-One to go live Topside."

Having steeled herself for the occasion, Jess had learned from Jay how to say it as it is. "I'm not finished, but this city may be, unless you really want to believe we're isolated from the surface. You're mistaken. I'm leaving voluntarily, and now I'm going to tell you what it's really like up there."

Jess launched into a vivid account detailing what had occurred, what she had seen on Beth's home screen—James be damned, he'd seen it too—and where their city was headed unless the Topsiders provided them with energy and water. Even then, there would be no guarantees.

After she had completed her presentation, the council members sat transfixed; Maggie and Mara shaking their heads at the effrontery of Jess to make up such a story.

Jess didn't ask for questions. With strong legs, she pushed back her chair, stood up straight, and walked out to say goodbye to Annie and Michelle. She packed up a few meager possessions, and left the city to meet with her man.

Jess could not hold back her enthusiasm when she saw him return in the old Mercedes, as though they hadn't seen one another in ages. After she got in the passenger side and immediately slid over to give him a quick kiss on the cheek, he handed her the paper bag filled with clothing. Even as he made the turn around to go back to the highway, she had already stripped off her garments, replacing them with jeans, T-shirt, and sneakers, finishing the operation with a New York Yankees baseball cap—all this with Carla trying to lick her face. She resisted the urge to throw her old clothing out the window. Instead, she folded it neatly and placed it into the bag.

"Time is running short. Honey, Ken and I are making plans to get back up north starting in a couple of days and do some serious work for a long time before winter sets in. Assuming you will go with us, you can see a lot of these trees turn yellow and red and lose their leaves. Ready to go back?" he teased.

"I will if it's an order," she teased in return.

"Your father doesn't want to go. It puts your mother in a bad position. She feels compelled to stay at home with him and that forces Beth to remain at home to take care of her guests. That leaves The Three Musketeers, plus Carla," Carter stated, tactfully.

"I'll do whatever I can to work," Jess offered, delighted to suddenly find herself a functioning part of team.

SEVEN

The following morning, Jess worked alongside Carter, Ken and Jay in the warehouse to carefully select crucial items needed for an extended stay in Sedona. A large U-Haul van was parked in the alley to compliment the other vehicles belonging to the group. The men considered this trip the following morning to be crucial in terms of completing the compound. Jess could not contain her excitement about beginning a completely new life. She had burned her bridge.

The radio Ken carried in his belt signaled a call coming in. He pulled it off and keyed the receiver. "This is Ken."

"Uh, hello, this is Brenda. Is this Salvage Enterprises?"

The work stopped. Carter and Jess made eye contact. Ken answered, "Yes, it is."

"Ken, we would like you to help us repair our city and maybe try to find the water Jess said might be there."

"When did you need this done?" Ken asked, looking at the others who appeared to be emotionally balanced between frustration and curiosity. Jay cocked his left hip and placed a fist on it, waiting patiently.

Brenda replied, "As soon as possible. It took a lot of arguing, but the council voted to approve your entrance to our city. The condition is that whoever comes in has to be an approved worker. I'm afraid the vote may swing the other way unless the work is started quickly."

"Let me call you back in a minute," Ken said, and keyed off the radio. Looking at the group around him, he shrugged. "Now what?"

Carter reached out for the radio and Ken handed it to him. "Brenda. This is Carter. We will present a plan at two mornings from now. I will be bringing Jay, Ken and Jess with me."

"Jess can't come. She left and she's not part of the work crew," Brenda stated, flatly.

"Yes, she is. She will be working with Jay, our Sider engineer, installing solar panels on the roof of the Pen. Unless you want to work with Jay yourself," Carter offered, grinning, watching Jess clap a hand to her forehead. Jay gave him a thumbs up.

"Will this Jay be coming into the city?" Brenda asked, after a long pause.

"Absolutely. Would you like to speak with him?" Carter paused after the stab, then continued, when he heard no reply. "Brenda, do you want this done or do you want to play word games? We were about to leave town for several weeks and you're cutting into our schedule. Is it yes or no?" Carter had reached his limit.

After another pause—Brenda could be heard discussing the conversation with another woman—she replied, "All right, in two days."

Carter switched off the radio.

The veins in Maggie's temples throbbed when she heard those words from Brenda, even though she had been in attendance when the vote had been cast. Immediately after the call, Brenda issued a single edict: SURFACE PEOPLE WILL BE COMING INTO OUR CITY. ANY BEHAVIOR THAT IMPEDES THEIR WORK WILL BE MET WITH THE STRICTEST PUNISHMENT.

All eyes were on Carter, as he stood before the city council, while Ken remained seated. Brenda could not believe what she was looking at. Hormones fairly oozed from her pores. She remembered that men wore wedding rings on the surface, not so this hunk. She definitely needed to have a private conversation with him. Although he knew Jess, that was beside the point.

Carter explained that his team would drill begin drilling one-half mild south of the city to try and hit a fracture line. If it were struck, the well would be lined, along with the addition of a pump and a filter. Then they would lay piping and a power line to the city.

Alex inquired, "Is there any down time for us?"

Ken shook his head. "Maybe a few hours when we shut off your water to cap the city line in order to add our own line over the top. Hopefully, we can do it in maybe three weeks. There is a limited amount of water pressure. You need yours and Phoenix needs theirs. We'll have to share. We'll have to tap into it during the morning hours when the crew is working, so prep the night before."

"In terms of providing you with energy, one thing we did a number of years ago, after things began to warm up, was to remove wind turbines from the tops of roofs. It's not a good place to put them because less height means less wind; no wind means no power. In any case, we installed them at the base. We've got enough of them in storage to put on top of the roof of the Pen to give you the power you need, although you won't have battery storage capabilities."

"How do we even get breezes, if we're under a high pressure dome," asked Philip, their resident engineer.

"Basically, they come from an interface of warm and cold air—different wind speeds, different temperatures, or horizontal air versus rising air. I'm thinking that your people can help Jay, Carter, and me with the installation. One major problem is that if the wind stops, so does your power. These turbines generate power when the wind is between 7-25 miles per hour. Without wind, you won't get any power to the well pump, or for anything else. Your ability to draw water will always be limited, but we don't think that will be an issue."

Once details were arranged, the primary heads of operation required another week to prepare for the operation. As forecast, with the assistance of underground city workers, a fracture line was indeed struck three weeks later. While the work crew Ken had hired worked on the well, the others worked inside the city installing new lighting in the city proper and new UV lighting in the Ring. Finally, the motor that operated the big fan was changed out for a low energy unit.

With the completion of the well, the elbows in the new line were bonded and the water switched to the new water source. This occurred in the morning hours. Burying the line would be done at a later date.

Jay proved to be a wonderful teacher and a delight to work with. He had the idea of turning the otherwise unused northern spoke into an uphill-downhill walking-running course when hiking or jogging could be used at all hours of the day. However, most citizens did their best to skirt him and the other Topsiders. As is the habit of people, a number of men and women identified with the trio, if only because of their unpopularity.

Her emotions in another state of flux, Jess spent little time communicating with life-long friends, opting to concentrate on physical labor. There were few who wished to communicate with her, considering her to be equivalent to a Sider—who wore Topsider clothing and climbed up and down ladders while wielding tools to install wind turbines on top of the Pen. Jess showed a surprising aptitude toward physical work. Her motivation and an exceptional memory impressed Carter. To her credit, she didn't fawn over him. She simply presented a cheerful countenance as she turned ratchet wrenches, all the while preparing for an uncertain future.

At last, the morning after completing the improvements to UL-One and finding themselves weeks behind schedule, Jess, Carla, Carter and Ken returned to Sedona.

That same evening, the bonding cement gave way after exposure to the desert's extreme heat. Once that happened, the pipes separated and the north corridor began to flood. Rivers of water ran down the graded corridor and began to pool around the kitchen hub.

EIGHT

The time of this occurrence is uncertain. The night trolley driver had been dozing with head down at a kitchen table when she was awakened to discover water swirling around her ankles. Her duty was to periodically look down each of the corridors to ensure that no red lights had been turned on outside a pod, which would indicate that assistance was requested. She sloshed out of the kitchen to find the walkway around the hub surrounded by water running down from the north corridor. Sounding the general alarm, she was already preparing herself to answer questions, when all the lights came on in the city.

As one of the first on the scene to learn of the problem, Philip had visited the drill site for a short period in the early morning on more than one occasion and knew the location for the shut-off valve. However, finding his way over a rock-strewn desert in the middle of the night lacked appeal. He did recall, however, that a switch had been created outside the north hatch that would permit use of Phoenix water, well water, or no water at all for just such an emergency. He called out to Gregor, who had responded to the alarm, and explained what happened. The men took the trolley the 200 yards up the long north corridor to locate the source of the leak.

It occurred to Philip at this time that a kitchen drain was present, in case of sink overflow, and that it might be closed with debris. After turning off the water, Philip directed Gregor find some bindings to hold the pipes together while he took care of other matters. Moments later, he was sloshing into the kitchen. Grabbing a ten-inch round metal knife sharpener, he felt for the screen, pulled it off, and ran the end of the metal pole up and down through the drain. Within a few seconds, he heard a distinct sucking sound and water began to swirl downward. He found Gregor at the Ropes and Ties store where they grabbed lengths of heavy fibrous straps and returned to where Gregor was using his height and size to reinsert one pipe into another and to bind them together. He turned on the water to find that a slow dripping had replaced the gushing torrent.

No damage had been done to any structure because the walls of the kitchen were not constructed with the gypsum board of old, but with virus capsid material totally impervious to anything man could throw at it. The material was initially developed by the same Jason Randolph who had destroyed the world, according to his own diary, and at the same time, had been instrumental in creating products that people could use to survive.

After Philip had reported to Brenda that the repairs would be completed within the hour, a sense of satisfaction overcame her. The crisis had been dealt with and no outside help had been necessary. There existed sufficient talent within her community to resolve physical problems, at least now that food and water issues were no longer a factor. Her people could sleep soundly.

Before breakfast in the morning, Philip and Gregor re-inspected their handiwork to ensure the two pipes were joined, when Philip said, "We're going to have to exhaust the moist air to prevent microbial growth. By the way, where's James?"

Gregor thought a moment and replied with a smirk, "I think he just got off his shift in hydro. We might find him in the Hub Junior trying to kiss up to Abike."

Philip nodded. "Let's walk over there. I'm going to get him to do some cleanup."

"What do you want me to do?" Gregor asked, always respectful of those who knew more than he.

"We're going to open the north hatch and the doors to the east and west. Then we'll speed up the big fan to push of the moist air.," Philip replied.

When the two men approached the café, Abike, who was facing them, saw them coming and turned around to return to her counter, leaving James alone, seated with his back to them. He called out to her. She chose not to face him and the approaching men.

"I have job for you," Philip stated flatly.

Surprised, James turned to face the two men. "What kind of a job?" he inquired, suspiciously.

"I want you to begin sweeping all the water around the hub down into the kitchen drain and keep sweeping until the place is dry. You can start with the north corridor."

"Dad, that's a lot . . ." James stammered.

"Gregor, if you would be so kind. Please escort our new assistant to his duties," Philip said. He turned to head up Spoke 1 toward the door to the Pen, wearing his own smirk. *There will be no more free rides on this train,* he thought.

What the men didn't factor in was the laws of physics, Philip's specialty. Although the walls would not absorb water, capillary action caused water to slowly inch up the seams between the walls of the kitchen and found association with the wiring. At 10:00 a.m., after James had finished three hours of water-sweeping—the fire started.

NINE

A story by Victor Hugo describes a five-ton cannon breaking free of its moorings on the deck of a ship. Subsequently, the canon rolls around, destroying both men and vessel, until it's finally subdued.

A loose cannon can destroy man and ship piece-by-piece. A fire is different. The absolute worst thing to happen on a ship on the open seas is a fire. Even if the ship hits rocky shoals or a coral reef, there is always a possibility that a few crew members can somehow make it to shore.

In the days of the wooden ships there were no high-pressure devices to pump water through hoses; only men with buckets, barrels of on-board water and long ropes. Just so with the inhabitants of the underground city, where water pressure was at a minimum.

Water had seeped into the main electrical panel to cause an electrical short in the one location where most of the electrical wiring for the city was located.

No Class C fire extinguishers were present. Indeed, there were no open flames and, other than brief flare-ups in the kitchen, which used electrical heat, a fire hadn't occurred in the history of the city. Even the kiln in the Yard used electricity. A crackling of the short was noticed by Maggie, who directed one of her assistants to get Philip and Jim Page, both of whom operated one of the electronics stores. Within a few short minutes, the two men arrived. When a worker pointed out the problem area, Philip emphatically stated, "Well, shuckers," which was about the extent of his cursing vocabulary. He directed, "We're going to need some light in here. Jim, hurry up and open the door to the Pen and I'll do the same to the door to the Yard. Meet you back here."

A moment later, sunlight and outdoor warmth flooded the two corridors. Philip had just returned to the kitchen when the worker was showing her discovery to another worker, who said, "Let's see what's going on," as she unlocked the panel that held the capsid wall in place and slid it back.

"No, don't," cried Philip. The wall cavity erupted into flame as oxygen hit the sparks. "I'll get some water," yelled the staff member, as toxic smoke billowed into the air from melted plastic.

Philip reprimanded, "No water. Not with an electrical fire. You'll either get electrocuted or make it spread." He went to the electrical panel and flipped off all the breakers. There was no Main. One by one he flipped the other switches and once again, but for the slight amount of sunlight entering two of the spokes, the city was plunged into darkness, without power to the fan, hydroponic pumps, city lighting, aquifer pump, kiln, stoves and ovens.

He and Jim removed their tunics and began to smother the fire, a procedure Philip had observed before joining the city, but had yet to experience. Within another minute the fire was out. In its wake was the smell of stinking plastic to dominate the airspace. "The whole thing is going to have to be rewired," he declared. The problem became: Where there's fire, there's smoke. Breezes from the outdoors pushed the rancid smoke into area surroundng the kitchen and into the corridors. No person born underground had ever seen or breathed smoke before, except from occasionally burned food. The coughing began and the fear of the effects of the smoke, combined with a remembrance of the influenza infection the populace of the city had recently incurred, provided an element of fear not unwarranted.

Philip apprised Brenda of the situation. "We can't fix it here. We need all new wiring," Frustrated, she went back to her pod to retrieve the radio and made an effort to reach *somebody.* She would have no clue what to do, if Jess had not given her the radio.

Brenda walked to the Yard. It was not possible to be surreptitious under these circumstances. At the far end of the Yard, she made the call. Jay answered. Brenda couldn't understand him at first, until it struck her that she was speaking to Jay, the Sider, whom she would now have to deal with directly. Hesitant to do so, she asked, "Yes, this is Brenda, is

Carter there?"

"No, he went somewhere. So did Ken. I don't know when they'll return. Can I be assistance?" Jay inquired, diplomatically.

Brenda's suspicious mind spun. *Was the Sider rubbing it in her face because he knew of their prejudicial beliefs, or was it a straightforward question?* She wondered whether she would have to be there when he did the work. That is, if he did the work. She explained the problem.

Jay returned, "Give me a couple hours to get together what you'll need. Ask Philip and one or two others to assist me. Oh, and I'll need you there, too."

"Me?" Brenda managed to stammer the single word. "I don't know anything about what you're doing. Why me?"

"Because I need somebody there in authority to follow my directives. Your people won't listen to me; they will listen to you," Jay stated in his straightforward manner.

Brenda thought furiously about how to handle the situation, when Jay added, "The smoke is going to be mostly in the corridors. The people can go into their pods where it will be less, or they can stay outside. You work out the rest. It could be late by the time we finish. No dinner tonight. Now, if it's all right with you, I'd like to get started."

Brenda began to ponder. *How do I deal with the people when a Sider shows up again?* She took the high road and reported what Jay had told her and announced that a Sider would be coming to do the work. "You all know him. He's really a nice guy."

Maggie clutched at her chest, feigning a heart attack. "A Sider in my kitchen? You're joking, aren't you?" She scowled.

Brenda did her best to console her. "Take it easy, Maggie. You don't have to be here when he does the work."

"It's him being here that's the problem—and all the bad energy he will leave behind," Maggie moaned.

"We'll have the minister bless the kitchen after he leaves the city, all right?" Brenda placed an arm around the other woman, who shrugged it off and walked away, complaining about the end of everything she had worked so hard for all these years. Brenda stared after her, shaking her head. She had heard about people getting senile with age and Maggie *was* 55 years old, the oldest person in the city.

In Maggie's eyes, Jess would be the loose cannon. To her, tendrils of bad luck had emerged from the dark side to destroy them all. Maggie's extreme views waxed and waned as the mood struck her and led the citizens to be curious about what rattled around in the woman's head. Brenda had long come to the decision that she didn't want to know—not because of the radical, overbearing nature of Maggie's views that set the standards for community superstitions, but for the fact that, damn it, Maggie made a lot of sense.

Jay stood in the corridor next to where the north

kitchen wall stood, looking at the melted mass of wires. "What a mess. Where's the micro-wire Jess brought?"

"It's in electronics. I'll get it, if I can borrow your flashlight," Philip responded. With a number of people following his light, Philip retrieved the wire and brought it to Jay. Working quickly and deftly, he and Philip had completed the work within three hours. Brenda stood nearby, transfixed by Jay's expert hands. She had never received any instructions from Jay, after all. Behind her, Maggie spoke in a breathy whisper, "What are you doing, Brenda, letting this Sider in here again. Are you crazy? Who do you think is responsible for this happening?"

"Go away, Maggie," Brenda turned on her.

"I won't go away. Next thing you know, my food will be poisoned," Maggie shot.

Brenda realized that Maggie could be going over the edge. Eccentricity aside, anti-social threats could not be permitted, especially when coming from the head chef, who had begun to envision problems with the food she prepared for the masses on a daily basis. A person couldn't be sent to Unit 7 as a punishment for becoming insane, could they? That said, she couldn't be ejected for the same reason, could she? As soon as the lights came back on, Brenda would find one of the doctors to get an opinion on how to proceed with this psychological mess.

At last, Jay looked up at Philip and stepped back. Philip slid the panels back, locking them in place, and flipped on the breakers to bring the city to life once again—until the flash storm raced through Phoenix.

TEN

The sun had set. Brenda, Maggie, Mara, Philip, and James sat near the entrance inside Drink More, a name Brenda found both amusing and painful when she considered her own past. The scent of garlic, mint, and lavender filled the air. The mid-day hour held sounds of children performing recitations in class, and Mara's assistants encouraging their students in the gym to work harder. The noisiest time was during and after dinner, when plates clattered.

At that time, card players became vocal in the central kitchen, after the tables had been cleared, while chess and checkers players tried to concentrate. Music came from individual pods that had their doors open. Life went on around them.

"Well, Brenda, the little vixen, Jess, is gone. Breaks my heart," offered Maggie, oblivious to James's presence.

"Amen to that," contributed Mara. "How about it, James, at least she's out of your hair and you can have your choice of women." This was an inaccurate statement. Rumor had it no woman wanted him, now that Abike had begun shopping elsewhere. The undeniable truth was that the surface had affected James in a dark way. Maggie called him *touched.*

"Mara, she was a friend, you know. She's a good person, something you wouldn't know about," James retorted, recognizing Mara's purposeful dig—pushing one of his hot buttons, yet strangely flip-flopping in the statements he made about Jess.

Suddenly, a terrible screeching sound made everyone in the café jump, as it echoed throughout the concrete walls of the corridors. Everyone in the area looked about themselves, wildly. The seated conversationalists sprang up and looked out at The Hub, where objects were being flung, seemingly at random, around the kitchen.

"Power surge," exclaimed Philip.

"Explain," Brenda urged.

"A surge of electricity came into the fan. That caused it to blow off three air ducts." To the observers, the configuration resembled an eight-legged spider that had lost three of its legs where they attached to the body. "The power station grid Topside probably got hit by lightning. It might be a transformer. We need to stop the fan." The others stared at the areas where Philip pointed. The gaps left by the detachment of the ducts permitted a windstorm to enter the immediate area from the openings. The wind increased in velocity as it circled The Hub and hit them forcefully.

"I'll get it," said James, making a move toward the kitchen.

Philip grabbed his arm. "James, be careful. Hug the walls."

"I got this," James told his father, touching some kind of pendant he always wore beneath his tunic. He knew enough to hug the walls or to crawl low because, whether wind or water, there will be less pressure in a pipe nearest its walls, which, in turn, can serve as a suction via negative pressure, even while the main air stream flowed. He knew that the power circuits were located behind a panel at the lower portion of the main entry door in the kitchen.

In order to reach the kitchen, he would have to deal with the high winds down the shaft. These would be most unpredictable nearest the rounded structure of the kitchen. Projectiles were another problem altogether, because the return air coming back down the corridors mixed with the force of the air from the broken connections to create a maelstrom that both sucked and blew small projectiles that had accumulated over the years.

Regular cleaning was a normal part of life within the city. Nonetheless, dust had accumulated for two decades. If viewed from the surface, it would appear as though a plume of smoke arose from holes in the ground, like an infinite number of flying insects just hatched after a first rain; or, as if the entire city beneath the surface might be on fire.

Using every ounce of strength in his thighs and shoulders, James inched along, flattening his chest against the wall, facing backwards, into the lesser wind near the wall of the corridor, surrounded by an assortment of small objects free-flying or bouncing off the floor and the walls. However, the negative pressure tended to pull objects out of enclosed spaces, such as from nearby pods that had their doors open, much as a tube connected to a water flow pulls gasses, vapors, or particles from another container due to the creation of a partial vacuum.

Fighting his own battle, numerous small objects were striking James on nearly every portion of his body. Something hard hit him on the right side of his head. Reflexively, he reached out with his right hand to clutch the area. This exposed his right flank to more injury. He took a quick look to get his orientation and dropped to the floor. Crawling the last few feet with head down, he reached the corridor that surrounded The Hub. He crawled through it, and finally stood to open one of the doors of the kitchen. Before he could disappear inside, a folding chair set against one of the outer walls lifted into the air and struck him in the head, edge-on. James went down again, somehow managing to crawl through the opening into the kitchen.

An instant later, the noise and wind stopped, although the lights remained dim. James had turned off the fan and, except for times when occasional repairs and maintenance were scheduled, the tunnels remained breezeless. The hum of the fan no longer served as eternal white noise, normally as much a part of the environment as the smell of spices.

Regardless of who had left the chair without replacing it, James could have saved himself the trouble, and his injury would have been spared, had he waited and counted to sixty, because in the next minute, their world became as quiet and dark as any person born in their city had experienced, when all the power went off in the night.

ELEVEN

To the citizens of the city, the familiar sound and familiar breeze of the always present air currents, provided some sense of normalcy. This was different. The blackness and total silence were so absolute that fear crawled down Brenda's spine—a fear genetically inbred in humans. Maggie could be heard reciting mumbo-jumbo, possibly praying to the gods of darkness, urging them to back off. Soon, screams from both men and women near and far broke through the blackness and reminded Brenda that, despite her fears, she wasn't dead after all. A primal fear of its own arose within her, demanding that she yell, to lessen the pain.

The darkness served as one dimension of fear. The absolute silence, in an otherwise noise-ridden city, served as another. Together, they served as a multiplier, which stripped away life as it had been known and inserted a vacuum with nothing of substance for the people to grasp, with nothing but screams to get sucked into the void.

Nothing could be done. It became a waiting game, as matters took their course. Flashlights were unheard of in a city where there had never been absolute darkness, or a need for such devices. As long as anybody could remember, lights had flickered on and off for short periods. In the old days, when that happened, backup generators on the surface took over. These were no longer operational.

The table began to shake, keeping time with Maggie's rocking. "Shut up, Maggie," Brenda ordered. "Philip, what do we do now?"

Philip, too, had been stunned by the darkness. Surprised by the sudden feeling of panic, he'd lost his focus on reality. Soon his rational mind arose. With a sigh, he said, "James probably pulled down several switches at once. He should have turned off power to the fan only. I've got to do it again. I have to turn on the switches for the fan and the lights."

"Good luck with that," Mara quipped, hanging on to Brenda's arm in a death grip.

Philip knew the length of his stride, having used it as a length of measurement on occasion, along with the length of his elbow and the width of his spread palm. Given he traveled in a straight line in the pitch blackness, he could count the steps to the wall of the kitchen. With arms outstretched, he walked forward and hit the wall after the fifth stride. He inched to the left several feet to find the opening. Entering the kitchen, he soon tripped over his son, hitting the control wall with his head. He felt for and found the control box located down low. An instant later dim light returned to the city. The fan remained still.

When Philip looked down, he saw blood running from a deep dent in the side of James's head. A pendant with a lion on it had spilled out onto the floor. Philip was half-way out the door when he ran into both doctors, who had exited the hospital at the sound of the screeching to see what was happening. They had seen James get hit, but couldn't get to him in the dark.

Alex called for a hauler trolley and within two minutes James lay in the hospital with a severe concussion. As though she had a switch in her own head, Maggie flipped back to normal.

Brenda walked over to Philip and put her arms around the man. "I'm so sorry. We all are. You know how we like to tease James. We didn't mean anything by it, did we Mara, Maggie?" She glared at the two women until they wilted under her withering gaze and said the right thing.

Brenda needed to get away from it all. She walked to the end of Spoke 3 and climbed the stairs to the Pen. Closing the door to the city, she found a nearby bench to relax and think. Within a few moments, sweat began to form. *Ah, yes, this is monsoon season, the humidity must be up. At least the storm has passed.*

Brenda tried to find a straw to grasp onto. She stood. Pacing pack and forth, she thought, *Events are spiraling out of control. It all started with Jess going to the surface. No, it started with Robert ap-*

proving the trip. All right, people were feeling a little sluggish. Next thing you know, the entire city is undergoing a makeover, from hydroponics, to energy, lighting, you name it. Surface people are running around in her city—even a Sider—for heaven's sake. Now the central fan is down, James is hurt, people busy coughing from the dust—what next?

A sense of loneliness overcame her. After two divorces and the doctors telling her she was incapable of having children, Brenda needed to be held. There were plenty of men who would do that, although there were none she trusted enough, or who had the sensitivity she needed at the moment. She could conjure up a thought of a single man who might be of solace, but he was currently elsewhere.

To her relief, the power returned an hour later, as did the few lights from the nearest and most occupied portion of Apache Junction. When Brenda returned downstairs, she found Philip and Gregor on ladders reattaching the air ducts to the central fan housing. According to Philip, several hours would be necessary to complete the task and to ensure the remaining ducts were securely fastened. Meanwhile, the dust level in their underground city remained at a critically high level. Persons exhibiting asthma symptoms were encouraged to wait out the repairs in the Pen or the Yard and to drink plenty of water. Many followed the advice. For now, there would be no food or fresh air below.

TWELVE

Rumor had it Mara's gym was as clean as her mind; it was small, always exuded an element of discomfort, and had never been properly ventilated. Complaints over the years had resulted in the usage of a single small exhaust fan standing on the floor just inside the doorway. Throughout the day, she or other instructors would tutor sweaty bodies who desired to practice dance, aerobics, wrestling, ballet, martial arts and gymnastics.

Mara, tired of gossiping with her friends, headed home at the Lights-Out chimes to find her husband scanning various diagrams of mother-boards on the home computer. She said in a low voice, "Jim, did you see who's going next door into Brenda's?"

"Not really, why?"

"Alex and Danny."

"So what?"

"So, Lights Out just happened. It's a strange time for a meeting."

     The City Beneath The Earth

Jim looked up from his screen, repeating himself. "Yeah, so what?"

She suggested, "Why don't you slip out the door, unlock the common wall panel and pull it out a half-inch." The practice was not uncommon in the city for purposes of eavesdropping. On rare occasions, a person would be caught unlocking or re-locking the clip that held a 15-foot common wall in place. The penalty for such an infraction was the publication of the names of the perpetrator(s).

Not anxious to incur his wife's vitriol, Jim reluctantly slipped out the door, to do as requested, looking both ways first to ensure no person walked the corridor. Within seconds, he had returned. "Let's see what's going on," Mara whispered.

The couple went to the far corner of their room, Mara leaning down, Jim standing, reluctantly, with ears pressed to the corner where the wall had been pulled away. First they heard small talk about the recent fire and how they'd been too jammed with respiratory complaints afterward to talk with Maggie about what she had on her mind and how great Philip was for their community, and it's too bad James isn't really getting any better although Philip thinks James needs a lot of hard work to give him a chance to come around. Apparently, James had lost a great deal of his memory. Too bad. Let's talk about Maggie's condition.

The doctors had not noticed the problem, but would be happy to speak with her, once Brenda directed the woman to consult with them. They would speak to Maggie about Siders and the issue of her promoting the theme of bad luck, associating it with her food. If they deemed it necessary, she would be pulled from kitchen duty and one or more of her assistants would have to take over temporarily, if not permanently.

After the doctors departed, Jim secured the wall within seconds, and Mara began to draft a missive to be sent out. "What are you doing?" Jim queried.

"Preparing a general post. I'll send it out after Maggie leaves the doctors' offices. Nobody will know where it came from. We don't have to sign it. Hell, all our news anyway is 'he said, she said'. People live on gossip. We got Jess to leave, didn't we?"

"Not really. She left because her parents left."

"Well, we stirred up the muck."

"You did, Mara. Leave me out of it."

"Whatever. It's our duty to let the people know that Maggie is down and out."

"You don't know that." Once again, Jim became offended at Mara's insistence to make trouble.

"Fine. If you want to be a coward, I'll do it. I should have known better than to ask you," Mara shot back.

"Hey, what's your problem? If you want excitement, why don't you join Jess on the surface?"

"No, thanks, you couldn't pay me enough to go Topside." She laughed, mockingly. "It'll never happen."

Maggie did visit with the doctors the next morning. Once she had left, Mara sent out a general post that read: Previous complaints and compliments about our meals are a matter of opinion. Many people think they are going downhill. There may be a reason for this school of thought. During our recent fire crisis, Maggie Nolana was overheard telling someone that we are all doomed because bad luck has contaminated our city and, in all likelihood, bad luck will soon contaminate our food. That's a frightening thought. What does that mean? She was seen visiting our doctors. Could it be regarding mental problems she is having? Let's hope not.

Shortly after hearing about Mara's post, Brenda excused herself from her shift in hydroponics. She returned to her pod to read what had been written and became furious, pondering: *Who had been standing around me when Maggie had said that to me? It could have been anyone. Mara is a likely candidate, but she was seen going outside the west gate with the others, and Jim was helping with the wiring. Hold on. The couple lives next door. Unless directly confronted, if asked, Mara would either lie or beat around the bush. She'd never implicate herself. On the other hand, Jim would answer truthfully, if pressured.*

Brenda brought big Gregor with her for the sake of appearances when she walked into Jim's electronics store. Jim saw her and did his best to look casual as Brenda strolled up to where he sat working on a home computer. "Do you know who wrote the general post about Maggie this morning? Yes or no?" she demanded.

"Well, actually, I did run across it." Jim did his best to screw up the courage to rat on his wife. He was more afraid of her than he was of Brenda.

"Yes or no?" Brenda stood with hands on hips.

After a quick glance at Gregor, who stood stolid, with arms folded, Jim said, "Yes."

"It was Mara, wasn't it," Brenda wasn't going to let this slide.

"Yes, it was Mara."

"I'm listening. So is Gregor. Let's hear it." Brenda drove the spear in deeper.

Jim told her everything that had transpired and how he was against it. He implored, visualizing the worst possible outcome for himself. "Come on, Brenda, you know how she is. I mean, she's always out to get somebody."

Brenda ended the conversation by saying simply, "Thanks, Jim. Gregor, come with me."

The two walked over to the gym where Mara was teaching an aerobics class. Standing in the doorway, Brenda waggled her finger at Mara, who directed her class to work on stretching until she returned. She walked over to Brenda and Gregor, wearing a look of smug confidence. Leading Mara into the hallway, Brenda asked her the same question, first stating that Jim had confessed. Mara responded, almost bemused by the fuss, "So what, Brenda, don't you think people have right to know if their food is going to be poisoned? Don't you want to know?"

"You spied on me, Mara. That's absolutely unacceptable. Worse, you incited an unnecessary panic in the city, and now nobody can trust Maggie until the doctors clear her. This time you've gone too far. Gregor, take her to Unit 7."

"Wait. Come on, Brenda, we're friends. We can talk this out," Mara beseeched, as Gregor gripped her by the elbow.

"The only thing we're going to talk about, Mara, is your ejection from UL-One. Wrap your brain around that bit of gossip," Brenda stated angrily, then turned and walked away. Gregor followed his directive, pulling along a shocked and tearful Mara in his wake, whose worst nightmare was about to be realized—ejection to the surface world.

Mara spent the remaining part of that day and that night incarcerated in Unit 7 until Gregor escorted the pleading, begging woman to the gate outside the Yard in the early morning, with a container of water as her sole companion.

PART 3

ONE

A month had passed since the repairs to UL-One had been completed. Now in late fall, the work crew neared completion of the Sedona project. The time had come for them to return to Phoenix to make preparations for a permanent move up north. In response to Ken's insistence that they try to pick up another travel trailer, and knowing that no usable unit would be available on RV lots after this period of time, Jay had found an old phone book. The book listed an Airstream manufacturing plant not far from the air force base.

By mid-afternoon, the tired travelers pulled up to the warehouse. Prepared for their arrival by radio, the vehicles were greeted by Beth, Jay, Susan and Robert. "Welcome back to more fun and games," Jay said as a greeting, lavishing attention on Carla.

Jess hugged her parents. "How was the drive?" Susan asked.

"A walk in the park," Jess answered, remembering her mixed experiences in a certain park, nearly a mile from where they stood.

Robert held his daughter close and said, "It must be pretty rough for you up there. Maybe we can fix that."

Jess was about to ask him what he meant when Jay said, "Listen, Beth and I just returned from the base a couple of hours ago. Radar is picking up a strong storm, possibly a series of storms coming in."

"And?" Carter groused, not having fully recovered from the journey.

"And UL-One needs to be warned," offered Beth.

"Can't it wait 'till morning?" He did not want to go back underground to do more work. He wanted to pack up the vehicles and get the hell out of Dodge.

"We've had plenty of big storms over the years," Jess said. "I don't see the problem."

"Not like this one," Beth answered. "I've been around to see these storms in person, which is something you haven't done. Expect the humidity to increase underground more than it normally would."

Jess got the point. Too much moisture for too long a period of time would result in the growth of mold on their plants. Disease would spread like wildfire. Carter suggested, "On the plus side, if the weather holds off, Jay can take my Mercedes tomorrow morning and check out the trailer place."

That seemed to satisfy both Ken and Jay. Ken said, "All right. For now, Beth, why don't you, Susan and Robert, go on home and tighten up the house. I'll drop off Carla there. Let's keep track of the radios. Jay has one. Carter, Beth, Jess have one each."

"And Brenda has one," Jess added. "She understands you can't call them underground to warn them. You'll just have to show up. There's one way to get in. It'll have to be through the north hatch. Nobody ever locks it."

Two hours later, sweat running in rivulets, Carter grabbed the handle of the driver's side door of the U-Haul in the alley. In its cargo space were two large, free-standing power generators, gallons of fuel oil, two dehumidifiers, hundreds of feet of cable and hoses, several small fans, six heaters and a box of humidity gauges. The side of the van advertised this model featuring CLOUD RIDE. Below that in smaller lettering was printed: Ride with pleasure: AM/FM/SAT/Tape Deck. Pick up all the stations wherever you go.

"Where did you get all this stuff?" Jess asked, before he could climb in.

Carter gave a quick shrug. "You don't spend 20 years scavenging and not come up with some loot. You never know what you need. Scavengers are usually sorry later for something they didn't pick up. That's why we accumulate so much junk and why we keep such close record—so we know exactly where everything is in the warehouse."

"Do you think you brought enough?" she asked.

The ludicrous statement almost caused Carter to laugh out loud until he realized this wonderfully intelligent woman schooled in the sciences, with whom he had fallen in love, had absolutely zero knowledge about such things. He patiently explained, "No, Baby, I don't believe it's nearly enough," and explained why he thought so in a sentence or two. "Go ahead and take my truck home. We'll keep in touch." He bent down to kiss her, a nine inch difference in their heights.

Arriving at the west gate to the underground city, Carter turned the big truck around to back in with Ken parking next to him in his SUV and lowered the hydrolic lift gate.The men got out and walked around to the north side to hike up the hill. To the south, black thunderheads towered to 55,000 feet. The men disappeared down the hatch. A few short minutes later, they reappeared at the west gate accompanied by Gregor, Philip, and Brenda, who unlocked the gate.

Ken directed, "Let's get this inside and downstairs." He had previously noted the presence of a concrete ramp next to the stairway for deliveries.

"Somebody explain to me what's going on, please—something about a storm?" Brenda said to Carter, ignoring Ken.

"I saw Jay at our warehouse a little while ago. He mentioned that you two had some electrical fun," Carter teased, as a reply.

Brenda's scrunched her nose. "Not too much fun. We're all hoping for some dull moments. Right now, it's dinner time, so why don't we meet downstairs here in Unit 7?"

Ken pointed to the south at the towering mass of black clouds well above the horizon. "Let's move and I'll explain."

The only personal objects in Unit 7 room were a pair of Nigerian Djembe hand drums set against one wall for use by the Contee family for their performances and practice sessions. These were stored next to a kettle drum. Other band members took their instruments home with them—instruments that came with the founding of the city. The wall between two units could be slid out during practice to make room for more members. Thus, Units 6 and 7 could be utilized during those times.

No wall hangings or drawings, beaded curtains, or personal art decorated the interior of Unit 7. No carpeting from the looms adorned the concrete floor. Everything blared white with the exception of the tan-colored wall panel separating the room from that of the next pod.

Gregor returned shortly with Alex, Danny, and two other able-bodied men who all entered the over-crowded pod. Carter began, "What a satellite at the base is picking up and what you're seeing outside is a major storm doing its best to push its way up here. It seems reasonable to expect several inches or more of rain for a number of days. Unfortunately, there is no way to predict anything with global weather patterns in disarray. Once the parched earth soaks up what it can, UL-One may flood. So will Phoenix. We need to take precautions."

Ken took over. "Our biggest concern is an increase in humidity. We'll be pulling in an excessive amount of moisture with the fan, so there won't be any cooling through skin evaporation in the humid air. Thus, we will sweat. That's the good news. We stand a real risk of mold growing on anything with cellulose. For example, paper and plant products, clothing, artwork, library books, sandals and ropes. It won't grow on concrete, glass or porcelain. It can also grow on human skin. How do we know this? We faced the same problem down in Houston when I worked there. I can tell you there is as possibility that the air will fill with spores. We may face a serious medical problem."

Ken gave a brief gesture of holding his hands outward directed to the doctors as a wait signal. "It's stalled right now, held back by a ridge of very high pressure. Beth, my wife, who worked at the base, says to expect the storm it to hit us sometime tonight or tomorrow once it pushes through. Beyond us here, there won't be anybody coming to the rescue, because those of us who live Topside are going to have our own problems."

"What do you think, Philip?" asked Carter.

Philip wasn't even certain he believed in the germ theory of disease. Infection of plants, yes. Disease in humans, no. For him, bad luck was alive and well—with another round of it looming in their immediate future. At this moment, he needed to play to the audience, not to popular sentiment. He declared, "There are a number of factors here: water intrusion and subsequent flooding, high humidity, microbial growth on organic material including books, leather and art supplies, and contamination of plant life in the rim. The air inlet is set above the fan on the surface. It's elbowed to keep free water from coming in, so we don't have to mess with that."

Carter added, "This discussion is on the wrong track. You have an entire mile of hydroponics ringing the city with spray misters in abundance. They add moisture to the air. So does human and plant respiration. Fifty dehumidifiers——we call them dehus——wouldn't be enough. So what we'll do is slow down our activities, turn the intake fan to low, stop using the misters, drain any open water sources that are in hydro, stop taking showers, and run heaters. We'll place the two dehus we have in the gym and library. We'll hook up hoses to them and run the hoses into the drain in the floor of the kitchen. People can take their special belongings to the heated rooms to keep them dry, plus we'll rig exhaust fans in those rooms to push out the air. "

Ken said, "Brenda, send out one of your general posts. Tell people to remove all wall hangings from every pod. Humidity will be highest between them and the wall and mold will grow on their backside before it starts on anything else. We need to keep the humidity down below 50% to keep point sources from cropping up. My guess is that you're typically running 30-to-35% here."

"How do you know so much about it?" Alex wanted to know.

"When I was going to school, I worked part-time

for a large fire and mold remediation company. They were accustomed to drying out homes whenever there was a water loss."

"I'll show Carter where the break to the water line occurred. It still needs some work," Brenda offered.

Carter had previously experienced Brenda's come-on charms. As she led him past the hub to the end of the north corridor, through which they had entered a short time earlier, Carter looked around him once again. With the new lighting they had installed, it might have been an indoor shopping mall, except for the presence of trolleys and the lack of windows.

Rather than take the hand-pump trolley, she opted to walk with him, the two of them alone, offering her assistance for anything he needed. When they reached the hatch, she stood very close to him and pointed upward to the break, ensuring he wouldn't miss the fragrance in her hair. He said "Thanks, Brenda. You're so sweet. I'll take it from here."

What's a girl to do? Frustrated, belaying an urge to tear at her hair, Brenda returned to her duty as mayor. Within a half-hour the entire city had been informed of events. Gregor and his work crew placed the equipment in locations suggested by Ken, and strung out enough cable to ensure there would be power to both the Phoenix grid, and when that failed, to the generators situated outside the door to the Yard. Electrical attachments would be run through an air register located in the wall next to the door.

Workers spent a long night laying power cords, attaching humidity meters to walls and making contingency plans for whatever might go wrong. The storm cooperated until noon. The black mountainous clouds moving in from northern Mexico had broken through the heat dome on their march north to begin the great deluge.

In the skeleton city of Phoenix, water flowed freely in the streets and over the curbs. Basins, gullies, and washes ran like river rapids, carrying tons of debris as bodies of water collided with one another, madly racing down other channels to overflow into buildings, which collapsed under the onslaught of the torrents and the tremendous weight of debris they carried. Wooden fences disintegrated and roofs were torn from their structures in the gale-force winds.

To Ken, this storm had bad intent written all over it. It was a living, breathing entity whose sole purpose was to wash the earth clean of . . . what? He had a strong urge to be at home, to ensure the safety of those living under his roof. He resisted the pull. After all, Robert was there—less than the equivalent of a fourth women in terms of work load, he thought. Jess was too forgiving and loving to set him straight. Susan and Beth would fill that particular void.

Annie knew a plant pathogen when she saw one. She didn't need a humidity gauge on the wall to inform her that her thousands of children might choke on water vapor. Now she worried, proclaiming, "We need surveillance of absolutely all crops every four hours. If a blight takes over one crop, it could spread everywhere. If that happens, we'll lose everything." She also had serious concerns about their stock of crickets. Once their surface became exposed to high humidity for a period of time, parasitic growth would become pervasive and the entire farm could be lost.

Both Ken and Carter found it remarkable that life went on as usual in the city during a time of crisis. Game players enjoyed their evening in the dining room, arts and crafts were created, people munched on slices of fruits and vegetables, read books on their home computers or visited one another inside their pods, leaving droplets and trails of sweat wherever they went. A few began making hand fans for distribution.

Ready for food, Ken and Carter took a break and entered The Hub Junior. Ambling up to the counter, they looked at a sign on the wall listing the food available. "How much for the fresh garden salad?" Carter asked.

"We don't buy and sell, we barter," said the proprietor, a middle-age man standing about five-eight—several inches shorter than his customers. "Say, you're the same guys who were here before to do the work on our water and all that."

The man had a genial personality that Carter took a liking to. "That's us."

"What's it like on the surface, anymore? I mean,

I came from Detroit originally. Rumor has it things must be pretty rough up there these days." The proprietor expressed sincerity in his quest for information. "By the way, my name is Jericho." He held out his hand.

"Every day is a struggle," Ken responded, taking Jericho's hand, more anxious to eat than to get into a lengthy discussion. After a slight pause, the proprietor asked, "It's getting like that down here, too. I heard everybody up there carries a gun. Do you both one?" asked Jericho, unable to hold back his curiosity.

"Yep," both said in unison.

"Do you think maybe I could see one, I mean, no offense . . ." Jericho said sheepishly.

The men reached behind their tan shirts, which they maintained out for cover. Each retrieved his weapon, dropped the magazine, checked the chamber and handed it to the man, who hefted each one in turn, then returned the weapons after looking down the sights. The men ejected a round from the magazine in their hand and gave them to the man, who hefted each one in turn. "Wow. What kind of bullets are these?"

Pointing at the copper-jacketed bullets in the man's hand, Carter said, "That one is a .45 and the other one is a 9 millimeter. They fragment when they hit the target. You want to cause the most damage without the bullet passing through a person to hit an innocent bystander. "

The proprietor absorbed this incredible wealth of

information—juicy stuff he could and would pass on, now that he was rapidly becoming an expert in surface weaponry. Amused at his admirer's curiosity, Carter told the proprietor. "Keep the rounds as a present for good luck."

The proprietor read the lettering stamped on the back of one of the rounds. "Wow, man. A real .45, just like they used with the old Tommy guns."

"Not exactly. These are more sophisticated. They didn't make them like this in those days," Carter contributed, happy to add to the proprietor's store of knowledge.

"Trade ya' food for these. Okay?" the proprietor offered, canting his head sideways, questioningly, encouragingly.

"Deal," Ken smiled, curious about what Jericho would give them for lunch.

Fifteen minutes later, the men imbibed a glass of lemon tea and a large soy-flour burrito rolled with slivers of soy patties, fresh lettuce, parsley, spearmint leaves, diced tomatoes, slices of jalapeno peppers—all garnished with fresh onions—a challenge to the taste buds.

Looking around as they ate, they couldn't help but marvel at the scores of products made from plant leaves, stems and roots; materials that plastics had replaced in their own world. Too late now. And if this present situation wasn't handled right, a huge hunk of remaining humanity could die almost overnight.

Actually, those tragic deaths did occur, only not

in the way they thought. Of the remaining three clusters of humanity they knew of, two of them would soon perish.

TWO

Within another hour, the immediate storm had passed. Shortly, another deluge began, this time heavier than the first. The entire sky became pitch black from one horizon to another. The power went out. Prepared for this eventuality, Ken and Carter employed flashlights to see that the humidity was approaching 55%, wherever the gauges had been stationed, while several areas of the ring were now close to 60%. The solar panels had stopped working. The humming generators gave life to the city.

Outside, the dark cloud mass moved northward; no others were in sight to the south. The clear sky promised a day of heat and drying-out. Any rain in the Yard had run out the holes at the bottom of the fence, and the pit used to obtain clay for pottery had filled to the top with water. Philip tossed a water pump connected to a hose into the pit and began to evacuate the water. Then he reversed the fan to blow out the moist indoor air in the city, although the mugginess would remain so throughout the day and into the next until the dry heat did what it did best. Better than anyone, Annie understood that if Jess had not brought back the fertilizer to give strength to the plant life, the same plants would not have been able to resist the assault. Jess had saved all their lives in more ways than one.

Carter soon found his home had been destroyed, along with Jay's residence. The warehouse had become filled with a randomized mixture of collapsed roofing materials, broken glass, and countless objects collected over the years. The power station was gone and so was the source of water and electricity. Carter, Jay, Wei, and Riki moved into Ken's home, which had incurred significant water damage to the upstairs rooms. It didn't matter anymore because the entire extended family made final preparations to vacate the premises.

Jay reported that he had found a completed Airstream unit they could take with them, while Wei and Beth expressed their concern about Luke Air Force Base and scheduled time to visit the base prior to leaving for Sedona. Susan and Robert opted to remain home to prepare dinner, and Jay wanted to work at the warehouse to find what they could save. There was no point in cleaning up after the storm; but several necessary items had to be found, if this was to be the last trip.

In Carter's truck, the Three Musketeers, plus Beth, Wei and two dogs, traveled the distance south to the base, which now lay barren. Only ghosts remained to suggest life had ever existed there. The water tower lay shattered on the ground, the water itself long-since evaporated on the scalding tarmac. The dormitories lay as kindling—the product of a micro-burst that killed every person within them and had blown apart the greenhouses. Bodies lay beneath the debris, or out in the sun.

The windowless building that once held satellite receivers shared space with overseas drone operations. This building stood apart from the others. Constructed of slump block filled with concrete and re-bar, its reinforced structure had been constructed to withstand anything but a direct bomb hit. As though it were a tease, the reinforced otherwise inaccessible door, stood open, with no personnel within, live or dead.

Beth and Wei found what they wanted—six military-grade, hand-held satellite radios that had been in operation days before during their last visit. These, along with their chargers, would enable them to communicate with anybody, anytime, anywhere on the surface the planet, which is to say, a small area now limited to the Desert Southwest and a small area several hours driving time from there. Although there would be a slight delay in receiving, as the signal bounced from one satellite to another to reach its destination, their ability to communicate gave improved by a quantum leap. Nobody argued when Ken mentioned that Brenda should be given one of the sat phones immediately. Ties could not be lost with this small remaining cluster of humanity.

While Beth and Wei removed usable electronics, Ken, Carter and Jess picked over the remains of the greenhouses. They gathered hundreds of yards of tubing, along with other materials needed for their own futures, while keeping a watchful eye for un- wanted guests, at the same time working quickly to escape the stench of hundreds of bodies rotting in the heat.

This time the men did find weapons: handguns, rifles, ammunition and cases of grenades of various ilk, including flash-bangs. They'd used them be- fore. In a fraction of a second, each grenade could emit seven million candle-power brightness and 170 decibels of sound. This intensity of light was enough to cause short-to-long-term blindness. In terms of the bang, they knew that whine of a jet engine is . . . was at 120-140 decibels and the human eardrum can rupture at 150. At 170 decibels the brain becomes disoriented and remains so for a lengthy period of time. Carter had the thought that if UL-One were ever invaded for their food and water, one of these would finish off the attackers inside a concrete cor- ridor, no problem, without a shot having been fired or leaving a body to be disposed of.

Ken reiterated his desire to pick up large gun safes, because the way things were going, the un- expected coming out of left field could not be ruled out.

THREE

The daughter of a Chinese industrialist and facing Chinese rule, Wei's father had fled Hong Kong to the United States, bringing his computer technology with him. Born a Sider, she had been one of the first mutants born in Asia when the disease finally reached the continent. An astoundingly fast learner and driven to succeed, she quickly climbed the ladder in the field of computer programming and wrote numerous groundbreaking papers on new techniques in tracking the tell-tale detritus left behind by hackers. She soon found herself in the field of cryptography working for the U.S. Military. Eventually, she ended up working at the military base in Houston, where she met Beth, Ken and Carter. At the collapse of the Houston base, they were all sent to Phoenix, where she met and married Jay. Wei and Beth made a team and played an integral role in obtaining data from satellite information systems.

Returning home, the explorers found Jay working with Susan and Robert. Jay had cut strips of deer meat, Robert had recovered a few remaining vegetables from Beth's greenhouse, and Susan had stir-fried the mix using propane. Except for the vegetables used for dinner, the remainder had been removed and frozen in preparation for the journey ahead.

In the garage, where boxes of propane bottles were stored, a humming generator connected to the freezer and to flooo on the ground floor. At the dinner table, cooled by an evaporative cooler, Ken reported that, from what he could ascertain, over two hundred people at the base and another hundred people in Apache Junction had lost their lives to the storm, as nature continued to whittle down the number of surviving humans. The dry-brittle buildings of the main business area, such as it was, could not withstand the flooding and the pounding rain. Gone were the stores that sold books, sweets, and shoes. The market and theater had disappeared.

The fanciful plan to connect UL-One water with Phoenix water had been scrapped early on for insurmountable reasons, one of which was that there was no manpower to find and lay the large-diameter piping necessary for the job, or to operate the heavy equipment necessary for the work. As far as anybody could tell, the last remnants of the city were gone.

Trying to remain upbeat, Carter shoveled a heap of instant mashed potatoes onto his plate, ignoring the two dogs cruising beneath the table looking for dropped food. He proclaimed, "Hey, look at the bright side. Tomorrow morning, an entire new life will begin for all of us."

"Amen to that," chimed the other seven.

Their schedule changed when the earthquake struck.

FOUR

Underground, at the sound of the general alarm, and even while citizens headed to safety, an immediate aftershock caused the collapse of the ceiling of the last fifty feet leading to the Yard. It took out the stairway, the portion of the Ring that ran beneath the stairs, and several of the pods at that end. Chunks of foot-thick concrete fell in Spokes 6 and 7 exposing the rebar reinforcement above it. A cloud of concrete dust filled the two spokes. People who were headed in that direction turned around and streamed toward the Pen at the opposite side of the city. Water lines in the two spokes ruptured and air ducts fell. The delicate balance of air within the city had been compromised, with strong drafts sending dust back into the city proper.

Philip ordered the opening of the door to the yard to permit positive pressure to blow out the dust in that direction. For that, Gregor volunteered to go outside the north gate and work his way around through the gate in the outer wall of the city in order to reach the door and open it. Philip increased the speed of the central fan. When Gregor returned, he reported the collapse of virtually the entire earthen wall surrounding the Yard, including the roof overhang that covered the pottery-making section and the kiln.

Brenda ran to the door of her pod and looked out. New cracks appeared in the ceiling and walls of her corridor. She needed to escape. She quickly ran back inside and grabbing the radio from beneath her pillow, she ran out to the Pen where she tried to get ahead of the flood of people going in the same direction. Once she climbed the stairs she called, frantically. "Hello, Carter, Jay, anybody. Are you there?"

Ken answered, "This is Ken. Yes, Brenda, we felt it too." Beth stood next to him, clutching his arm.

Brenda pleaded, "Ken, we need your help. The ends of Spokes 6 and 7 collapsed. We can't get out that way to the Yard. The dust is terrible. There are cracks in other spokes, too."

Jess reached for the radio, when Carter's hand stayed her. He whispered, "No, let it play out."

Ken pursed his lips. Looking the others, he said, to Brenda, "Did anybody get hurt?"

"No, thank God," she said. "We're trained to immediately come to the hub whenever we feel a tremor. We do have a few people injured."

Ken told her, "I don't know what I can do. Moral support won't move concrete blocks. I presume your solar power is still working and so is your water supply. What you need is heavy equipment or manpower. You have the manpower. There is no heavy equipment that will work inside those corridors, let alone even get down into your city. You'll have do it yourselves. We can't help you."

"There must be something you can do? Aren't there a lot of doctors experienced in trauma out there, at least?" Brenda implored.

Ken shook his head grimly, his dark hair laced with grey strands. "Unfortunately, there aren't. There is no hospital and there are no doctors anymore. You've got the last two. We'd really like to help you, but there is nothing we can do that you can't. I'm afraid you'll have to use your own resources."

"Wait. Brenda, this is Carter." He took a deep breath. "Ask if any of your people want to leave your city and come live with us. We'll meet with you at breakfast a day from now. Will that work?"

"Oh, my, yes, yes," signed Brenda weakly. She hit the off button. She thought, *He's right. There's nothing they can do.* Holding her face in both hands, she began to sob. "We can't end like this."

At the conclusion of the call, Carter placed a hand on Jess's. The other seven stood watching and listening. In his obtuse manner, Jay said, "Ken's right. Their situation will be the same whether we get involved or not. If we do, it will create serious problems for us. We'll get hung up helping them and lose valuable time to save ourselves—time we are rapidly running out of. We need a tomorrow for all of us. "

"Maybe I should go over there and see what I can do," Robert offered. The look given him by seven pairs of eyes caused him to say, "All right, bad idea."

Jess felt torn again. Her city was dying, piece-by-piece. And if she had been there, not knowing at all about her new surface friends, she, too, would be helpless. Reluctantly, Jess assented, then asked, "Can we check on them, if and when some of us return, for whatever reason?"

"Absolutely," Carter agreed, hugging her tenderly, understanding her pain. "Let's try to get a little rest now. It's going to be a very long day. We have a lot more packing to do and, hopefully, we'll have a passenger or two. Maybe your people can assist us, rather than us helping them."

"Carter, it can't end like this." Jess began to cry, almost as though she had heard Brenda's sobs.

FIVE

Carter, Ken, and Jess appeared as scheduled. There was no more finger pointing, no more accusations, no more bad luck signs; only a group of people concerned for their lives. A large number of people clustered around the trio. Jess, possessed more color than when she had left the city. She wore a short-sleeved and tan work shirt over muscular arms, blue jeans, work boots and a baseball cap over the red hair she had requested Beth and her mother cut to no more than four inches in length. A holster attached to the rear waistband of pants held her weapon—a Beretta 9 mm. At one time, she was a seedling that had broken through crusty soil to sprout into the open air of the surface. Now she belonged to Carter. Most of all, she belonged to herself, sworn to be the master of her own destiny—a religious convert, in her own manner.

The damage to UL-One went beyond Brenda's description. Aftershocks would surely cause the complete collapse of the two spokes. Numerous cracks had also appeared in Spoke 4 and 5. These could be expected to widen. Brenda ordered their evacuation, with the gym to serve as the holding place for their contents until arrangements could be made to find housing for the displaced families.

Carter and Ken took turns, describing in detail what he and his people had accomplished, who was on-site and outlined plans for the future. To the rapt attention of the audience, Jess told, in frank honesty, of her own physical struggles, leaving out anything related to personal feelings.

"We'll take our chances here," Maggie insisted.

"No. We will put it out for general information and see who's interested in going with them now," Brenda instructed. The fewer in her city, the better for everyone.

"You say Susan is living with you?" Annie inquired. She and Susan had been closest friends for years. They had shared stories of their past lives and their present adventures, such as they were. Susan was Annie's best student. In a recent sudden shock, Susan had told her that she was leaving the next day. Just like that.

Jess nodded. "Absolutely. My mom misses you, Annie."

Ken said, "We have room for a handful of people right now. That's it. The surface is dead; no power, no water, no people, at least as far as we can tell. The weather is generally harsh and the workload is heavy."

"Why would anybody want to go?" somebody else asked, not accusingly.

"Why would anybody want to stay?" Jess responded, shocked at her own question, wondering if hypocrisy was the proper word to define her actions, versus her life-long beliefs she held before her escape from the city of her birth. "Call it another chance for survival. UL-One may have served its purpose, perhaps as a reservoir for humans. Maybe it's time to move on."

Alex and Danny began conferring. Danny asked, "What do you have for living accommodations at the present time?"

Brenda voiced concern. "You're not thinking about leaving us, are you?"

"We're just asking. People want to know what they're getting into," Alex replied.

Carter sighed. "Understand something, my friends, we don't run a trolley service that can come and go at every call. We have room to take four or five right now. Unlike you, we have seasons. These limit our time to build housing. When we do, the units are going to be a fraction in size of what you are living in now. Furthermore, for the rest, you will have to wait several months to move out of here. There is nothing else we can do, absolutely nothing. Sorry."

One hour later, Carter and Jess found themselves in a dilemma: 42 people had signed up to leave UL-One. This whole earthquake situation had caught everyone off-guard. The endeavor called for at least one more trip down, to Ken's chagrin. For the moment, four were chosen: Annie, her son Gregor, his wife, Michelle, and their eighteen-month-old son, Will. Gregor had long been an admirer of Jess, who seemed to be doing fine—unlike James—and if Annie, his mother, could find the courage to leave, so could he. It would also stop Michelle from complaining about how much she missed Jess.

In addition to serious damage to the spokes, the earthquake had also destroyed a portion of the food production facility. Thus, bags of coir could be appropriated by Annie for use in the new development. A great benefit that emerged from the trip down was that 25 inflexible panels, that separated the now abandoned rooms in the corridors, could be slid out and loaded onto the truck. Each measured seven-by-fifteen feet and thinner than a sheet of paper, which fit through the door at the top of the Pen on a diagonal. In addition, another dozen panels were stored in the north corridor. Ostensibly, they were to be used by the builders of the city to construct an activity center outside in the Yard, but were never used due to a time constraint issue. When stacked, the panels measured two inches in total thickness. They served no further purpose in the city, but would be invaluable up north. When taken to the truck, there was no reason not to toss them on top of the other items already present. Ken handed Brenda a sat phone and told her to call on alternate Sunday mornings after breakfast.

Loading of the truck took another hour, and by

8:00 a.m., both vehicles left the underground city, with the new passengers in the Mercedes. Carter valued the big dually too much to knock around in it, preferring to use it for more serious ventures. For getting around town, he used the sedan. It had the same seating capacity, but was more comfortable and took the rough roads better. If and whenever it died, he would be sorry.

A few moment after the visitors and the four citizens had departed, Brenda began to think. Her small distillery had not been destroyed in the ring. With Annie gone, few would complain if she ramped up production of alcohol and, why not, get some serious *Cannibis* growth and get the kitchen to make some cookies with her special recipe, all to reduce tension in the city. The good news? Unit 7 had been destroyed. No more jail time. Things were beginning to look up.

Carter explained, "We're going to move fast, so don't try to figure anything out now. The first thing you're going to need is clothing." He drove to Ken's house, where the extended family quickly became reunited.

Raiding the closets yielded coats, pants and shirts that to fit the three adults. "In a few minutes we're going shopping to try and find you suitable shoes and clothes for the little guy," Ken declared. "After that, we've got a mobile home to pick up before we head out."

An hour later, Carter parked the Mercedes next

to a walk-in door at the Airstream plant that Jay had broken when he had previously inspected the building. Carter entered the door while Ken backed up the U-Haul to a large rolling door next to it. A moment later the rolling door opened. Ken backed the truck in further, until the trailer hitch touched the front coupling of the mobile home. Damage to the roof and the loss of several windows in the large building permitted sufficient light to enter. Inside stood numerous trailers in various stages of construction and destruction.

Jess led the guests into the single completed 24 foot-long Airstream. Opening the door, she announced, "This is the one we're taking with us."

A moment later Gregor declared, "Man, I have first dibs on this," while his son, Will, bounced on seats and Annie and Michelle opened cabinets, exploring all the nooks and crannies.

Jess smiled. "Gregor. Don't get too excited. It's not a 450 square foot pod. This may be your new home for your entire family for some time."

Ken disappeared for a several minutes and came back with an armful of devices. "I found these in the supply room."

Carter came over and said, "No kidding. A drone, a controller and a monitor."

"What's a drone?" Jess asked.

Carter replied, "It's like an airplane or helicopter that you fly remotely. It sends back signals that you pick up on your computer screen so you can see what it sees. In the old days they used to be as big as small airplanes. They could listen to everything you say and carried weapons."

"What are you going to use it for?" Jess inquired.

Carter shrugged. "Don't know yet. We'll see if Wei can get this system operational so we can look around our new home to get an aerial view of our neighborhood."

The men began discussing the trip home and how the Big Hole, as they called it, would be negotiated. Listening patiently Jess offered, "Hey, guys . . ." Whenever she began a sentence with those words, it could spell trouble. "When you get to the Big Hole, why don't you place one of the panels over it cross-ways. It'll cover it completely. Put a small boulder on each end to keep it from blowing away. Then drive right over it. It won't even flex. Leave it there for future trips. By leaving it in place, it will also prevent further erosion of the hole. If we don't do anything, the hole will become so large the road may become completely impassable. Furthermore, just before the Big Hole, there's a cluster of potholes that you take forever to get through. Another panel placed over these holes will, in sum, save a good 20 minutes driving time."

Jess was referring to the fact that the panels were so strong they could serve as the outer coating of a spaceship. In fact, they had served in such a manner. Initially, the spaceship was the size of a virus that had spent millions of years inside a rock traveling through outer space until it landed on Earth. Jason Randolph discovered a way to grow it and harvest the shell or capsid, after which Wilbur Gottlieb made products from it.

Carter said, cheerfully, "Honey, I could kiss you. I mean, we must have ESP. I was about to suggest the same thing to Ken."

"Bullshit, you were," Ken snorted.

"What is the meaning of 'bullshit'?" asked Jess. "You men use the word a lot."

"Aside from change, it's the other constant in life," Carter explained, without going into detail.

"It means ridiculous nonsense that is part of every person's life, whether rich or poor," Ken contributed.

Prior to leaving the house, Robert had declared, "I'd like to go with you, but I have to take care of some things here. I'll come up later."

Susan looked at him with narrowed eyes. "Robert, they won't let you in. They won't listen to a word you say and will throw you out on sight. Besides, they don't need more people now. They need less."

Robert looked at his wife as if to say, *"Oh, spare me. They've known me as their leader since the beginning."*

Carter tossed Robert the keys to Beth's truck and handed him a sat phone. "Don't wreck the car," he said, curtly, and walked out the door to join the caravan, wondering whether he'd ever see Robert or Beth's truck again.

To Carter's great delight, Robert had steadfastly refused to go to with them to Sedona. After working with the man and now living with him, Carter had had his fill of the man. He considered him to be a control freak and a complainer. He reviewed what he had learned about the man. Thanks to his gift of gab, Robert started out selling homes, moved up to selling businesses, then spent 20 years running a small town, manipulating, cajoling, creating wedges, getting things to go his way—like a spoiled rich kid. After that, he moved in with Ken and Beth, trying to do what he always did.

The caravan began the long journey northward. The U-Haul had been loaded with the old household freezer packed with meats, a new freezer obtained from an appliance store, along with equipment from the warehouse, salvage from the base, and a few personal items.

The slow-moving vehicles were delayed further when the mobile home got a flat tire going over the pass. Jess was driving Carter's truck to the rear of the chain of vehicles, behind the trailer, when she saw the tire blow. "Call it in," she said to Gregor, who sat next to her. He did as requested and each picked up their radio to receive the information. All the vehicles stopped.

"Somebody shoot me if I ever talk about making this trip again," Ken moaned.

"I'll have to shoot you twice. We have to make at least two more round trips to get all the refugees," Carter answered.

"Okay, do it before we go," Ken suggested. "By the way, I'd like to suggest we find ourselves a large school bus so we can do it in a single trip."

"Good idea, but it won't be this time. Let's see if we can find a bus when we get to back Sedona," Carter suggested.

"Good thing we thought to bring a spare tire," Ken said, cold wind whipping around him.

"Yep. Trouble is, it's in the back of the big truck and we'll have to unhitch the trailer so we can drop the lift gate to get to it," Carter replied.

"Why didn't we leave one of the spares in the trailer itself?" Ken queried.

"Because we're not too bright," Carter answered. "Let's see if we can fix stupid."

The men retrieved the jack from a side panel in the truck, loosened the hitch and raised the tongue. Carter pulled the U-Haul forward a couple of inches to free the trailer. The tires were the last items to be loaded. "While you're there, take out the other spare. I'll throw it in the trailer," Ken said. "Murphy's law, you know." Within 20-minutes, the operation had been completed and the trip resumed.

SIX

Robert waited half-an-hour, then wrote a note thanking Ken and Beth for their hospitality—it was the proper thing to do; told his wife and daughter he loved them, and said he was moving back to UL-One. He grabbed the keys to Beth's Silverado and headed south to the underground city, expecting to be welcomed with open arms.

Feeling empowered and wth anticipation, Robert climbed down into the north hatch to walk the long corridor in the blessed coolness of the city. The dust from the fallen concrete had not been completely cleared out of the air. He counted it as a good sign when he reached the 12-foot-wide walkway encircling the hub and immediately ran into Maggie. She told him to stay there and hurried off to collect Brenda. Robert stood in place, wearing surface clothing and receiving stares from curious passers-by, who recognized him, but chose not to show it. Shortly, Maggie returned with Brenda, who stood stolidly in front of him with Maggie standing to her right. Both women were dealing with their own personal aftershocks and were in no mood to see any Topsider, especially Robert, walk in to their city. Brenda gave consideration to locking the hatch to keep out unwanted vermin, but decided to hold off on that decision for the moment.

Standing with hands hanging at her sides, ready to throw a fist at the visitor, she bored into him with her eyes and said, "Maggie tells me you said something about coming back. What does that mean?"

Instead of being welcomed with open arms, Robert sensed a challenge. That was fine. He decided to disarm the situation by being honest. "It means the world up there is too crazy. I should have let Susan go on her own, so I decided to come back here to help."

Brenda tried to process the insanity behind the statement, wondering if Maggie would try to tear Robert's eyes out, and if she would stand there to watch it happen, or, more likely, to join her in the act. Poised for action, she told Robert something he didn't want to hear. "Look, you can't come back unless you're part of an approved Topsider repair team. You're not. The addendum to the city charter is quite clear about that. And 'no' to your next question; it isn't up to the council, it's up to me. If Gregor were here, I'd call him, but I have no doubt there will be several men who would like to see justice served. On second thought, I think we"ll do it ourselves. What do you say, Maggie?"

Robert felt sucker-punched in the gut. Maggie took a step forward. Robert, almost breathless, snorted, "What's the matter, Brenda, are you afraid I'll take your job?"

Brenda's eyes blazed fire and indignation, her lips in a half-snarl. The declaration could not be clearer: *No entry beyond this barrier.* "Call it what you want, Robert. You're making a fool out of yourself," she snapped, spraying spittle on the man in front of her. "Of all people, you should understand the rules. You drilled them into us every chance you got, until you let your own daughter break them. I mean, you just walk in here? Are you nuts? Topside did get to you, didn't it? Get out, now, Robert. Your home is not here, not anymore."

Robert finally grasped the reality of the situation. Blanching, he gave a wry smile. He wanted to tell them about the big house he was living in and the great car he drove, but thought better of it. They'd despise him even more, if he did so.

Without a retort, Robert turned around to stiffly walk back up the corridor, out the hatch, down the hill and into the car. Weeks of planning for nothing, waiting for the opportunity. When it did come, it did so as a good sign. He could move back to where he belonged.

After Robert's abrupt entry and departure, Brenda humphed. She turned to Maggie and offered, "I never did like that guy," whereupon Maggie declared, "There's a shot of bad luck for you. Obviously things aren't going well for him. Maybe Susan left him. He always was a slacker. "

Once back at Ken's house, Robert tore up the notes and flopped onto the hot sofa with no operational evaporative cooler because they had taken the generator. The hour was not yet 8:00 a.m., two hours after the others had departed. Left with no choice, he would have to go up north. It should be no problem. Maybe he could help them cook or something. In a rare moment of conciliation, he drove to the warehouse to see if he could find something to bring up with him.

That's right. He remembered now. *They were out of room to carry things and had asked him to pick up . . . what was it . . . space heaters or fans?*

He pulled into the rear of the building to avoid the rubble left over when half the roof collapsed during the deluge. He stopped the car and got out. The damage had been extensive. When the northern portion of the roof collapsed, it took with it numerous rows of three-tiered shelves. Countless items collected over the years were randomized and mixed in with lumber from the ceiling and shelves. Broken shards of glass from the upper windows glistened between salvaged goods, small and large. No lights were on, no fans moved the air. Walking deeper into the building, he tried to remember where anything was located. He hadn't paid that much attention despite the time he had put into working on the inventory, which, now that he thought about it, they had taken with them. Or was it in the office?

Robert gave up after several minutes of poking

through the rubble, kicking apart pieces.. Despondent, he walked to the car, reflecting on his life. What had he ever done to hurt anyone? Hadn't he been successful in real estate because he could relate to people? Hadn't he been elected—well, appointed—mayor of a city? Carter didn't like him, Jess's dog didn't like him, neither did Jay's dog, and Ken never did like him. He had his suspicions of Jay. Did Susan? He gave a brief thought about going to the air base, until he remembered that it, too, was gone.

He pondered the map they had given him. He knew Arizona. Tracing the route with his finger, he began to plan. The car had almost a full tank of gas, the tires were good and if it rained, the windshield wipers still worked. With careful planning, he could make it safely to the northern city in two to three hours. Okay, add a half-hour for the unexpected. No cars would be on the road. He'd be there well before noon, easy. The problem would be to find the campground. He should have listened when they told him where it was, but he had his mind on other things. He did have the satellite radio. He'd call when he got in the area of Munds National Park, but not now. Let it be a surprise. He pocketed the map, grabbed a bottle of water, his toothbrush, and some clothes, not especially looking forward to Plan B.

SEVEN

Jess drove Carter's truck. As passengers, she carried Michelle, little Will, Annie, Susan and Gregor. On the way, she shared the evolution of the feelings she had encountered through her transition in order to assist her passengers in understanding the emotions each would face in the coming days and weeks. The mention of the benefits of a hot water soak perked their interest. "Unless you brought bathing suits, it'll be in the raw. Be prepared for that," Jess teasingly announced.

Night had fallen by the time the encampment had been reached. Beth and Susan had packed a cold chest full of food prior to leaving the house the night before and the group huddled around the campfire eating sandwiches. The small community had trippled in number, which now included two dogs.

After Carter assigned sleeping spaces and good-nights had been said, he and Jess remained by the fire, pleased that the long journey was over and they could enjoy quiet time together. Carla's chin lay on her master's leg while she read. Carter had wrapped his arm around Jess. He thought about how full his plate had become since meeting her. He had thought of little else since their first meeting and, somehow, here they were.

Jess could feel her man thinking by the occasional twitches of his fingers on her arms. She felt connected to Carter, the fire, Carla, the forest, the breeze—like long threads of mold mycelium belonging to a single universal truth from which they had all stemmed.

Her fertile mind and excellent memory rapidly absorbed what she read. The forest around them had changed considerably from what the books described—books graciously provided free of charge by the Sedona Chamber of Commerce. At the moment she was absorbed in *Plant life of the Coconino National Forest*. As she read, the found that altitude, amount of precipitation, temperature, and slope of the mountain were four factors affecting the type of life in a region. She should be looking for edible plants that survive in very wet conditions during cool to moderate temperatures. That opened up a lot of possibilities. Like a detective trying to solve a mystery in an Agatha Christie novel, she pulled out the book *Pictorial Review of Edible Wild Plants of Arizona* and began to read. She soon found that the nutritious nasturtiums, especially watercress, might be found in the local summer, such as it was. Indeed, it was one of their staples back home. She had already found wild parsley, related to carrot and anise.

Pausing in her reading, her mind wandered and, like a hummingbird curious about her red hair, so she wondered about the galaxy of stars she had seen her very first night out in the park. She knew that particular night was forever impressed upon her soul. "Carter, tell me about the stars," she requested, softly.

"Baby, I'm no astronomer."

"Tell me."

Carter patiently told her what he knew about the planets, the galaxy, the universe, and make-believe starships. Whether he was correct in all that he told her, who would say otherwise. After he finished, wondering about what might have been, she began to cry, softly.

Carter relaxed his arm around her and asked, "What's the matter, sweetheart? What did I say to hurt you?"

"It's not that. It's just . . . what happened, Carter?"

"You mean, why did it happen? There is no why. No other life form asks why. They deal with life on a moment-to-moment basis. And what if they did ask the question? Would that help their survival? Does it help ours? Something beyond our control did this. We can't go back in time, although I might suggest that right now our planet is a little pissed off."

"What does that mean?"

Carter secured his arm around her again. "It's like a dog shaking off unwanted dirt," he answered, grimly.

Jess overcame her emotional lapse and decided to give her man something else to think about. She rehearsed the lines and tone in her mind once again, finally saying with a note of gentle annoyance, "Don't squeeze so hard, love. The baby might complain."

Carter let her go and sat up straight. "Uh, what, how, I mean . . ." He stumbled over the words.

Jess milked the moment. "Let me explain to you how it works and exactly and precisely what happened." Jess went into lurid detail to such an extent she could have sworn that, by the flickering red-orange light of the fire, Carter had blushed before he carried her off into the trailer. Carla followed to watch.

In the morning, Jay had already unloaded the panels from the truck when the other men arrived. Ken assigned tasks for each person. Jay and Wei began to draw up plans for 30 small apartments, some single and others double in size to accommodate from one to three persons each, with room for a small common area. Enough panels would remain to build a windbreak on the north and east outside a row of heated outhouses. The windbreak would prove to be a major factor in reducing wind velocity and accompanying energy consumption.

Carter sent Jess off to do more exploration of the

immediate area, something he had been wanting to do for some time. Rather than going straight ahead north or toward the right, she and Carla headed to the left, a direction not yet explored. After several minutes of fighting underbrush and low-hanging branches, she came to a large plastic sign at eye level. Brushing off the dirt and debris from its face she read: Coconino National Forest. The map told her she was at a starting point with lines marked as trails meandering into various directions. Writing beneath the map admonished the traveler to:

Stay on the Path, Do not Litter, Do not pick up Souvenirs, Laws will be Strictly Enforced.

To the left of the sign was a large paved area she took to be a parking lot with a single-story building badly in need of a paint job, but otherwise seemingly intact. Walking over to the structure for a closer look, she saw a wooden sign above the doorway that read:

Munds National Forest Tourist Center.

Beneath it was carved Welcome to Navajo Country. The area, including the building, encompassed some 6000 square feet, with the building itself occupying one-fifth of that. Three outhouses stood intact next to the building and to its rear. Forest lay on all sides, except for a paved drive from the south that, ostensibly, originated in the eastern portion of Sedona—the left fork of the branch once the bridge had been crossed.

According to Carter, aside from hunting, virtually all the time the men had spent up here revolved around construction-related activities, their time limited by the weather of the day. Still, she was surprised the building and the lot had escaped their discovery. It might have provided them with an immediate home. Warily, Jess leaned against the glass entrance door, expecting it to be locked. Instead, it opened easily, almost throwing her off her feet. A strong gust of wind blew in behind her. Whoever had left must have done so in a hurry with no concern for lockup. Cautiously, she entered with rifle in hand and Carla at her side. "Go look for people," she commanded. Carla went off to explore the rooms and returned moments later, not finding any surprises. Several long-dead plants stood dried out in floor pots with odd-looking whitish-mounds on the under-surface of their leaves. A counter stood near the entrance with its racks of pamphlets to her left. A few chairs were in order against one wall, along with a leather sofa. Behind a reception desk she found booklets entitled *Complete Trail Guide to Munds for the Serious Hiker* and *Pictorial Review of Edible Wild Plants of Arizona*. She took one of each and placed them in her pack. The room gave way to a large back room with an oaken table surrounded by six chairs, a second room designated as a break room measuring some 8' x 10' with a small fridge, table and chairs, and another room of the same size that held filing cabinets and a small desk. Finally, another door proved to be a his/hers bathroom. Exploring the filing cabinets and the desk revealed no surprises, such as those she had encountered during her foray into the hospital at Fort Huachuca.

About to leave the building, a whining sound caught her attention. Carla began barking. What appeared to be a large mosquito passed in front of her eyes. She swatted away at the insect, which she took to be a stinger, and quickly left the building, ensuring the door closed behind her and feeling good about the discovery of an intact building. It had no serious roof leaks and no broken windows, but the insect attack disturbed her. The men were right in that the local surroundings had not been weather-ravaged, unlike the city proper a few miles away.

Jess saw no easy path into the woods. With a wary Carla at her side, she wended her way by taking the path of least resistance until she came to another hot spring, this one twice as large as any they had seen thus far. Beyond the spring lay a good-size body of water nearly half the size of their compound. A mat of growth covered its surface. Carla sniffed at the water and turned away. Jess set down her pack and stuck a finger into the warmth. Like the water of the various hot springs, the brackish water tasted alkaline; yet a gold mine lay on its surface —Watercress. She walked around the edge of the pond to where she could grab the plant and began to haul it in. She allowed it to drain before placing it into her backpack to be washed off later. Mushrooms grew everywhere. Familiar with *Coprinus* and *Agaricus*, she collected those. She knew enough not to pick the colored varieties.

Quite pleased with her discoveries, Jess looked around to maintain her bearings. At some point she would have to return. It would be helpful to know what the backside looked like when approached from a different direction. If she possessed a compass, she would have to make a huge compensation, due to the shift of the magnetic pole, as Ken had pointed out.

Jess was about to move on when Carla shot off. She loosened her rifle from her shoulder in preparation for the unknown, until her dog returned with a rabbit in her teeth, tail held high. This, too, went into the backpack, weighing but a fraction of what it had been when she and James had loaded it with magazines and books.

What caused her to think of James so much here in the wilderness, of all places? He wouldn't be happy here having to depend on himself. Had he ever known true happiness? What would happen to the rest of his life? It might be possible some woman would want a man diminished in many ways, yet creative in others. And now that she thought of it, she wondered if her father was well and what time he might arrive.

Jess found the air surprisingly warm compared with the other areas they had previously explored, perhaps ten degrees warmer. She removed her parka and hung it over a tree branch. No wind made it through the undergrowth. The tops of the trees swayed to provide a swishing sound. Concentrating on the sounds, she quickly learned to associate them with wind velocity, using the spinning of the wind-mill as a guidepost. At the moment, fifteen miles per hour would be about right, quite enough to gener-ate enough electricity for their needs. At night, she would find herself listening to the sound of air mov-ing over and through the trees and to the changes in the intensity of cicada-sounds, as the insects rubbed their legs together in response to temperature. From what she had read, the males would rub legs together to attract females. When the temperature decreased, the rubbing would slow. To her perception, there ex-isted a correlation between the rate of chirping and wind velocity so that wind-chill had to be factored into the equation.

Looking for specific plants, she found more pars-ley along with wild carrots. She also found the in-sect population to be an endless nuisance, as they attacked her face and neck. She donned the surgical gloves. Although her arms were covered with the flannel shirt, that didn't protect her neck. She set down her pack and paused to reconnoiter when she saw another rabbit. "Stay," she commanded Carla, who sat, watching. Jess unslung her .22 rifle, taking careful aim. She hesitated for an instant, thinking about taking a life, when the rabbit ran off out of sight. Jess had a long talk with herself on the return to the camp. This was food. Out here it meant sur-vival. She would not make that mistake again.

Returning to camp and ashamed to tell Carter about her missed opportunity to get another rabbit, Jess unpacked her loot, excitedly telling him about the building and her discoveries. She saw spray misters going into the greenhouse which now encompassed 800 square feet of three-tiers of plants with panels serving to naturally insulate the sides of the structure. In addition, Annie had brought with her a cage of crickets. She expected to have enough for a continuous supply of powder within a few months and planned to house them with the plants in a section of their own.

Carter said, "You found a whole house? Damn. That makes me feel bad. We will definitely go back for a closer look. Why don't you get these veggies washed and I'll start cleaning the rabbit." Fortunately for her, he didn't comment on the fact that there was no bullet entrance into the rabbit, only teeth marks around its neck.

"I forget to tell you. There's what I think might be a stinger loose in that building. It may have blown in when I first entered. I got out right after that," Jess reported. Carter grunted.

She poured fresh water from a carboy to wash the dirt and small bugs from the edibles, deep in thought. When she had told him about the baby, he asked the typical male question about how she knew. When she gave him the details, he made her laugh, asking in typical Carter fashion, "Are you sure it's yours?"

Her mother had been told, and her father would

be very pleased to learn about a grandchild. Maybe the news would bring Carter and her father a little closer together. She felt certain that things could get better. Assailed by that thought, Jess declared, "Carter, I want to know where my father is."

Carter looked down before answering. "I knew you'd ask, so I tried to call him on his frequency two or three times. He didn't answer."

"Why didn't you tell me?" Jess asked.

"Because I figured he would pick up when he wanted to and I could give you positive news," Carter replied. "Maybe he lost the radio, or left it behind or turned it off."

"Or something happened to him," Jess stated, unhappily.

"Look, I can't tell you where he is, but maybe when Brenda calls on Sunday, we can find out where he isn't."

When she did call at the appointed time, Brenda reported that there were betwen 40 and 50 people who still wanted to leave the city, including Alex and his family. Carter informed her that it would be a good four months until they were ready with a new residence hall to accommodate the refugees, but to keep in touch.

Jess motioned for Carter to hand her the sat phone. He did so, saddened that Jess had to undergo this tribulation. "Brenda, this is Jess. Have you seen my father? He was supposed to be here earlier in the week."

"He came down here several mornings ago wanting to get in," Brenda said.

"What happened?" Jess asked, knowing the answer.

"I told him to get out, that nobody wants him here. So he left. Maggie and I sent him on his away. Plain talk," Brenda said with finality.

Carter shook his head sadly at Brenda's cruel words. Jess said, "If you see him…"

"We won't," Brenda stated, not letting Jess complete her sentence. "He wasn't too happy about it, I'm afraid. But rules are rules."

"Yes, they are," Jess agreed, and signed off. There was a long pause before she said, "It was as though my father had turned into a different person, don't you think?" Jess asked, tears beginning to form.

"Most definitely out of his element," Carter responded, wistfully.

"Did that ever happen to you?"

Carter turned briefly to look at her. "Oh, yeah. Sometimes you get into a different crowd of people outside your comfort zone, or into a completely different situation in which you have no experience whatsoever. You try to adapt, but it's more than that. I've done some really dumb things. When I look back on them, I have absolutely no explanation as to what drove me to say or do those things. How can I be so smart in one place and so thoughtless in another? It makes me want to crawl under a rock sometimes when I think about them. There are memories I will take to the grave with me."

Shocked to find out her superman was human after all, Jess's admiration for him increased. She contemplated: *What had she regretted? Where would she be today if she had stuck it out with James? Would it be living the humdrum life, or would the time come when she would feel like crawling under a rock to hide from the world?* She had to ask, "What did you do when you felt like that?" She felt connected to Carter, Carla, the fire, the forest, the breeze—although, she did miss the vast open spaces of the desert.

Carter's mood turned more positive, "I do my best to look at what I have accomplished and how they outweigh the mistakes I've made. If you don't, it'll eat you up. I always try to look to the future and do as many things as possible to gain experience. The poet in me holds that my greatest trial will be to overcome my greatest triumph. Also, I try to be as productive as I can be, trying not to kill time. If you do that, you could cause serious damage to eternity."

"What?"

"Something out of Thoreau's Walden," Carter said. He went on, "I still have morbid thoughts, but I try not to get emotionally involved with them. To he honest, there's a lot of buried rage inside of me. It's part of my driving force. Maybe someday it'll get cleaned out. "

EIGHT

Carter proclaimed Jess to be the head explorer, based on her success in finding edible plants and the visitors' center, a title which she took seriously. After the men had gone into town to find an additional generator, Jess had the urge to go exploring. Just a quick trip. She grabbed her .22 rifle and radio to head off across the bridge, into the deeper woods—Carla at her side. Walking quickly, she passed a number of hot springs and found the insects to be somewhat less in this area, possibly due to the heat given off from the springs. Soon, she came to flat area with minimal vegetation approximating the size of their present compound. She could envision Ken leveling the area for construction of new buildings.

Moving on, she approached a hillock covered with vegetation. It looked like a low mesa cleared by several yards around much of its rocky base. A large crack in the granite greeted her. As she looked inside, she saw sunlight entering from occasional cracks in the walls of rock. Entering the chamber, she stood aghast. Carla sniffed the air, not yet ready to explore. Once they had entered, they heard the sound of squealing rats or field mice scurrying away,

The size and depth of the cavern astounded Jess and gave her a flush of nostalgia for home. Walking forward slowly, she saw evidence that heavy machinery had been used on the ground and the walls to smooth and level them, therefore, more entrances to the well-hidden location would be present. Could this be the lost city she had read about, the one Gottlieb had tried to start, but had given up on for some reason?

She was about to explore further when a rumble of thunder caused her to halt her investigation and exit the way she had entered. They had gone but a quarter-mile when Carla suddenly yelped and bit at one of her paws. She lay on the ground licking it, under a canopy so dense that little light showed through.

Jess sat next to her and put down the rifle to check on her partner. There was no evidence of a bite mark, although in was difficult to see fine details in the gloom. She decided they had better return quickly, but found Carla unable to walk. Now feeling concerned, Jess looked around and realized she had no idea from which direction they had come. She stood and carefully checked the ground to see if any footprints were visible, but the gloom revealed nothing in the earth to her untrained eye. Even if she knew where to go, Carla would be too heavy for her to carry. She decided to radio for help. When she tried to make the call, she found the radio was dead. It had been given to her, specifically. It was her responsibility to ensure her own unit functioned before going anywhere. She had committed a serious mistake and Carter would surely scold her, although no worse than she was scolding herself at the moment.

Looking around, she smelled, put a wet finger in the air and used every trick she could think of to find her direction. She needed to go north-by-northwest. The wind usually came from that direction, but there was no breeze where she stood. The sun rose in the east and set in the west, but she couldn't see the sun for the canopy. Moss generally grew on the north side of the trees, but thanks to The Mars Virus, it grew around the entire circumference of a tree, when it was present at all.

How long had she been gone? An hour or two? Somebody must know she was missing. Another mistake. She didn't tell anyone she was leaving. In a quandary, she smiled to herself, remembering the rifle. She would fire off a round. Somebody would hear the shot and come looking. The problem was that she had brought the .22 for hunting small animals and large birds. It wasn't the Marlin or the Winchester and the sound of it might not be heard. It was worth a try. Picking up the gun, she racked a round into the chamber and thumbed off the safety—no round entered. She had neglected to load it after Carter cleaned it the night before. She mentally kicked herself. It was her responsibility to ensure all her equipment functioned properly all the time. If she had cleaned her own weapon instead of relying on someone else, this wouldn't have happened. This wasn't UL-One, when a single scream would bring scores of people to your doorstep; this was real life—where a single mistake could mean your life.

She still had an option. Her Beretta held six rounds in the magazine and one in the chamber. She pulled it from beneath her waistband and fired off a round, then another a minute later. That left five. Jay and Wei could recognize the sound of a handgun, including her Beretta. She waited a couple of minutes, then fired off a third round. Seconds later she heard a distant rifle shot in acknowledgment. She immediately responded with a forth shot. This time the repeat rifle shot was closer. Finally, she fired a fifth round and within minutes Riki came bounding through the brush, followed by Jay.

Too ashamed to tell Jay about her failures and the hard lesson she had learned, Jess merely told him that Carla got bitten by something and that she was too heavy to carry. She also told him about her discovery of the cavern. Dutifully, Jay picked up the heavy dog with his muscular arms and the two dogs and two humans emerged from the trees into a torrent of rain. Once inside the house, under the light of a bright bulb, and to Carla's great relief, Jay quickly found an embedded thorn.

Once called the Witch from Hell, Jess was now treasured as the Goddess of Good Fortune. That term became reinforced a day later while several of the men had driven to out to collect pallets of bricks at a brickyard. She and Carla were hunting beyond the building site near where she had gotten lost. She almost stepped on a wild turkey hidden in tall grass. The hen became aggressive toward them, suggesting a nest might be nearby. While the dog kept the turkey at bay, Jess found a clutch of 15 eggs hidden beneath heavy vegetation. There was no way she could bring back the turkey alive, so she rigged a carrier and returned with the clutch, running into her Jay and Wei. Jess gave them more reason for excitement when she pointed out that, according to the books she had read about wild life in the region, hens born from this clutch would weigh 10 pounds—with the toms weighing as much as 24 pounds. Construction of housing for the turkeys must become a project of paramount importance. The envisioned the new grounds she had discovered might work a site to construct a turkey farm, a project which Jay immediately undertook.

How do you build the roof, Jay? Jess inquired.

"That's the easy part. You build it upside down. Lay the panels on the ground and run a lot of hot solder along the joints wherever you want your dividers. It's so light you can flip it over and set it into grooves you first make in the ground. Pour in your concrete and you're good to go. Same thing we did for the residence hall."

Once completed, the farm would be totally impervious to weather changes and the eggs would be kept warm under cloth with a heater close at hand. It would take them approximately one month to hatch and they would have to be watched constantly.

According to Jess, a wild turkey in captivity will not lay eggs in a large clutch, but will lay 100 eggs per year, or about one egg every three days. At 40% larger than a chicken egg, the turkey egg goes farther as a meal serving. With enough turkey hens, the large eggs would serve the entire population amply, if served on a rotational basis when mixed with other foods.

During their visit to the brickyard, Gregor had found an old farm bell which he hung outside the house. Jess worked out a coding system to advise anybody within earshot of incoming weather systems, calls to gather, and other variables. Construction of the residence hall had barely been completed when winter entered. Rescue of the remaining people in UL-One would have to wait until the spring.

At last, forced indoors and armed with board games, cards, and musical instruments, the separate households occasionally gathered in the meeting hall when weather permitted. Brenda had missed her bi-monthly call, fueling a growing concern for the underground city. When she did call, she inquired as to the status of the compound, because more earthquake rumblings were occurring in her city.

In April, Jess gave birth to twins, a boy and a girl. She named the girl Tracy, after Susan's mother, and named the boy Vincent, after Carter's father, adding the middle name of Robert. She did not want for attention. Not only was Annie, ostensibly the most knowledgeable person on the planet about the growth of food products and their nutritional value, she also turned out to be the perfect nurse, who possessed prior experience in preparing easily digestible foods for growing infants. She proudly announced to Jess that she would serve as nanny for the children, explaining, "In Russia we call it niania or nanechka. From now on the children will call me niania."

Furthermore, Michelle, who was still nursing little Will, happily volunteered to care for the twins when requested to do so.

Two weeks after Jess had given birth, spring arrived almost in a moment and exceptionally early for the region, an event that drew suspicions, considering the whimsical nature of the weather. As they were soon to find out, the pendulum swings two ways.

NINE

Carter was wrong on two counts. The stingers he and Jess had encountered were not local. They wre of the few that annually left their climatic region early—outliers as it were. Their seasonality varied. The main body was born in that same pass between Phoenix and the higher country before the stretch to Sedona.

As many life forms prosper in interfaces, so the stingers and greens rigidly held to the edge of the bubble—the windy interface between the very hot temperature to the south and the milder weather to the north. Their life cycle was such that the mosquito-like stingers laid their eggs in a prey without causing its death during the insects' short one-day life-span. The prey included both mammals and reptiles. The proteolytic enzyme extruded by the proboscis softened the skin to make way for the eggs to be inserted. Once hatched, scores of eggs quickly turned into larvae, which soon became caterpillar-like greens. Those inched out of the subject without killing it, made their way out of the subject onto the earth, up the trees and out to the stems and the leaves, where they ate until they grew to a point where they ceased their activity. At this point, a cocoon was formed on the underside of the leaf. Within the cocoon, a metamorphosis occurred and a stinger emerged to begin the cycle, once again.

Both stingers and greens were prone to be eaten by birds. As such, the greens had developed their poisonous defenses, as Jess had guessed. Like clockwork, triggered by the onset of cooler weather in the fall, or warm weather in the spring, they normally stayed very local; the typical behavior of common household mosquitoes. However, on this occasion, rather than northern winds bringing about a cold snap signaling cool fall weather, the mass of cocoons was fooled by a sharp influx of hot air from the south. Millions of cocoons hatched within quickly, releasing the temperature-sensitive stingers to be pushed far to the north to freeze to death in the more northern clime of Flagstaff. On their way to death, they found an abundance of suitable subjects in the Munds National Forest that made for an ideal locale for purposes of egg laying in the wide variety of mammals and reptiles—and for the formation of more cocoons.

Carla heard it before the humans did—a whine similar to that of a high-speed power drill. She began to bark madly. Activity in the compound ceased as a dark cloud could be seen coming up from the south. Not knowing what it was, but alerted to danger, Jess ran to the bell and ringing the Emergency-Emergency sound—a continuous unceasing ringing. "Everybody get indoors," she yelled, just as the first stingers flew in. Stingers or not, the others took shelter.

Ken and Carter had just closed the hood of the U-Haul in the parking lot, when they heard the non-stop clanging of the bell, rather than paced-out rings. At the same time, Carter's radio went off. He heard Jess yell about the stingers. "Got it," he said. He and Ken closed the doors to the cab and Carter started the truck. He drove it to the entrance of the compound, where the men could see if they could help in any way.

At least all structures were tight: the greenhouse, meeting hall, home, and even the outhouses were leak-proof with every crack and crevice sealed. Energy was too hard to come by to afford its loss through leaky doors and windows. Missing were Wei and Jay, who were exploring upstream in a deep canyon, trying to find the trout lake. Absent since the evening before, the couple was expected to return momentarily. Habitually, they sent Riki ahead to alert the camp of their arrival. This had not occurred.

The black cloud engulfed the compound with no casualties reported. All three buildings were in tight lockdown. Pointing southward, the air turbines spun so rapidly they did their small damage to the incoming herd.

The hours passed. The big truck sat idling, providing fresh air to the men who dared not open their windows. The sat phone rang and Ken picked up. "Ken, it's Jay. We were holed up in a cave for the night when they came in this morning. Riki warned us. We had a fire going. That seems to be working to keep them away."

The dragonflies appeared from nowhere. Drawn to this new feast, they were capable of eating up to a hundred mosquitoes a day. Soon, happy to eat both stingers and dragonflies, the birds appeared. Flycatchers, swallows, kingfishers, falcons and kites arrived by the hundreds to add to the insanity of the airborne maelstrom of activity. An occasional bird would fall to the ground, having been struck in a vital area by one or more stingers. The forest, too, had become alive with aerial activity, though the open spaces at the compound provided for better attack angles. For every stinger eaten, a thousand survived.

Stupefied, Ken and Carter watched the aerial activity through the windshield of the truck that was rapidly spotted over by bird droppings of various colors, depending on the food habits of the bird species. All of droppings were specked with black particles. The day passed slowly; darkness fell. The men waited another hour, watching, guiltily listening to music on the CD player. A two-inch thick carpet of black-winged insects covered every horizontal surface inside the compound, along with the hood and roof of the truck, and all visible points between. In the light of the headlights, no more flying insects could be seen——no more black flakes of snow blowing in the wind. The abnormally large dragonflies and the birds had disappeared.

Shortly, the tarantulas appeared by the scores to feast on the unmoving insects, until they, too, departed, having eaten their fill. These were not the typical 3-4 inch tarantulas of old, but an almost hairless mutant variety with a leg span twice that size.

Ken looked at Carter, circling his finger round and round to signify the insanity of the random events they had just witnessed. Picking up his radio, he called Jess. "We're going to take a chance and see if we can find Jay and Wei."

Jess replied, "Best to do it now. We don't know if these things will come to life in the morning. Maybe they're taking a time out."

"Got it." Carter backed out the U-Haul and drove to the parking lot, where he and Ken quickly got into Carter's truck. He checked their store of water and each took a good drink. Ken called the couple to request their position. An hour later, at the All Clear ringing of the bells, people began to emerge from their own cocoons of hiding. A wind had come up to scatter piles of the black insects. None moved. Cautiously crunching through the insects, Annie opened the door to the greenhouse and came over to Jess. Hearing her footsteps, Jess looked up and said, "To think, the week I was here I never saw a single one."

Too late. As soon as she said it, Jess knew she had given away her secret. Less than a year before, her third trip to the surface had been under the guise of female problem that required more serious medical attention. Only Ken, Carter, and her parents knew of her trickery. Noting Annie's look, Jess sheepishly said, "Well, I did sort of need attention, in a manner of speaking."

Annie began laughing and retraced her steps to the greenhouse. A moment later, Susan and Michelle could be heard laughing. Annie returned to find Jess brushing her clothing, ostensibly, to free it from insects that might be invisible in the darkness. "I've never been so scared in my life," Annie said, becoming serious, sweeping her arm outward to include the black mass covering the ground.

Jess continued with the brushing. "They're not nocturnal. They're more like butterflies that rest at night or like other insects that go into deep torpor." She was referring to their combined years of experiences in hydroponics. The Mars Virus made any green plant grow faster in the presence of ultraviolet light. In, UL-One, the regulation of growth occurred by creating variations in light cycles, the most frequently used was the basic day-night diurnal cycle. A 24-hour light might be provided to provide for faster growth. Many insects followed a diurnal cycle and would go into a resting state when the lights were off, then come back to life in the light. The activities of other species might be triggered by changes in temperature, barometric pressure, or humidity.

"What do we do now?" Annie asked.

The wind had switched directions 180 degrees and now came down from the north. The temperature had dropped by 20 degrees or more in a matter of minutes.

"We play it safe." Jess said. "We have time until first light. Make preparations for an extended stay indoors. Eat lightly and prepare food stores. Above all, don't track a single one of these things indoors. That's the hard part. Once they wake up indoors, and I'm not saying they will, then we're fucked."

Taken aback for an instant, Annie laughed again. Amused, she wanted to say, *So much for hanging around military guys.* Instead, she grunted, "No, Jess, we're fucked if all these millions of creatures wake up and start looking for some live meat to lay their eggs in."

Each group ensured their particular residence was free of insects and took every step possible to check for the smallest air leak where even an ant might enter. In addition, crude toilet arrangements were made for. Life can have its rough edges when the best that can be offered is that nothing will happen.

That night nobody slept well. Each person awaited a sting, trying to keep every single inch of their body covered. If mosquitoes didn't care about drilling through soft material, why should stingers?

An eternity later, dawn broke. The blanket of the insects began to twitch as one, like a pulsating single life form awakening out of hibernation, required by the laws of nature to deposit their eggs. Those watching through the windows saw the movement. Wind found its way through cracks between the rocks, causing pockets of black stingers to swirl like small black swirling tornados. The dogs began their bark as the whine began, then reached a crescendo, the mass of blackness rising like a giant magic carpet, the sound echoing off the boulders of the compound. Jess put her arm around Carla's neck and said to her, "Yes, I 'm scared, too." Her babies began to cry.

As an orchestra conductor raises his wand, the mass of blackness continued to rise to the top of the rocks until the sleeting rain and gale-force wind cut through their millions, decimating their delicate bodies, scattering them southward again.

With the blades of the wind turbines locked to prevent over-rotating, the power provided by the water wheel was sufficient to provide internal warmth and lighting to the structures. Pockets of stingers remained in crevices. Jess contacted the others and warned that danger lurked. They must remain indoors for at least another day. Carter and Ken did not heed that warning. Instead, protecting themselves from head to foot, they rigged hand pumps to five-gallon containers of kerosene to search out the smallest crevice and spray the insects that had not yet taken flight.

SJessshould have followed her own advice. In front of the house, she screamed and grabbed at her right ankle. She backed inside and closed the door. The two men ran to the house and Carter stopped outside the door. "Brush me off," he ordered.

"They're stingers, not greens," argued Ken, who

began brushing off his partner, who did the same in return.

They entered the house and closed the door. Jess lay on floor trying to take off her boot. "Grab some alcohol," Carter yelled. Ken ran to the supply closet and pulled out a bottle of isopropyl rubbing alcohol. Carter had removed Jess's boot and sock and had pulled up her pant leg. Apparently, the pant leg had ridden up over the boot to expose the flesh of the leg. Carter poured a liberal amount of alcohol on the wound. Pulling out his pocket knife from his belt, he flicked open the blade and cut the wound so that it bled freely. Jess writhed in pain.

Carter carried her to the sofa. There was a knock at the door. Ken opened it a crack to see Annie, Michelle, and Susan. "Brush yourselves off," he directed.

"We already did," Annie said as Ken let the women into the house. Jess lay on her left side, her left arm outstretched with her head on it while Carter worked on the wound.

"Get me a single-edged razor," he ordered to no one in particular. A moment later he began cutting the blackening tissue around the wound that now measured more than a half-inch in diameter. He poured more alcohol on it.

"This is bullshit," Jess yelled. "Give me childbirth any day over this."

"Does that mean you want to try for another baby now, honey?" Carter grinned, looking at the others.

"Not funny," she moaned.

"No sense of humor," Ken said.

"Get out of here," Annie ordered, pushed Carter aside. "That hole is going to leave a nice scar."

Michelle brought bandages, which Annie used to wrap the wound. Susan felt Jess's forehead and declared, "She's got a fever."

Jess lay on the sofa two days, moaning, sweating, talking in her half-sleep about growing up, her mother and father, people she had known, her love for Carter, flipping from one subject to another until she fell into a deep sleep while Michelle nursed the babies. On the third morning, she awoke and declared, "I'm hungry." She tried to stand, but fell back down when she put weight on her right foot where clean bandages adorned the outside of her right lower shin.

Riki and Carla lay on the floor next to her. They had awakened when she did. Carla began to lick her face. "From now on I think I'll start putting mint oil on my legs, not just the exposed parts of my body."

"Good idea," Carter commented. "Let me get you a crutch."

"Don't need one," said Jess, who stood again, testing the leg, limping around the house. "It's only pain. Pain never hurt anyone," she announced, mimicking one of Ken's favorite lines.

"Breakfast will be ready in a few minutes," Beth announced from the kitchen, raising her voice to overcome a hard spring rain that began in earnest.

Anxious to get on the move again, Carter said, "Great. After we eat, we have got to pick up our refugees. Those poor folks must be hanging on by a thread."

Ken would drive the U-Haul, Carter would drive the 90-passenger school bus that had printed on its side: SEDONA PUBLIC SCHOOL DISTRICT, while Gregor, who had become an excellent driver of all the vehicles, now sat behind the wheel of Carter's dually. Jess opted to remain home, preferring to care for her twins. Given time for conversion, the bus was a much better choice for habitation than a mobile home. School buses were steel-framed on a steel body with a diesel engine that had been maintained by shop mechanics. Plus, each bus had an escape door.

TEN

Two hours after the men had gone and during a lull in the storm, the dogs began barking wildly. Jess stopped caulking the outside windows of the trailer and looked up. The last thing in the world she expected to see was a half-dozen men on horseback ride into camp coming from the direction of Oak Creek upstream. Carter had said this used to be Navajo country. If she hadn't been a fan of Western movies, she might have felt like the Incas when Cortez and his men rode up and they thought horse and man were fused into single animal. She saw bows strung across the shoulders of four of the long-haired men; the other two carried rifles. The crew presented a soggy sight. Most appeared to be middle-aged, with deep lines in their faces, and baggy eyes. One older man rode next to the largest man of the group in terms of height and weight. Two of the men were Siders. The visitors' clothing was an eclectic mix. A few wore long-sleeve shirts made of furs; others wore long-sleeved Western shirts. Pants were either blue jeans or cargoes. Some wore boots, others moccasins. She noted a pair of binoculars hanging from the neck of the older man.

What would Carter do? She remembered his words. *Anybody who lives this long out here is a survivalist, knows how to use a weapon, and didn't make it this far by being polite.*

Hushing the dogs, she reached for her own rifle. Limping away from the trailer, she nodded her head upward, waiting for one of them to speak, hoping her shaking wasn't evident. She didn't trust herself to speak without a quaver.

One of the middle-age Indian-looking men spoke first. "Nice little community you have here. You wouldn't happen to have a doctor in the house would you?"

"Maybe," replied Jess.

"My name is John. We're curious. Where do you folks come from?"

Jess pointed with her chin southward, while keeping her eye on John. "Down there. Where are you coming from?"

John pointed his chin to the east. "Over there."

Jess wanted to call her men, even though they were on the road. If she did, she knew they would turn around and come back. She didn't want that. The mission was too important. She'd deal with him later.

"Your colloquial English is pretty good," Jess observed.

Now John began to laugh. "You mean for an Indian? I've got a PhD in Mechanical Engineering from Northern Arizona University, otherwise known as NAU. That went nowhere fast when this whole mess hit. These other guys aren't too shabby, either. My father here was the one who raised the funds to send me to the school where he attended. Now that we've broken the ice, I'll ask you again. Is there a doctor here or not?"

Without replying, Jess told Carla and Rikki to fetch Jay and Michelle. The dogs ran off and within two minutes, returned with them both. When they arrived, Jay and the two Siders on horseback nodded at each other without speaking and Jess said to Michelle quietly, "I might need you to take care of my babies for a little while. Will that be all right?"

"Of course, Jess, anything I can do to help," Michelle responded.

Jess related to Jay what John had told her, when John asked Jay, "Are you the smart one around here, or the guy in charge?"

Jay shrugged, "Neither, according to my wife. What do you know about Stokes' Law?"

"Which aspect? The fluorescence part or the gravity part?"

And off the two went discussing physics until Jay broke it off. Tuning to Jess he said, "I don't know about the PhD part, but he knows what he's talking about."

Instead of leaving, Jay remained. There was no way he would leave Jess alone with these men. Both dogs growled softly. He gave a soft command to stay them. Jess held on to her rifle.

"It's okay. They're not used to strangers," Jess explained, which was not true—only certain strangers.

"What do you need?" Jess asked.

"Fix a broken leg," replied John. One of my men slid down a canyon trail. Got scraped up pretty bad, too."

"Got any hooch?" asked Jay.

"Everything from tequila to Jack to Southern Comfort. Got some wine, too. Take your pick. If you want, you can follow me along the road. That'll get us within a couple hundred yards that way. You'll have hike down to one of our caves," explained John. "It's going to get messy in the mud. My men will take the trail back with their horses."

"Okay, Jay and I can set it," Jess told him. "Michelle, we're going with these people for a while."

"No problem," Michelle said, and turned to walk into the house to check on the two children, looking forward to relieving the pressure in her breasts.

"Just a minute," Jay said. He walked back to the meeting hall, spoke with Wei a moment, and returned with a doctor's bag. He joined Jess at Ken's SUV with the two dogs. Jess made a mental check to ensure her gun was holstered in her rear waistband beneath her shirt, then she knelt down to whisper something to the dogs, both of which licked her face in understanding. Now weighing sixty pounds Carla had outgrown expectations with another year of growth ahead of her. Riki, her brother, was larger.

Jess followed the man on horseback for two miles east along a winding road, then stopped and dismounted. Tying off his horse, he waited for the other to join him in the torrent.

The group emerged from the car at the top of the cliffs and, leaving their rifles in the car, half slid, half walked down a trail, grabbing onto trees as they descended. Jay tried to hang onto the bag and maintain his balance, the struggling dogs doing their best to survive the descent. Jess's ankle screamed at the torture. She was more concerned about infection than pain. The lazy creek below had become roiling, foaming rapids as waterfalls cascaded from the top of the cliff hundreds of feet to the river below, intermingling with the deluge as it fell. Within the canyon wall on the other side of the river, dark holes were noted through the mist, suggesting the presence of caves. On their left side, the path branched into the forest. Straight ahead lay a ledge a good hundred feet above the water line and on the same ledge to the right lay the mouth of a cave. John led them inside, the dogs shaking themselves repeatedly.

"How did you go on horseback from here?" Jess asked.

"That little fork up the trail there. It leads in your direction. It's faster than on the road when it's not raining," John disclosed.

A fire burned within a large cave. Next to the fire lay a man on a blanket. Behind him in other areas of the cave were sleeping bags, bedding, and a wide variety of supplies. An empty bottle lay next to the man.

"I'll get get him another one," John announced. He disappeared deep into the cave and returned shortly with a full bottle of Southern Comfort. Jay took it and poured a quantity it over the wound, then handed the remained to the man on the floor who began to groan from the burn of the alcohol on the open wound.

Jess and Jay set a compound fracture of the right tibia, about six inches above the ankle. After applying a splint to the leg, they tended to a number scrapes on that same side of his body.

The other riders appeared. Where they had left their horses could not be determined. John, with rifle in hand, pointed it at the two visitors. "Have a seat, folks. We have a compound to raid."

Neither Jess nor Jay were completely surprised. "Why didn't you just run in and take it over to start with?" Jay asked.

"Well, to tell the truth, we were getting set to do that come nightfall. We wanted to make sure your big friends wouldn't be back for a long time. My guess is that they won't be; not with them taking the U-Haul, the truck and the bus. Then my brother had to bust his leg. Now that you were so kind to fix him, my friends are ready to go. They're not as polite as we are. Don't believe me, check out a couple of the larger caves." John pointed with his thumb. "I mean, you don't know how many years we've been waiting. First, your two guys show up and start to build.

They come back I don't know how many times, while we're living in caves, no less. Then things take off and you've got a whole city for the taking."

Jay gave the strong direct command while John's mouth continued to move. "Riki, Carla, attack!" Less than a second later, both dogs, awaiting this opportunity, had clamped onto John's upper legs, shaking their heads, their strong Sider jaw muscles ripping into the femoral artery. John screamed as blood spurted outward rhythmically, with each beat of his heart, striking Jess. At the same time, Jess pulled out her pistol. *If it's about your life, do not stop to think. Just react.* She fired two quick rounds, striking John in the upper chest, knocking him backward. Before he hit the ground, she shot him a third time. The angle was wrong and the round hit him in lower gut. The other five men in the cave ran outside, forgetting to use their own weapons, losing their power of reason at witnessing the viciousness of the snarling dogs.

"Attack!" Jess now commanded pointing out. Within short seconds, the dogs bounded after the running men. At the same time, Jay picked up the rifle and ran out after the dogs. Jess heard several screams from a number of throats intermingled by shots from the rifle followed by complete silence. The entire episode lasted no longer than a minute.

Jay returned with the dogs. "That's one problem solved, at least for the moment," he declared.

"Anything left in that bottle?" Jess said, visibly shaking. Jay handed her the bottle and she took a strong pull of the burning liquor followed by a slight shiver. "If I had to hazard a guess, I'd say the boys are going have a few nests to clean out when they return."

"What was with the Indian-looking thing?" Jay asked.

Jess checked the rounds remaining in her weapon and holstered it. Her voice hardened. "I don't think they tried to look like Indians. I think that's just how they dress. John probably hand-picked his team for the ride-up, but apparently they're not much in a fire fight, at least that's what Carter might say. Probably inexperienced because there aren't too many people to practice on. Anyway, if we need horses, we know where to find them. Now, let's get out of here before the others try to find out who shot their friends."

Jay said, "If you take the medical bag and the dogs along that trail, I'll get to the top and bring back the car. Meet you back home."

The four left the cave. Within a minute Jess found the trail to the west, accompanied by two wolf descendants, one on each side. They belonged to ages long past, licking flesh from their teeth, looking for more meat to tear, protecting. Jess, in her turn, found herself having devolved with them. For long moments, she bewallowed in the feeling of being an early human from 50,000 years in the past, shambling through the muck beneath a dense canopy of trees in the bleakness of a cold dreary death-filled morning—a cavewoman from a past long dead, as a child conceived out of the mists of dawn, lacking only a club. She saw herself thusly, as a convert to surface life—one who had killed another human whose blood had stained her clothing, accompanied by two feral meat eaters as intimate companions.

Tell that story to the city council and see how many want to join us now, she thought, tramping, limping through the mud, laughing, baying out loud, like a mad woman with total reckless abandon at the lunacy of it all—an entirely new dimension to life, the ultimate in total release, consequences be damned.

Jess and the dogs soon passed a corral with numerous horses within. She and the dogs maintained a pace as quickly as they dared along the horse-trodden muddy path, occasionally slipping. She had shoved the reality of what had occurred to the back her mind, opting to deal with it once she found safety.

Jay's climb up the hill took too long. Slipping and backsliding in the mud, he grabbed at tree trunks and roots, while rain pounded him like a pronged hammer beating meat to a pulp. Even his strong legs began to tire before he eventually reached the car. Soaked and muddy, he took one last look behind him before driving off. The hour was not yet noon. Cautiously, wending his way around the curves in the road, not waiting until he returned home, he called on the sat phone. He had a brief concern about how mad Ken might get when he saw how Jay had muddied the interior of his car.

"Carter here."

"Ken here."

In their respective vehicles, each the men carried both a sat phone and a radio with them. Gregor in the truck carried a radio. Jay explained what had happened. The men listened patiently. Carter was the first to speak. Grimly, he said, "We're going to have to come right back. They won't attack today. The remainder will have to reorganize, probably wait till tonight. There must a second-in-command there. They don't know what this John guy told you in the cave, so they'll probably stick with the original plan. I know the trail they're talking about. I was on it last year."

What Carter didn't mention was that they had found Beth's SUV off the road in a ditch with Robert dead at the wheel before the Sedona side of the pass. They surmised that he had hit a pothole and had cracked his head against the steering wheel when he went off the road. He had tried to get out, but got hung up by the seat belt. He was found him hanging out of the car door, semi-frozen. The icy rain had quickly finished him. Carter had winched out the car and left it in the roadway to bring back on the return trip. Robert could be buried in Sedona.

When Jay had finished his tale, and having regained a measure of her sanity, Jess's voice cut in. "And don't start telling me about how I made bad decisions and could have been killed. What's the point of you teaching me how to take care of myself, if you criticize me when I do it?"

"Guess that shut your mouth," Ken said, listening in.

After Jess and Jay went into more detail about what they knew of the cave, Carter told her, "We're closer to UL-One than we are to you. We'll drop off the U-Haul and the bus, make a quick check in with Brenda and head back right away. In my car. We'll bring Gregor with us. He needs to get initiated. It'll be after dark when we get back. You should be all right until then, but keep an eye out. We'll pay a social call on these guys and drive back down here in a few days. Otherwise, it'll take too long to get the passengers loaded, take the slow caravan back up there, and then go pay our social call. It won't work and I don't want to lose that time."

Jess heard Ken in the background saying something about making the sons of bitches pay for them having to drive so much and complained about getting saddle sores.

At last, exhausted, Jess reached the front door of the house. Gasping for air, the enormity of shooting a person dead struck her and she retched several times, with the rain quickly washing away her previous meal, the remaining alcohol in her stomach and the splatters of John's blood on her shirt. Her ankle burned like a blow torch had been applied to it.

In another moment, Jay arrived. Once back indoors, She found her babies sleeping with Michelle reading a book. Jess quickly related to Michelle about what had happened while stripping down and putting on a change of clothing. Jay tended to her leg, cleaning the wound and replacing the bandage, then placing her leg in front of the floor heater to dry out. Michelle bade her good evening and departed, anxious to hear more details of the adventure that would surely be retold in the morning. What was this about the men coming right back?

Wishing for a fast-food restaurant to grab a hamburger and fries to eat along the way, the three men returned, with Carter driving Beth's SUV while Ken and Gregor led the way in Carter's truck.

The two vehicles arrived after nightfall. Strung out after nearly twelve hours of tense road travel—the trip down had taken an hour longer than the return—they were bug-eyed and wide awake, ready for a diversion. It didn't take them long to head to the kitchen. Jess had informed Beth and Michelle of their impending arrival and the three women watched the men put down a great portion of turkey and vegetables.

"Can't wait to drive down there again," Ken said sarcastically.

"You want me to drive both the truck and the bus back up through the pass on the return trip?" Carter chided.

"Yes," Ken responded.

"Gregor, are you too used up to have a heart-to-heart talk with some bad guys? It'll give you a chance to get off your lazy butt and stretch your legs. That's all you do is sit around." If nothing else, Gregor had proved to be a workhorse, who had quickly learned to put up with manly barbs thrown at him by his new friends.

"Well, now that you put it that way," he responded, intrigued by the possibility of morphing from a songster-poet-strongman into a soldier. If Jess, his idol, could do it, so could he.

The men filled their growling stomachs with Beth and Michelle hovering over them like mothers. After eating, Ken and Carter packed what they needed for a fight, providing Gregor with the necessary firepower he might need. In the dark, with a glimmer of moonlight and a couple of small penlights to guide them, the men began to trek through rain that now came from different directions, changing its mind as a pregnant woman might desire strawberries and ice cream, only to order up a pound of chocolates instead.

Carter had considered asking Jay to be part of the operation. He had shown a different side of his intellectual, workaholic self when finishing off the potential marauders after the dogs had taken them down. However, he and Wei were heavily involved in drawing specs for a trout screen to be placed in the creek, having failed on two previous occasions. Either the mesh was too large or too small. Carter about-faced after seeing what they were up to and passed on asking him the question.

Carter had to smile. He had once asked Jay, "Did you know that Wei's entire body is simply a life support system for a giant brain?" to which the genius had replied, "Thanks for the insight. I'll be sure to write that down in case I forget."

Not much later in the evening, after caring for the twins and feeding Carla in her trailer, Jess thought she heard distant booms of thunder coming from the canyon. Carla lay asleep, twitching. She had returned to the roots of her ancient wolf ancestors, on the prowl for game, at the behest of her human masters. Three of those masters were also returning to their own roots, seeking revenge on those bent on subjugating their families, those who would take by force from others who had worked a lifetime for what they possessed.

Two hours passed before the men returned, bemoaning the loss of several flash-bang grenades. Bullets could be replaced.

"What happened?" Jess inquired.

Ken reported, "We cleaned out the caves on this side of the river. We saw smoke coming from caves on the other side, but we couldn't get to the bridge that was down maybe a few hundred yards from us. We'll have to go after them some other time, although I suspect they may clear out now. The hail was crazy. We did find the corral you mentioned and let the horses go. There were maybe fifteen of them."

"You let them go? Why didn't you bring some of them back?" Jess queried.

Carter had to chuckle. "Do you know anything about horses? I don't. Do you know how to groom or clean them, how much food it takes to feed them, to care for their medical needs? The answer is 'no'—and neither does anybody I know of. Therefore, I them go. They'll be fine in the wild."

Carter then turned contemplative. "I've been thinking. With the creek running as much as it is and the climate getting milder, maybe we should give Flagstaff another try. It's less than a 30 mile drive, but probably the most scenic route in the country-—I mean spires, canyons, changing cliff colors, lakes, overlooks, you name it. You'd love it, Jess. If we can get there, it means we can we might be able to set up a colony. We can do it in a day for a quick look-see."

"I definitely would like to be a part of that," Gregor said, as he dropped the magazine from his rifle to confirm it was empty. At that, the men said goodnight as utter fatigue washed over them. They had completely forgotten that, on the return to Sedona, they had brought back Beth's SUV, after they had tranferred Robert's body to the bed of Carter's truck where it still lay.

ELEVEN

Carter did not sleep soundly. Either he was driving all night or shooting all night, or both. When he did get into a deeper sleep near morning, some inner annoyance poked at him—some unfinished business—something to do with the trip. When he let go of trying to remember, it popped into his head. He sat up with a start. Jess and Carla were outside, Robert was dead in the back of the truck, and he was in a heap of trouble.

Carter tried to calculate what he would say when he looked over toward where he had parked and saw Ken standing there with Jess, Susan, and Gregor. They saw him and Jess gave a short wave of the hand. He had neglected to put on a hat or a windbreaker, but somehow it didn't matter.

He walked over to them, streeling himself for the worst. He saw Susan crying. "It's my fault. Why didn't I insist that it was all right if he didn't follow me. If I had, he'd be alive today. He knew he'd made a mistake and tried to return."

Remembering his own brother's death in prison, Carter said, gently, "Shoulda', coulda', woulda'. We all have those. It's not on you. It was his decision to make the move Topside. Susan, you can't wrap yourself in blame."

Distracted for a moment by her mother's crying, Jess returned to what she wanted to do in the first place when she said to Carter, "Oh, sweetheart, thank you so much for bringing back my daddy. Ken and Gregor told me how you risked your life in the terrible storm to pull him from the car. They told you it was too dangerous for you to go out, but you did it anyway. You're my hero." At that she buried her head in his chest and threw her arms around his waist. He looked at Ken and Gregor who both grinned. Ken gave a wink.

Jess pulled away and said, Mom and I would like to have a ceremony for him, all right?"

"Of course, my dear, anything you want," Carter agreed, gladly.

During the burial of Robert in the forest just outside the compound, Jess reflected on her early-on perceived greatness of her father——a greatness on the surface overlaying a fragile support system beneath——a man who would never know his grandchildren, nor they, him. She had written a eulogy based on words she had read, things she had learned from both Carter and her parents, along with her own ideas.

In a firm voice, she read what she and Susan had

prepared. "Even the most backwater, tranquil place cannot escape the vicissitudes of life's turbulence. All succumb to the inevitable. We like to think we're in control of events, but life has other plans that override ours. It's the nature of humans to have regrets. Sometimes we get a second chance, but usually we try to recover at least a piece of driftwood from the shipwreck to hang onto, to carry us to the next adventure. The learning process is based on doing things wrong and learning from them. It's as much a part of the survival mechanism as is fight or flight. A goal is like a magnet and will pull us toward it as long as it's kept in sight. Don't let unpredictable adverse events deter you. Rest in peace."

Upon adjournment of the ceremony, Annie suggested that the compound be named after Jessica and thought that Sekah City would be an appropriate name for their little community. The group approved the appellation, to the protestations of Jess, who proposed that the residence hall be named Whitmore Hall, to the protestations of Jay and Wei. Ken proposed building a doghouse named after Carter, where he might reside, now that he had become a father.

Weary from their ordeal the day before, the three men required some days of rest, as did Jess.

On the third morning after their return, Wei announced that she had managed to recharge the batteries of the drone, the monitor and the charger, and it should be ready to go, at which point Ken said, "I'm still getting over my war injuries from the round trip to UL-one. Let's give it a try. I want another day for R and R, anyway, before doing it again."

On the kitchen counter, Wei turned on the monitor and said, "I used to make these years ago. This one has a battery life of about half-an hour, call it 25 minutes to be safe. With its four rotors, it can fly up to 70 miles per hour. I recharged the batteries on both the monitor and the drone to get them operational."

Wei turned on the laptop and the monitor. A picture of them all staring at the drone came on the screen, sent from the camera built into the underside of the device. The picture zoomed in and out as she played with the controls.

"Let's go outside," Wei declared. "Jess, carry the drone and set it on the ground."

Jess did so and an instant later, four propellers began spinning. The drone lifted off with a whizzing sound until it cleared the rocks of their compound. The image began to shake side-to-side. "Too much wind. I'll have to stay low," Wei said. She flew the drone out to the creek, where she remained a few feet above the surface of the water. At one point, she tried to lift higher and ran into the same problem. Dropping to a lower elevation, she continued onward to the east. The watchers were able to see the road on the far side of the creek until the watercourse took a sharp turn northward where the road continued straight. A bridge spanned the creek. A dirt road lead northward into the trees. Suddenly, a water wheel came into view. Braking hard, the drone came to a stop and hovered, slowing, inspecting the wheel "The wheel is stuck with debris," Wei announced. "That's a serious wheel. Maybe five or six feet in diameter. Somebody had money."

"A project for you and Jay," Ken told her.

"Great. We need something to do," Wei answered, sarcastically.

She followed the road beneath a canopy of trees as though she were driving through a foggy tunnel, until 100 yards later a large two-story house appeared, surrounded by a chain-link fence topped with razor wire.

"Anybody see a wind turbine?" Ken asked.

Wei maneuvered the drone in a circle, but no wind turbine could be seen. "It looks like they didn't want anybody to notice them," Ken offered.

The home had been cleared of vegetation on four sides with some 10 yards of open space between it and the surrounding fence. A large garage stood to the left of the house with the door partially open. Wei flew the drone into the garage. The image of two ATVs appeared. Both possessed windshields and a roof. "Pull in closer. Let's see what it says on the side."

Wei maneuvered the drone to hover next to the words. Ken read, "Toyota 1000 cc, DOHV. Very nice. We can use those. I'll bet if we look around that garage, we'll find an ATV charger, if somebody doesn't shoot us first."

"Good luck with an old battery," Carter noted.

"The weather's been cool to cold. It's worth a

try," Ken countered. "We can tow one of them back here and use our electricity for the charger."

Keeping track of the flying time, and hoping somebody unseen didn't shoot her down, Wei flew the perimeter of the home and noted cameras beneath the eaves on four sides. Beneath an overhang at the rear of the home, she stopped at a window that had been broken out almost completely. Carefully, she maneuvered the drone through the window into a large kitchen. Two fully-dressed skeletons lay on the floor, one with a rifle next to it, the other with a handgun. Some feet distant lay two more skeletons. A rifle and a shotgun lay nearby.

"Shootout," said Carter, unnecessarily.

The three had seen their share of dead bodies in either combat or on the base. None had seen skeletons. The men more easily processed the vision, while Jess drew back in fright, as a shiver ran through her.

The image in the large family room displayed a completely furnished home with a downstairs master bedroom and bath, as well as an upstairs loft area with three more bedrooms and another bath. "That's a big house for two people," Ken observed. "I wonder what happened to the others."

"We're running short on time. Got to bring her back," Wei announced. Within two minutes the drone landed outside the door to their home.

"I'm going over there," Jess said. "Who wants to go with me?" She turned to her dog, "Carla, go bring Michelle."

Ken and Carter volunteered to go. Carter asked, "Wei, see if Jay wants to go with us.

Wei said, "He's working on plans for the residence hall. He wants it built in the lot next to the visitor's center. I don't want to disturb him. He has a dark side you don't want to know about. If you three are going, then let me recharge the battery first so we can keep a watchful eye on you from here. Take your radios."

"What dark side?" Jess asked.

Wei shrugged. "Oh, he gets depressed sometimes. He never got over the guilt of betraying the Randolphs when they hired him in his early years after his entreaties that they do so, and then he turned on them. Years later, Jason forgave him, but Linda never did. You know the story. He carries it around like extra baggage during the day and has occasional nightmares about it."

An hour later, the three rifle-carrying investigators exited Carter's truck. They walked across the bridge and up the gravel road beneath the canopy of trees with Carla in the lead, until the home came into view, invisible from the stream.

"We're here," Ken said softly into the radio.

A minute later the drone appeared from their left. The trio came to the front gate of the fence, which stood partially open. A heavy chain lay on the ground accompanied by a pair of long-handled bolt cutters. Entering onto the property, Jess pointed to the garage and said, "Go see." Carla ran through the door and a shuffling sound could be heard followed by a small squeal. The dog emerged with racoon in her mouth. With all eyes checking in every direction, the three entered the garage, moving cautiously to take a quick look at the ATVs. "Good find. We can make them work, no problem," Ken said. "I get the sense the owners may not have much to say about it."

They left the garage and followed the drone that had circled back to the broken rear window. "I got this," Jess said. "You big guys won't make it through." She cleaned out the remaining glass with the butt of her rifle and stepped through the low window. A moment later, she opened the rear door, cringing at the sight of the skeletons and trying desperately to avoid touching them. Carla entered and waited for the command to search, then bounded off to look in the various rooms, both downstairs and upstairs.

"Got to bring her back." Wei's voice came from the radio. "Let me know if you need me." The drone buzzed away.

The home smelled like a combination of moisture and dust. Standing in the large living room, Carter said, glumly, "Boy, do I feel ridiculous. Years of building and this place was waiting for us all the time, just like the other building Jess found."

"Tell me about it," Ken replied, rubbing his head, taking in the expanse of the home that exceeded in size the one he had lived in for the past two decades.

"Neither of you get it," Jess chided, standing her ground, looking from one to the other. "Don't you guys read? We're explorers. When you explore, you make discoveries and you do things with those discoveries. Ken discovered the drone, which led to the discovery of the house. You would never have found this house on your own. Furthermore, our compound is starting to prove its worth, so your efforts are bearing fruit. That's called a long-term investment."

Carter grinned and scratched a corner of one eye, growing accustomed to the pelting, and conceded, "She's right, I guess. Let's think about cleaning up this place. We'll have Jay, Wei and Gregor work on the wheel that serves this property after they get our wheel going first."

He explained to Jess that a water wheel operated on the same basic principle as a wind turbine in that a moving wheel spins a shaft within a generator to produce electricity. A slow-moving creek will spin a small, four-foot diameter wheel enough to provide for sufficient domestic lighting, given proper electric parts. The larger one serving this particular house could generate several times that amount of electricity.

Beth faced a problem. As head chef, she wondered how she could provide enough food for two meals a day for the large family. Hunting had its limits in a small area. Annie had brought along a cage of crickets, but it would take several more weeks before a continuous supply of the insects would be available for consumption. Given a female cricket will lay seven eggs per day on average, they would require a good home to do so. With Susan and Wei's help, she had constructed a habitat for the crickets and their eggs at one section of the greenhouse that now measured some 21 x 35 feet and possessed three tiers of food crops.

Events were progressing too smoothly. Brenda was the variable. She would not let it go.

TWELVE

Brenda inquired as to their status on the third afternoon of what they facetiously termed to be their vacation. The three men were not anxious to return to Phoenix. To their way of thinking, the citizen of UL-One had waited so long to vacate that a few more days wouldn't matter. Carter collared Gregor and insisted he go with him and Ken to Flagstaff. Reluctantly, he consented, wanting to continue cleaning the water wheel that served the New House.

The road to the northern city required a climb of 2500 feet to a final elevation of 6900 feet. Icy patches existed on the roadways, especially many within the city proper. The altitude and steepness of the climb guaranteed that heavy cold air masses would readily slide downhill to affect the northern Verde Valley region. Many of the city's more sheltered buildings remained intact. The riches available in the city would not be plundered, unless their group did the plundering. There appeared to be no others to do it. There were no fireplaces burning, no lights on, no movement but for blowing drifts of snow in a white, ghostly city without energy.

Surely, treasures could be found here, such as those recovered from the caves of the marauders. Those materials included camping equipment, warm-weather clothing, blankets, sleeping bags, freeze-dried foods, frozen deer meat and even bear skins; coffees, teas, and, of course, a cache of booze large enough to fill a liquor store. Add weapons to the list that ranged from slingshots to compound bows to AK-47s. Several individual pieces of equipment bore the name of the Flagstaff store from which it had been obtained.

During that Flagstaff visit, Brenda called, to report that aftershocks had knocked down the back half of Spokes 4 and 5. "We lost a lot of our citrus growing in that quadrant of the Ring along with what was at the outer rim in 6 and 7. So we've got more panels for you." Her voice was shaky, clearly trying to hold back tears, as she offered the incentive of more panels as a token reward for their services.

Mid-afternoon of the following day, just as Carter's truck pulled next to the big vehicles outside the rubble of what was once the west gate of UL-One, Wei called to say she and Jay had at last achieved success in constructing the right-sized screen for catching mature trout. It worked well without impeding the water flow. As long as somebody checked and cleaned the net on a regular basis, fish could be added to the menu beginning immediately.

In the eyes of the inhabitants of Sekah City, this particular trip to Phoenix promised to be monumental for a number of reasons: A large group of refugees would be joining their growing township which included a staff of medically trained persons, such as they were; more of the priceless panels would be brought back; and Carter would retrieve the Mercedes to provide them with another operational vehicle.

As a group, the three men walked around to the north hatch to enter the city to find Brenda. When they did, she did not present the picture of a poised mature, mayor in control of the city. She showed unmistakable signs of sleeplessness with her hair in disarray and darkening circles beneath her eyes. She smelled of alcohol. "It's good to see all of you," she sang, giving Carter a chesty hug, ignoring the other three, who watched, bemused at her antics.

Carter lightly patted her on the back. "I'm so sorry for your losses," he offered, genuinely heartbroken at the loss of more human life, but unwilling to hold her in the way she wanted him to hold her. "Why don't you get together everyone who wants to leave and we'll meet in the kitchen to talk," he said.

The temperature in the city had warmed and the breeze generated by the big fan had also increased due to the rubble that had disturbed the balance of air flow. Concrete dust filled the air.

The four spent the night in the hospital pods, the only spaces available. Another full day of work loomed ahead before the passengers could board the bus. Thirty-seven of those who wanted to go were earmarked for Whitmore Hall. Alex, his wife and young son, would be housed in the new medical center. The Contees wanted to go, as did Philip and Jim Page, who was hot after Abike. Jericho, the restauranteur, whom Ken and Carter had previouly met, expressed a desire of becoming a small independent businessman in the new community and wanted to be a hunter.

Preparing to leave the next morning, Ken asked, "What about you, Brenda? Are you staying?"

Brenda appeared to be gathering her thoughts before she replied, "Initially, I wanted to go begin a new life with you, then I decided against it and decided my place was here, you know, to manage the city." She paused in her narrative.

Carter breathed a mental sigh, relieved there would be one less element of strife for their community.

Brenda began anew. "So I talked about it at length with Danny and he assured me that if he were appointed as new mayor, he would take care of things. So I'm free to go live with you Topside."

Brenda's joining their community would not be a disaster. Carter could see a potential worst-case scenario looming. Close to 200 persons remained behind.

Having finished loading personal belongings and passengers, the men held a final meeting prior to getting into their respective vehicles. Each person carried their own food and water. Gregor, now feeling completely comfortable with the men asked, "Carter, how are you going to deal with Brenda?"

"I'd rather be chased by a stinger than be chased by her," Carter bemoaned.

"She'll want to get her liquor still going, but this time Annie won't allow it," Gregor contributed.

Ken noted, "Getting liquor isn't a problem for us, if we want it. We certainly don't need to make our own. We could place her in Whitmore hall with a roommate. That should keep her quiet in the evenings, if what you've told me about her is true. How about if we put her under my direction. I'll deal with her like a drill sergeant training a new recruit. I'll make her responsible for cleaning up the new house and the barn. We'll assign a work crew to work under her direction. She'll answer to me. The crew will hike two miles each way to work and back, which should keep her and them out of trouble."

"She'd have to get the skeletons out, as well?" Carter suggested.

"Absolutely," both men said in unison.

THIRTEEN

Beth and Susan worked furiously with Jay and Wei to prepare enough food to feed 50 people upon their arrival. Eating utensils had already been procured for the event and Annie had proposed feeding the masses in shifts, similar to what they were accustomed to doing. The immigrants would first get situated in Whitmore Hall, then brought in three shifts to the meeting hall for dinner.

Nothwithstanding the trip over the pass, thinking that the tales of weather extremes were part of an elaborate practical joke, the group arrived on a perfectly beautiful day with clear skies and a slight breeze that carried forest scents.

The day following the return of immigrants, Gregor drove them, as a group, to various clothing stores to pick out suitable wear. Although the weather became warmer in general, it also became more extreme. One day the heat pushed up from the south. The next three days saw freezing rain push down from the north accompanied by lightning flashes, as thunder rolled off into the distance; hot rain fell on the fourth day, followed by a week of clear weather with high winds.

The surprise registered on the faces of the Gomez family, when they first entered their combination home/medical center, could not be matched. The outside of the structure had been freshly painted, albeit with paint poorly mixed and still damp. The front area served for reception and waiting. On the wall hung a few of the tapestries Jess and James had brought to Beth during their visit in another life. Volunteers converted the conference room into a bedroom replete with three cots, bedding and a sleeping bag each; and the manila folders previously filling the file cabinets were emptyied, save the folders themselves, waiting to be filled with patients' records. Two bookcases stood against the wall where the potted plants had been, ready to receive a variety of new found medical books. In addition, search crews returned with a major haul of medical supplies recovered from various local hospitals and clinics in Sedona and Flagstaff.

When Alex and his family first moved into the visitors' center, they requested a clean room to be added on for more delicate surgical procedures. This task proved to be extremely difficult. Air purifiers might remove dust, but bacteria were a different story. Wet mopping with vinegar and chlorine bleach, abundant usage of alcohol, simplicity, sterile instruments maintained through use of a small autoclave, and a lot of UV lighting were the best that could be achieved. None of this guaranteed that infection would not occur, although it did tend to lean the luck needle toward the direction of good and, exceeded what they had at their old home. Dental equipment needed to be added.

Completion of the second wind turbine and second greenhouse soon occurred along with the conversion of the visitor's center into a habitable building complete with heat and power.

Alex made the observation that, although he was one of the two doctors in UL-One who had performed vasectomies on married men with a child, the process could be reversed. Business for the medical family increased, thereafter with no infections reported. Carter appointed Susan as Minister of Education, who, in turn, appointed Jess to the position of Minister of Science.

Carter directed Philip to construct a separate facility to process turkey products and to construct a main kitchen with the new plot across the bridge. Jim Page, who had fallen in love with Abike, now occupied the bedroom at the rear of the meeting hall with her and her father. The two ATVs served as shuttles between the turkey farm and Sekah City, a quarter-mile to the north, after Ken had bladed a path with the front-end loader. Food became plentiful with protein supplied by turkey, eggs, crickets, fish, rabbits and occasional birds. Every able-bodied person worked rotational shifts in one of the two greenhouses. Others foraged for watercress, parsley, mints and other vegetables in the surrounding forest. Lime production provided for fresh drinks and by-products.

Enough musical instruments had been obtained from numerous sources so that each person might have his or her own, which evolved into the creation of an orchestra to include string instruments, along with replacement strings, lesson books and musical scores. Flutes, piccolos, two trumpets, and a trombone comprised the wind instruments. Boxes of replacement reeds for oboes and clarinets were in sufficient number to warrant taking the instruments. A set of bongo drums rounded out the list.

Soon, each of the three areas would have its own water well and energy sources. In addition to the wind turbine, a 48 kW liquid-cooled whole-home generator had been placed along with a diesel fuel storage tank to provide for all their electrical needs. Two large greenhouses provided basic foodstuffs.

A newly formed city council passed a noise ordinance in response to those playing musical instruments after hours, while Ken and Carter began classes in constructino and auto mechanics. Meanwhile, Annie began dating Philip Okimura.

Carla's litter of six puppies did not look like they came from a union of the two dogs in their encampment, Carla and Riki. Jess now remembered that, months before, when looking for Carla, she had found her mating with what could only be described as a true wolf—a dog that stood two-and-a-half feet at the shoulder and must have weighed close to 100 pounds, not the mere 15-20 pound weight of a coyote. There would be no gene pool problem in their dog population for some time. How did the wolf get there? she wondered. Then she recalled that Beth had told her that the land bridge between Alaska and Siberia had reappeared, the same land bridge that had connected the two continents across the Bering Strait during the last ice age some 100,000 years in the past.

The Flagstaff International Airport yielded a virtually limitless supply of diesel and aviation fuel, much of which was brought back to the camps in a tanker truck.

In the world of old, a number of companies had installed wind turbines in Flagstaff. Within months, the overcrowded community began to arise and thrive. The strength and longevity of this emergence would depend on the vagaries of climatic conditions instituted by The Mars Virus.

FOURTEEN

"It's too bad Flagstaff won't work for us to set up a colony. We'd never get enough energy generated to overcome the winters. At least we can bring back all the wind turbines and anything else we might want," Carter said.

Beth complained, "Honestly, Carter, I don't understand why you don't open up Sedona. It's right there for the taking. Oak Creek runs through the city."

Carter took a breath and hung his head a moment, as if in remembrance. "I'll tell you why not. Because what happened there scares the hell out of me."

Beth laughed, "Oh, you mean that little half-mile diameter tornado that leveled the place and you're afraid it's going to happen again?"

Not afraid to look Carter in the eye, Wei piled on, announcing, "Wait a minute. You pack us in here like a can of sardines and all the time you're afraid of the big bad wolf? What a wimp. Moving away makes sense. The insects are bigger than they've ever been and we're living in the middle of them." At that, she scratched an imaginary itch.

Jess didn't know whose side to take. They were both right in a way, although she would hesitate to call her husband a wimp. Concerned citizen might be a more appropriate term.

Carter looked like he got caught red-handed stealing money from his mother's purse by both his mother and his father. He scratched his head and turned away.

Wei felt badly. She had touched a nerve in Carter. Jess had shared with her what Carter had told of his tragic background. Trying to deflect, she placed a hand on Carter's arm. "I have an idea. We've all been to Sedona a number of times to collect whatever. How about we go back and give it a serious look from the standpoint of some making a move there. We have enough transportation. All we need is food and energy. It's a no brainer. There's a whole row of B & Bs that are like small hotels located off the beaten path at 179A before it winds through the forest. They might be run-down, but, basically, they're appear to be undamaged from the outside. Plus, the creek runs right behind them. It beats living in a trailer, or in those cubicles we built for the newcomers. And, if nothing else, we do have a good work force."

Carter scratched his head, doing his best not to admit to himself that his own prejudice had kept him from considering the buildings, until this point in time. "I'm not saying yes, but we'll take Jay and Philip and Ken."

"I'm going, too," Jess insisted, glancing at Michelle, in a mental request to watch the babies for her. Michelle gladly consented with a toothy smile.

"All right, then," Carter directed. "We'll take two cars and both dogs. Let's see how many of them are workable and how many rooms they have in total."

Jess winked at Wei.

Twenty minutes later, two vehicles pulled in front of a bed and breakfast. The wind gusted to 40 miles per hour. Undeterred by inclement weather, Jay, Carter and Rikki got out of their vehicle. Ken had reminded them that he was teaching a class in auto mechanics and had to move inside the meeting hall with his class. He wouldn't be couldn't go with them.

Jess and Philip walked another fifty yards to the second building and entered the unlocked front door with Carla. The apparent damage to the downstairs area appeared to be in the kitchen, where the back wall was rotted and the counter had pulled away. A broken window above the counter had permitted rain to enter over the years.

While Jess patiently checked out the downstairs area, Philip went upstairs. Satisfied that the rooms she had seen were acceptable in terms of size and sleeping capacity—she'd slept in a lot worse—she noticed a rear deck off the kitchen. Through the window she could see that rusted tables and chairs lay strewn over the deck. Once she opened the door and stepped out, Carla began barking madly.

Jess froze in place. Eight feet away stood a coyote, patches of fur missing, head hanging down, eyes looking up, white foam dripping from its mouth, wind blowing the foam to the side before it could hit the ground "No, Carla, stay," Jess commanded. A new emotion gripped her. A sense of cold fear ran from her core to radiate outward. Her bowels stirred. Sweat broke out on her forehead and armpits, to chill her further. This was different than an instant's reaction, when she had shot John in the cave. At this moment, a fear of imminent and terrible death looked her in the eyes. She remembered Carter's words. *Rabies. Any sudden move could cause it to attack.*

She mentally rehearsed the movements she would have to make in order to draw and fire her weapon. Once she made a sudden move, the animal might attack. One bite and she would look like the dog in front of her in a few days. Slowly, smoothly, she reached her right hand behind her back with her eyes locked onto those of the coyote's. The coyote's eyes suddenly shifted slightly off of Jess's.

"I've got this, Jess." It was Carter's voice behind her.

"So do I," she replied. Each of them fired and each hit the target. Carter's shot next to Jess's right ear was painful, but at least the animal was down, out of its misery.

"In all, I'd say we found maybe twenty rooms that are acceptable," Carter summarized, as Beth tasted the stew and declared it ready to eat.

"With another ten that can be repaired," added Philip.

Ken said, "That's not a lot and they're scattered."

"We may be better off building homes from scratch." This from Jay.

"Why don't you and Wei start working on finding a location where you can do that," Carter suggested.

"Great idea," Wei replied. "We need something to do."

EPILOGUE

Winter would soon be rearing its ugly head. With Jess expecting her third child, she and Carter were returning from inspecting the repairs to the water wheel now serving the New House. Carter turned his truck onto the bridge that lead to their compound when he hit the brakes hard, looking through the windshield. He turned off the engine, grabbed the binoculars from the glove box, and exited the truck.

"What is it?" Jess asked, who clambered out to stand next to him.

"It's a plane," Carter said, handing her the binoculars. "See." He pointed at a black speck some 45 degrees above the horizon with a white line behind it. Knowing Jess would ask details if he didn't get them in first, he told her, "That's a vapor trail caused by hot engine exhaust gases and the white is from ice crystals that form. Look to the front of that line."

"Wow, a real plane," Jess exclaimed, lifting the binoculars to her eyes.

"It's more than that, my dear. It's not a passenger plane. It looks like it might be a military jet. It's going too fast for private plane——definitely moving faster than the speed of sound. I'd say it's up at least to 40,000 feet, above most of the bad weather and traveling from northwest to southeast. Which could mean it's going from maybe Washington or Oregon to New Mexico. Texas would be too far unless it stops to refuel. It's probably going from one military base to another. Let's see. If it was going from Seattle to, say, Albuquerque, that would be less than fifteen hundred miles, well within the range of most jets. Maybe the two places made contact with one another and then lost contact, so one sent a plane down to the other place to talk about it."

"I thought you said there was nothing up north?"

"Apparently, I was wrong," Carter admitted.

The pair watched the plane until it passed out of sight. As they climbed back into the truck, Carter said, "Let's see if Beth can pick up anything on the military wave bands."

Beth and a few others were standing outside when Jess and Carter arrived. Jess said, excitedly, "We saw it, too. Carter thinks you should get out your radio and scan the military frequencies.

Beth needed a fix—a return to old habits. Preparing food for the masses took a lot of time, even with ample assistance. She went to the bedroom that she and Ken shared, rummaged in a box and pulled out her old tube-operated transoceanic radio. Jess played with her children, waiting for her aunt to return with her prize possession. In a moment, Beth brought the radio into the kitchen, set it on the counter and attached the plug to a power lead. Turning on the instrument and with well-practiced patience, she began to scroll through the wavelengths on her list like a child reunited with a favorite toy. Various squeaks and squawks filled the airways. She did her usual fiddling and finagling, moving from station to station, playing with her personal six-sided Rubik's Cube, across six bands of shortwave. Beth stopped occasionally, listening, adjusting, fine tuning, concentrating, slowly scrolling. She stopped again to listen. The others thought they heard occasional voices over the radio. In an instant, she jumped up and ran out the door.

"Where are you going?" Jess yelled after her.

"Be right back. Don't touch a thing," Beth yelled behind her.

They waited for several minutes until Beth returned out of breath with Wei and Onoyu on her heels. All three appeared eager with excitement.

Beth sat on the chair, almost knocking it over. She stuck her nose up to the radio to ensure the frequency was the same one she had left it on. Jess stood between the Wei and Onoyu. Fine tuning to 20 MHz, Beth turned up the volume and looked at Wei, whose eyes were elsewhere, almost as though she were looking at sounds, concentrating. "It's Chinese, Cantonese to be specific. It's more sing-song—more tonal—than Mandarin. A lot of words with an 'ah' sound. The two languages can't understand each other, but they read the same script. Weird, huh? It is . . . was the most widely spoken language in the world. It could be anywhere. From what I can understand, he's a former tech worker, isolated with his family, been trying to make contact. My guess is he's in Hong Kong. With all the shortwave jammers that are down in China, he's able to transmit, weather permitting, of course. I'm also going to guess that he doesn't want anybody to know where he is, exactly."

Beth turned the dial to another wave band. She turned to look at the Nigerian. As was his character, Onoyu rambled. "Are you asking me if that is Nigerian English? You will not find a shortwave transmitter in my country, especially where the operator is a female like this one. Therefore, she is educated and probably moved to South Africa, perhaps even to Egypt. She may have worked for the military or the government there."

Beth made a note of the wavelength and continued to scroll. Stopping at another, she declared, "Aussie," tears forming, hands trembling. It became a guessing game. The first to declare gets a point. She scrolled further. "South Korean," Wei announced. "Castilian Spanish," Wei announced at another stop.

Other humans were out there. It wasn't as though people were coming out of hibernation; they had been there all the time. Apparently climatic conditions were temporarily cooperating enough to permit wave transmission to go through, as a high amount of electrical activity throughout the world interfered with signal transmission and reception. How long the freakish return to normality would last was impossible to tell.

Jess was about to ask Wei if she could build them a transmitter, when she realized that the woman could and would, if requested to do so. "Wei, can we determine the exact location of any of these calls?"

"Not without them giving us the information," Wei answered. "Theoretically, the location of a signal can be triangulated, once there is a concerted effort to do so. We don't have a clue as to what's out there in terms of people or technology, other than to know that where there's one, there's the other."

Jess wasn't alone in reading between the lines. Bad guys versus good guys. Sometimes, it's not a good idea to let people know you're alive, let alone where you are. She left unsaid her idea to build a transmitter. Let minds greater than hers make that decision.

Carter and Ken stood behind the three women watching Beth re-scan the frequency bands. The Chinese guy and the Korean guy had disappeared, the Aussie was still there, as were two or three others, one of them a woman broadcasting from France. They couldn't catch the name of the city. It wouldn't be Paris. Paris was long gone. So was the port of Marseilles and any other port on the planet. On satellite feeds, Beth had personally seen the Seine overflow to an unprecedented amount accompanied by rainfall that did not cease. Just as a hot air pocket covered the Desert Southwest, so did a rain pocket cover all but the southern part of Europe that is now desert.

Carter said, "Good job, Beth. Keep us posted as to late developments. We'll lay low for now. We don't need any more excitement. By the way, when's Jay planning to come back from Flag?"

"Fairly soon, I think," Ken reported. "Did you put our makeup on the shopping list, like Beth asked?"

Carter replied, "Yes, I did. Gregor and Onoyu each have a copy. Jay said he can remember it. I also told him to bring back as many sets of chess, checkers and decks of cards he could find; eyeglasses, too. Our people are ready to go on strike, if they don't. He should be calling soon to let us know when they reach their first stop."

At that very moment Ken's sat phone squawked. "That's probably Jay now. I'll put it on speaker." Pulling the phone off his belt, he pushed a button and brought it up to his lips. "This is Ken," he answered, cheerily.

"Ken, thank God. It's Danny Gomez. You've got to help us, please. The city is collapsing. We have nobody else to turn to. I want to leave. We all want to leave."

Time stopped. Ken exhaled, hung his head down, shook it back and forth a couple of times and looked up at Carter with sad eyes. "Hold on a second, Danny," he said. Then, "Let me call you right back."

Jess mouthed, "What do we do now?"

"Maybe we can make use of the caves for now," Wei suggested, glancing at the two men. "I mean, there are a lot of them available from what hear."

"Holy smokes," Jess almost shouted. "I totally forgot about the cavern."

"What cavern?" Ken asked.

Jess described the huge dry cavern that Gottlieb's men had hollowed out of the mesa she had discovered. "Between that and the caves we might be able to shelter a lot of people until we can build enough housing in Sedona."

Carter put a hand to his forehead, massaging, then said, "We're going to have a look at this place right now. Ken, tell Danny to hang on. We're getting there as soon as we can. Then call Jay up in Flag. Tell him we may need to add some supplies to the list including another school bus or two. Noting a stern look from Beth, he added, "including a lot more makeup."

Synopsis of other books by Mark R. Sneller

The Mars Virus

Cancer researcher Jason Randolph and his geologist friend, Don Jennings, decide to search for life in a meteorite the geologist found in Antarctica years before. What's the worst that can happen? Everybody tried it, from NASA to the Russians, *and nobody found a thing.*

Suddenly, in Lincoln, Nebraska, a nightmarish discovery by the scientists threatens not only mankind and all life on Earth, but the stability of the planet itself, while Randolph and Jennings try to make hay before the sun stops shining.

Toxic Exposure

Dr. Jeffrey Shenero, rough-hewn professor, adventurer, and mold expert, finds himself embroiled in a lawsuit by a man-eating shark because he didn't find mold in her home. She is circling. He is blindsided by the attack.

At the same time he becomes embroiled in a national scandal surrounding a school controversy in which a demonic teacher is hard at work poisoning the educational system of the country. Do the two women know each other?

Jeff is partnered with Frank Bennett, his best friend and an environmental attorney with his own dark past, and Billy Kirk, a handsome television broadcaster, who wants to play by the book, but has an eye on his own future. He wants to move up the ladder of success and will bend the rules, if it becomes necessary.

Dying to Read

A terrible sickness awaits those who read newspapers and certain magazines. The ink holds a poison that was extracted from a deadly mold. Many children and pets of the readers become affected when they get touched by those, who handled certain print items.

Mold expert and professor, Dr. Jeffrey Shenero, gets pulled into a diabolical and original plot designed and carried out by terrorists. Countless persons are threatened and many have died.

An epidemic and national panic ensue as Shenero and his mathematician friend and genius, Dr. Paul Anderson, stumble onto the truth and the nature of the plot. Attempts are made by members of the U.S. Government, who are working in concert with the terrorists, to persuade Shenero and Anderson to think twice about revealing their findings.

In a fast-moving adventure full of eccentric characters the mold expert gets help from his brilliant graduate students and his intelligent and alluring secretary, Carmen.

Then, Jeff learns that poisonings by the terrorists are in progress in other aspects of everyday American life, not only print ink; even as they come after him.

Greener Cleaner Indoor Air 2nd Edition

Re-edited and enlarged, the 2nd Edition boasts over 120 articles written by award-winning scientist Dr. Mark R. Sneller. Greener Cleaner Indoor Air is an invaluable reference guide promoting longer life. Covering virtually every aspect of the range of particles (and toxic gases) we breathe every day, you will learn how to reduce, if not eliminate, them from your home air and save money at the same time.

Considering the book to be of such value, the country of South Korea purchased the rights to download the e-version to its citizens.